THE N
HOLIDA

ANN McINTOSH

MILLS & BOON

Ann McIntosh was born in the tropics, lived in the frozen north for a number of years, and now resides in sunny central Florida with her husband. She's a proud mama to three grown children, loves tea, crafting, animals (except reptiles!), bacon and the ocean. She believes in the power of romance to heal, inspire and provide hope in our complex world.

Juliette Hyland began crafting heroes and heroines in high school. She lives in Ohio, USA, with her Prince Charming, who has patiently listened to many rants regarding characters failing to follow their outline. When not working on fun and flirty happily-ever-afters, Juliette can be found spending time with her beautiful daughters, giant dogs or sewing uneven stitches with her sewing machine.

THE NURSE'S HOLIDAY SWAP

ANN McINTOSH

A PUPPY ON THE 34TH WARD

JULIETTE HYLAND

MILLS & BOON

First published in Great Britain 2023
by Mills & Boon, an imprint of HarperCollins*Publishers* Ltd,
1 London Bridge Street, London, SE1 9GF

www.harpercollins.co.uk

HarperCollins*Publishers* Macken House, 39/40 Mayor Street Upper, Dublin 1, D01 C9W8, Ireland

The Nurse's Holiday Swap © 2023 Harlequin Enterprises ULC

Special thanks and acknowledgement are given to Ann McIntosh for her contribution to the Boston Christmas Miracles miniseries.

A Puppy on the 34th Ward © 2023 Harlequin Enterprises ULC

Special thanks and acknowledgement are given to Juliette Hyland for her contribution to the Boston Christmas Miracles miniseries.

ISBN: 978-0-263-30620-0

10/23

MIX
Paper | Supporting responsible forestry
FSC
www.fsc.org
FSC™ C007454

CHAPTER ONE

OUTSIDE HIS KITCHEN window the morning sky was gray and the bare branches of the maple tree whipped in the cold December wind. The aspect did nothing to improve Dr. Javier Pascal's rather sour mood as he contemplated the day ahead.

The hospital board meeting the night before had been fractious. The chief of surgery's complaint against pediatric surgeon Ben Murphy had been clearly valid, and Ben's previous infractions hadn't helped. Although Ben was admittedly the most skilled pediatric surgeon at Boston Beacon Hospital, his surly attitude had strained everyone's patience to the breaking point.

Even Javi's, and that took quite a bit of doing.

Being head of Pediatrics meant it fell to Javi to tell the surgeon he had until the end of the year to change his behavior. If he didn't, they'd have to let him go.

It certainly wasn't the way Javi wanted to start the month leading up to Christmas.

Plus, one of their nurses had given a week's notice, and another, Abbie, had decided to take a sabbatical to Hawaii, switching places with a nurse from Molokai. That new temporary nurse was fully qualified, of course, but also an unknown quantity, and Javi didn't much care for disruptions in the smooth running of his department.

His need for order and routine was already being severely

tested today, and he hadn't even gotten up from the breakfast table.

"Papi?"

Realizing he'd been staring out the window rather than concentrating on his plate or his daughter, Javi gave himself a mental shake and, forcing a smile, turned his gaze to meet Mabel's.

"Yes, *mija*?"

"Will you take me Christmas shopping?"

Ouch.

The day was going from bad to worse.

He felt his smile wavering, and shored it up through sheer willpower.

"I thought you were going with Oma?"

Mabel's eyebrows twitched together, but she nodded too. "She's taking me tomorrow to buy a gift for Dad because she says we need to mail it soon or he won't get it in time for Christmas. But I want to go with you another time. I can't buy Oma's gift with her there, can I?"

"No, *mija*, you can't," he replied, keeping his voice even with the greatest of efforts. "That would spoil the surprise."

Mabel's brown eyes suddenly twinkled, and her hopeful expression seared Javi to the soul. "So you'll take me? Maybe next week or after school is out for the holidays?"

He'd been about to suggest she ask his mother, her other grandmother, to take her instead, but the words shriveled on his tongue and he couldn't deny her.

Mabel asked so little of him most of the time.

"Yes, I will." He hoped she didn't hear the resignation in his tone, and apparently she didn't, since all the six-year-old did was beam and bounce a few times in her seat, setting her dark ponytail dancing. "Now, finish up quickly for me so you won't be late for school."

"Yes, Papi," she said, adding, "Thank you," before obediently turning her attention back to her food.

And the tight hug and smacking kiss she later gave him before running into the schoolyard warmed him all the way through.

But after dropping her off, while on his way to the hospital, he found himself still brooding over their conversation.

It was times like this that he really missed Michael—and resented him too.

Christmas had been Javi's ex-husband's favorite time of year, and he'd been the one who'd made it over-the-top spectacular. He'd arranged outings and shopping trips, baked cookies with Mabel after they'd adopted her. Not to mention the skating, skiing and tobogganing outings, along with the drive out to the farm to pick a tree and the evening specifically planned for decorating the house.

Which was why Javi couldn't understand why, two years ago, Michael had chosen Christmas to ask for a divorce. To inform Javi how unhappy and stifled he'd felt and that he'd signed up with a medical rescue service, which was sending him to Africa early in the new year.

It had turned what was already for Javi a fraught and somewhat chaotic time of year into a reminder of heartbreak.

In a strange way, Javi understood why Michael had become so restless and discontented. Their mutual friend, Hugh, had died while on assignment with a group of flying doctors in the Australian outback. Each time they'd gotten together over the years, Hugh would tell them about his job, making it sound like one grand adventure. And afterward, Michael would be quiet and moody, obviously resenting his staider working life.

Stupidly, Javi had thought adopting Mabel would help Michael settle down. After all, it was Michael who'd suggested they apply to adopt, while Javi had been a little more cautious about the disruption being parents would bring to his orderly, quiet life.

Now, as a single parent, Javi could say without reservation Mabel that was the best thing that had ever happened to him. If it weren't for her, he wasn't sure just how he'd have gotten through the divorce and kept himself on track at work.

Every time he thought he couldn't go on, he'd see her beautiful little face, those big brown eyes, and he'd find the strength to continue.

And it was his love for his daughter that now made him consider the upcoming Christmas season with new resolve.

Ever since their divorce Javi had left it to Mabel's grandmothers to pick up the slack around the season because he hadn't the heart to fully participate. There had been too many memories attached to the holidays. He'd met Michael at a Christmas party, and the attraction between them had been so intense, they'd almost instantly become inseparable. Their seven years together had been the happiest Javi had known, the dissolution of their marriage the worst of times.

But now, with Mabel in mind, wasn't it appropriate to let go of his antipathy for the holidays and make it special for her, instead of depending on others to do so?

It wouldn't be easy. Michael had been the extrovert to Javi's more introverted personality, but Mabel deserved the best Javi could provide for her—and not just financially. She deserved the happy memories Javi himself had of childhood Christmases. Coming from a large, boisterous Hispanic family, Christmas had been a chaotic, wonderful affair, filled with outings and family get-togethers. Since his family was now scattered all over the country, he couldn't offer Mabel the exact same experience, but he could do a lot better than he had been to this point.

Offer his parents a better time of it too, rather than moping about, letting them take the lead on the seasonal activities and do all the work to make it bright and cheerful. Mamita and Papa had always supported him, even when they didn't fully understand him. It must have been difficult for his conservative and slightly old-fashioned mother and father to wrap their head around what it meant to have a pansexual son. Explaining to them what that meant—that gender meant nothing to him when it came to attraction and love—had been hard, but to their credit, they'd never made a big deal about it.

And that acceptance had allowed him to live his life openly and without fear or shame.

Not every person in his situation was so lucky, and he knew he had so much to be grateful for.

Now would be a great time to start showing it.

Turning into the hospital parking garage and driving toward his reserved space, Javi made a promise to himself to do right by Mabel and his parents this year.

Then he put the entire thought of the holidays out of his mind and turned his attention to the upcoming workday.

He'd need to be on his toes to keep the department running smoothly, especially with the chat he had to have with Ben Murphy. Hopefully, even now when medical personnel was short, he'd be able to find a replacement for the departing Heather and the new nurse would settle in without too much trouble.

The last thing they needed was to have to babysit Ailani Kekoa during the rush of patients engendered by the flu and other respiratory illnesses going around.

The trouble with having an adventure after a lifetime of craving it but being unable to satisfy the urge was that it left you feeling completely unprepared.

But Ailani refused to give in to the shivers of apprehension crawling in waves over her skin as her new friend Bryn steered her car toward Boston Beacon Hospital.

Making the decision to do a three-month life swap with another nurse, Abbie, had been not just stepping out of her comfort zone but rather like leaping off a cliff into the sea for the first time.

Terrifying and thrilling all at once.

The swap had come with an apartment, car, job and room-mate, Bryn, who Ailani had discovered was also an RN, although she wasn't working as one at the moment. Ailani didn't know why, since although she and Bryn had become fast friends almost immediately, the other woman hadn't said. And Ailani didn't believe in prying for information others didn't want to give of their own accord.

However, Bryn worked with therapy dogs like her own golden retriever, Honey, now ensconced in the back seat, wearing a bright holiday sweater and what could only be termed a grin on her face.

"Are you cold?" Bryn asked, obviously concerned. "I can turn the heater up higher if you want."

Ailani shook her head, sending her friend a small smile. "I'm fine. I should be, since I have on enough clothing for five people."

Bryn gave her a sideways glance, her lips quirking to one side in a half smile. "Once you get used to the cold, you'll find it's better to wear just two or three layers, depending on whether you're going to be inside or out."

Somehow Ailani doubted she'd ever get used to winter. The frigid air stung the skin and hurt her nose when she inhaled, despite the fact that Bryn assured her it wasn't really *that* cold yet. There'd been a little snow since she arrived, just enough to send light whirls like tiny blossoms blowing in the breeze along the ground. Nothing like what Ailani had expected.

In fact, one of the things on her adventure list—experiencing a white Christmas—had been the impetus for this trip. And now it sounded as if it might not even happen.

"Oh, we usually get most of our snow in January or February," Bryn had said when Ailani had asked why there was no snow on the ground after she'd arrived five days earlier. "Sometimes we get a white Christmas, but more often it's just frosty and gray."

Well, that would be a disappointment—no doubt about it. She'd assured Tutu that was the main reason she was going on the trip, and although her grandmother had shaken her head, Ailani was sure the older woman had kind of wished she could see snow too. It was something about the faraway look she'd gotten in her eyes, as though imagining the pristine white landscape glistening with holiday lights.

"You can see snow in those sappy Christmas movies you like to watch, and without risking pneumonia," Uncle Makoa had inserted, his brows drawn together. "No need to go all the way to Boston to do that."

But it had already been too late for any of their objections. Ailani had made all the arrangements with Abbie, Boston Beacon and Molokai Regional and even booked her ticket. When she'd told them as much, Uncle Makoa had made a derisive sound in the back of his throat and gotten up to leave the room.

Wanting to call him back, Ailani had bitten her lip to stop the words from emerging.

It was past time for Uncle to realize she was going to live her life on her own terms, not his or Tutu's.

Now that she understood why they'd always held her back from doing anything even remotely adventurous, she'd figured the only way to break the cycle was to just go for it.

Whatever *it* happened to be.

That was what her mother had done, and although it hadn't ended too well for her, at least she'd *lived*.

Ailani wanted to do the same, and no one was going to stop her.

No matter how much she loved them.

She was thirty, just a year younger than her mother had been when she'd died. If that wasn't impetus to get out and explore life more, then she didn't know what was.

A chilly, damp nose touched her ear, making Ailani jump and sputter with laughter. Turning, she looked over her shoulder at the golden retriever on the back seat who, although tethered into a safety harness, had somehow managed to reach her. Liquid brown eyes looked back—offering comfort, Ailani thought fancifully.

"Honey, girl, I'm cold enough as it is without you adding that nose to the mix."

The dog's mouth opened, seemingly about to answer but instead just smiled, tongue hanging out.

"Are you nervous about your first day?" Bryn maneuvered the vehicle down a busy road that went past Boston Common.

"A little," Ailani admitted, reaching back as best she could with all those layers binding around her arm to ruffle Honey's head. "Do you think that's why Honey touched me?"

Bryn shrugged slightly, her indicator on for the left-hand turn into the hospital parking garage.

"Could be. Or maybe she was just tired of being ignored."

Ailani laughed the way she knew Bryn wanted her to, but at the same time she gained new respect for Honey as a therapy dog. Up to now, she'd only seen Honey the couch sneak and Honey the goofball, who'd do anything for some peanut butter. She'd yet to experience Honey in her work capacity— offering comfort to the children on the wards—but already she knew the dog would be amazing at it.

After all, just that little interaction had lowered Ailani's heart rate and allowed her to catch a full breath as Bryn found a parking spot and pulled in.

"Okay, my friend," Bryn said after they'd gotten into the hospital and taken the elevator to the second floor. "I'm going to have to leave you here. You have a great first day, okay?"

"Thanks, *hoaloha*."

Giving Bryn a hug and Honey a last pat, Ailani went off to find the head nurse and report in.

Leigh Wachowski had an almost bruising handshake and shrewd blue eyes.

"Good to meet you," she said, then started walking toward a door marked Staff Only, which she held open for Ailani. "You'll miss morning briefing since I'm sending you up to the administrative office to get your key card and ID, and after today you should come in through the staff entrance. That corridor leads to the staff room, where you can swap your outdoor shoes and stow your belongings. We'll go there now so you can take off your coat. Otherwise you'll be sweating in no time."

Ailani didn't bother to mention she already had perspiration running down her back.

No need to advertise the fact that when it came to winter, she had no idea what she was doing! Best not to take the chance that it might be seen as a sign of general incompetence and silliness.

After she'd stripped down to scrubs and a thick cardigan, she set out to follow Nurse Wachowski's directions.

"When you get back, I'll show you around and introduce you to some of the staff," the older woman said as Ailani was heading toward the elevator.

But when she got back to the nurses' station after filling out more forms, getting her picture taken and receiving her badge and card, Leigh was nowhere to be found.

"She was called away, up to the administrative floor," the nurse said as he got up to answer a buzzer. "Just stay here for a minute. When I get back, I'll try to figure out what to do with you."

The words made her sound like she was some kind of package or a waste of space rather than a competent, experienced nurse. A bubble of annoyance rose in her throat, but the other nurse had already brushed past her and was heading off down the hallway, leaving Ailani standing, uncomfortably, on her own.

"Nurse Kekoa?"

The smooth, deep voice, coming from directly behind her, made Ailani jump. Spinning around, she found herself looking at a broad chest. Strange to find her gaze fixated on the V of the white dress shirt, which exposed a tanned throat and a little swathe of straight, dark hairs.

Looking up caused her heart to do a strange flip as she found herself the focus of a pair of beautiful hazel eyes surrounded by long straight lashes and set in a decidedly handsome face.

Remembering she'd been asked a question, she stuttered, "Y-yes, that's me."

"Dr. Javier Pascal, head of Pediatrics," he said by way of introduction, thrusting out a large, long-fingered hand in greeting.

Taking it was instinctual, but Ailani had to stop herself from pulling her own hand back when a zing of electricity shot up her arm on contact.

"Nice to meet you, Dr. Pascal." After a firm shake, she eased her fingers from his grasp. "I'm just waiting for Nurse Wachowski to continue my orientation."

"She'll be unavailable for a while yet," Dr. Pascal said. "I'll be showing you around instead."

"Oh." Why did she hesitate and wonder if she was about to go through a trial by fire? Pulling herself together by taking a deep breath, she added, "Thank you, Doctor."

His eyebrows twitched together slightly, but his only verbal response was a dispassionate, "Follow me."

And all there was left to do was fall into step beside the tall doctor and remind herself not to think of Javier Pascal as an intriguing man but only as her boss.

CHAPTER TWO

A STRANGE SENSE of unreality settled over Javier as he set out to show Nurse Ailani Kekoa around the ward and introduce her to other members of staff. Professionalism was second nature to him, and he was glad of that fact today since it allowed him to carry on as though nothing untoward was happening.

Inside, though, he was shaken.

The effect Ailani had on his equilibrium was completely unexpected.

And unwanted.

Looking down into her dark brown wide-set eyes had caused his heart to literally skip a beat, and now, as they walked along the corridor, it took everything he had inside to sound normal. To point out the various areas she needed to familiarize herself with and ask the questions he needed to so as to gauge her competence. Not to stare at her lovely, soft profile or try to get another whiff of her gentle, flowery scent.

"The hospital is probably busier than the one on Molokai," he said, unable to stop himself from watching her gaze dart from one area to another. When she looked up at him, though, he quickly turned away, reluctant to get trapped in her eyes again.

"Much busier," she agreed, her tone firm and confident. "But I don't view that as a bad thing. I wanted to stretch myself, and this will be a great place to do that."

He had an almost overwhelming urge to ask her to elaborate on that statement. Why did she want to stretch herself? What was her life like back in Hawaii?

Everything.

He wanted to know everything about her, but none of it was relevant or his business or even remotely appropriate. Falling back on his habitual detachment and the cool, businesslike persona he'd developed as a shield against unwanted emotion, he reluctantly changed the subject.

"At this time of year, besides the usual injuries and diseases we see all the time, we have an increase in respiratory ailments," he stated. They were standing outside a patient's door, looking in at six-year-old Mason, who was on oxygen, while his mother sat beside him, holding his hand. "I'm guessing this isn't as big an issue for you in Hawaii."

"Actually, we had a noticeable spike in both RSV and flu in younger children last year," she told him. "It got quite intense for a while. Boston Beacon serves a larger population, so it'll obviously be busier, but I'm familiar with the protocols."

"We've been fortunate this year that we've had no fatalities, but every child who comes in with symptoms has to be properly tested to make sure what we're dealing with."

She nodded, sending him a sideways glance as though recognizing that he was testing her and expected a response to prove she did, indeed, understand what needed to happen and why.

She didn't hesitate but immediately said, "It's standard knowledge that while the symptoms of various diseases may be similar, the treatments and infection control practices differ. The main concern is ensuring patients get the proper care and that their stay in the hospital is minimized."

No fault to be found there.

"Definitely."

Just then, a nearby door opened and Nick stepped out into

the corridor. When he glanced their way, Javi gestured him over and made the introductions.

"Dr. Nick Walker, this is Nurse Ailani Kekoa."

"Nice to meet you," Nick said as they shook hands.

Was it his imagination, or did Nick's smile seem brighter than usual?

Quickly squelching a little spurt of annoyance, Javi continued, "Dr. Walker is our newest pediatrician. Today is his first day on the floor, in fact."

And it was equally irritating to him when Ailani started making small talk with the other man, bonding over their comparative newness on the ward. As soon as Javi saw the opportunity, he interrupted and took Ailani to meet someone else, exasperated now with himself for those instances of what felt like protectiveness.

Or, he admitted to himself, jealousy.

When he saw Kalista Mitchell near one of the nurses' stations, he guided Ailani that way.

"Kalista." Hearing her name had the internist looking up, startled out of her perusal of the file in her hand. "Here on a consult?"

She nodded. "Urgent Care is slammed today. They called me in to examine a six-year-old girl, and they're sending her up right now."

"This is Nurse Ailani Kekoa." As the two women shook hands, he continued, "When we've finished her orientation, I'll send her in to shadow whichever of the nurses is working with you. She'll see a lot of RSV and flu patients, but it'll also be good for her to work on some of the consults too."

With a shrug, Kalista replied, "Sure." Then she immediately turned back to the chart in her hands, effectively—almost rudely—ending the conversation.

As they walked on, Javi wondered if Ailani was put off by Kalista's abrupt manner, but the woman beside him seemed totally unfazed. Not that it mattered whether she was or not, really. They were all professionals, and Javi demanded professional behavior from every member of staff, no matter what.

Speaking of which…

Ben Murphy strode toward them, the habitual scowl on his face even more pronounced than usual. You'd think that their talk this morning, instead of convincing him to change his attitude, had actually made it worse.

"Ben…"

The other man barely paused, his gaze flicking dismissively from Javier to Ailani and then back.

"Yes?" he growled.

"I'd like to introduce—"

"Yeah. Hi. I'm in a hurry."

Then, before Javi could even get another word out, Ben brushed past and walked away.

"Oh, my." No mistaking the amusement in Ailani's voice as they both turned to watch Ben disappear into the distance.

"He's one of the best pediatric surgeons I've ever seen," Javi replied, knowing he sounded defensive. Ben had been through the emotional wringer and deserved *some* slack. Unfortunately, he'd run out of rope now. "And his bedside manner is exemplary."

"Hmm." Ailani turned bright, laughing eyes his way, making Javi forget how to breathe. "I'll bear that in mind the next time he's rude."

"Please do," he said, trying for a quelling tone but somehow seeming to fail because her lips quirked and the twinkle in her eyes didn't abate. Clearly she wasn't easily subdued, and that made her even more attractive.

"Dr. Pascal." Hearing Leigh Wachowski's voice was a relief since it gave him an excuse to wrench his gaze away from Ailani's. The charge nurse bustled up, shaking her head. "HR finally got finished with me, so I'll take over Ailani's orientation."

Ridiculously, he wanted to object, despite the pile of paperwork he needed to get through before doing his next set of rounds. But to do so might lead to raised eyebrows and unwanted speculation.

"Thanks, Leigh." He hoped his tone wasn't as grudgeful as he felt. "I want Ailani paired with whoever is assisting Dr. Mitchell. Kalista has a patient coming up from Urgent Care."

"Will do," the charge nurse replied.

"Thank you for the tour, Dr. Pascal." Ailani's smile was bright, and it took everything Javi had not to grin back at her. Something about this woman made him feel light—in contrast to the weight of his position, which often made him solemn and serious at work. "I'm sure you have far more important things to do."

"You're welcome." Turning, he took off along the hallway toward his office, needing to put some distance between them, even though he fancifully thought her scent followed, teasing him all the way.

Ailani watched Dr. Pascal walk away before realizing Leigh had already started off in the other direction. Scrambling to catch up, she got abreast of the other woman.

"I'm sorry to have abandoned you like that," Leigh said. "We've had a nurse give notice unexpectedly and, of course, the administrators picked this morning to call me up to talk about it."

"No problem. Dr. Pascal was very informative."

Ailani stopped herself from looking back the way they'd come. There was something magnetic about the head of Pediatrics she couldn't explain, even to herself, but now was not the time to dwell on it. Yes, Dr. Pascal was gorgeous and his voice slid like warm silk into her ears, but that was beside the point, right? It was more important she do the best job possible and prove that despite the difference in the number of patients at Boston Beacon versus Molokai Regional, she'd be able to cope. Making the most of this orientation would be a good start.

The environment—with its hustle and bustle, familiar scents and vernacular—made her feel she'd be okay. But the one thing she feared, above all others, was not being able to handle the job that was affording her this once-in-a-lifetime opportunity.

While the position itself was a temporary one, almost incidental to the reasons she'd come to Boston, Ailani had always prided herself on her work ethic.

She had to admit, though, that Molokai Regional was usually more laid back and had a slower pace than this busy inner-city hospital.

"He's really great to work with," Leigh said, bringing Ailani back to the topic of Dr. Pascal, just when she'd been trying to banish him from her mind. "Even when his husband divorced him a couple of years ago, he didn't bring his problems to the hospital. Was a bit more solemn than usual, but he got on with things just the same."

A twist of regret made Ailani's lips turn down. So Javier Pascal was gay, eh? What a shame.

But then she couldn't help silently laughing at herself. Whether he was or wasn't didn't really matter. The last thing on her mind was any kind of fling while she was in Boston.

Well, it should've been the last thing on her mind, but the yummy Dr. Pascal brought it front and center.

So it was actually a good thing he was gay!

"I'm going to pair you up with Brian, since Dr. Pascal wants you working with Dr. Mitchell on her case. When you're finished in there, I'll assign you elsewhere."

They were approaching the main nurses' station, where a nursing assistant was busy rummaging through a stack of boxes, pulling out Christmas ornaments.

"Patty," Leigh said when they were within earshot. "Keep

a look out for any glass ornaments, okay? Someone donated a bunch last year and we tried to pick them out, but I'm not sure we got them all. If you see them, put them aside. I'll donate them."

"Getting ready for the season, huh?"

Leigh grabbed a chart while replying, "We're big on Christmas around here. It helps the kids' morale. We always do a special Christmas wish for one of the kids, plus a Santa Dash and bake sale to raise funds for Camp Heartlight."

"Camp Heartlight?"

Leigh was perusing the chart but still replied. "Yeah. It's a special summer camp for children with heart conditions. We do different fundraisers all through the year but make most of our money off the bake sale and Santa Dash each year.

"Oh," she added as she looked up from the file. "And we do a Secret Santa gift exchange among the staff."

"Nice." Now that was something she could get into. "I ran the one at Molokai, and although I'm sure it was tiny in comparison, I could help out there. Who's in charge of that?"

Leigh scowled. "Well, Heather, the person who was in charge of it, is the one who's leaving in a few days, so I guess I am." Then her face brightened. "Do you want to take it over?"

Ailani quickly shook her head. "Nope. I'm not confident enough to do that, but I'll definitely help out."

Leigh gave her a grateful glance and replied, "If you could ask around for people wanting to participate and give me the list, I'd appreciate it. One less thing for me to do."

"Sure, I can do that."

It would be a good way to introduce herself to staff members and get to know them a little better.

Then it was time to pair up with Brian and go assist Dr. Mitchell.

On the way to the room where their patient was going to be put, she asked the other nurse if he wanted in on the Secret

Santa, and he agreed. It was a good confidence booster, since Ailani had already started worrying that, being new, no one would agree to take part. Having Brian say yes made the entire situation a little less stressful.

But just before they got to the room, Leigh came trotting over.

"Ailani, change of plans. The Urgent Care clinic is sending up another patient, and I need you there instead." She smiled slightly. "Throwing you in the deep end. Feel up to it?"

"Of course," Ailani replied, making her voice firm and strong although her heart was pounding.

"This way."

As Leigh led the way, she said, "Normally Urgent Care will examine the patients and only those needing further intervention are sent up to the wards. But they're so busy right now, and this little guy is sick enough that they made the decision to have him examined up here instead of making him wait."

They got to the room just as their patient, Kyrie Powers, was wheeled along from the elevator, and Ailani held the door open for the orderly to push the gurney through.

Kyrie turned out to be a slight-framed eleven-year-old, whose dark face had a pinched appearance and ashen cast. His mother hovered outside the door as they got him from the gurney into the bed. Just as they'd settled him in, Dr. Pascal came into the room, and Ailani's breath caught in her throat before she looked away and concentrated on her patient.

As Javier Pascal introduced himself to Mrs. Powers and Kyrie, Ailani busied herself, making sure the saline line was straight and operational. Then she placed a kidney dish to hand in case Kyrie needed to throw up, and checked both his temperature and oxygen levels. All the while she kept an eye on the doctor in case he asked for or needed something—and because she was interested to see what his bedside manner was like.

Meanwhile, Javier was asking a series of questions, none

of which the youngster seemed inclined to answer. Instead, it was his mother who told them that Kyrie had complained a couple of times about not feeling well, then about having stomach aches.

"Not feeling well how?" Javier asked, looking at Kyrie.

He twisted his mouth and looked away from the doctor, accidentally meeting Ailani's gaze. When she smiled at him, he closed his eyes and tilted his head up toward the ceiling, clearly ignoring her friendly overture.

"When I asked him, he complained that he felt tired, and I thought he was trying to get out of school or football practice."

Kyrie's eyes flew open, and he gave his mother a glare, his lips opening as though to dispute her words. Then he clamped his lips together and closed his eyes again.

"He tried to get out of school before, and I just thought this was another one of those times…"

She started to cry quietly, and as Ailani grabbed a couple of tissues to hand to Mrs. Powers, she saw Kyrie's bottom lip tremble.

Dr. Pascal looked from his patient to the little boy's mother and back.

Then he said, in an almost offhand way, "Kyrie, if I'm going to help you, you need to work with me, okay? Your mom might know what you told her, but you're the only one who knows exactly what you've been feeling—what you've been going through."

Kyrie took a deep breath and his lashes lifted, just a little, but he still didn't speak.

Dr. Pascal moved closer to the head of the bed and said, in a man-to-man sort of tone, "Kyrie, it's up to you to point me in the right direction. There are a lot of different things that might be happening to you, but until you give me all the information I need, I'm in the dark."

And somehow that prosaic, stark pronouncement got the

youngster to open up and give them a comprehensive list of his symptoms and ailments.

Javier nodded. "Thank you. That's really helpful. Mrs. Powers, could I have a word with you outside?"

When the doctor and Mrs. Powers left the room, Kyrie frowned, his gaze fixed on the door, as if he thought he could hear them through it.

"They'll be right back," Ailani said, taking a leaf out of Javier Pascal's book and not overtly trying to be soothing. It seemed the doctor had quickly gauged the best way to deal with their grumpy, unhelpful preteen.

Kyrie's glance was scathing. "I'm old enough for that doctor to say what's wrong with me in here," he groused. "Didn't he just say I wasn't a baby?"

"That's true," Ailani agreed, keeping her expression serious, although the fierce look on his face somehow made her want to smile. "But the fact is that Dr. Pascal still doesn't know what's wrong with you, and he won't know until we've done some tests."

"So what's he saying to Mom, then?"

Although she could guess, Ailani made a big deal of shrugging. "I don't know. I'm in here with you, aren't I? And darn it if I didn't forget my bionic hearing aids at home this morning."

His lips twitched, and his nostrils flared. Keeping his mouth closed, he stretched his chin down, doing his very best to keep his amusement from showing. But when their gazes clashed, and Ailani crossed her eyes at him, there was nothing Kyrie Powers could do to stop his peals of laughter.

CHAPTER THREE

BY LUNCHTIME, Javi needed a break. One that took him away from the hospital and into a quieter, less stress-inducing atmosphere. So, instead of going down to the hospital cafeteria, he headed over to the nearby coffee shop, Full of Beans, hoping to find a quiet table. Grabbing an herbal tea and ordering a panini, he settled onto a padded bench at the back of the room with a sigh.

The wards were getting close to capacity, as unfortunately often happened at this time of the year. As a parent, it was scary just how similar to a petri dish schools and extracurricular activities were. As a doctor, it was his job to ensure that every one of the children who came to the hospital received the best care possible and didn't get any sicker.

There was always that specter hanging over the pediatric ward. Kids came in with a wide variety of illnesses but over winter respiratory illnesses were a huge scourge, and because they were so transmissible extra precautions had to be in place.

One of those precautions was to ensure the ward was properly staffed. With Heather leaving unexpectedly, it wasn't going to be easy to replace her, especially with a general shortage of nurses post-pandemic.

At least he didn't have to worry about Ailani Kekoa. Not only had he been impressed by her no-fuss handling of her first patient at Boston Beacon, but the sound of Kyrie Powers laughter coming from the room had startled both Javi and the little boy's mother.

"Oh," Mrs. Powers had gasped. "I was beginning to think I'd never hear that sound again. Whatever that nurse is doing, I hope she continues."

After his examination, he'd referred Kyrie Powers to Kalista Mitchell, who had finished with her previous patient and been able to immediately take over from him.

Kali had been forthright, as usual, in her evaluation of Ailani's competence, saying, "She's good. I have no complaints about her at all." Then she'd surprised him when she'd added, "I like her."

It wasn't that Kali was unfriendly, but she had the reputation of being aloof and wasn't known to try to develop any kind of connections within the hospital. Javi couldn't think of anyone Kali had gotten close to at work, although he could be wrong, since he wasn't keeping tabs on the internist.

Somehow, Javi wasn't surprised Ailani had seemed to instantly be able to bridge Kali's natural reticence, if not bond with the young doctor. There was something very appealing about the nurse's outgoing personality, twinkling eyes and wide smile, which she tossed about with a total lack of discrimination.

Although why he'd want her to be a little less free with that beaming grin, he didn't want to contemplate.

He also didn't want to think about why Ailani Kekoa was lingering in his mind the way she was. Didn't he have enough going on without that? His sister, Lena, and her family were coming from California on Christmas Day, and his mother was beside herself with excitement. With his sister, brother-in-law, niece and nephew in attendance, his parents' home would be a hive of activity. The expectation would be that he and Mabel would spend a lot of time there so she could be with her cousins. However, he'd also have to somehow ensure that his ex-in-laws weren't left out.

Michael might have walked away from their marriage, but that didn't mean that Joan and Ronald Edwards should be shut out of Mabel's life. They genuinely loved their granddaughter and still treated Javi with the same love and respect they always had.

And although Joan and Mamita were on the best of terms, with all the excitement of Lena coming for Christmas from California, Javi would have to make sure the Edwardses weren't forgotten.

He moved his cup out of the way as the waitress brought his sandwich, and he smiled in thanks. But for a few minutes he ignored his meal, staring sightlessly across the room, contemplating how much more chaotic Christmas would now be and how little he liked chaos.

"If you're just going to breathe over that sandwich instead of eating it," came a cheeky voice from over by the counter, "you might want to consider giving it to someone else before it gets cold."

Looking up, meeting Ailani's twinkling gaze and seeing her wide smile somehow made the band around his chest ease a bit. He was even able to chuckle.

"If you have time, come and join me and make sure I eat up like a good boy."

He didn't know where those words came from, especially since he'd spent a great deal of time that morning trying to stop himself thinking about her.

And still somehow wanting to, although he had no business doing so.

Now it was too late to back out, and if he were being honest with himself, he didn't really consider that option.

She'd be a good distraction from his whirling thoughts and no doubt would be an entertaining lunch companion.

* * *

Surprised at Javier's lighthearted reaction to her teasing, Ailani felt her eyebrows go up when he spoke but kept smiling as she picked up her coffee and ready-made sandwich, then headed his way.

"What do I look like, Dr. Pascal, your mother?"

"Not even a little," he replied, standing politely as she got to the table and tilting his head, as though giving her question far more consideration than it warranted. "Except maybe for the hair. Hers is long and wavy too, but grayer."

Ailani couldn't help a little spurt of laughter breaking free as she plopped down into her chair and sighed with pleasure at being off her feet. Who knew the serious Dr. Pascal would have such a quirky sense of humor, almost as offbeat as her own?

"Well, I'm glad to hear that's the only similarity, Doctor."

"Please, outside of the hospital, feel free to call me Javier— or Javi, if you prefer. How's your first day going?"

The invitation to call him by his first name gave her a silly little glow of pleasure. He'd settled back into his seat and picked up his sandwich, and Ailani found herself looking at his hands, admiring them, and forced her gaze away.

She was becoming almost ridiculously obsessed with looking at this man and all his delicious attributes. Unwrapping her sandwich gave her something else to focus on, thankfully, but she had to swallow before she trusted herself to speak normally.

"It's going really well. Busier than I'm used to," she added. "But I think I'm keeping up without too much of a problem. The ward is set up in a way that makes navigating it easy for me, even though it's my first day, and everyone's been very helpful."

"Glad to hear it." He paused, glancing down at his plate for an instant, and Ailani couldn't help noticing how long his lashes were. "By the way, I haven't told you how impressed

I was that you got Kyrie Powers to laugh. That would have been the last thing I expected to hear from outside that door."

Again, the pleasure she got from his words seemed excessive, but she couldn't seem to help feeling that way. His approval meant a lot.

"He's scared and trying to be brave, I think. Dr. Mitchell ordered a bunch of tests, and he was a real trooper when the phlebotomist was doing his thing."

"You got on okay with Kalista Mitchell?" he asked in what sounded to her like an overly casual tone, and it piqued her interest.

Although she wondered why he'd ask only about that specific doctor, she replied, "Sure. She's easy to work with, and it turns out we share a ridiculous sense of humor. When I asked her if she wanted in on the Secret Santa, she said she was having a *No-Christmas* Christmas this year, and I said instead of *Noel*, for her it was *Hell No*." She couldn't help giggling at the memory. "It was all downhill from there—going back and forth with silly wordplay, until I called her Scrooge McMitchell and we had to stop because we were laughing too hard. We were afraid we'd disturb the patients."

Dr. Pascal chuckled, shaking his head. "Did all your teasing change her mind about the holidays?"

It was Ailani's turn to shake her head, and she took a moment to chew and swallow before she answered. "It wasn't meant to. Not everyone is as into Christmas as I am. It's her prerogative not to participate, although I think she said she'd make a donation toward the camp fund, so it's not as if she's completely ignoring it."

That earned her a sharp look from those gorgeous hazel eyes. "Most people would have tried to talk her into participating anyway."

Ailani snorted. "That's no way to behave—trying to get people to do things they don't want to. I mean, she's not hurting anyone, so why fuss at her? She's an adult, and it's her decision."

Besides, there was something about Kali—as she'd been given permission to call the other woman—that reminded Ailani of her uncle Makoa. Maybe, like him, she found the holidays and all the hubbub overwhelming or filled with sad associations.

Unlike Makoa, Ailani liked Christmas because it featured in some of her favorite memories of her parents. Somewhere along the line she'd decided that since they'd always made the holidays so much fun, it was a time to honor them by making the season bright for others too, whenever she could.

Which reminded her...

"Hey, would you like to take part in the Secret Santa? I'm collecting the names for Leigh."

He seemed to hesitate before saying, "How did you get roped into that on your first day?"

Noticing he hadn't answered her question but not wanting to push, she shrugged. "Apparently the nurse who was in charge of it is leaving, so Leigh had to take it on. It's not a big deal, really. All I'm doing is getting names."

He nodded, but when next he spoke it was on a completely different subject.

"So, what made you decide to come to Boston? I mean, I can see Abbie wanting to spend winter in Hawaii but can't understand someone from there wanting to come here."

The change in the conversation came so quickly, it took Ailani by surprise. Since she'd just taken a bite of her food, she had a moment to formulate a reply.

Not one hundred percent sure she wanted to go too deeply into her story, she planned to give him a short, sanitized version.

"I have a list—like an adventures-to-go-on list—and a

white Christmas is on it. So when I heard about the chance to do a life-swap with Abbie, it was a no-brainer. I'd never be able to afford this otherwise."

His eyebrows dipped together for an instant, and then he looked merely curious. "You mean a bucket list?"

"I don't like calling it that, but yeah, I guess so."

Javier's gaze sharpened. "Why don't you like that term?"

"Oh, I just don't."

There was no way she'd tell him about finding her mother's list—with that heading—and that one of the adventures she'd embarked on had led to her death.

He seemed friendly enough, but they were still strangers after all.

"What else is on your list?" he asked, and she thought there was a bit of an edge to his tone. "What other adventures do you have planned?"

"Oh, there are other trips I'd like to take, and maybe live in a different part of the world, but right now I have a few that I'm hoping to cross off while I'm here—like build a snow-man." She knew it probably sounded silly to him, and she lifted her chin slightly. "I've always wanted to do that. Go tobogganing too. Just snowy-type stuff that you all probably take for granted."

"I'm sure you'll get the chance, at some point anyway. It might not be—"

"Until after Christmas," she finished with him, then gave an exaggerated sigh. "I know, I know. Maybe no white Christmas. Blah, blah, blah. Bryn keeps telling me to manage my expectations, but I refuse to give up hope that it'll snow for the holidays."

She struck a dramatic pose, hoping to make him smile and chase that solemn expression from his eyes. "I will not allow Grinches to steal my dream!"

It only partially worked, as his lips quirked upward but his gaze retained a hint of shadows, as though something she'd said had caused him pain. Then he relaxed, and his smile widened into a more genuine grin, which made his eyes sparkle and Ailani's heart do a little jig.

"If I remember correctly, the Grinch only stole presents, not dreams."

"I disagree," she said. As both were finished, they got up and started clearing away their debris. "What he was *trying* to steal were presents *and* dreams."

And they continued the completely nonsensical argument all the way back to the hospital.

While they were going up in the elevator together, Ailani suddenly remembered the Secret Santa exchange and, despite the niggling thought that he wasn't interested, again asked him about joining in.

"Well," he said, sounding almost surprised at himself, although why that was she had no idea. "You can add my name to that list."

"Awesome," she replied.

It was only later, when she told Leigh about it in passing, that she found out Dr. Pascal hadn't taken part in any of the Christmas events for the last couple years.

"Hopefully he's finally getting over his husband leaving," the charge nurse said, scowling. "He's too young to just have work and his little girl to look after. Maybe he'll even start dating again. He deserves to be happy."

Ailani murmured noncommittally. Javier Pascal's private life was no business of hers, although she liked him and rather hoped they might become friends.

She'd enjoyed his company at lunch, and he'd said that if she was available around the same time the following day they could eat together again.

What she had to avoid, she reminded herself, was getting a silly crush on him because he was as delicious as pineapple upside-down cake. And since she was allergic to pineapple, equally off-limits!

CHAPTER FOUR

AILANI HAD ALWAYS enjoyed driving, and since she and Abbie had exchanged cars as well as jobs and apartments, she had no hesitation about driving to work the next morning.

"I'll take you in whenever I'm visiting the ward with Honey," Bryn had said after Ailani had first arrived in Boston. "But there'll be other times when I need to be at the therapy-dog association so I can't give you a lift."

"That's no problem," she'd told the other woman. "Although I have no sense of direction, between the navigation system in the car and the one on my phone, I'll get there. Not too sure about after it snows though. That's something I have no experience with—at all."

Bryn had chuckled, replying, "I wouldn't worry too much about that. Every year it seems everyone forgets how to drive on snow, and the first few days are a mess. You'll fit right in."

Although they'd both laughed, Bryn had also made sure to take Ailani on public transport a few times, to ensure she had alternatives. All in all, her roommate and new friend had been wonderful—welcoming and helpful, without being overbearing. It helped Ailani feel a lot less lonely and like a fish out of water, even before she'd started at Boston Beacon.

And having lunch with Javier Pascal the day before had also helped a lot.

But, Ailani told herself sternly as she inched along in the

morning traffic, she was going to have to get her head on straight about him.

He was handsome, warm and engaging, and had the knack of making her want to tell him far more than she'd intended to tell anyone here. But she needed to keep reminding herself that developing anything other than friendly feelings toward him would be courting disaster.

Yet somehow, she always seemed to find herself thinking about him in less-than-innocent ways.

It was something about those gorgeous hazel eyes, sparkling with intelligence—sometimes serious, sometimes good-humored—that made heat gather beneath her skin. Not to mention the fact that he had lips made for kissing and the most beautiful hands she'd ever seen on a man. Hands and fingers she'd already imagined touching her intimately, and that had caused a dangerous melting feeling to invade her belly.

She definitely had to get control of herself!

She hadn't come all this way to complicate her life with feelings of unrequited lust for a man who clearly wouldn't be interested in her that way.

It was nice to think they might develop a true friendship though. She'd been so sheltered after going to live with Tutu and Uncle Makoa that her cousins had been her closest friends until she'd gone to the Big Island to nursing school. At that point she'd been pretty shy but soon had figured out how to break out of her shell. It didn't mean she was indiscriminate about who she got close to. In fact, she took her few friendships very seriously, but she thought herself lucky in having the ability to know, almost immediately, whether there was true friend potential in the people she met.

Bryn had been one. Kali another. And yes, Javier Pascal was also in the mix.

Unfortunately, with him, she couldn't help wishing there could be more, but she'd keep working on it.

"Finally," she muttered to herself as the hospital came into view.

Getting used to the heaviness of the traffic and how long it took to get the few miles from the apartment to work was another thing she found difficult. She didn't think she'd ever take the more laid-back lifestyle of Molokai for granted again.

Yet she liked the hustle and bustle of Boston and the hospital here too. It suited her restless energy better than she'd expected—so far anyway. After all, this was only day two.

After finding a spot to park in the garage, she got out of the car and shivered as a gust of cold air smacked her in the face, making her gasp. Then she shook her head and chuckled, remembering how excited Bryn had seemed about the "warm" weather that morning.

If this was warm, Ailani wasn't sure she was in any way ready for the cold!

"And still no snow," she said aloud, taking a moment to shake a fist, as though at the sky.

The burst of warm laughter made her spin around, heat rushing to her cheeks.

"Are you still fussing about the lack of snow?" Javier asked, coming across the parking garage toward her. He looked particularly yummy wearing a pair of dress pants and a tweedy jacket open over his buttoned-down shirt.

"I want snow, darn it," she replied, trying to hold on to the light tone although her heart was pounding like a crazy thing. "It shouldn't be this cold without it snowing."

"Listen," he said as he came abreast of her and she turned to walk alongside him toward the entrance to the hospital. "You should take my advice and stop tempting the snow gods. If you cause an artic event, we'll never forgive you."

"Well, at least it's early in the month. There's still time."

Javier held the door open for her and waited while she preceded him into the building.

"Yes, thankfully there's still time before Christmas. I have to take my daughter shopping, and I have no idea what to get anyone. My ex used to do most of the present buying."

Sympathy was her first impulse, but he didn't sound sad, just resigned, so as they stepped into the elevator, she replied, "Well, then it's time you put on your thinking cap and come up with some ideas. How old is your daughter?"

His laughter was unexpected but somehow a relief. "I haven't heard that expression in decades. Probably not since grade school." And he chuckled again when she stuck out her tongue at him. "Mabel's six, and just now you reminded me of her. Although I'd have to have a stern talk with her if I saw her sticking out her tongue at anyone."

"Lucky for me, then, that I'm not six and you're not responsible for my questionable behavior."

"That is indeed true," he said, his tone stern, his eyes twinkling merrily. "I wouldn't know how to cope."

The elevator stopped on the next floor, and two nurses and another doctor got on, nodding and murmuring good morning, and that was the end of the conversation. Javier and Ailani parted company when she got off at Pediatrics and he stayed on, saying he had a meeting in Administration.

At the morning meeting, Ailani was brought up to speed on the patients she'd be working with that day, including Kyrie Powers, who'd been kept in overnight.

"As you know, yesterday Dr. Mitchell ordered a urine cortisol test, so we had to take samples through the night. He's also scheduled for an ACTH stimulation test as soon as the cortisol test is over."

"Poor little guy. He must be exhausted."

The nurse she was taking over from snorted. "He probably is, but it's just made him testier."

Ailani started her rounds, and by the time she got to Kyrie's room, he was in there alone and awake. When she smiled and greeted him, all she got in response was a scowl.

"Do I have to pee in the bottle again?"

The truculent question was fired at her like a bullet, but Ailani kept smiling as she picked up his chart.

"Ooh, someone's spicy today. I get that way when I don't get enough sleep too. And yes," she added. "One more urine test, then you're done."

His dramatic groan made her want to laugh, but she held it in, not wanting to annoy him any more than he already was.

From the direction of the tests, Ailani suspected Kali was thinking some kind of adrenal issue was causing Kyrie's illness, and her heart went out to him. If that was the case, he'd probably be on medication for the rest of his life and have to watch for situations that could cause flare-ups.

With that in mind, and remembering the conversation between Javi and Mrs. Powers the day before, after his urine test, Ailani tried to draw him out about what was happening in his life. Stress could, after all, exacerbate adrenal problems, leading to the symptoms he'd exhibited.

Keeping her voice casual, she said, "So, you play football?"

"Yeah," he said, but there was no enthusiasm in his voice.

"You don't sound too happy about it. Don't you like it?"

"I don't mind it."

"Are you good at it?"

He shrugged, but his lips were turned down at the corners and his eyes seemed moist, as if he was holding back tears.

"I used to be," he said, so low it was little better than a whisper. "Then the other boys started getting bigger, and I couldn't keep up with them like I used to."

Making a show of labeling the sample and not looking at him, she said, "You know, people grow at different rates. Maybe it's just not your time yet. Or maybe whatever is happening that brought you here has been interfering with your strength."

"I wanted to quit." It sounded like the admission was dragged out of him, from somewhere deep down in his belly. "The guys all started teasing me, calling me Peewee and things like that. But Dad played in college, and he was so happy when I got on the team, I didn't want to…"

His voice faded, and she knew he was trying not to cry from the sniffles and snuffling coming from the bed.

Putting the sample into the collection tray, she pulled some tissues out of the box beside the bed. When she looked at him, it was to find he'd turned his face away, but she stepped up beside the bed and gently pressed the tissues into his hands.

"Listen, *makamaka uuku*." She kept her voice soft and gentle. "It's okay to be afraid and to cry when you are. And sometimes, no matter how hard it is, you have to be honest with those you love. Even if you're sure they'll be hurt or disappointed. The people who love us will understand."

He looked at her, still trying to hold back the tears, and in a strangled voice said, "But everyone's been telling me I have to be brave and strong. Crying is for babies, and I don't want my dad to think I can't be what he wants me to be."

"Bravery doesn't come from ignoring the way you feel. It's not about pretending you aren't afraid, but being afraid, dealing with the fear and then going on. That's real strength."

And she held him, patting his back as great gulping sobs overcame him, and he finally let go and let all he was feeling out.

"There you go. You're all right. I got you."

When his rush of tears had passed, she gave him more tissues so he could blow his nose and got a clean cloth from the bathroom to wipe his face.

"Feeling better, *makamaka uuku*?"

"Yeah." His voice was still watery and his eyes were red,

but his face had lost some of the pinched expression it had be-fore. "What was that you called me? *Maka*-something? What's that mean?"

"Makamaka uuku?" When he nodded, she told him, "It means 'little friend' in Hawaiian."

"Oh, cool. Can you teach me some other words, so I can tell the other kids when I go back to school?"

So, she did, until Kali Mitchell came in to oversee the first part of the ACTH test, accompanied by the phlebotomy team. Then, after making some notes in his file, Ailani stepped out of the room to continue her rounds, coming to a halt when she saw Javi standing nearby.

Something in his expression made a rush of heat suffuse her body, settling in her face and making her blush.

"Good job," he said, nodding toward the door she'd just come out of. "Really good job."

He must have heard her comforting Kyrie, although she hadn't noticed. Suddenly, under Javi's frankly approving gaze, the damp spot on the front of her scrub top felt like a badge of honor. Although it wasn't the first time she'd held a little one so they could cry and, in this case, she hoped she'd done some good, she'd never felt prouder.

When Javi turned to walk away, she couldn't help watching him for a few moments more before continuing on her rounds, trying to slow the frantic hammering of her heart.

Because of his early morning encounter with Ailani, Javi had started his work day in a good mood, but as the morning pro-gressed that began to fade.

The administrative team was having problems finding a new nurse and had suggested hiring a traveling nurse through an agency, which would play hell with the department's bud-get. Not to mention the fact that he disliked having temporary staff. To his way of thinking, they might not feel as though they had any skin in the game, and it could lead to less-than-stellar performance.

Not that anyone was saying anything of the kind about Ailani. In fact, her praises were being sung all around Pediatrics. Charge Nurse Leigh mentioned just how helpful and useful she was, and Kali Mitchell had stopped by Javi's office to tell him Ailani had gone above and beyond with her patient.

"Kyrie Powers opened up to Ailani," she'd said in her brisk, no-nonsense way, not realizing Javi had witnessed it for himself. "His admission that he'd been having problems in school might not help in diagnosing his condition, but it might explain why his symptoms escalated the way they did."

"Do you have a diagnosis?" he asked, hoping for the little boy's sake it didn't take much longer to find one.

"From everything I've seen, I believe he has some type of adrenal disease, perhaps Addison's, but I'm waiting for the results of the ACTH test to make it definitive. If I'm right, stress, like what he's been under in school, can precipitate a crisis."

Seeing Ailani interact with Kyrie had moved Javi in a way he found almost shocking. He was used to working with medical staff who were compassionate and well-versed in how to speak to their patients, but Ailani's sweetness had been overwhelmingly touching.

Now, running a little late because of another call from Admin, he hurried down to the street on his way to the coffee shop, ridiculously eager to spend some more time with Ailani.

Being with her was so easy, so relaxing. She was smart and funny and made him laugh in a way that he hadn't in far too long. No doubt it helped that she didn't treat him as though he were fragile and potentially about to break—the way other members of staff, who'd known him longer, were inclined to.

That was one of the difficulties of working in the type of environment he'd tried to foster since taking over as head of Pediatrics. People were liable to know a great deal more about your private life than you might like. Yet the current staff worked well together, and he liked to think it was because he'd allowed a more family-type atmosphere to develop.

His predecessor had been a very good administrator and an adequate doctor, but he'd been a poor people manager. He'd seemed incapable of considering the nurses, in particular, as worthy of his respect and consideration. While he'd been less likely to treat the doctors with the same contempt, even they, especially residents, had been subject to Dr. Benoit's high-handed treatment.

He'd been notorious for requesting nurses be transferred out of the department, seemingly on a whim. But the truth was he'd done it because, in his mind, they hadn't treated him with the deference he'd thought he deserved.

It had taken Javi almost a year to get the department running the way he wanted it to, and he'd be the first to admit his preoccupation over that time hadn't helped his marriage. Yet he'd gained enough distance to see where both he and Michael had fallen down on the job of keeping their relationship on track. Now he could look back at everything without feeling as though he'd utterly and completely failed.

And the relief was unmistakable.

Pushing open the door to Full of Beans, seeing Ailani grinning and waving from the same table they'd sat at the day before immediately lightened his spirit. He found himself smiling and felt the cares and concerns of the morning fall away as he headed her way.

Later, he told the more cautious part of his nature. *Later we can think about why she has this effect on me. Right now, I just want to enjoy it.*

CHAPTER FIVE

AILANI SIGHED, leaning back in her chair, cupping her coffee between her hands to warm them up. Lunch had just started, but she was already wishing to herself that it would go on longer.

There was something about Javi—as he'd said she could call him outside the hospital—that both soothed her restless soul and energized her at the same time.

Who knew that was even possible?

He brought up Kyrie Powers, and she found herself being more honest with him than she'd normally be with anyone she'd known for such a short time.

"It's hard when you're a child trying to protect everyone else around you. He's so smart and so afraid, trying not to disappoint his dad, being strong for his mom. In a way, he needed permission to do the best thing for himself, although I didn't say it to him like that."

Javi's brows lowered slightly. "You think his parents have been pushing him too hard?"

"Not at all." She'd met Mr. Powers as well as Kyrie's mother, and they'd both seemed perfectly reasonable and desperately worried about their son. Having dealt with a wide variety of parent/child relationships, Ailani felt confident in her opinion. "They know he's smart, and before he got sick, he was doing well on the football field, but it seemed they were living a well-balanced life.

"No. I think it's Kyrie that was pushing himself, and because he couldn't understand what was happening to his body, he thought he wasn't good enough. That he wasn't living up to what his father wanted and expected. He needed a good cry and someone he felt he wouldn't be letting down when he cried on them—as well as someone to point out what he was going through wasn't his fault."

Javi gave her a long look, his gaze so searching she felt it down to her toes and had to force herself not to look away.

"I know you're an experienced nurse, but why do I feel as though there's personal experience behind that particular insight?"

She hesitated for a moment, turning the question over in her head before replying. And she found herself speaking slowly, feeling for the right words as she went.

"It's not the same, really, but I definitely understand having to realize when you can't live under the weight of expectations, whether they're your own or someone else's." His gaze was trained on hers, and although she sort of wanted to look away, she found she couldn't. "I lost my parents when I was eight."

"I'm sorry."

He looked it too, his face tightening as though feeling her pain. Ailani shrugged, not because it didn't still hurt all these years later, but because she didn't want his sympathy, really.

"It was a long time ago, so don't stress it." She knew she sounded terse but didn't apologize. "What happened, though, was that Tutu—my grandmother—and my uncle Makoa raised me and kept me so sheltered I wasn't allowed to do anything that was remotely risky. I went through all the emotions a child does when they lose their parents—was it somehow my fault? What else horrible was going to happen? Then I realized that Tutu and Uncle would get upset if I climbed too high in a tree or wanted to go down to the cliffs with my cousins without an adult, and I thought that if I defied them, they'd leave me too."

She took a deep breath, looking down at her plate so as not to remain caught in that intent hazel gaze, which somehow scorched her in a way the past no longer did.

"So, what happened?"

Exhaling, she picked up the remains of her sandwich and replied, "An older cousin gave me a box of things that had belonged to my parents, and I got to read my mother's diaries. They were an eye-opener. My mom had this extraordinary, adventuresome spirit. There were all these entries about the things she'd done before she had me, all the places she'd been. And there was a list—she'd labeled it her bucket list—with stuff crossed off. But there were a bunch of things she hadn't gotten a chance to do."

"So you decided to do them for her?"

There was a note in his voice that had her looking back up at him, not knowing what expression to expect to find on his face, but his expression was curiously blank. She dropped her gaze again.

"Well, really, I finally realized that I had to live my own life, no matter how Tutu and Uncle felt about it, just like my mom had. I know they were just trying to protect me, afraid something would happen to me and they'd lose that last connection to my mom. But it wasn't my job to make them feel better by denying my own needs."

She wouldn't admit how hard it had been, especially knowing Uncle Makoa really struggled with change because of his ADHD and autism. Yet even Tutu had eventually told Ailani she understood, although she didn't like the thought of her granddaughter doing what she'd called *lōlō* things—crazy things.

"Was that when you went into nursing?"

Surprised, she looked up and chuckled. "Oh, no. I was already a nurse. That was the one thing they agreed on, although I had to go to the Big Island to study. My high school guidance counselor talked them into it after I did an aptitude test. There was also a grant I got that paid for my training as long as I agreed to go back to Molokai and work for five years. I only read my mom's diary a couple of years ago and decided I really needed to get a move on if I wanted to experience any other kind of life."

She didn't add the fact that her mom being only a year older than she was right now had galvanized her into action. There were some things that were far better left unsaid.

Javi smiled, but it didn't seem as natural as usual, and she couldn't help wondering what part of her story it was, exactly, that made him look that way.

"Anyway, all this is my long-winded way of saying something that I'm sure you already know, which is that kids often get the story wrong or take on responsibilities that really aren't theirs to bear."

He nodded, and now he was the one who looked down.

"When Michael—my ex-husband—left, the one thing I asked of him was that he reassure Mabel that his decision didn't have anything at all to do with her." Moving his cup back and forth between his fingers was a giveaway to how difficult it was for him to talk about. "We'd only adopted her about a year and a half before, and she'd had difficulty settling in, so I was afraid his leaving would confuse and upset her."

His low-voiced confession made her heart ache—both for him and for his daughter.

"Did it?"

"A little. But thankfully both my parents and his rallied around us and helped us both get through it. And whatever else I could say about my ex, he's been a reliable, if long-distance, presence in Mabel's life."

"I'm glad."

Her voice wavered, but there was nothing she could do about that, and when their eyes met his gaze was so warm and yet so vulnerable, it took everything she had inside to tear hers away.

The last thing she needed were these protective impulses that made her want to find his ex and give him a good slap. Nor did she appreciate the sense of longing combined with the urge to comfort him.

Javier Pascal didn't need—and most likely didn't want—her compassion, just like she didn't want his sympathy. And all of this soul baring made her stomach hollow and saddened her heart.

So, clearing her throat, she did a complete one-eighty, hoping he'd follow her lead.

"By the way, do you know if there's anywhere around here that I can buy some inexpensive Christmas decorations? Bryn says she's hibernating this year, and I need something Christmassy around the place, even if she doesn't."

Thankfully, he took the hint and nodded. "There's a big craft store in Cambridge, and they always have a bunch of seasonal decorations. What?" he asked when she gave him a surprised look. "I have a little girl. Of course I know where the craft stores are."

"Ahh…" Glad for the lightening of the mood, she couldn't resist teasing him. "So that's your story, and you're sticking to it?"

Giving her a haughty look, he replied, "Yes. Although I'll admit to you, if you promise not to tell anyone, that once upon a time I was considering a career in the arts. A decision had to be made, and medicine won."

Now that was a shocker. "Really?"

Javi shook his head, his expression disapproving. "You find me that one-dimensional? All I am and could possibly be is a man of science? Without soul or sensibilities?"

Laughing, still not sure whether to believe him or not, she

wrinkled her nose. "You're being ridiculous. Of course I don't find you one-dimensional. Although right now, I'm not sure whether I find you truthful, and that's the real question."

It was only when he relaxed back against his chair that she realized they'd both been leaning toward each other, not quite able to touch but very close across the small table.

"It's absolutely true. I was the only person in my year who won prizes for both science and art in high school. Of course, I wanted to pursue the art. Who wouldn't, in comparison to eleven or more years of studying, along with crippling student loan debt?"

Intrigued, she asked, "So what happened?"

"My father," he replied with such a wealth of meaning in those two words, Ailani couldn't help hooting with laughter. "He made it clear that if I wanted to be an artist, I would be doing it on my own time, in my own house, not his. He'd support me getting what he called a real profession, and art was not one."

"Oh dear," she said as he looked at his watch and she realized it was time to go. "So, do you draw or paint or anything anymore?"

Rising, he shook his head, and she thought she saw a flash of regret in his eyes.

"Who has time? Priorities shift, and it's all I can do to keep work and fatherhood under control. Maybe one day I'll get back to it—when I'm old and retired."

For some reason, hearing him say it that way made her sad again, and she reacted the way she usually did when conversations got too hard or deep.

By teasing him some more.

"Don't you just mean when you retire? You're already pretty old."

And his outraged expression had her howling again.

* * *

Even as they laughed and joked their way back to the hospital, Javi's brain was turning over all he'd learned about Ailani over lunch.

Orphaned at eight. Overly sheltered and protected by her relatives, who probably feared losing her just as much as she feared losing them. Suddenly awakened to the reality of the type of woman her mother was and wanting to following in her footsteps.

A woman who probably had itchy feet and had resented being stuck in one place all the time.

Sounded horribly, heartbreakingly familiar to Javi.

Why, he wondered, did he seem to be attracted to the same type of person, over and over again?

Outgoing, exuberant and longing for more than just a regular, settled, steady life?

Then he mentally shrugged and reassured himself that no matter how interesting and attractive he found Ailani, there wouldn't be anything more than friendship between them.

Despite recognizing that he was more or less over the heartbreak of the divorce, he'd already made the decision to concentrate on Mabel and his job. Nothing else. He had neither the time nor the emotional currency to pursue anything other than those two most important responsibilities. Not even for a fling. Not that there could be anything else with a woman who was only going to be in Boston for three months and who was no doubt already planning her next adventure.

"See you on the floor," Ailani said when they got back to the door of the staff room.

And then, with a wave, she went in, leaving him to continue on his way. He had only a few minutes to get his gear and head out onto the wards, since today was one of his rotation days. Normally he took at least one day of the weekend off to spend with Mabel, but one of the staff pediatricians, Dr.

Iain MacKenzie, was off at a conference and wasn't due back until Monday. It was another shortage in staff that made him feel as though he was standing with his finger in the dike, trying to stem a deluge.

He'd gotten a call earlier, too, about a young boy coming in from Providence, Rhode Island, to be operated on by Ben Murphy. Thankfully his pediatrician, Dr. Dylan Geller, was coming along to support the family and provide a familiar face and had agreed to help in the pediatric outpatient clinic while he was here.

Right now, they needed all the help they could get.

If he could just find a suitable nurse...

As Javi shucked his jacket and reached for his white coat, his brain turned away from where it should've been—on work—and back to his private life. And Ailani.

He'd never been a one-night-stand kind of man or even a friends-with-benefits type, and since Michael had left he'd avoided the dating scene altogether, not wanting to get involved again. Especially not with Mabel to think about.

His daughter deserved his complete attention and to be taken into consideration whenever a life decision needed to be made.

But why was he thinking about life decisions and Ailani in the same train of thought?

Maybe, he thought, pausing with his hand on the doorknob, this was all part and parcel of deciding it was time to move past the pain Michael had caused? Was all this—the attraction to Ailani, in particular—just an offshoot of him contemplating a new future? One without the shadow of his divorce and heartbreak hanging over him?

A glance at his watch had him muttering a curse and swiftly pushing all those thoughts aside. If he didn't leave his office right this minute, he'd be late.

And Dr. Javi Pascal was never late. Not if it could be avoided.

CHAPTER SIX

LEIGH WAS AT the nurses' desk and heaved an audible sigh of relief when she saw Ailani was back on the floor.

"Thank goodness," she said, thrusting a file into Ailani's hands. "Tricia just had to leave because she started running a fever, and we had an influx of patients in the hour you were gone. It's nuts."

"Where is my patient?" she asked, looking at the file and noting there was no room number on it.

"He's coming in now. Brought in from the park by ambulance. They took him to Radiology, but he should be on the ward any minute now." She checked the board and added, "Room 205 is empty, so direct them there."

There was a children's section to the emergency room, and the kids were sent up to the ward only if they needed additional attention. As she moved toward the room Leigh had indicated, Ailani read the notes she'd been provided with, and her heart did a little dip.

Isaac Barone, age eight, had taken a tumble off playground equipment. He had lacerations to the back of his head and above one eye and a potential fracture to the right arm. The emergency room notes said he was conscious and alert, with no overt signs of concussion, but what gave Ailani that sinking feeling was the last notation.

Father suffered from epilepsy. Deceased after grand mal seizure.

Unless they were filled to capacity, a couple of gashes and a broken arm would probably be taken care of in the emergency area. The only reason she could think of for Isaac to be sent up to the ward was if there was a concern his injuries had been caused by a seizure.

Pushing that thought aside, she prepared the room, ensuring all the equipment necessary was on hand. The turnover in the rooms had been phenomenal over the two days she'd been on staff, and it was a constant chore to keep the supplies in place. Just before she'd gone to lunch, there'd still been a toddler in 205, the little girl on a nebulizer because of RSV.

Hopefully she was no longer there because her illness had improved to the point where she could be discharged.

Ailani made a mental note to check when she got a chance.

After her quick inventory check, she headed toward the elevators, just as the doors opened and a stretcher was pushed out by one of the orderlies. The swathe of bandages over the wan face of the little boy lying on it and the terrified expression of the woman walking beside it told their own tale.

"205," Ailani told the orderly as the gurney came alongside her, and she turned to walk beside it. "Hi, Isaac, I'm Ailani, and I'm going to help take care of you. Are you Mom?" she asked the ashen-faced lady.

"Yes," she replied, her voice wobbling. "Yes, I'm Isaac's mom."

"Okay, well, you're in good hands now. This way."

"Radiology is sending the results. They're a little backed up, so they asked me to tell you it'll be a couple of minutes," the orderly said.

"Thank you." The results would be coming through on the computer system so whichever doctor was looking after Isaac could access them.

They were in the room now, and Mrs. Barone reluctantly stepped aside so that Ailani and the orderly could help Isaac from the gurney to the bed. The little boy caught his breath sharply, no doubt because his arm got joggled, but otherwise he was stoic, clearly trying not to cry.

Ailani was just wondering which of the doctors would be examining and treating Isaac when Javi slipped in through the door past the departing orderly.

"Mrs. Barone, Isaac, I'm Dr. Pascal."

At the sight of him, her heart did a little tip-tap, but Ailani ignored it and went on making Isaac comfortable. It would be interesting, and very informative, to see the type of tone he set. Whether he adjusted his mannerisms to suit these particular people or spoke to Isaac the same way he had Kyrie.

Both members of the Barone family were watching him with what looked like absolute terror, and she knew that the specter of epilepsy must've been hanging over their heads.

How traumatic it must've been to think Isaac was exhibiting the same signs as his father and might suffer the same fate.

Javi gave first Mrs. Barone then Isaac a smile so gentle and compassionate, Ailani swore she could feel the tension in the room ease.

"I see from the record that you fell off some playground equipment. Can you tell me what happened?"

As he spoke, Javi started his examination. Even though the little boy had been seen in the pediatric ER, he obviously needed to take a look at Isaac for himself.

"I…" Isaac's voice caught, and he shook his head, wincing. Then, taking a deep breath, he said, "I was doing tricks on the monkey bars—flipping and stuff like that—then I fell."

Javi was working his way down Isaac's body, avoiding the right arm as best he could and without taking off the bandage wrapped around his head to hold the dressings in place.

"Do you remember falling?"

A pause as Isaac seemed to be thinking back, his eyes blinking slowly and tracking up and left and then to the side.

"Yes," he said slowly. "I think so. There was a girl there, and she said something to me. I looked at her, and then I was falling."

"Good," Javi said, glancing up at Mrs. Barone. "That's very good."

And it was. Most people with seizures had no memory of the onset and what had happened during the time they'd been seizing.

Ailani felt lighter at his words and smiled although no one was paying any attention. Javi smiled too and rested his hand on Isaac's shoulder, lightly rubbing it.

"Well, I'm going to take a look at the cut on the back of your head, but the doctor in the ER said it needs stitches, so I'm afraid you're going to have a bit of a bald spot for a while."

Isaac groaned. "Aww, that's gonna look stupid. Do you have to shave it?"

"Afraid so, man." Javi somehow made his expression serious, while Ailani just wanted to giggle at the entire situation. "I also took a look at your X-rays. You have what they call a greenstick fracture of your radius—one of the bones in your arm—so I'm going to give you a cast to go with the bald spot."

"I don't mind the cast so much, but the bald spot? That's just stupid."

"Isaac," his mother said, an admonishing tone to the way she said his name.

"Hey," Javi continued. "What's your favorite sports team?"

"Bruins all the way," Isaac said. "That was my dad's favorite team too."

Mrs. Barone sucked in a breath, and Ailani instinctively reached out to touch her arm, hoping to keep the other woman calm now that they had Isaac more relaxed.

"Mine too," Javi said. "How about I put the *B* logo on your cast? Would you like that?"

"Yeah!"

"Then that's what we'll do. You can show all your friends when you get back to school on Monday, okay?"

And Isaac's enthusiastic agreement even brought a smile to his worried mother's face.

From the corner of his eye, Javi saw Ailani reach out to Isaac's mother, and he heaved an internal sigh of relief. Often their patients were a lot easier to deal with than their parents.

Not that he blamed them in the slightest. He felt sorry for any doctor who'd have to treat Mabel if anything happened to her. Javi knew he'd be in Papa Bear mode and a monster to deal with.

He liked the way Ailani did what needed to be done without fuss. She already had sutures and cast material to hand, even before he'd arrived in the room. There was no doubt in his mind that she'd also seen the notation about Isaac's father suffering from epilepsy and had interpreted Isaac's report of falling correctly.

Doing the stitches first—and getting them out of the way—made sense. While neither the stitches nor having the cast put on would be pleasant, the latter would be a little less traumatic. Between Isaac's mother and Ailani, they kept him still until the local anesthetic did its job, and it didn't take long for Javi to get the laceration closed up.

Ailani, as part of her distraction technique, got Isaac talking about hockey by the simple method of asking him what the Bruins were.

Eyes wide, he asked, "You don't know what the Bruins are?"

"Nope," she said with one of her cheeky grins. "I know *bruin* means *bear*, but besides that I have no clue."

"Don't you know about hockey?"

"Oh, you mean on ice? Hold still," she admonished as he started nodding. "Where I come from there's no ice to skate on."

By the time Isaac had told her more than she'd probably ever wanted to know about ice hockey and she'd told him a bit about Hawaii, Javi had stitched his head, applied a butterfly bandage to the cut over his eye and almost finished the cast.

Mrs. Barone was looking a lot more relaxed too.

There was a certain positive, cheery energy about Ailani that Javi was sure made all the difference.

As he was stripping off his gloves, Isaac was admiring the Boston Bruins logo inscribed on his cast and asking if he could color it in once the yellow material was dry.

"Of course. If your mom will let you use a permanent marker, it'll last until you take it off in four to six weeks."

"Cool!"

Ailani was saying something softly to Mrs. Barone, and the other lady was nodding, not quite smiling but certainly not as stressed as she had been at the beginning.

"Mrs. Barone." Both she and Ailani looked up at him, and Javi felt a weird impulse to blush under their combined attentions. "I'd like to speak to you about Isaac's care going forward, and Admin will have a few documents for you to sign."

"Of course." Mrs. Barone got up, sending her son, who looked so small and vulnerable in the hospital bed, a tender glance. "I'll be right back, sweetheart."

"I'll be here with you until your mom gets back," Ailani reassured the little boy, and Javi was relieved when Isaac nodded.

Outside, he stopped Mrs. Barone just down the corridor with a hand on her arm. "I see from Isaac's file that his father suffered from grand mal seizures, and I know that must have been at the forefront of your mind when he fell."

He could see the strain that immediately tightened her face.

"Yes. The little girl who spoke to him said he looked at her in a weird way, and…"

Her voice faded and, seeing her sway slightly, Javi put his hand on her shoulder to steady her.

"The fact that he remembers falling is a good sign, and although I'm going to ask you to watch him for any signs of concussion, I think he's fit to be released."

She opened her mouth as though to argue and then closed it again. Her brows were knitted, and she frowned, shaking her head.

"Your nurse said you're head of Pediatrics and a really good doctor so I can trust your judgment, but do you blame me for being worried?"

"Not at all," he replied, giving her shoulder a little squeeze and ignoring the spurt of warmth he felt at hearing what Ailani had said about him. "If it were my daughter, I'd be beyond worried. But the reality is that your son has had a traumatic experience and I'd like to give him a chance to recover somewhat from it before we do anything more.

"Once he's healed a bit, discuss with your primary care physician the benefits of having an electroencephalogram to rule out epilepsy. In the meantime, you can watch him and see if he exhibits any signs of the disease. If he does—even the smallest sign—you bring him right back here, and we'll run the tests then."

Mrs. Barone's gaze roamed his face, as though searching for the answers to all of life's questions there. Sighing, she nodded.

"I know you're making sense," she said in a small voice that wavered and threatened to crack. "But after what I've been through—what we've been through—it's hard not to want definitive answers right away."

"I know." It was almost impossible to reassure her any further than he had. "It's up to you to make the decision, and I'll support you however you need."

Taking a deep breath and then blowing it out, she straightened her spine and lifted her chin. "I have to believe that if you thought he was in danger, you'd tell me to have the test right away."

"I would," he said, nodding.

"Then I'll wait and keep an eye on Isaac." Her lips tightened, the corners turning down. "He was there, when his father seized that last time. I don't want him to be scared that it will happen to him. If I think he's fretting about it, I'm bringing him in right away. It's not right for an eight-year-old to have those kinds of fears."

"You're right," Javi agreed. "And it's not right for you to have them either. If you have any doubts, you let us know, and we'll schedule the electroencephalogram. Do you want me to speak to him about it and reassure him?"

"If you would, that would be amazing." He could see her relief and nodded before taking her to the nurses' station to sign the discharge forms.

But when he got back, it was to find a smiling Isaac, as calm as calm could be, as Ailani kept him occupied and relaxed.

"Nurse Ailani told me I can trust you to take care of me," he said when Javi broached the subject of epilepsy and their plan to wait for a while before doing any tests. "And if Mom says I'll be okay, then I believe you all."

After they'd taken their leave of the Barones and were heading back to the nurses' station, Javi asked, "What did you say to him? I was expecting a bit of a scene when I mentioned the epilepsy."

She shrugged slightly, sending him a sideways glance from beneath her dark, straight lashes. "He actually brought it up with me, and I told him that we knew about his dad and would do everything we could to figure out whether he had it or not, but it didn't make sense for him to worry about it. If he had it, we'd find out and treat it. If he didn't, worrying about it wouldn't be productive. I reminded him that he had a bone to mend and hair to grow back so he should concentrate on that."

"Concentrate on growing back his hair?" Javi couldn't help the little snort of laughter that broke from his throat.

"Yep." Ailani's grin could have lit the entire ward in the event of a power outage. "He's still annoyed about the bald spot. It just seemed like a good diversion."

And they were still chuckling when they got to the desk to receive their next assignments.

CHAPTER SEVEN

MONDAY MORNING FOUND Ailani running late for work, when, going downstairs, she found Abbie's car had a flat.

"Dammit," she muttered, thankful that she'd noticed it immediately but still annoyed.

She'd learned the various departure times that got her to the hospital with plenty of time to get out of her coat and boots and make it to the morning meeting. If she or Bryn were driving, she could leave later than if she were taking the subway, which felt somehow counterintuitive.

Shouldn't public transportation, which didn't get snarled by traffic, be quicker over such a short trip? But because of the train schedule, it wasn't.

Then, realizing she was wasting time she didn't have, she set off toward the subway station at a trot. Anywhere there was moisture on the ground was now coated with a thin sheet of ice. Although her anxiety built every time one of her feet skidded, she refused to allow herself to stop or turn back.

However, at the subway entrance, there was no mistaking her exhale as anything other than relief.

Rush hour hadn't started fully, but the car was still full. A glance at her watch told her that she was definitely going to miss the morning meeting, and she made a quick call to the floor telephone, leaving a message when the call went unanswered.

Then, as they had many, many times over the last few days, her thoughts drifted easily to Javi Pascal.

Now there was a conundrum.

She kept telling herself he was just being friendly—trying to help her fit in and feel welcome—and that she was reciprocating. However, there was a fine line between befriending someone and being on the cusp of falling for them, and she knew she was already doing a tightrope act with Javi.

Trying to convince herself all she felt was an innocent liking for the handsome man was a nonstarter, and she was honest enough to admit it. No, there was definitely more to this feeling of wanting to be around him, to get to know him better. And when he looked at her with those gorgeous eyes...

"Whew," she said aloud, remembering the sensation of losing her breath, her heart thumping, her insides warming to dangerous levels.

When a nearby woman gave her a surprised, interrogative glance, Ailani shook her head and looked away, aware that her cheeks had darkened with a blush.

The problem was everyone at work talked about his ex-husband and there seemed to be no doubt in anyone's mind that Javi was gay.

So, was it just her imagination furnishing some of his glances with less than innocent interest? Was she so deluded—or desperate—that she was hallucinating the electricity between them? It had been a while since she'd been involved in a relationship, so maybe she was out of practice reading the signs accurately.

In reality, the only way to find out would be to ask him, but it seemed ridiculous to do that on so short an acquaintance. After all, they'd known each other all of three days. Surely that wasn't long enough to even give credence to any kind of emotional connection, was it?

Besides, emotional connections came in all kinds of shapes and packages. Probably, by the time they'd known each other for a month or so, she'd realize it was more of a fraternal affection.

At least, she rather hoped so.

Either way, it couldn't be allowed to grow into anything else because, even if somehow it turned out he was as interested in her as she was in him, it couldn't go anywhere. She was only going to be in Boston for three months.

There was her family to go back to and a whole lot more world out there to explore.

Finally, the train pulled into her station, and Ailani joined the people going up to the sidewalk. It was only as the icy wind struck that she remembered she'd dressed for driving, not walking. Under Bryn's guidance, she'd worked out the proper attire for taking public transportation versus the car. Now the wind cut through the thin scrub pants, and although she was wearing her winter coat and walking as quickly as possible, Ailani shivered.

The sun was just a golden smudge on the horizon between the buildings. The sidewalks were still slick with ice, and she struggled to keep her footing while avoiding oncoming commuters.

As she hurried along, Ailani moved closer to a van parked alongside the sidewalk. A workman was leaning into the open side door, but as Ailani came abreast of him, he suddenly turned, whatever he had in his hand slamming into her thigh.

She'd been mid-step, her other leg lifted, and the impact sent her flying. Landing on her tote saved her chest from the worst of the fall and kept her head from slamming into the pavement. But her elbow struck hard, sending an explosion of agony through her arm so intense she couldn't even cry out.

Trying to catch her breath, she sat up gingerly, holding the wrist of her injured arm and blinking against the tears gathering in her eyes.

"Are you alright? I'm sorry—I didn't see you." The workman was stooping beside her, his face creased with concern. "Can you stand? I can call an ambulance."

"Give me a sec," Ailani managed to say as she took stock. "I think I'm okay."

"Your leg is bleeding." A woman had stopped too and pointed to Ailani's thigh. "We're right by the hospital. If you can walk, I'll take you into the emergency room."

"No. It's fine." Although pain, like a series of electric shocks, was still firing up her arm, there was only a small amount of blood staining around the tear in her scrub pants. "I work there, so I'll get looked at when I get inside."

Getting to her feet with help from the onlookers, she somehow found a smile for everyone gathered around. All she wanted to do was get away from the over-solicitous onlookers, so with one last reassurance to the man who'd hit her, she continued on her way despite the trembling of her legs.

Shock was definitely setting in, and although it took her only about five minutes to make it to the staff entrance of the hospital, her teeth were chattering and she was shaking.

Once in the staff locker room, she dropped onto the nearest bench and took a couple of deep breaths, trying to collect herself. She was already late, and there was no time for hysterics. Besides, she wasn't really hurt—just a little banged up.

After carefully getting her coat off, hissing as her elbow complained, she took off her boots and then bent to put on her rubber shoes. That was when the cut on her leg stung, reminding her it was there.

A glance revealed there was more blood around the rip in her scrubs than she'd thought.

"Dammit," she muttered, just as the door opened and Javi strode in.

"Hey," he said, giving her a smile. "Didn't see you at the morning briefing. Everything okay?"

"Had a flat," she said, covering the spot where she'd been cut with her hand and trying to sound normal although she was still trembling and felt close to tears. "So I took the train."

But Javi obviously wasn't fooled. He moved closer.

"A flat tire wouldn't upset you this much." At any other time she might have taken exception to his assumption, but just then she couldn't. "What's wrong with your leg? Let me see."

"I took a little tumble," she replied, reluctantly moving her hand. "Nothing serious. I just need to—"

"You just need to come with me so I can take a proper look at that laceration," he said in a tone that brooked no argument. "What cut you—do you know?"

"No, I don't," she replied, trying to maintain control. "But you know I'm a nurse, right, and can take care of myself?"

"Normally I'd agree with you, but you're pale and shaking, and you're cradling your left arm as though it hurts too. What kind of doctor—what kind of friend—would I be if I just walked away and left you to deal with it by yourself?"

How was she to argue with that, especially since her throat had closed and she had to look down so he wouldn't realize she had teared up? As she blinked away the moisture in her eyes, she saw his hand, outstretched, and instinctively took it.

"Come on," he said softly, tugging gently to urge her to her feet. "Let's get you patched up."

"I need another pair of scrub pants," she said, embarrassed by the way her voice hitched. "Give me a second."

He waited by the door as she went to the cupboard where the scrubs were kept and grabbed a pair, then he let her precede him into the corridor beyond.

"Let's get one of the other nurses to come in with us, in case I need something," he said as he guided her toward the nurses' station. Spying a nurse there, he hailed her. "Carol, do you have a couple of minutes? Ailani took a tumble, and I want to examine her laceration."

"Oh, my gosh," the other nurse said, coming out from behind the desk immediately. "Of course. Are you okay, Ailani?"

"Yes," she muttered, now totally humiliated. "It was so

dumb. A workman swung around as I was passing and bashed into me. Between that and the ice, I went flying."

"Room Four is empty, Dr. Pascal," Carol said, before continuing, "Girl, don't feel silly. I fall at least once a year on the ice, even without anyone's help."

Ailani smiled, feeling a bit better, and as the three of them went into the exam room, it occurred to her that Javi had asked Carol to join them so there'd be no chatter on the ward. And she was extra glad of his foresight when he turned his back so Carol could help her take off the ruined scrubs.

When Ailani was seated on the table with a drape over her lap, Carol said, "She's ready for you, Dr. Pascal."

"Great." He came over and before looking at her leg, quipped, "You're a little bigger than my usual patients, but not by much."

Ailani snorted, glad he was joking because it had suddenly occurred to her that he'd actually be touching her, and her insides had started quivering. Not with shock, but with anticipation.

"I took down the last person who tried to tease me about my height," she replied, trying to give him a hard stare.

Javi just laughed. "Okay, tigress. I'll not mention your vertical challenges again."

And Ailani just gave a growl, as if annoyed, while Carol chuckled.

"Did you hit your head at all?" he asked, gently palpating her skull through her hair before she could answer.

Just that impersonal touch made her heart rate kick into a higher gear, but she somehow found the wherewithal to reply, "I don't think so."

"Good." He'd done a comprehensive examination of her head and now turned his attention to her leg. "I'll take a look at that elbow when I'm finished with your leg."

"It's fine," she said, bending and flexing first her fingers and then the elbow itself. "I just hit my un-funny bone."

Carol snorted a laugh. "That's the perfect name for it."

"Right?" Ailani forced herself to concentrate on the other nurse, trying to ignore the sensation of Javi's fingers on her skin. Even though he was wearing gloves and it was a clinical setting, the knowledge that he was touching her sent sparks of awareness through her nerve endings.

"It's not too deep, but the edges are pretty ragged," Javi said. "Once it's cleaned up, I'll close it with a butterfly bandage and a gauze pad." Carol handed him the cleaning solution. "When last did you have a tetanus shot?"

"Last year," she said through gritted teeth as the cut throbbed under his attentions. "We're on a mandatory schedule of every ten years."

"Good."

She found herself watching his hands as they moved with precision and skill and had to turn her gaze elsewhere. Not because she couldn't bear to see what he was doing, but because she felt as though her temperature was rising.

Javi Pascal was far too attractive for her peace of mind.

Carol glanced at her watch. "Dr. Pascal, it's almost time for Catrina to head up to the OR."

Ailani recognized the name. Catrina was a little cancer patient slated to have a bone marrow transplant that day. Hoping to mitigate the effect Javi was having on her with his proximity, Ailani asked, "Are you taking her up?"

"No," Carol said. "I forgot you're new here. When we have little ones going for transplants, we all line the hallway and cheer them on." Her eyes clouded for a moment. "She's such a sweetie—I'd hate to miss it."

They all developed favorites on the wards, especially when the child had been there for a while, so Ailani understood Carol's words.

"I'm pretty much done here," Javi said as he reached for the gauze pad to put over the now-cleaned and bandaged laceration.

"You good?" Carol asked Ailani.

For an instant she hesitated but then told herself not to be silly. "Yep. Go ahead."

"We'll be out in a minute," Javi added, applying one more strip of tape to hold the gauze pad in place.

As Carol left, he asked, "How's the elbow?"

"It's fine. Hardly hurts at all anymore."

Those penetrating hazel eyes locked on hers, searching and sending heat cascading through her veins.

"If you're in pain, you could go home. No one would blame you."

"Don't be silly," she replied. Her breath wanted to catch in her chest. He was so close his warmth and delicious scent touched her, making her heart beat erratically. "I... I'm fine. Besides, we're short-staffed."

She didn't think he moved, but suddenly the moment seemed incredibly intimate.

"Well, if you have to leave, just let them know I said you could."

It suddenly occurred to her that with the way they were positioned, if she lifted her chin just a little, she'd be perfectly positioned for his kiss, and her heart went from thumping to racing.

What are you thinking?

Totally flustered, she forced her gaze down to her lap and away from the temptation he offered. Had she really been about to make a fool of herself with a man who wasn't just gay but her boss too? Imagining the warmth in his gaze was more than friendly concern?

Gathering her composure and giving her head a mental shake, she straightened, making her face impassive.

"Don't fuss." She made her voice as firm as she could, adding a bit of a shooing gesture with her right hand in emphasis. "Go back to work, and I'll be out in a minute."

Javi's gaze dropped to where her bare legs poked out from beneath the drape, and she immediately felt naked.

Exposed.

Funny how when he'd been bandaging her up that hadn't even crossed her mind!

"Right," he said, abruptly turning for the door. "See you on the ward."

And it was only when the door closed behind him that she could breathe again.

Ten minutes after he'd left Ailani in the examination room, Javi was still grappling with the effect of their encounter.

He'd almost kissed her.

If she'd given him even the slightest hint of interest—and despite them being in the hospital—he'd have gladly succumbed to her allure.

Now, as he stood with the rest of the staff lining the hallway, his gaze sought out Ailani where she stood quietly talking to one of the other nurses. The more he saw of her, the more they interacted, the more fascinating he found her. Luckily, she didn't seem to share his interest—and that, he told himself firmly, was a very good thing. It dialed back the temptation to manageable levels.

Just then the gurney with Catrina was wheeled into the corridor, and the traditional send-off of clapping and cheers began. The little girl, weak as she was, still found the strength to smile and wave as though she was royalty, leaving hardly a dry eye on the ward when she entered the elevator.

As though unable to help himself, Javi gravitated to Ailani's side, and when she looked up at him, her big brown eyes still swimming with tears, his heart just about melted.

"Oh, gosh," she said. "That was so moving. I have to remember to tell the staff in Molokai about this. It's a wonderful way to encourage our little patients, isn't it?"

Mention of her home in Hawaii was just the reminder he needed that they would only ever be friends, no matter what else he felt, and allowed him to smile and nod.

"It lifts their spirits," he agreed. "And the staff's too."

"If you can consider bawling my eyes out a spirit lifter," she replied tartly, making him grin. "I have to go wash my face. Lunch later?"

"Sure," he replied before thinking it through.

But he had to call off their lunch when he found himself dealing with some administrative matters, which precluded leaving the hospital. When he texted Ailani to let her know, she answered:

NP

Leaving him wondering why it was he felt so disappointed while she was simply nonchalant.

Part of him—the sensible part—wanted to leave it like that but couldn't help remembering how pale and shaken she'd been that morning. As it got close to the end of both their shifts, he went looking for her, finding her just leaving a patient's room.

"Hey," he said, making his voice as casual as he could. "I'm going to drive you home and change that tire for you."

"You don't have to do that," she said immediately, reminding him how independent she was. "I can deal with it."

Giving her a long look, he shook his head. "I think the words you're looking for are, 'Thanks, friend. I appreciate it.'"

Ailani gave one of those adorable snorts of laughter and mimicked his head shake.

"No, that really wasn't what I was going for, and yes, I do appreciate it, but I am capable of changing a tire."

"Did you check the spare? If it's flat too, you'll need transport to get a new tire. And," he added as her lips opened, "if Bryn isn't around, you're stuck waiting for her to get home."

Apparently that was the deciding argument because she agreed, and thirty minutes later found them back at the apartment building, and he was hefting the spare out of the trunk.

"Looks fine," she said when he dropped the tire and it bounced. "I can take it from here."

"How's your elbow?" he asked, already pulling out the jack. "And your leg. I'm guessing bending down isn't too comfortable for you just now."

The sound she made was somewhere between annoyance and amusement. "You're not going to give in, are you?"

"Nope." He made sure to keep his back to her so she couldn't see him grinning. "I'm as immovable as a mountain."

"I think the words you were looking for were 'stubborn as a mule,'" she replied, echoing his earlier teasing and making him laugh out loud.

It didn't take long for him to get the tire changed, replace the tools and deposit the flat tire into the trunk.

"Yes, yes," she said after he'd closed the trunk and before he could say a word. "I'll take it to be repaired as soon as I can, but I volunteered to work some extra shifts this week because we're so short-staffed. It'll have to wait until my day off."

"Well, I suggest not driving it too much in the meantime."

Ailani's face fell. "I was planning to go to that craft store you told me about tomorrow evening. I *need* some festive cheer in the apartment."

"I'll take you after work." He glanced at his watch and added, "I'd take you this evening, but I have to go pick up Mabel from my mom and dad's. I hardly spent any time with her on the weekend because of work."

The look she gave him sent tingles up and down his spine and made him feel ten feet tall.

"You're such a good father."

She was like a magnet to him, and Javi found himself stepping forward, getting closer to where she leaned against the side of the car.

"I have—" Before he could finish saying he had a little time and ask her if she wanted a quick drink, his phone rang, the ringtone one he instantly recognized. Frowning as he pulled the phone from his pocket, he said, "Excuse me. I need to take this. It's my ex."

He connected the call with a swipe. "Michael. What's up?"

As Michael started talking, Javi was only giving his ex-husband some of his attention. The rest—the majority—was focused on the woman who lightly touched his arm, then waggled her fingers in goodbye, mouthing, *Thanks*.

Javi realized, as he watched Ailani heading into the building, that he'd hardly heard a word Michael was saying, too busy wishing he was free to follow her inside.

Wishing his life were somehow different than it was so there could be room for her in it.

CHAPTER EIGHT

STANDING STOCK STILL just inside the door of the craft store the following evening, Ailani just stared at the mass of Christmas displays and swiftly moving people.

"Wow," she breathed. "Where do I even start?"

Javi chuckled. "Your eyes are so wide right now, you look like Mabel when I took her to Disneyland last year."

"It's better than a theme park," she said. "It's nirvana, even for someone like me who isn't particularly into crafts."

"No matter what you like, there's something in here for you," he replied. "They make sure of it. No one gets out of here without buying something."

"I don't plan to spend a lot." Although she could already see at least eight things she wanted. Make that ten, including the huge gnome figures, which wouldn't fit into the apartment without a shoehorn. "And I know you probably don't have a lot of time, but could we walk around a bit?"

"I'm in no rush. Mabel had a dance class this afternoon, and my ex's mother, Joan, usually takes her, then they go back to Joan's place for dinner. I have a couple of hours before I have to pick her up, and they live quite close to here."

"Oh, if they're close by, I can take the train back to the apartment. I don't want to take you out of your way."

"Don't be silly. I don't mind driving you back." Javi took

her arm gently and urged her farther into the store. "Let's start over here and work our way around."

Ailani felt like a kid in a candy store, who wanted every new thing they saw. But she'd decided on a budget and was determined to stick to it.

Besides, when would she find the time to take up any of the intriguing-looking hobbies displayed around the store?

"I've never been very interested in crafts," she admitted to Javi as they stood in an aisle filled with wooden cutouts, boxes and birdhouses. "But somehow, right now all I can think about is painting a bunch of stuff I know I'd probably never use, even if I got around to actually painting them when I got them home."

He laughed. "You'd be the perfect customer if you weren't so disciplined. I'm sure they salivate over people who can't resist the urge to buy, even when they know for a fact they're wasting their money."

"Yeah." Ailani sighed and put the birdhouse she'd been examining back on the shelf. "I came in here for Christmas decorations, but right now all I can think is how sweet that birdhouse would look in my garden back home."

"You like gardening?"

They strolled past a holiday display of yarn, and Ailani had to stop and finger a skein. It was so soft and would make a gorgeous scarf—if she knew how to knit.

"I love gardening. It's in my blood, I guess you'd say. My mother's family has lived and farmed in the same place for generations, and while I'm not a part of the business, I had my own plot to grow whatever I liked, from I was a little child."

"You still live with your grandmother?"

"No, I have my own place in Kaunakakai, close to the hospital. Do you think I'd send poor Abbie to live with Tutu?" She giggled at the thought. "My grandmother would be all up in her business."

They wandered through a section of art frames, and as they got to the fine-art supplies, she noticed Javi slow down, so she did too. While they continued to chat, she watched him run his fingers over displays of pencils, gently rifle the pages of sketchbooks and pick up brushes to test their softness with his thumb.

There was both familiarity and wistfulness in his movements, she thought, leading her to ask, "Do you have a favorite medium to work in?"

"I'd say watercolors," he replied, rather absently, as he was investigating a small set of something or other with concentrated focus. "Something about the way you have to plan the layering of the paint always fascinated me."

Then he put whatever it was he was looking at back on the shelf, and Ailani thought she heard him sigh.

"Do you do art with your daughter?"

He smiled but shook his head. "Not really. I mean, she's only six, drawing stick figures and coloring all over the place. Maybe I will when she's older."

Putting her hand on his arm, Ailani stopped him from continuing on his way.

"Are you waiting to see if she'll be the next Picasso or something?"

Javi's eyebrows dipped together over his nose, and he shook his head. "Of course not."

"Then why haven't you been drawing and coloring with her? It would be a great way for you two to spend time together, doing something you both enjoy. I bet she'd be super excited."

He hesitated, his brow wrinkling. Then his head tilted, and he gave a little shrug. "It's funny, and rather sad, but I never even thought about it from the point of view of sharing the love of art with her. In fact, once I made the decision to drop my dreams of becoming an artist and go into medicine instead, I stopped creating art all together."

The regret in his voice washed Ailani, and she gave his arm a squeeze. "I can see how that could happen. You're a very focused person. You must be, to already be the head of Pediatrics at such a large hospital."

She gave him a smile and then, realizing she still had a hold of his arm, gave it another squeeze before releasing it. Their gazes had locked, and the intensity in his expression made her heart give a funny little thump before beginning to race.

He looked both lost and needy, as though he was searching her eyes for something—something secret or mystic—that only she could provide and that she ached to be able to give him.

Then he blinked and looked away.

Running his hand across his nape, he tried to smile, but there was something askew about the movement of his lips before he spoke. "'Already made it to head of Pediatrics'? 'Already'? Weren't you the one who called me old the other day, like I was on the brink of retiring?"

To her, the joke sounded forced, and her answering laugh was almost painful to produce since she had to get it out past the ball of sympathetic pain in her throat.

"Come on, then, *elemakule*. Enough of your doddering around. Let's go find me some decorations."

He seemed to relax, but Ailani thought there was still tension around his eyes when he asked, "What did you just call me?"

"Old man," she replied, snickering. "Now let's shuffle along. We need to get you home to bed soon, huh?"

Although the sound he made and the look he gave her made her laugh out loud, something in his expression also made heat wash through her veins.

And she had to turn away, hoping he didn't notice the blush on her cheeks and rightfully interpret it as her reaction to the thought of tucking up in bed with him.

* * *

Why did Ailani have to mention bed?

Javi trailed after her as she went down another aisle, staying back to give himself a chance to regain his calm.

Right after the words had left her lips and he'd growled in feigned annoyance at her sassing had followed a surge of desire. He'd had to bite his tongue so as not to tell her that she was more than welcome to tuck him in—as long as she came to bed with him.

Came for him too.

The sensation of her hand on his arm, the warmth in her eyes, the sweet curve of her lips had all produced in him a rush of need.

He wanted to cover those lips with his and turn that warmth to heat.

Yet they hadn't really known each other very long, and he had no way to gauge whether she was actually interested in him in any way other than as a friend. She knew he'd been married to a man and hadn't asked anything else. Here, in the middle of a store, only a few days into their relationship—however it was categorized—wasn't the time or place to broach the kind of conversation he was tempted to initiate.

Besides, it was always complicated, explaining his sexuality to people, and there had even been times when he'd had potential partners shy away from him on learning he was pansexual.

No.

Already he was learning to treasure the friendship blossoming between them. What he had to do, he told himself, was appreciate it for what it was, for however long she was in Boston, and not rock the boat.

"Hey," she said, stopping suddenly at a stack-out display. "Look at these. Wouldn't your daughter like one of these for Christmas?" Javi pulled his thoughts back to the moment and looked at the display of kits, as Ailani continued, "There are a bunch of choices, from science experiments to crafts and building projects. I'm sure you could find something she'd like."

Looking through the various boxes, he found himself a little overwhelmed by how many there were, then he realized the kits were all for different ages. Being able to disregard the ones too old for Mabel's age group cut it down to a manageable amount.

"If you're not sure what she'd like, get a few," Ailani said, as she watched him vacillate back-and-forth between the four he thought might be fun for Mabel. "It'll be informative to see what she finds interesting, and there'll be the added bonus of you being able to help her, if she needs it. Daddy/daughter time, for the win."

"I like the way you think," he replied, gathering up three of the boxes. "I think she'd love these. Thanks."

"You're welcome."

Her grin threatened to melt him altogether, and he rushed to find something to say. "This is a far better suggestion than my ex's. He wants to get her a puppy."

"Really?"

"Yeah," Javi said, wondering what she'd think when she heard he'd refused to allow it.

"What did you say?"

"I told him no."

"Good for you," she replied, surprising him. "Giving animals as gifts when you're not around to take responsibility for them is wrong. Should I give him props for at least asking?"

A little stunned, Javi shook his head. This woman seemed destined to continuously astonish him.

"Yes, but I had to warn him that I'd speak to his parents too, to make sure he doesn't do an end run around me. Michael wouldn't hesitate to do that if he really wanted to."

"Huh."

That little snort released a band Javi hadn't even realized had tightened around his chest and remained there since the conversation with Michael the night before. Somehow it was easy to speak to Ailani about anything, and right now he desperately wanted someone to be a sounding board about the dog.

"I know Mabel would love to have a dog, and I hope one day we'll be in a position to have one, but I just can't see how we'd be able to manage that right now. The poor thing would be by itself in the house all day, and when we finally get home, looking after it would be one more thing I have to navigate by myself."

Ailani nodded and gave him a look of rueful understanding. "I get it, believe me. It wouldn't be fair to you or the dog."

Her agreement didn't make him feel that much better. Scrubbing a hand across his nape, Javi said, "I feel like the bad guy, again, you know? Mabel loves animals, and when she's older and more able to take on the responsibility, I'll happily get her a dog. Having Michael suggest it and having to say no makes me feel as if I'm coming between them, which I've tried so hard not to do."

Ailani's eyes narrowed, and she seemed set to say something but hesitated.

"What?"

"Well," she said slowly, "have you considered a cat? Or two?"

"What?" he said again, this time in disbelief.

"Think about it. Cats are low maintenance in comparison to dogs. Yes, feeding them, cleaning the litter box and all the rest is additional work, but it's far less than walking and training a dog. Besides, you and your ex can each get Mabel one, they'll keep each other company and you won't feel like the bad guy, again."

Her words triggered something in his brain which had nothing to do with getting a pet but that he'd never actually considered before.

How had he never noticed that Michael got to do all the fun things with Mabel while leaving Javi to deal with all the day-to-day chores and make the hard, sometimes hurtful decisions?

Maybe instead of only concentrating on making Christmas special for Mabel, he needed to seriously think about the dynamic that had existed in the house before Michael left and adjust it now that he was gone.

"Hey," Ailani said softly. "I'm sorry if I spoke out of turn. I just thought—"

"No," he said, grinning so wide, so damn happy he wanted to grab her and dance her around the store. "No. You're a wonder. A marvel. Thank you!"

Buoyed by this new sense of relief and resolve, he leaned down to cup one of her cheeks and planted a kiss on the other.

And he allowed himself the luxury of letting his lips linger far longer than he should on the soft velvet of her skin, inhaling her scent as he did.

"Wow. Who'd have thought you were such a cat fan," she said, sounding as breathless as he felt when he finally straightened.

"No one said just because there are dog people and cat people that there can't be dog *and* cat people, now did they?"

As the words left his mouth, he recognized the double meaning and wished he had the guts to segue from speaking about pets to speaking about people.

Himself, in particular.

But before he could, she was already replying, and the chance was lost.

"True, *hoaloha*. Friend," she added as he raised his eyebrows at her. "That means *friend*."

"Hoaloha," he repeated. "I like that. And I like that we're friends."

"Me too," she replied, but her cheeks flushed as she spoke, and she turned away, adding, "Come on, or you'll be late picking up Mabel, and I don't want that."

CHAPTER NINE

THE NEXT DAY was a bit of a blur for Ailani, as they had a sharp influx of children in the outpatient clinic and she was sent to lend a hand there. While there wasn't much time to chat, it gave her a chance to spend a bit of time with Dr. Dylan Geller and also Kali, who was helping out.

There was a certain aura around them when they were together—a certain familiarity—that made Ailani wonder about their relationship, but when she mentioned it, Kali explained.

"He's staying with me during the holidays. Well, not with me," she went on, "I mean, Jen is my roommate and his sister, and she told him he could use her room at the apartment over Christmas since she's out of town," she said all in a rush, but her cheeks were pink as she spoke. "But it's all good. I mean, Dylan and I see each other a lot now and since we slept together six years ago it's awkward, but we'll get over it and…" She seemed to have run out of words at this point.

"No worries. I think we all have things we'd rather forget in our past," was all Ailani said in reply, although she wasn't completely buying the explanation.

Yet despite whatever was happening between them, Kali was as focused as ever, and Dylan also seemed extremely competent when treating and diagnosing their patients. Ailani liked that he'd traveled all the way from Providence to offer support to his patient and Jiyan's mother, since she was a widow and, apparently, his friend too.

Unfortunately, with Javi off, it meant Ailani was without her usual lunch companion again.

Silly to feel lonely and out of sorts as she sat in the staff lunch room and ate her salad. The night before, she'd realized she didn't want to go over to the coffee shop if Javi wasn't there, so she'd brought food from home.

As it turned out, it was a good excuse to also not accept Dr. MacKenzie's tentative invitation to lunch. She'd met the pediatrician on his return the day before, and although he seemed okay, he reminded her of a long, skinny wading bird, with a shock of red feathers on its head.

But it wasn't as though she and Javi were out of contact during that time. In fact, she'd messaged him the night before, sending a video of the apartment after it was decorated. His response had made her giggle.

WTH? Did you go back out and buy more stuff? There's no way a stocking, a gnome and some fake snow could stretch that far!

She responded:

LOL! No. Bryn decided she felt Christmassy after all and had a ton of ornaments and decorations. We even had hot chocolate afterward.

Seeing the mind-blown emoji he'd sent had made her nod in agreement. It had been the last thing she'd expected. Well, maybe the second to last, with Bryn getting ready to go back to work as an RN squeaking by for first place.

They'd chatted a little more, and after he'd wished her good-night, she'd gone to bed and dreamed that those warm, firm lips had drifted from her cheek to her mouth.

Just the memory of that innocent kiss had the power to

make her heart race, the way it had at the time. Every sensation of those moments lingered in her brain. His hand, strong and somehow commanding, on one cheek. His mouth resting against the other, causing heat to radiate out, not just into her face but throughout her entire body.

How would it feel to kiss Javi fully? To be kissed by him? To have that long, muscular body against hers while those strong arms held her?

Ailani knew she shouldn't have these fantasies but couldn't seem to help herself.

Then there was the sweet way he spoke about his daughter, which also melted Ailani's heart.

She couldn't help feeling for him as he tried to navigate life as a single parent. Maybe she was reading between the lines and coming up with the wrong end of the stick, but it sounded as though Javi's ex had been happy to be the fun parent, leaving Javi to pick up the slack. She'd seen that before in many families. One parent had all the enjoyment, while the other did the hard work.

Hopefully Javi would come to realize it didn't have to be that way and started interacting on a different level with Mabel. All children needed a firm hand, but they also needed to know the softer, more relaxed side of their parents.

Javi seemed to be thinking along those lines too when he texted her on his day off.

I've been thinking about what you said about the cat. I'm not even sure Mabel likes them though. None of the family has them as pets.

She'd thought about that for a moment and then replied:

Is there some way to expose her to them without getting her expectations up?

His reply was a while in coming, and Ailani didn't see it until after work:

I just found out there's a cat café here in Boston.

She'd laughed to herself when she saw that.

So you'll take her there?

Another long pause, and then:

I called, and they said that would be a good way to gauge her reaction to them and also make sure she isn't allergic. I hadn't even though of that.

He'd added a hand-to-face emoji, and Ailani had responded with the same, along with:

Don't feel bad. Two medical professionals, and neither of us even considered allergies, although we deal with the effects every day!

Then Javi added:

And they're attached to a shelter, so the cats she'll meet are all up for adoption.

Later that evening, when her phone rang, she thought it would be Tutu, but when she saw Javi's name on the screen instead, her heart leapt.

"Hey," she said, striving for a casual note. "What's up?"

"Nothing much." He sounded totally casual and relaxed too, which made Ailani, in turn, glad and ridiculously annoyed.

"I just put Mabel to bed and thought I'd see how your day in Urgent Care went."

"It was a hustle. Can I tell you? Lots of kids and traumatized parents. Dr. Geller was great though, and we had both Kali and Dr. Jeong helping out at various times. Dr. Jeong is a real sweetheart, isn't she? It's the first time I've worked with her, although I've glimpsed her around the hospital."

"Yes, Izzy is nice. She's a huge favorite with everyone because she always seems to be in a good mood."

It made her want to say Izzy Jeong balanced out the grumpy Ben Murphy, but she bit her tongue and instead asked, "When are you planning to take Mabel to the cat café?"

"I'm not sure. I'm working tomorrow through to Saturday, but my ex-mother-in-law is taking Mabel to New York on Friday evening to see the Rockettes and do some shopping. They won't be back until Sunday, so it'll have to be after they get back."

"Ooh…" Ailani reached over and pulled her journal off the bedside table, flipping it to her adventure list. "I'm adding *New York City during the holiday season* to my list of things to experience. I always watch the Thanksgiving Day parade and the tree-lighting ceremony. I don't know why I didn't think of putting it down as something I want to do. Have you ever been?"

There was a little pause, and then he replied, "I have, and it's worth the visit."

Something in his tone told her not to ask anything more, and after a few more minutes of idle chatter, he said good-night.

As they hung up, she was left with the sense that she'd touched a sore spot, although there was no way to know exactly what it was or how to soothe it. Even if that was something she had the right to do, which she most certainly didn't!

Going back to work the morning after a day off for Javi usually took a self pep-talk, but not that Thursday. Instead, he found himself eager. Raring to go.

And he was honest enough to know it was because he'd see Ailani.

She'd been constantly on his mind since he'd dropped her off after their trip to the craft store. Partway through the day before, as he'd taken care of chores around the house, he'd realized just how often thoughts of her had played through his mind.

The sound of her laughter, and the lovely cadence of her voice. Her sassy personality, which intrigued, amused and stimulated him by turns. Intellectually, he couldn't remember anyone he'd enjoyed talking to—or sparring with—more.

And then there was his physical response to her. The softness of her skin beneath his mouth, and the urge he'd had to gently turn her face toward his and see if she'd allow him to kiss those delicious lips.

He longed to know how it would feel to embrace her, and that desire was twisting him up inside. Even while telling himself there really was no place in his life at this point for a relationship that would go nowhere, there was no mistaking the attraction he felt. Thankfully, Ailani seemed completely content to simply allow their friendship to grow and for them to enjoy each other's company without strings.

If he hadn't already needed a reminder about why friendship would have to be enough, her comment about adding New York to her list of adventures certainly provided one. He definitely didn't need to get involved with another person who had itchy feet.

However, conversing with her and hearing her advice—which seemed wise beyond her years—had already encouraged change in his life.

He couldn't wait to show her the evidence of that and talk further to her about his plans for Christmas with Mabel.

He'd have to wait until they met up for lunch, though, since she was seconded to the urgent care clinic again that morning and he had a small mountain of paperwork to deal with. That included the employment papers for Bryn Bedford, who he'd approached about returning to nursing, specifically on the pediatric ward here at Boston Beacon. He'd long known she was an RN but didn't know why she'd left the profession. Not that it mattered, now that her recommendations and employment records had been verified and she'd accepted the job. Javi was just glad to fill the nursing position with someone he already felt would both fit in and be an asset to the department.

Plowing his way through charts, assignments and memos from the administrative staff, Javi was so focused on what he was doing, he actually started when his phone rang. Glancing at the caller ID, he immediately accepted the call.

"Hi, Joan. How're you?"

His ex-mother-in-law's warm, motherly voice sounded far away, as though she had him on Speaker and had put the phone down while she walked around. "I'm well, thank you. I'm sorry to bother you, but I wanted to have a quick chat before Mabel, Ronny and I leave for New York tomorrow."

Leaning back in his chair, Javi shifted the phone from one side to the other as he replied, "It's no trouble. What do you need?"

"Oh, I don't *need* anything, really. Just wanted to say how much we're looking forward to the trip and to thank you again for letting us take her."

"Not at all," he replied, once more aware of how lucky he was to have Joan as a part of his family. "I should be thanking you. There was no way I could take time off just now to do it myself."

The one time Mabel had gone to see the lights in NYC, she'd been too young to enjoy them, although Michael had insisted they go as a family.

"It really is our pleasure. Ronny's beside himself with excitement. You'd think he was the six-year-old."

Javi chuckled. "I can believe that." Michael was more like his father than his mother, temperamentally. When Joan went silent for a few moments, Javi started shuffling the papers on his desk, his mind drifting back toward work, and asked, "Was there anything else?"

"I spoke to Michael last night..." The way her voice trailed off caught and held Javi's attention, but he waited, silently, for her to continue. "He's still talking about Mabel getting a puppy for Christmas. I've refused to help him circumvent your wishes," she added quickly. "But..."

There was no need for Joan to continue. Javi knew the drill. Michael, for all his charming manners, could also be a complete pit bull when it came to getting his way. If his mother wouldn't help him, he'd find someone else who would, totally disregarding Javi's wishes or needs.

Suppressing a sigh of annoyance, Javi said, "I have an alternative in mind that might be acceptable to us both, but I need some time to figure it out. Can you stall him for me, please?"

"I'll do my best."

After they hung up, Javi tilted his chair back, clasped his hand behind his head, inhaled and then blew out a long breath, trying to release the annoyance tightening his shoulders. It irked him to have to ask Joan to get further involved in the situation, but there was no escaping the fact that Michael could reach out to any of his myriad friends and have them acquire a dog. He wouldn't bother to tell them that Javi was against it—had, in fact, expressly forbidden it—and if he did mention it, it would be couched as Javi being difficult.

When they'd been married, Javi had developed a variety of ways to deal with Michael's selfishness, and although it had annoyed and occasionally angered him, after a while he'd hardly noticed. Now it was just flat-out aggravating, and Javi couldn't help wondering how on earth Michael's fellow medical personnel were putting up with him in the field.

Shaking his head, he had to acknowledge that, besides that one major personality flaw, his ex-husband really wasn't a bad person. He was an amazing doctor, had charm and warmth and the ability to make others like and respect him. No doubt, to those not having to deal with him on a very personal level, those attributes balanced out any periodic stubbornness.

Suddenly, his brain switched from his ex to Ailani, almost seamlessly. The need to see her, to tell her about this latest shot across the bow from Michael, had him glancing at his watch and huffing with annoyance at how early it still was.

He didn't know why, but he felt better after talking to Ailani about things. It was probably her lack of judgment toward him and her commonsense way of looking at each situation. In the wake of his divorce, he'd lost many friends, simply because he'd been too hurt and wrapped up in taking care of Mabel to sustain those relationships.

Now what a relief it was to have someone he felt comfortable talking to, even if it meant battling constantly with his less-than-innocent urges toward her.

Totally distracted now, it was a relief to have his phone buzz and see that he was needed on the ward. Hurrying out of his office, he pushed aside all thoughts other than work but couldn't help scanning the corridors, hoping for a glimpse of Ailani.

CHAPTER TEN

FULL OF BEANS was full when Ailani and Javi got there, and after pausing at the door to see if there was a table available, Javi suggested they eat somewhere else.

"I don't mind," she said. "As long as I'm not late getting back. Poor Pat is going a bit bonkers today, trying to make sure everyone's taken care of."

It was the first time she'd worked with Pat as charge nurse and, while she liked her, Ailani thought she wasn't quite as effective as Leigh.

"Thank goodness Bryn starts tomorrow," Javi replied, putting his hand on the small of her back to guide her farther along the road, toward a red brick building. "All of the charge nurses are complaining about the difficulty brought on by the staff shortage."

"I'm sure Bryn will make a big difference," Ailani said, looking up at the sign over the door Javi was reaching out to open. "She's really looking forward to getting back into nursing. I promised to help her get ready for her first day, although she's so organized, I don't think she needs anything more than a cheering section."

"And that means you can get a day off too." The deli was bigger than the coffee shop and not as full. "I can't tell you how much we all appreciate you taking on the extra shifts, but you must be exhausted now."

She was but refused to admit it.

"I'm fine. My grandmother says I have way too much energy for time off anyway." She chuckled, perusing the menu on the wall behind the counter. "Of course, that was always when she wanted me to work with her and Uncle Makoa on my days off from the hospital."

He chuckled, his hand warm and firm against her back again as they moved closer to the front of the line.

"I think I'd like your *tutu* if I met her," he said. "She sounds like my kind of lady."

Ailani was pretty sure Tutu would like Javi if she met him too, but she didn't say so, although why she hesitated, she didn't know.

She'd spoken to Javi about her family and mentioned him in passing to Tutu on the phone, but something inside was whispering that she should keep the two parts of her life separate.

"I'll be glad of the days off," she said instead, reverting to the previous subject. "I haven't contributed anything to the bake sale yet, just because I haven't had the time."

"What are you making?"

"I'm not sure yet." A patron sitting at a nearby table had just taken a bite out of a sandwich that looked so delicious it made Ailani's mouth water. "I wonder what it is that man is eating. Do you know?"

"Umm…maybe pastrami on rye?"

"Okay, I'm having that," she replied before continuing their prior conversation. "I'm going to go to the supermarket tomorrow morning to pick up supplies for my baking spree. I'm considering pineapple upside-down cake, but I like using fresh pineapple instead of canned, so we'll see if that works out."

"Yum!" He sounded so enthusiastic, Ailani giggled. "I'll make sure to bring cash on Monday. That's when you're back on, isn't it?"

"Yes. Three whole days off. Unheard of."

She injected as much enthusiasm into her words as she could. It wasn't that she didn't want the time off. In fact, she desperately needed it so as to catch up on rest and chores alike. The problem was that she'd missed interacting with Javi so much when he hadn't been at work, she was almost dreading those three lonely days.

"What—"

She didn't find out what he was about to ask because suddenly an excited female voice interrupted him.

"Javier? Javier Pascal. Is that you?"

Both Ailani and Javi turned at the same time, but while he broke into a big smile, Ailani could only stare.

The woman enthusiastically hugging Javi was tall, blonde, beautiful and obviously a huge fan of his.

"Georgia Musgrave. I haven't seen you in ages." Javi held the woman by her shoulders, his gaze roaming her face. "You haven't changed."

Georgia scoffed. "Don't be ridiculous. It's been at least ten years. Of course I've changed—and not for the better, despite the fillers and working out like a maniac at the gym."

"How's your husband?"

The way she wrinkled her nose should have made her look silly, but somehow it didn't. "He's fine. Still at the bank. How's yours?"

Ailani turned away, not wanting to eavesdrop on the rest of the conversation. It was none of her business anyway, and there she'd been, staring and listening like a nosy neighbor.

Impossible, however, not to hear Javi say, "We divorced about two years ago."

"Oh, I'm sorry," Georgia replied and then dropped her voice to an intimate whisper that didn't reach Ailani's ears.

"No," she heard Javi say. "Nothing like that, Georgie. You definitely haven't changed a bit."

They were at the counter now, and having forgotten what

Javi said the sandwich she'd wanted was, Ailani order an Italian sub instead. Then she turned, putting a smile of her face. "Hey, Javi. What do you want?"

"Did you get the pastrami, like you wanted?" He came up beside her, the blonde Georgia trailing along behind.

"Changed my mind," she said, not wanting to let on that she'd been so focused on him and Georgia that she'd forgotten what he'd said.

"Well, I'll get one, and you can try it. If you like it, then you can order it next time."

"Sure. Thanks." Then, since it was only polite, she smiled at Georgia and said, "Hi. I'm Ailani."

"Georgia," the other woman said, sticking out her hand to shake while her sparkling blue eyes gave Ailani a comprehensive once-over. "Nice to meet you. You work with this mutt?"

"Hey, hey," Javi said, chuckling. "None of your name-calling. It doesn't look good for the head of Pediatrics to be called a mutt, even if it's done affectionately."

"Who said it was affectionately?" Georgia quipped, taking the words right out of Ailani's mouth.

She snickered, which earned her a laughing look from the other woman and a mock scowl from Javi.

"I'm surrounded by cruelty," he said. "I expected it from you, Georgia, but you?" He pointed at Ailani and then shook his head. "Who am I kidding? I'm completely unsurprised."

Georgia laughed, then looked at her phone, and grimaced. "I'd love to stay and catch up, but I gotta run. I'm due in court, and my client is probably waiting. Nice to meet you, Ailani. Let's get together soon, Javi."

Javi and Georgia embraced once more, then Ailani watched the other woman stride away and couldn't help wondering what the relationship between her and Javi really was. There was a familiarity there—something beyond simple friendship—she was sure.

But he was gay, wasn't he?

Almost as though reading her mind, after he'd ordered, and they'd found a table nearby and sat down, he said, "It was great seeing Georgia again."

"She's a good friend, huh?" When his eyebrows rose, she hurriedly said, "There was just something about the way you spoke to each other..."

About to add that it reminded her of her first serious boyfriend who, once they'd gotten past the hurt of their breakup, she'd remained friends with, Ailani bit her cheek to hold back the words.

Javi looked down at the ticket in his hand and then back up to meet Ailani's gaze. His jaw firmed as though he was clenching it, but his expression was calmly neutral when he finally replied.

"Yes. Georgia and I almost got married about ten years ago."

Javi held his breath, searching Ailani's face to see what her reaction would be to his statement.

Seeing Georgia at this particular time, while in Ailani's company, had presented an opportunity Javi couldn't pass up. In the back of his mind, he'd been wondering when and how to explain his sexuality. It wasn't a topic easily brought up out of the blue. In fact, it wasn't something he felt compelled to even speak about to most people. Yet the urge to tell Ailani had been growing and growing, and her response suddenly felt like the most important thing in his world.

Her eyes had widened, and her lips parted—whether in shock or in preparation for speech was still in question—but her gaze stayed on his, searching, no doubt, for some clarity.

"Go ahead," he told her, wanting to get it over with. "Ask whatever you want."

Ailani tilted her head, her eyebrows coming together so little wrinkles appeared on her forehead but, to his relief, there was nothing but curiosity in her eyes.

"I'd rather you just tell me what you want me to know," she finally said. "That way I don't inadvertently say something hurtful."

Javi couldn't help smiling at this newest indication of her commonsense approach to life, and her lips quirked up at the edges in response.

Not quite a smile, but close.

"I'm pansexual," he said. "And it's something I've known and acknowledged since I was in my teens."

The faint lines on her brow smoothed out, and now her smile was more genuine. "I think I know what that means, in comparison to being bisexual," she said. "But explain it to me anyway, just so I'm sure I'm on the right track."

Something loosened in his chest—a knot he hadn't even realized was there, pulled tight with tension that, with her calm words, unraveled, leaving him free to breathe easily again.

"I guess the simplest way to explain it is that gender—or gender identity—doesn't play into whether I'm attracted to someone or not." The intent way she was listening, even leaning forward a bit over the table, brought a rush of warmth through his chest. "I know there's some controversy over the difference between pan- and bisexuality, but that's the easiest way I know to tell the difference."

She seemed to consider that for a moment, and then she nodded. "Okay, makes sense to me." Then she said, "I do have questions I'd love to ask, but I don't want you to think I'm just being nosy—although I definitely am."

That made him laugh, just as the woman at the counter called their numbers for collection. Getting up, he replied, "Let me grab our sandwiches, and then you can be as nosy as you like. I really don't mind."

And he didn't.

In fact, there was something incredibly freeing about talking to Ailani about his past and the journey he'd embarked on as a teen to understand, and accept, himself.

"I'd figured out that I was bisexual very early on," he said, prompted by Ailani's obvious interest and her question regarding how he figured out he was pansexual. "And back then pansexuality wasn't really being discussed the way it is now, although the definition isn't at all new. I'm lucky enough to have the type of family that were willing to accept me, even if they didn't fully understand."

"Very lucky," she said, nodding. "Not every teen in that situation is."

"I know that, only too well. A friend I went to school with was kicked out of his house for being gay."

"So, how did you make the mental step from bisexual to pan?"

Swallowing the bite of sandwich he'd been chewing, he wiped his mouth before replying. "In college I met someone who didn't conform to any gender stereotypes. They were the first person I'd met who was clearly and openly gender neutral, and I fell head over heels for them." He couldn't help smiling as he remembered Cal. "They were the one who, over many nights spent talking and analyzing, suggested I was pansexual. It didn't mean anything much to me at the time—I would have agreed if Cal said I was a purple polka-dotted wolfman—but over time I realized they were right."

"What happened to your friend—Cal?"

"They went on to become an advocate for LGBTQI rights. We still keep in touch, but Cal is like a whirlwind, always rushing here and there, while I'm the quintessential homebody. We usually only get together if Cal comes to Boston for some reason, and it's often just a quick drink because they're so busy."

Ailani concentrated on her meal for a moment, and he wondered what she was thinking. Then she looked up, meeting his gaze again. A little spot of mayo beside her mouth made him want to lean over the table and kiss it away, an impulse that had him breaking eye contact and checking his watch.

"Almost finished?" he asked, wadding up his garbage.

"Yes." She answered, absently wiping her mouth, her thoughts obviously elsewhere.

Was she reconsidering their friendship now that he'd opened up to her about his sexuality? Had what he'd said made her uncomfortable? Was there something he needed to say to reassure her—in whatever way she needed reassuring?

How was he to even figure that out, he wondered, a sour taste rising in the back of his throat as he got up to toss the paper in his hand away.

Ailani had risen too, her handbag over her shoulder. Once she'd thrown away her trash, they headed to the door, silently weaving their way through the other lunchtime patrons. The tension he'd felt dissipate while they'd been talking slowly started tightening across his chest again, and Javi mentally fumbled for something to say.

As they stepped out the door, Ailani's phone pinged, and she looked at it, her brow creasing slightly.

"Hang on a second," she said, stepping to one side so as not to block the sidewalk. "I just need to…"

As she tapped away at the phone, Javi let himself stare at her in a way he made every effort not to when she wasn't concentrating on something else. Ailani was beautiful, but he knew it wasn't her looks that really attracted him but her personality and character, which shone out from within.

Yet, he reminded himself, she wasn't someone he could afford to get involved with. They worked together—he, in fact, as her ultimate supervisor—and Boston was only a temporary waypoint in her life. He owed his allegiance and concern to Mabel and the life they had together. If Ailani was somehow uncomfortable with him, now that she knew his truth, then this was the time to find that out, rather than try to maintain an unsustainable friendship.

Before he could look away, her eyes met his and widened, becoming dark and unfathomable, making his heart rate kick up a notch.

Then, she blinked, and the moment, which had felt somehow way more intimate than such a brief instant should have, passed.

"Do you want to go to an NFL game on Sunday?" she asked. "Kali Mitchell has tickets."

And with that question, asked without tentativeness or even a hint of reluctance, Javi knew everything would be okay.

"Sure," he replied, trying to rein in the grin pulling at his lips. "I'd really enjoy that."

And the opportunity to spend some more time with her, but with others around, so he wouldn't be tempted to do something stupid.

CHAPTER ELEVEN

THE FOLLOWING MORNING was a bit of a mad rush as Ailani and Bryn got themselves together and out the door to go to the hospital. Despite Bryn insisting that Ailani didn't have to go with her, Ailani had already made up her mind.

"Friends don't let friends go back into nursing alone," she joked, trying to ease some of the stress she could see Bryn was under. "I'm walking you in, *hoaloha*, to make sure you don't try to make a run for it."

"But it's your first day off in ages," Bryn all but wailed. "You should sleep in."

Ailani shrugged. "I never do, so it's not like I'm going to be missing out. Besides, I have to take my cake in for the sale. Yes, yes, I know, you could take it for me, but that's not going to happen, so just accept the inevitable."

If she were being honest with herself, Ailani was also hoping to see Javi but didn't count on it. Her plan really was to go in with Bryn, hopefully keeping her friend calm and collected before her shift, drop off the cake and head back home to do chores.

No way was she going to hang around like a lovesick schoolgirl, hoping that Javi just might show himself.

She was still trying to process all he'd told her the day before. In fact, it had been so much of a revelation, she'd felt as if all the weariness of the past week had fallen away during that conversation, leaving her restless and full of energy. As a result, she'd stopped at the supermarket on the way home, bought the ingredients for pineapple upside-down cake and baked it.

Unable to resist, she'd taken a picture of the dessert as it cooled and sent it to Javi.

OMG... I thought you were bringing it in on Monday?

The drooling emoji he'd added had given the message the perfect finishing touch and made her giggle.

I changed my mind, since we're going to the football game on Sunday. I wasn't sure I'd feel up to baking after that.

Smart. I'm wearing my stretchy pants tomorrow. I'm guessing there's no way I can buy the entire cake from you under the table, is there???

No! But if you're nice to me I'll make you a smaller one, just for you and Mabel alone.

I love my daughter, more than my own life, but no one told me that parenthood meant sharing my cake...

That had made her laugh even harder, but although it would have been easier to have the conversation over a phone call, neither had suggested it or taken the initiative to call the other.

Maybe he'd also been still processing the fact that he'd opened up to her in that way?

Javi must've been aware that everyone—or at least everyone she'd talked to since she'd started at the hospital—took it for granted he was gay. Entrusting her with the knowledge of his pansexuality made her feel both honored and confused.

Sure, they'd been well on the way to developing a great friendship. In fact, in her mind, they already had one, and she thought he felt the same way too. However, she wasn't sure why he'd confide something that personal to her.

If it was a mark of his trust in her, then that was one thing. If it was because he was interested in her, not just as a friend but as something more, then she wasn't sure how to proceed.

And she really didn't like not knowing what to do next.

There was no way she'd let him know just how attracted to him she was, even knowing there was a chance the attraction wasn't one-sided.

Too many reasons not to, including her pride, the short amount of time she'd be in Boston and, most importantly, the knowledge that doing so might very well sever the bond between them.

She'd rather keep Javi as a friend than risk destroying the relationship.

Well aware of how contrary she was being, given that she'd been practically drooling over him since they'd met, she nevertheless resolved to keep their relationship on a platonic basis.

When they got to the hospital, she put down the cake so as to hug Bryn outside the locker room.

"Have a great day, *hoaloha*. Honey and I will be at home waiting to hear all about your first day back."

"You sound like you're my mother and this is my first day of school." Bryn laughed, as Ailani had meant her to, but returned the hug before entering the staff room.

Going along to the break room, Ailani backed through the doorway so as to not have to put the cake down again. When she turned around, there was Javi, and her heart did that silly hop-skip-jump it often did when she saw him.

"Morning," he said, grinning. "Is that my cake?"

Collecting herself, she mock-frowned at him as she put the

sheet cake on the table. "I can't believe you're skulking around in the break room, waiting for the cake to arrive."

Javi chuckled, watching as she opened the carrier to unwrap the cake. "I'm quite sure it won't last more than an hour once everybody knows it's here." He gave a little groan of appreciation as the plastic wrap came off and the scent of sugary goodness wafted through the air. "Oh, that smells like heaven. Give me a piece—immediately."

Laughing, Ailani slid a square of the already cut-up cake onto a paper plate. "You're not going to eat that now, are you? It's not even seven."

Javi was already reaching for a fork. "One of the best things about being an adult is that you get to eat cake for breakfast if you want."

"As long as your child isn't watching, right?"

"True."

"Well, you can be the official taster. Let me know if it's okay. I used my *tutu*'s recipe, but I swear mine never turns out as good as hers."

Javi put a forkful of cake into his mouth, and his eyes rolled back in seeming ecstasy.

"Oh-mm-gug…" he mumbled. He swallowed, then shook his head. "So good. Ambrosial."

Ailani couldn't help the rush of pleasure his words brought, but she kept her tone light as she replied, "Glad to hear. I never know how it tastes until someone else tells me." At his inquiring look, she said, "I'm—ironically—allergic to eating pineapple, although not to touching it."

"That's tragic." He paused, another forkful poised before his lips. "I weep for you."

She snorted. "I feel your sympathy as you stand there stuffing your *waha*."

He couldn't respond, his *waha* too full of cake, but the twinkle in his eyes and sheer amusement in his expression had her blood fizzing like soda.

This man was lethally attractive, even while scoffing cake as if he hadn't eaten in years.

He finished the slice and was eyeing the rest of the cake when he said, "Mabel's off to New York right after school. Feel like having dinner with me tonight?"

How casually he asked. And although she felt her pulse speed up, she feigned interest in the rest of the baked goods on the table so as not to betray any hint of excitement.

"Sure, if you don't feel like enjoying some alone time while you can."

"That actually sounds great." He shoved a five-dollar note into the money jar on the table and glanced at his watch. Ailani felt her heart sink, thinking he'd changed his mind, but then he continued, "But dinner with you counts as me time, so that's just as good."

"I'd love to, then." She couldn't hide the enthusiasm in her voice and then asked herself why she'd want to. They enjoyed each other's company, so Javi would understand. "Text me later, when you have more time, and let me know where you want to meet."

"Will do," he said, just as the door opened and a small knot of nurses came in.

In the midst of the hubbub about the items on offer for the bake sale, Javi slipped out the door, and Ailani followed not long after to go home and take care of her chores.

Javi had wanted to invite Ailani to his home to have dinner there, but at the last minute the words had stuck in his throat. It would be unwise, at this point, to be alone with Ailani in what could very easily become an intimate setting.

And she'd been wrong about him probably wanting alone time. Actually, before meeting her, he'd probably have relished the weekend—not being without Mabel, who was the light of his life, but being without the responsibility of parenthood. However now just the thought of being at home alone when he could be enjoying Ailani's company annoyed him.

How often did he have the chance to socialize?

He was honest enough to admit to himself that since the divorce he hadn't even tried to make time for a social life, nor had he really wanted to. Consumed with taking care of his daughter and getting past the hurt and heartbreak, he'd let the thought of meeting with friends slide away.

No one wanted to feel as though they were the odd one out or the focus of pity. Being a single parent, even one with supportive grandparents in the wings, had presented a built-in excuse as to why he was unavailable.

Having dinner with Ailani was in a different category all together though. Truthfully, he felt as if for the first time in a long time, he was doing something just for himself.

Something to make himself, and only himself, happy.

Thankfully, Ailani clearly saw their dinner out as something other than a date. He'd been prepared to pick her up and drive her to the restaurant, but having her say she'd meet him there brought their relationship back into better focus.

They'd be dining as friends and workmates who were both at loose ends, and the same applied to their proposed outing on Sunday to the football game.

All this Javi reminded himself of as he approached the restaurant where they'd agreed to meet that evening, still in the clothes he'd worn to work. When he'd said he would be finished at the hospital by five, Ailani had suggested they meet just after that for an early meal, and he'd agreed.

Pulling the door open, he saw her already sitting at the bar. His heart did a backflip, and he forgot all the explanations and excuses that had been going through his head all day.

She hadn't seen him yet but was looking down at the phone

propped up in front of her on the bar. The dark green velvet of her dress hugged her body, and the curve of her cheek, visible in profile, was so purely beautiful, his heart clenched all over again.

There was something about her that drew him so strongly he found his steps growing longer, quicker in an effort to get to her as expeditiously as possible.

He'd just forced himself to slow down and regained some semblance of control when she looked up and, seeing him, smiled.

And just like that, Javi understood the danger he'd been courting.

The danger he was already in.

CHAPTER TWELVE

AILANI LOOKED UP, and a sensation like a strike of electricity went through her veins when she saw Javi striding across the restaurant toward her.

There was something in his expression, in the gleaming, hooded gaze that made her breath hitch in her suddenly dry throat.

Then, when he was two steps away, he smiled, and the stricture in her chest eased a bit, and she found enough air in her lungs to say, "Hi."

If her voice sounded as breathless as she thought it did, Javi didn't seem to notice. Getting up onto the stool beside her, he looked at her—not directly, but in the mirror behind the bar.

"You look nice. That color suits you."

"I couldn't resist it," she admitted, smoothing her hand along her thigh, reveling in the soft slide of the fabric. "I've always wanted a velvet dress or blouse but couldn't justify having one in a tropical climate."

They made similar small talk until the hostess came to tell them their table was ready, and although it seemed normal on the surface, Ailani thought there was a strange aura between them.

Perhaps, though, it was just her. Aware of Javi's every move or breath, she was on edge, her usual easygoing attitude toward life severely lacking. She knew her disquiet sprang from the residue of that expression on his face when she'd seen him coming toward her at the bar. It made her think she really wasn't imagining the chemistry between them but also had her wondering what, if anything, to do about it.

He hadn't said or done anything overt, which led her to believe that he, too, was reluctant to pursue anything more than friendship. While she had no idea what his reasons for that might be, in her mind the risks of letting their relationship develop into something more intimate outweighed the potential benefits.

After all, when you got right down to it, he was her boss. Was it worth the possibility of destroying both a personal and a professional relationship just because she couldn't control her libido?

But there was no denying the tension swirling across the table, and it, more than anything else, made her wonder if she should cut the evening short, even though she hadn't even ordered yet.

Then Javi seemed to relax, dissipating the strain between them with a genuine smile.

"You didn't tell me poor Kali got punched in the face in Urgent Care," he said after the waitress had brought them menus. "She came by to tell me how you saved the day with, of all things, a wireless speaker."

"Never leave home without one," she said, giggling when he gave her a disbelieving look. "And suitable playlists for any occasion."

"Music has charms to soothe the savage breast?"

"Yes, even when it's on a two-year-old."

That made him laugh, and Ailani relaxed even more.

It was probably just her own self-consciousness and hyperawareness of him that had caused her earlier stress, she decided.

"Oh," he said suddenly, reaching into his jacket pocket. "I thought you'd like to see this."

The piece of paper he passed across the table to her had been carefully folded in four but seemed to have been in his pocket for a while, since the edges were a little dog-eared.

"I'd meant to show that to you yesterday when we were at lunch, but I forgot." There was no need to explain why it had slipped his mind. "I wanted you to see what Mabel and I did a few nights ago."

Unfolding it revealed a drawing, done on a long piece of paper, and the composition of it made her both smile and get a little misty-eyed too. Animals, each skillfully outlined, although cartoonishly drawn and garishly colored, romped between twists of green and brown, obviously meant to be trees and foliage.

"You drew this with Mabel?"

He smiled, and the tenderness in that lifting of his lips made her sigh.

"Yes. Instead of rushing back to the house to cook, I stopped and picked up some takeout so when we got home we could just spend time together. I asked her what she wanted to do, and when she said she wanted us to draw together, it felt like a sign, you know?

"She wanted me to draw the animals and she'd color in the forest, so that's what we did."

"It's lovely, Javi." And she meant it. Not just the picture itself, which she wished she could put in her bag and take home, but the knowledge that maybe, somehow, she'd played a small part in its creation.

The waitress came back to take their order, and Ailani carefully refolded the picture and reluctantly handed it back. When they were alone again, Javi sighed, leaning back in his chair.

"I needed to thank you, for what you said to me. For opening my eyes to something I hadn't given any thought to."

The intimacy between them was back, and although she knew she shouldn't be, Ailani was glad. This closeness had nothing to do with romantic feelings or sexual desire. This was friendship, pure and simple.

"What was that?"

"After talking to you that night in the craft store, I realized I'd fallen into a rut and needed to figure out how to get out."

"What kind of rut?"

Rubbing his palm over the five o'clock shadow on his cheek, Javi seemed to be considering his words carefully before he spoke. "I'd gotten so caught up in taking care of everything—even before Michael left—that I'd lost sight of the fact life isn't all about work or making sure Mabel eats nutritious meals or does her homework. Somewhere along the line I forgot that life should also be fun. Unstructured fun, just for the heck of it.

"I'd run around doing everything necessary to keep the house and my job running smoothly, and Michael got to hang out with Mabel, doing all the fun things. That's no way to build the best type of relationship with my child."

"There has to be a balance," she agreed, her heart aching for him.

"Exactly." He paused, taking a sip of his beer. "I've also depended on my parents and Michael's parents too much. I know I've needed help and they've been glad to provide it, but I think it's time I get my own house in order so they're not put in a position where they feel they *have* to help."

"What are you thinking of doing?"

Funny how, although she asked the question, she'd already envisioned him looking for a new spouse. One who'd be able to teach Javi how to relax more, take more time for himself and Mabel too.

"I'm considering getting a housekeeper." He said it as though it was a terrifying idea. "One who can drive Mabel home from school and take care of some of the chores, so she and I can spend more time together."

"And you won't be as stressed," Ailani added before taking a sip of water. "I'm surprised you didn't have one before."

"It didn't seem that important before. Sure, Michael and I both had stressful jobs, and when we adopted Mabel, it made sense to have a cleaner come in weekly, but I was sure we could manage between us. And it worked, until…"

Until Michael left.

The words hung in the air, and Ailani looked for any signs of sorrow, pain or anger in Javi's expression, but despite his seeming not to want to say the words, his eyes were clear and untroubled.

"Yeah," he said quietly. "I've been leaning on Mabel's grandparents too much. Feeling sorry for myself too much too. Well, up until recently."

She knew better than to think she might have had anything to do with his improved mood, but that didn't stop her from wishing that were the case.

"I'm glad for you." And she was, despite her confused emotions. "And for Mabel too. I've often thought how hard it must be to be a really good parent when you're miserable or sad, you know?"

"Yes," he nodded, and now a little flash of pain crossed his face. "But even then, most of us try to do the very best we can."

She thought of Tutu and Uncle Makoa and all of her mother's relatives, rallying around her after her parents had died. Then, even in the midst of her own pain and fear, she remembered Tutu walking into the house in Honolulu, her eyes red and swollen from crying. Remembered how the older woman had pulled her close and whispered that she would always take care of Ailani. Protect her.

And in Javi's words, she understood now that Tutu and Uncle had in fact done the very best they could for her. Whether she agreed with all of their choices was immaterial. The important bit was that they'd tried their hardest.

When she said as much to Javi, he nodded but didn't comment on her words.

Instead, with a shrug that seemed designed to rid himself of whatever emotion he'd just experienced, Javi asked, "What else do you have on that list of yours that I can help with while you're here?"

The change of subject, along with the reminder that she wouldn't be in Boston for very long, caused a pang, almost like grief. But she dredged up a smile from somewhere. "I was thinking of finding a rink and trying my hand—or really my feet—at ice skating. After talking to Isaac last week, I felt as though I was missing out, never having been on the ice."

Javi grinned. "I'd have thought you'd want to see a hockey game instead. If Isaac couldn't convince you how amazing hockey is, I don't think anyone could."

She shared his amusement. Isaac had been so caught up in telling her every rule he could think of that it had been an effective distraction.

"I actually thought about it, but the tickets were expensive." No use mentioning that she didn't want to go alone, the only companion she could think of was him and she didn't want him to think her needy by asking if he'd go too. He was already being nice enough to go to the Patriots game with her. "So, I thought I'd go skating instead. See how it stacks up to Rollerblading."

"Hey," he said, his eyes suddenly twinkling. "How about we go after we've eaten? The rink Mabel and I go to rents skates."

She bit back the instinct to immediately say yes as her mind went to the physical contact they might make as she tried to skate.

"Oh, I didn't plan on doing it tonight," she said quickly, scrambling for a valid excuse. "I... I don't think I'm dressed for it."

Javi raised his eyebrows, as if wondering why she was trying to refuse the invitation. "Unless you were planning on doing a triple Salchow your first time on the ice, you'd be okay with what you're wearing."

What she'd been picturing was more along the lines of a couple's dance routine, romantic and somehow sexually charged, as the best pairs were able to pull off. The ridiculousness of that thought made her giggle-snort and fall back on her sassy mouth to get out of the corner she'd gotten herself stuck in.

"What? You don't think I can do a triple *whatchamacallit*?" She tilted her chin up and narrowed her eyes. "Don't underestimate me, Javier Pascal."

And so it was that after dinner, Ailani found herself at the indoor rink with Javi kneeling at her feet, helping her put on her skates.

Thankfully, he'd had enough sense to stop at a nearby shoe store so they could both buy appropriate socks, since her tights and his dress socks wouldn't be sufficient.

"Our ankles would be a mess," he'd explained. "And your tights would probably be ruined."

"And here I was more worried about putting my feet into a pair of skates goodness knows how many other people have worn," she'd quipped, earning a chuckle from him. "Instead of visions of sugar plums, I had visions of ringworm."

"Ugh" was his response, but he was laughing at the same time. "Come on, let's see how you do."

Getting out onto the ice wasn't hard, but once on it, Ailani felt the first shiver of apprehension. But Javi held both her hands and gave her pointers on what to do with her feet so she could propel herself along in small increments.

"It's harder than it looks," she said, feeling as though she might end up in a split at any moment.

"You're doing great." He didn't seem to mind the death

grip she had on his fingers. "Use the inside edge of the toe... and push."

To Ailani's surprise, she got the hang of it fairly quickly, but Javi didn't seem in a rush to let go of her, and she didn't insist on it.

"Okay, you're doing great," he said when she was gliding along, if not gracefully then at least competently. "I'm going switch to skating beside you."

Suiting action to words, he let go of one of her hands and swished around so they were facing the same way. When he put his arm loosely around her waist, holding her hand in his, Ailani tensed.

"Relax," he crooned. "You're fine. I'm not going to let you fall."

"You better not," she pretend-groused, hoping he didn't notice the breathiness of her voice.

It wasn't the thought of falling that had her stiffening but the sensation of being so close to Javi, his scent surrounding her, the hard, muscular body supporting hers.

Difficult—no, impossible—to ignore the way her body reacted to his proximity. The tingles of awareness and desire flitting over her skin and into her blood.

Friends, she reminded herself. *He's my friend.* And this type of reaction to his nearness was both pathetic and dangerous to her emotional health.

"Everything okay?" Ailani shivered as his breath ruffled through the hair at her temple. "Are you too cold?"

"Yes. No." Annoyed with herself and her flights of fancy, she snorted. "I'm fine, and no, I'm not too cold."

But he didn't seem convinced.

"Let's do one more circuit and then call it a night. Tomorrow some muscles you didn't even know you had will probably be sore as it is."

"But I haven't done my triple thingy yet," she said, wishing they could stay like this, practically joined at the hip, a little longer.

"Well, I'd suggest waiting until you've had a chance to get yourself one of those competition dresses before you try." The amusement in his voice made her smile too. "Because if you've waited this long to buy and wear a velvet dress, I'd think you wouldn't want to destroy it so quickly. Trying to jump in it would probably shred it."

"Darn it, I think you're right." She put grudging agreement into her tone, although even the thought of doing anything more intricate than hanging on to his arm and sliding slowly around the edge of the rink was laughable. "Next time, though, I'm going for it."

That made him chuckle, as she'd meant him to, but it was with real regret that she let him lead her off the ice.

After they'd returned their skates and were walking together through the parking lot to where they'd parked side by side, Javi asked, "Did you put my address into your navigation system for Sunday?"

He'd suggested that since his home was in Norwood, south of Boston and relatively close to Foxborough, Ailani would meet him there on Sunday, and they'd use a rideshare service to get to Gillette Stadium. Javi had gone over it a couple of times already, and as they got to the cars, Ailani leaned against her door and gave him a cheeky grin.

"Yes, Tutu," she said slowly, with elaborate care, the same way she'd say it if it were her actual grandmother nagging her about something. A spark of annoyance made her voice quicken as she continued, "We've gone over this already. You even showed me the best route on the map."

Javi crossed his arms and gave her long, level look, somewhat spoiled by the twinkle in his eyes. "Are you or are you not the same woman who confessed to having a terrible sense of direction?"

"Yes, but—"

"I believe the way you explained it was to say if I put you in a paper bag, even without being shaken up, you couldn't find your way back out?"

Somehow being reminded of her own words didn't lessen her irritation, even as she confessed, "Yes, that's true."

"Then stop with the sass and humor me, okay? Wanting to make sure you're going to be safe and find your way without complications isn't a bad impulse, is it?"

"No," she said, having to admit that much, although she was still irrationally aggravated. "But you know I'm not a child, right?"

He just shook his head, not a shred of amusement left on his face. "Is that how you think I see you?"

Something in the timbre of his voice made Ailani's face suddenly blazing hot, but she held his gaze, even as her exasperation drained away. "No, although sometimes it sounds that way."

His eyebrows rose. "Since when has a normal concern for a friend become some kind of overbearing parental thing? I didn't get that memo."

She knew she was perhaps overreacting, but hadn't she spent enough of her life being coddled? Although she couldn't say exactly why she didn't want that from Javi too, she knew she didn't.

It was bearable from Tutu and Uncle Makoa, but not Javi.

"I've had enough of being treated as though I'm fragile or unable to take care of myself. Please don't do that."

His face tightened and then, as he exhaled, relaxed again. "One of the things I liked about you from the moment we met is that you didn't treat me in the same way other people did—as though because of my divorce I was somehow breakable. People have been tiptoeing around me, treating me with gentle care for the last two years, and I let them because at the time it made things easier. No one was pushing me to get on with my personal life—pushing me to live. So, yeah, I get what you're saying."

When she opened her mouth to express relief that he understood, Javi held up his hand, forestalling her.

"But I think there's a big difference between treating someone like they're made of glass and being genuinely concerned for a friend's safety and comfort. You're not used to driving in a city this size. That in itself is enough to give me cause for worry. Add to that your self-avowed directional challenge, and I'd be a pretty crappy friend if I wasn't anxious."

His words stunned her to silence, and before she could find her voice, Javi reached past her and opened the driver's door of her car.

"Text me when you get home," he said as she moved to get in. Before she could sit down, he stopped her with a gentle hand on one cheek and bent to kiss the other. "So I know you're safe."

And she still hadn't said a word when he closed the door and watched as she started the car, but her mind was whirling and her heart felt too full of emotion for any close dissection of their conversation.

CHAPTER THIRTEEN

SUNDAY DAWNED BRIGHT and crisp, the thermometer in Javi's kitchen proclaiming it to be cold as well. Dragging himself out of bed far earlier than he'd wanted but later than usual, he set about making coffee, rubbing sleep from his eyes and yawning.

He hadn't felt this tired in a long time, but the day before had been rushed and a little frantic at the hospital, and even with the nursing shortage dealt with, it had been all-hands-on-deck.

His last patient for the day, a two-year-old girl named Kinsey, had been so very ill, he'd been loath to leave until they'd figured out her diagnosis.

"What's happening to my baby?" her mother had wailed over and over again, her husband failing to comfort her. The hubbub she'd created had sharpened the tension on the entire ward to the point where Javi had been forced to ask her to compose herself or step outside the hospital until she could.

"I'm sorry," he'd said firmly, feeling like a lout. "But you're disturbing and upsetting all the other patients and their families as well as Kinsey, and it's just not acceptable."

Mrs. Noonan had stared at him as though he were some type of monster, while Mr. Noonan's look had clearly said, *Better you than me.*

Before she could say whatever had been bubbling up inside her, Javi had dropped his voice almost to a whisper and said, "Your daughter is very ill and needs to be kept as calm as possible while we investigate and try to make a diagnosis. She'll stay quiet if you do. Can I count on you to do that?"

She'd given him such a look of dislike, he'd thought she'd defy him just for the sake of it, but somehow she'd collected himself and calmed down.

It had crossed Javi's mind how much easier the entire situation would have been if Ailani had been on duty, but then he'd thought it unfair to the nurses he'd been working with at the time. While Ailani had a knack of calming and soothing both patients and parents, other members of staff were equally adept. It was more likely his preoccupation with her creating those thoughts.

He'd missed seeing her smiling face on the ward or hearing her often-cheeky laughter. It seemed almost impossible to him now to think they'd only known each other for such a short time. Thinking of her was like thinking of a lifelong friend or a member of family, except there was no friend or family member who also aroused him physically, the way she did.

But he'd learned his lesson with Michael. He'd always been prone to instant love—the type of immediate, intense attraction he'd felt on meeting more than one of his exes, which had eventually culminated in his marriage. Hindsight now showed a man far too eager to subsume himself in relationships, assuming the person he was so caught up in felt the same way. Rushing into serious attachment without giving it the deep thought a relationship deserved.

It was the one area of his life where it could be said his innate practicality and carefulness deserted him.

And now the one relationship he had to put before all others was the one with his daughter. Mabel had to be considered in everything he did, especially now that Michael had decamped to Africa and showed no interest in coming back to Boston to live.

So, no matter how Ailani made his heart beat faster or how intriguing he found her, for the first time in his life he knew he had to be practical—if not for his own sake, then for Mabel's.

There was no place in their lives, in his life, for a temporary relationship. One that could break not only his heart but Mabel's too.

Not that Ailani showed any signs of being interested in him as anything more than a friend. A fact he should've been thankful for but actually slightly resented. How like him to be alone in fighting the attraction. To be the only one who had battled the urge to pull closer as they'd skated, to kiss that luscious mouth instead of pressing a chaste salute to her cheek.

That velvet dress had driven him almost crazy with the need to touch and to trace the contours of that sweetly rounded body beneath its softness. Having his arm around her waist, his hand on her side had been intensely arousing. So much so that it still amazed him that they'd kept their feet beneath them, with her being a beginner skater and him almost shaky with desire.

All of which had led to very disturbed sleep the last couple of nights.

Ailani not only constantly inhabited his brain when he was awake but now also had taken it over in sleep.

Yawning again, wishing his mind had allowed him to rest a little longer, he poured himself a cup of coffee, then moved into the four-seasons room next to the kitchen to drink it. Outside, the trees, now bare of leaves, thrust spindly branches into the air, and a cardinal and a blue jay took turns fussing at each other, competing for supremacy at the feeder. Normally Javi loved watching the avian inhabitants coming to his garden, but at the moment his concentration kept sliding back to Ailani.

They hadn't talked about that flash of temper she'd displayed the night they'd gone skating, when she'd seemed to think he'd been treating her like a child or something. In fact, they hadn't spoken at all the day before, which was unusual, since one or the other usually texted, just to ask how the day went.

Was she still annoyed at him? Or was she—correctly, if he was being honest—worried that his concern masked something deeper than just friendship?

He knew why he needed to put the brakes on his feelings, but to his mind, there was no reason for her not to give him some indication that she was interested in him, unless she wasn't.

No one in their right mind wanted to be the recipient of unrequited love any more than the person in the throes of it wanted to be.

But was he really falling for Ailani, or was it another instance of him, desperate for companionship, imagining emotions that didn't actually exist?

Frustrated with himself, Javi strode back into the house. Checking his phone, he figured he had enough time to do a couple loads of laundry before Ailani came over to go to the game. Better to spend that time in useful activity than to sit around brooding.

By the time he heard the doorbell ring at eleven, he'd not only done the laundry but also some cleaning and had changed into his Patriots shirt.

Ailani shook her head as she stepped into the foyer.

"I wish I'd thought to bring my jersey with me," she said as he helped her take off her coat.

"Are you a Patriots fan?" he asked in surprise.

"Nope," she replied, giggling in that sassy way she had. "San Francisco 49ers all the way. I'd stand out in the crowd wearing it though, wouldn't I?"

And just as Javi couldn't help laughing with her, he also couldn't help feeling as if the earth had shifted—none too subtly—under his feet.

* * *

Ailani dragged her gaze away from Javi's and pretended to look around the entranceway to his home.

Driving through the neighborhood, she'd at first been surprised at the size of the houses. Surely a single man with one child didn't need a place as big as these were? Then she remembered he'd been married and that probably he and Michael had chosen the house together when they'd wed or when they'd decided to adopt their daughter.

And it was none of her business, was it?

But she had to admit the interior of the house had a homey atmosphere. Somehow she'd pictured Javi running around after poor Mabel, picking up after her before she'd even finished playing with a toy. However, she could see the space looked lived-in and comfortable, with a scattering of both toys and adult books in the living room, which was off to her right.

"Come through to the kitchen," he said, leading the way. "I just need to finish up in here before I go."

Suddenly, she realized what was missing.

"You haven't decorated for Christmas."

He turned a slightly shame-faced expression her way. "With everything that's been happening at work and with Mabel being busy with her grandparents, I haven't had a chance. I'm planning to do it this coming week."

"I'm surprised Mabel hasn't been at you about it. I used to nag Tutu to decorate as soon as Thanksgiving was over."

"Your family is big into Christmas?" he asked as he held up a cup, clearly offering her some coffee.

"Yes, please," she said about the coffee. "And no, Tutu isn't very interested in Christmas. All that *Mele Kalikimaka* annoys her, to be honest. She let me decorate because she knows I love it, but it's not her thing at all."

As she climbed onto one of the stools beside a granite coffee bar, he said, "Yet you decorate and seem to be pretty passionate about the season, although your grandmother isn't. Why?"

She shrugged, taking the cup he offered and taking a sip of her coffee. Wondering how much of herself she wanted to tell this man who was on the verge of stealing her heart, although she was determined not to let him know that.

"After my parents died, I moved to Molokai from Honolulu," she said, trying to answer without revealing more than she should. "Tutu was more traditional than my parents. There's a movement to resuscitate and recapture our heritage as Hawaiians, and on Molokai, Tutu is heavily involved in that. She hasn't been able to totally abandon the path her parents were on—devoted to the West and all its theology—but at the same time, she feels strongly the old ways of our ancestors are important too.

"For me, it was a matter of sentiment, I guess you could say. I had great memories of my parents at Christmas, and being immersed in the season made me feel closer to them."

Javi was leaning on the counter, his gaze intent on hers, and Ailani felt a shiver run along her spine.

"You have a lot of memories of your parents?"

It seemed a strange question, but Ailani nodded, saying, "I do. And I'm glad, since until I was given my mother's journals that was really all I knew about them."

"Your family didn't speak about them to you?"

"A little." Her mood darkened momentarily as she looked back. "But Tutu was devastated at the loss of her daughter, and I guess no one wanted to make her sad. I know I didn't."

"What did you find out about your parents from your mom's journal?"

That they loved me. That if they'd had even a hint that they might not return from that trip, they wouldn't have gone. That I was the most important person in their lives.

Ailani took a gulp of coffee and swallowed the lump in her throat with it before answering.

"They were adventurous and fun. My dad was a bit of a joker but also a pretty shrewd businessman, while my mom liked to sail and surf, when she wasn't flying all over the place as a flight attendant." Turning inward for a moment, she allowed memories to flood her—of trips to the beach; dinners where the three of them laughed as they ate; of bedtimes, when they'd read her stories, each making up funny voices for the characters. "I've been without them for three times as long as I had them, and I still miss them every day."

The expression in Javi's eyes made Ailani's heart clench.

"I'm sorry." His voice was deep and so full of sympathy she had to blink not to get teary-eyed. "I didn't mean to make you sad."

Setting down her cup, she hopped off the stool, briskly replying, "You haven't." Normally, she'd have had some kind of joke or a snappy comeback for him, but somehow she just couldn't manage that just then. "May I use your bathroom?"

"Down the hall, to the left," he said, and she felt those hazel eyes remain on her as she beat a hasty retreat.

Wondering why this particular man, at this particular time, had the ability to make her open up in ways no one else ever could.

CHAPTER FOURTEEN

THE SEATS AT Gillette Stadium were really good ones, right on the fifty-yard line, and Ailani enjoyed the game immensely. Seeing her first ever live NFL game was almost as much fun as watching Kali doing her best to pretend there was nothing between her and Dylan.

It was there, in Kali's body language. The stiff way she sat when he put his arm across the back of her chair without realizing that, at the same time, she was leaning ever so slightly toward him.

Recognizing it in her friend, Ailani made the conscious effort to not do the same to Javi.

And it was an effort. Just as it was to laugh and joke and try to pretend everything hadn't changed.

She'd realized she couldn't be his friend anymore. Not with the increasing depths of her feelings toward him.

This was all new territory for her, and she didn't know how to navigate it. She'd fallen for guys before, but never to the extent where she'd contemplated getting very serious. Reading her mother's journal had shown her a relationship unlike any she'd experienced. Her parents had fallen in love almost on sight. Had shared things with each other that they'd never told anyone else. Seemingly had been bound, soul to soul, in a way that almost made her glad they'd died together.

She wasn't sure how either of them would have survived without the other.

While she wasn't at that stage with Javi, somehow she could see it happening. Could see herself getting so entwined and attached, she'd never want to let him go or be without him. By the end of the game, with both Javi and Kali jubilant at the Patriots' win, Ailani knew she had to put some distance between herself and Javi.

Give herself some time to figure out how to handle these feelings growing inside her. Decide whether they were manageable or if she needed to cut and run.

So, when they were on their way back to his house in the rideshare and he invited her to have dinner with him, she refused.

"I'm back on early shift tomorrow and still have some things to take care of. I was actually surprised they didn't switch me over to nights this week."

"Usually you'd do a month of days before they switched you over to nights," he said, his gaze so intent it was giving her goose bumps. "You're going to have to eat this evening anyway, aren't you? We could do that now, although it's a little early, so you'll still have time for whatever it is you need to do."

So tempting to just give in, especially since it was what she wanted to do anyway, but she stuck to her guns. "Nope. I'm still full of hot dogs and soda. I'm going to head home."

He seemed to take her refusal at face value, but she was hyperaware of his gaze on her for the remainder of the ride, and thankfully he made no effort to kiss her cheek before she got into her car.

It would have been hard not to turn into the kiss—let her mouth meet his, just to see how it would feel.

But she'd decided that discretion was the better part of valor—or whatever the heck the saying was—and that she wouldn't spend any more time with Javi than she had to.

Which meant only at work—not in the café at lunch or anywhere else.

Thankfully he was off that Monday, and when he texted her, she kept her responses short and light, warding off any further invitations by telling him how busy she was outside of work.

Although Ailani had hoped he'd be swamped with paperwork on Tuesday, he was on the ward, but they didn't have occasion to work any cases together. Her spirits were incredibly low—so much so that she found herself battling tears as she nebulized a limp baby who was exhausted from coughing.

She'd learned a long time ago that her mental state often affected the children she worked with, so she began to hum the tune of "Aloha 'Oe," which made her feel better, although rather homesick.

But it was a good feeling, in a way. Things might have taken a turn she hadn't expected here in Boston, but no matter what, Tutu and Uncle were there on Molokai, waiting for her to return.

She hadn't really known what she would find in Boston. It had just been the place she'd had the opportunity to go to, where she might see a white Christmas. Now she wondered if it had all been a terrible mistake, and a part of her longed to go home to escape the threat of heartache hanging over her.

What was it, she wondered as she hummed and rocked the little girl against her chest, that drew her to Javi? Sure, when she'd been a bit younger, she'd craved a home and children of her own, wanting to know what it was her own mother had felt at Ailani's birth. Mom had written so lovingly and glowingly about motherhood that the first time Ailani had read her words, she'd cried. It had been tempting, then, to dream about feeling the way her mother had about her husband and child, but eventually Ailani had started to wonder if she was even capable of that depth of emotion.

All her friends had fallen in love, with varying levels of

happiness and success, but she never had. Infatuation and desire were what she'd experienced, but none of it had felt like what her mother had described.

What she felt when around Javi was suspiciously close though.

When they drew for Secret Santa and Ailani realized she'd gotten Javi's name, she couldn't help wondering why fate was insisting on messing with her.

"Are you okay?" Bryn asked that evening when she got home. Honey made a beeline over to Ailani and rested her head on her lap.

"Of course," she replied, dredging up a smile.

Bryn gave her a narrow-eyed look but didn't push it when Ailani changed the subject.

On Wednesday afternoon, Isaac came back in to have his stitches removed, and his mother waved to Ailani as she passed the door to the examination room.

Sticking her head in and making sure she wasn't interrupting, she said, "Hi, Isaac. How're you?"

The little boy beamed, saying, "Hi, Nurse Ailani. I'm good, thank you."

Javi looked up, his gaze strangely dark, and then swiftly turned his attention back to the little boy's head as Mrs. Barone said, "Nurse Ailani. Just a moment, please."

As Ailani waited, the other woman exited the room, pulling the door closed behind her.

"I just wanted to thank you for what you said to Isaac when he was here before," Mrs. Barone said, taking Ailani's hand. "It made all the difference to him." She actually gave a little chuckle as she added, "He's been so funny. When I call out and ask him what he's doing, sometimes he tells me, 'Concentrating on growing my hair back.'"

Ailani laughed with her, glad to hear the cheerfulness in

the other woman's tone. The last time they'd seen each other, Mrs. Barone had, justifiably, been in a bit of a state.

Just then the door opened, and Javi was there, looking out. "Mrs. Barone, if you could…"

"Sure."

With another quick squeeze of Ailani's hand, she turned back into the room. A glance at Javi's interrogatory gaze, which seemed to clearly say he knew she was avoiding him, had Ailani hurrying away.

Going to the nurses' station to pick up a file, she was surprised to see a little girl sitting behind the desk, a workbook in front of her. With her dark hair done up in two pigtails and the tip of her tongue caught between her teeth in concentration, she was absolutely adorable.

Hearing Ailani come up beside her, she looked up, and Ailani's heart did a little flip, recognizing Mabel from one of the pictures in Javi's house.

"Hi," Mabel said with the self-possession of a much-older child. "I'm Mabel."

"Hi, Mabel. I'm Ailani."

The little girl's eyes widened. "I like your name. Where'd you get it?"

Ailani couldn't help grinning. Mabel made it sound as if she'd bought the name somewhere rather than having been given it by her parents.

"It's Hawaiian. Do you know where Hawaii is?"

"Yes." The little girl nodded. "My daddy showed it to me on a map. It's out in the middle of the sea, right?"

"Yep. That's the place." Ailani added, "I like your name too."

Mabel gave her a look that was so like Javi's when he was trying to judge if Ailani was joking or not, it made Ailani's heart clench.

"A lady at my dance class said it was old-fashioned."

"Well, that doesn't mean it isn't beautiful, does it?"

"I guess not."

"Does your daddy know you're here?" It felt silly to ask, but who knew?

"Papi does," she said, looking back down at her worksheet. "Daddy's far away, in Africa. My *abuela* couldn't come and get me from school, so I had to come here instead of going to her house."

"Ahh... I see." So *Papi* for Javi and *Daddy* for his ex?

Mabel looked up again and said, "Did you come here from Hawaii with your family?"

"Nope," she replied, trying to be upbeat, although that homesick feeling she'd experienced before tugged at her heart again. "I'm here by myself, until spring."

Before Mabel could answer, Bryn came up to the desk, with Honey in tow. Between explaining why Mabel was there and the little girl's delight with meeting the dog, Ailani didn't leave quickly enough to avoid Javi.

"Careful, Javi. Someone will be asking you for a golden retriever soon," Bryn said with a laugh, earning her a sharp shake of the head from Javi.

Then Bryn and Honey went off to make their rounds, and Ailani realized Javi was standing directly between her and the way out from behind the desk.

"Papi?"

Javi looked over at his daughter, the edges of his lips lifting into a smile so sweetly loving, it made Ailani want to cry.

"Yes, *mija*?"

"Nurse Ailani is all alone here for Christmas."

It wasn't a question but a statement, and Ailani felt her cheeks heat with embarrassment.

"Not *all* alone," she said quickly. "I've made friends here."

"But no family, right?"

"No," she admitted reluctantly, not sure where this conversation was going. "No family."

Mabel turned her attention back to Javi. "It's not fair, Papi. Nurse Ailani doesn't have anybody to go shopping with or decorate her house with."

It was on the tip of her tongue to say her house was already decorated, but Mabel went on without giving her a chance.

"Can Nurse Ailani come with us on Friday when you take me shopping?"

"That's up to Ailani," Javi said in a tone so quelling, Ailani felt as though her stomach became hollow. "She may have other plans."

Then, suddenly, she was the focus of two pairs of eyes— one dark and appealing, the other hazel and veiled, although she thought there was a hint of hurt beneath.

How could she refuse when she really, really wanted to accept?

"I'd love to," she said, and although filled with trepidation at the thought of the outing, she couldn't help smiling when Mabel bounced with excitement in her chair.

Javi stepped aside to let Ailani out from behind the nurses' desk and watched her walk away. To say he was surprised that she'd agreed to go shopping with them was an understatement.

When Mabel had suggested it, he'd been quite sure she'd refuse.

Just then, he saw his mother walking toward them from the direction of the elevator, and he said to Mabel, "Here comes Abuela. Pack up your workbook."

"Yes, Papi." Ever obedient, Mabel closed her book and picked up her bag to put it in. "Papi?"

"Yes, *mija*?"

"Can I get a dog?"

"Let's talk about that another time, okay?"

His daughter gave him one of those too-adult looks she did so well and replied, "That usually means no."

His mother got to them at that point, and Javi leaned down to receive her kiss.

"I'm so sorry, Javi, but when the dentist said I should come in right away, I had to go. If not, they wouldn't have been able to fix my broken tooth until next week. I didn't expect it to take so long either."

"It's fine, Mamita. Mabel wasn't any trouble at all."

"And I met a nice nurse from Hawaii and a *bee-yoo-ti-ful* dog named Honey." Javi was helping Mabel with her backpack as she filled her grandmother in on everything that had happened. "Nurse Ailani is coming with us to go Christmas shopping on Friday, and I asked Papi for a dog, but he said we'd have to talk about it another time, and I think that means no."

Javi's mother laughed as she put her hand on her granddaughter's head and guided her back along the corridor toward the elevators.

"Is that so?" she said, the fond amusement in her tone a balm to Javi's stormy emotions. "What else happened today?"

"Wait," Mabel suddenly said, stepping out from beneath her grandmother's hand and turning to run back to Javi, who stooped to catch her flying form. "I didn't say goodbye."

Javi hugged her tight, his entire mood lifting because of his sweet daughter and the love he had for her.

"Goodbye, *mija*. I'll see you in a little while, okay? I love you."

"Love you too, Papi."

And as he watched her skip back to where his mother waited and waved to them again as they both looked his way, Javi was reminded of what was truly important in his life.

His family.

Keeping them safe.

Making them happy.

But that didn't mean that he wasn't going to have a few choice words with Ailani Kekoa and find out what was going on. The sudden cooling of their friendship had left him floundering, wondering if it was something he'd said or done to make it happen.

He didn't plan to spend any more nights tossing and turning, trying to figure it out. They were adults, and whether Ailani liked it or not, they were going to discuss it.

Tracking her down to a patient's room, he stood outside, watching as she adjusted the nebulizer, which was being held by the mother of one of their most ill patients. As she gently soothed what looked like both the baby and her mother, Javi felt that rush of tenderness and longing she so effortlessly engendered in him.

Maybe it was stupid to confront her about the last few days. It might've been smarter to just let things ride, letting the friendship dwindle without fighting for it. But something deep within told him he shouldn't do that. That he'd spend a lot of time—perhaps the rest of his life—wondering what had gone so drastically wrong.

Feeling as though he was skulking outside the room just made his sense of unease increase, so he went back to his office and texted Ailani, asking if she'd stop in for a moment. Twenty minutes later, she knocked on his door, her handbag on her shoulder and coat over her arm.

"Hi. You wanted to see me?"

There was something akin to wariness in her eyes, and Javi made sure to keep his expression as unrevealing as he could, although it hurt to see it. And he knew he couldn't press her about her change of attitude, out of fear of hurting her in some way he couldn't see or fathom.

"Yeah. Listen, I'm sorry Mabel put you on the spot like that. If you really don't want to go shopping with us—"

Ailani inhaled a long breath, her gaze steady on his, and

when she exhaled, it was as though she deflated slightly. "Before we get to the shopping trip, can I apologize for the last few days? I've just had some stuff on my mind and needed a bit of alone time to think it all through. I don't want you to think it's anything you've done. I've just been...preoccupied."

"It's fine," he said, trying to sound as though it hadn't hurt, more concerned for her than for himself. "Is there anything I can do to help?"

"No." Coming fully into his office, she sank down into one of his guest chairs. "I've just been...a little homesick."

Definitely nothing he could do about that, and hearing it made him remember why he needed to work on keeping his emotional distance from this winsome woman. In the blink of an eye, she'd be gone.

"I'm sorry to hear."

She flapped a hand. "It's okay. But to answer your original question, I'd love to go shopping with you and Mabel. She's adorable, Javi, and I'd hate to disappoint her. As long as you're okay with it."

"I am." He made his voice decisive so she'd have no doubts. "I was thinking after I've picked her up from school, I'd take her to the cat café and then to the mall. If we have time I'll take her to the Holiday Market at Seaport. If she's too tired, we can go another day. Will that work for you?"

"Sure. Where do you want me to meet you?"

"I'll pick you up," he said decisively. "Mabel is off at two thirty, and I'll text you when I'm on my way."

"Okay," she said, getting up and hitching her bag back up onto her shoulder. "I'll see you tomorrow."

Then she was gone, leaving behind a hint of her fresh scent and a man who wasn't sure whether she'd been completely truthful with him or not.

CHAPTER FIFTEEN

THE TEMPERATURE DROPPED on Friday, but the sky remained stubbornly clear of clouds, making Ailani complain to Bryn that they'd all jinxed her.

"I came here for a white Christmas, and everyone I've told has said it probably won't happen. I think you've all sent it out into the universe and I'm gonna be disappointed."

Bryn had laughed on her way out the door, leaving Ailani to consider her day off with a mixture of anxiety and excitement.

She was honest enough with herself to realize she'd rather have Javi's friendship and companionship while she was in Boston than keep him at arm's length. The two days when they'd hardly communicated had been the loneliest she'd experienced since leaving Molokai. She wasn't sure when Javi had become so important to her, but he was, and her new plan was to enjoy being with him as much as possible.

In two and a half months, she'd be gone.

Not a lot of time to spend with someone who was as important to her as Javi had become.

Rather than sit around all day, worrying about the upcoming excursion, Ailani put Honey into her crate and went to buy Javi's Secret Santa present. She'd planned to buy a few small gifts for her new friends, Bryn and Kali, but figured those could be acquired on the shopping trip that afternoon.

Getting back to the apartment and still as restless as before, she took Honey out for a brisk walk, and then, finally, it was time to get ready.

I'm on my way.

Javi's text had her heart rate going through the roof, but at least she had enough time to calm down before he sent a second text saying he was outside.

"Hi, Nurse Ailani."

Mabel, although strapped into in her booster seat, still managed to bounce up and down in excitement as Ailani got in through the passenger door.

"Hello, Mabel. Are you all ready to go shopping?"

"Yes!"

"I thought maybe we could stop and have a snack first," Javi said, exchanging a smile with Ailani before turning his attention back to the road. "Doesn't Abuela give you something to eat when you get home?"

"Yes. I like when she gives me apples or a cookie and some milk," Mabel said with that tendency young children had to list off everything they could think of under the circumstances. "Or toast and jam. Or a piece of cake, but not too much, okay?"

Javi snorted, drawing Ailani's gaze.

"That sounded just like my mom," he said softly, while Mabel kept listing foods her *abuela* had given her. "I've never heard her mimic her that way before."

Ailani giggled. "I'm guessing she probably does a really good impression of you too when she wants."

The sideways glance he sent her way made her laugh even harder.

"I hope not."

By the time they pulled up outside of the café, Ailani was pretty sure she knew the entire contents of Mrs. Pascal's cupboards and fridge.

Javi opened the door for Mabel, who'd already unbuckled herself from the booster, and Ailani's heart melted when the little girl took up position between the two adults and reached for both their hands.

Walking into the café, Ailani felt the tug on her hand as Mabel came to a complete stop, staring around.

"Papi," she whispered. "There're cats here."

"Yes." Javi was watching his daughter's face, while Ailani was watching his. "Would you like to pet some?"

"Yes, *please*," Mabel replied, jigging from one foot to the other in excitement.

One of the waitstaff came over to greet them. When Javi explained that Mabel loved animals but hadn't spent any time with kitties, the young lady led them to one of the tables, then took Mabel to where one of the cats was lying on the back of a bench.

"This is Buster," she told Mabel, who was standing with her hands clasped behind her back as though too afraid to reach out toward the gray-and-white fur. "He's very gentle, and he likes little kids. Would you like to touch him?"

Mabel looked back at her father, and Javi, still smiling, nodded.

"Yes, please."

The young woman, whose nametag read Julie, took Mabel's hand and showed her how to stroke the now purring Buster.

"Never ruffle their fur," she said. "Always stroke them from their heads down toward their tails, okay?"

"They don't like when you do it the other way?"

"Nope, they don't. If you do that, you might meet the murder mittens."

"The what?" Mabel giggled at the name. "What are murder mittens?"

"Their claws."

Buster got up and stretched, causing Mabel to put her hands behind her back again.

"Does she always stand like that?" Ailani asked Javi. "Clasping her hands behind her that way?"

He laughed softly.

"That's her *abuela*," he replied. "My mother taught all of her children to stand that way, especially in shops. We could look but not touch."

"Ingenious." Ailani couldn't help chuckling with him. "I'd love to see her try to teach any of my little cousins that trick. They're unholy terrors, those boys."

"Are those your uncle Makoa's kids?"

"No. Uncle never married." Julie was leading Mabel over to another cat, the seemingly smitten Buster following. "It's not something we talk about a lot, but he has autism, along with ADHD and issues with depression. He almost got married once, according to my mom's diary, but it seems as though the woman broke it off at the last minute, and he never tried again."

"It's hard," Javi replied absently, and when she glanced at him out of the corner of her eye, he was watching Mabel, a little smile lightening his face. "When things don't work out, sometimes the sense of failure is as bad as the feelings of loss."

Was that how he felt about the end of his marriage? That he'd been a failure? Somehow lacking?

Ailani wanted to ask but bit the inside of her cheek to hold back the words. Getting too caught up in Javi's life and backstory would only make the inevitable parting that much harder.

"She's doing really well," she said, bringing the conversation back onto safer territory. "What do you think?"

"I think we may have found the solution that will satisfy everyone, at least for a while," he answered.

Just then another cat, which had been circling around behind Mabel and Julie, came right over and jumped into Javi's lap. For a moment, feline and human looked into each other's eyes, and then the cat leaned forward to rub its cheek against Javi's face.

"That's what they do when they're claiming you," Ailani told him, sotto voce, so Mabel wouldn't hear. "I think she's not the only one who'll be getting a pet."

"Hush, you." He was trying for a quelling tone, but Ailani just laughed, watching him stroke the cat, who was clearly exactly where she wanted to be.

Javi had to admit that the cat café was a huge hit and, since Mabel showed no signs of allergies, getting her a cat might be the ultimate Christmas present.

She was still talking about them when they got to the mall.

"Buster is my favorite," she said, over and over. "But I love Clara Meow too. Clara liked you, Papi."

"That she did," Javi agreed. "I'm still picking her fur off my clothes."

But although he tried to make it a grumble, he was actually quite exhilarated by the experience. They'd always had animals growing up, and it was time to allow Mabel to have the same joy he and his siblings had had.

After they got to the mall and Mabel decided she wanted to shop first and then go see Santa, Javi whispered into Ailani's ear, "Can you take her into one of the shops for a moment? I want to send an email to Michael with the idea."

"Of course." Her eyes were sparkling, and he got the feeling she was deriving as much enjoyment out of the situation as he was.

Emailing Michael was always the best way to get through to him, since Javi never knew if he was working or when. The time difference made it tricky, but Javi wanted to get the question of the cat settled as soon as possible. Embedding a couple of the pictures he'd taken of Mabel sitting on the floor, surrounded by cats and looking like she was in heaven, he hoped the pleasure on their daughter's face would seal the deal.

He'd decided against getting her a kitten for the simple reason that an older cat, whose temperament was already known and that was litter trained, would make the transition that much easier. He wasn't sure Buster was up for adoption, but if he was, Javi thought the gray would be perfect.

Having sent the email, he wandered into the store he'd seen Ailani and Mabel go into and paused by the door, watching the two of them. Ailani was showing Mabel how to spray scent onto one of those little strips of white paper, dry it by wafting it through the air and then sniff it.

"But I wanted to spray it on me," Mabel said. "So I'd smell nice, like you."

"But you want to make sure you like it first," Ailani told her. "It's awful walking around not liking how you smell and you can't get it off until you have a bath."

"Oh." The little girl seemed to be considering that, her head tilted to one side. "Okay."

And as the afternoon progressed into evening, Javi became aware of something he hadn't fully considered when planning the outing.

Mabel seemed to be as enamored with Ailani as her father knew himself to be. It was in the way she watched what Ailani did and then tried to imitate her actions, and the way she appealed for Ailani's opinion in almost everything she did. Javi wondered if he should feel slighted as Mabel conferred with Ailani, rather than him, about the perfect presents for her grandmothers but realized he didn't mind.

Ailani was so sweet to Mabel, making her feel comfortable and important. The most vital thing, as far as Javi was concerned, was that Mabel was happy.

They joined the line to see Santa, and Javi could see that his daughter was flagging. Lifting her up and putting her on his hip, he said, "We'll see Santa, then get something to eat, okay?"

"Yes, Papi," she sighed, snuggling into his neck.

He kissed the top of her head and then caught Ailani's gaze resting on them, and his heart sped up. But before he could interpret the expression on her face, she'd turned away.

Mabel made it through the visit with Santa but fell asleep in her booster seat as Javi drove to pick up the takeout Chinese food he'd ordered. He was kicking himself for not arranging things differently as he turned the car toward Ailani's apartment.

"If I had someone to watch Mabel, I'd invite you to have dinner with us and drop you home afterward, but I'm afraid I don't."

"It's fine," she said, sounding content and a little tired too. "Thanks for buying me some food too. Honey and I are grateful."

He chuckled just as his phone vibrated, and he saw he had an email come in from Michael. As eager as he was to see what it said, he waited until he'd drawn up in front of Ailani's apartment before reaching for the phone.

"Hang on," he told her as she reached for the handle. "Let's see if today's trip was worthwhile."

Michael's reply was succinct and to the point:

Yes!

He turned the phone so that Ailani could see it, and she punched the air, obviously as elated as he was.

He had no time to react when she leaned across the console and, after whispering, "Good night," pressed her lips to his.

Javi froze, every muscle in his body locking up, every nerve ending seemingly attached to where those gorgeous, soft lips rested against his mouth.

Before he could react, put his arms around her and try to drag her closer, it was over, and Ailani was opening her door.

Then she was gone, leaving him with the lingering, tantalizing scent of warm skin and the sensation of having been offered a glimpse of heaven, only to have it snatched away again.

CHAPTER SIXTEEN

AILANI WORKED THE weekend and was glad of it. The hustle and bustle took her mind off the shopping trip with Javi and Mabel—and off the kiss she'd been unable to resist stealing from him.

He'd looked so ecstatic when he'd read the text from his ex, his face alight with pleasure and relief, there was nothing she could have done to stop herself.

But it was the entirety of the afternoon and evening that she kept going back to.

Being with them had opened up a space in her chest, leaving her with a longing that had nothing to do with her attraction to him and everything to do with the sense of belonging she'd felt with them.

Mabel was a treasure.

Ailani had always liked children—she wouldn't have specialized in pediatric care if she didn't. But, except for a while after reading her mom's journals, there'd never been an overwhelming longing to have any of her own. Or, if she thought about it, it was in an abstract, *maybe one day* sort of way.

Javi and Mabel had changed that, all in one short shopping trip.

She felt like a part of a family with them. Felt as though her presence mattered in a fundamental way. The way Mabel had looked at her, looked to her for advice or comfort or com-

panionship had melted Ailani's heart in a way nothing else
ever had.

She'd been worried that she was falling in love with Javi.
Now she was doubly worried that she was falling for the entire
Pascal package—both father and daughter making her long
for a life she knew she couldn't have.

Thankfully, her impulsive kiss didn't seem to have created
any problems between her and Javi. She'd worried that he'd
misinterpreted it—actually worried that he'd *correctly* interpreted it!—and that it would cause strain on their relationship
again. But on the day after it had happened, he'd been back to
texting her the way he usually did.

Do you want to come over on Sunday to help us decorate
after you get off work? If you think you'll be too tired, it's
not a big deal.

But it was a big deal to her, who craved their company and
the warmth she felt in it. Of course, she'd never say so, but she
fell back on banter to disguise her pleasure at the invitation.

You're finally getting around to it, huh? I'd love to.

You sound like Mabel. "Papi, all my friends' houses are already decorated." I'm the most henpecked man in the
Greater Boston area.

Hahaha. Yeah, right. What time should I come over?

Come straight from work if you like. I'll have a meal for you
and everything ready to go. I know you probably won't want
to be out too late.

I'm off on Monday, so it's not a big deal. I'll probably take a rideshare too, since they say there's a chance of freezing rain.

And suddenly the weekend took on a whole new, and improved, atmosphere.

Because she was on shift, she couldn't compete in the Santa Dash taking place that Saturday. But, as she'd told Bryn when it had first come up, there was no way she'd be willing to run in that cold anyway.

She didn't know how any of them could do it, but many members of staff, including Kali, Bryn, Dylan, Nick, and even grumpy Ben Murphy were in the lineup. Honey was too, looking snazzy in a pair of reindeer antlers as she and Bryn had left the apartment that morning.

Then, Nick, who'd gone all out and turned up in an actual Santa suit, came by to visit with the children on the ward afterward, Bryn and Honey going around with him. Ailani was glad they'd come back to the ward when they did because one of the patients Bryn was especially concerned about was being readmitted for the second time.

Telling them Susie was on her way up from the emergency room put a bit of a damper on the holiday spirit, but the other children enjoyed the candy canes Nick handed out.

"Have you finished your shopping?" she asked Kali as they met up at the nurses' station unexpectedly.

"I have," Kali said with a sly little smile, so unlike her usual rather stern demeanor that it piqued Ailani's interest even more than seeing her and Dylan at the game had. "And even though I'm not interested in Christmas, I've decided instead to celebrate the holidays, just a little."

"What's that now?"

"I know, I know. 'Scrooge McMitchell' and all that," Kali

said with that same little smirk and a twinkle in her eyes. "But even Scrooge McDuck took in the triplets, right?"

Just then a call came from one of the rooms, and Ailani had to go before they could continue their silly banter.

"Good for you," she called to Kali as she strode away. "But don't think I won't still call you Scrooge McMitchell. It has a certain ring to it."

And the sound of her friend's laughter followed her down the hallway and made her smile widen.

By Sunday evening, Ailani was a bundle of nerves about her visit to Javi and Mabel's house. It was one thing to walk around a mall or go out to eat, but she wasn't at all sure how Mabel would feel about having a woman she hardly knew in her home.

But Ailani found she shouldn't have worried.

"Nurse Ailani!" Mabel was capering around, frolicking like a puppy around Javi's legs when he opened the door. "We have pizza and sodas and all the decorations in boxes. And Papi bought the tree yesterday, and we found some insects in it, and he had to take them outside, and I told him not to because it was too cold, but he said they'd be okay. And Oma bought me some books. Not for Christmas, she said, but just because I'd been so good."

Ailani couldn't stop laughing at the run-on commentary and the way Javi ruefully shook his head at his daughter's excitement.

"I think it was a praying mantis nest," he said in an aside when Mabel had run off—still chattering away—to fetch a book she wanted to show Ailani. "In the tree. I shudder to think of waking up one morning and finding the place overrun with them."

Ailani gave a little shudder, partially at the thought of the insect but mostly because Javi was helping her take off her coat and his fingers had brushed her neck. "I don't mind them outside, but not in the house. I totally agree with you on that."

"Papi said he would bake cookies with me this weekend." Mabel was back, book in hand but forgotten as her brain skipped off to this new topic. "But then Oma wanted me to help her make cake, so I went there instead. Papi, are we still going to make cookies?"

"I don't know, sweetheart. Honestly, I'm not very good at baking."

Mabel gave him a sweet smile and wag of her finger. "Mrs. Durant says that just because you're not good at something doesn't mean you shouldn't try."

"Her class teacher," he explained. "We'll see."

"That usually means no," Mabel told Ailani, pursing her mouth for a moment as though in disapproval. Then she smiled again. "But Papi *might* change his mind and try."

It was, Ailani thought to herself as the evening went on, one of the best nights of her life.

They ate the pizza by the fireplace in the living room, Mabel telling her all about her school and the friends she had there and then asking Ailani about Hawaii.

"Papi showed me some pictures," she said. "Of the birds and the sea and people on boards flying through the water. Do you know how to do that?"

"Yes, I know how to surf. It's a lot of fun."

"I want to try one day. Can we surf here, Papi?"

What a treasure she was. So smart and sweet. How lucky Javi was to have her for a daughter.

It made her wonder what type of person his ex was to so easily leave these two behind. Obviously, he must've been a dedicated doctor since Javi had said he was serving with an international medical team, but what kind of man left his husband and daughter like that?

This husband. This daughter.

While Javi adjusted the lights he'd already strung on the tree the evening before, Mabel and Ailani went through the boxes of ornaments. Then they decorated the mantlepiece, the banisters of the staircase leading up to the bedrooms and the occasional tables in the living room.

"Remember to leave some decorations for the kitchen," Javi said.

"Okay, Papi."

But even as she agreed, she put another snowman ornament on the already-overcrowded table beside her, making Ailani suppress a smile.

Trimming the tree with Mabel was a trip too, as the little girl had very decided ideas of where each and every ornament needed to go.

By the time they'd finished, the little girl's eyelids were getting heavy and she seemed too tired to have much to say.

Javi had made them all hot chocolate, and Mabel drank only half of hers before she began to nod.

"Come on, *mija*." Javi got up from off the floor where they all were sitting and reached out for his daughter, who was drowsing in front of the fire. "Time for bed."

Mabel got to her feet, weaving a little as though drunk.

"I have to kiss Nurse Ailani good-night first, Papi."

And when those little arms went around her and the sticky little mouth found and kissed Ailani's cheek, it was all she could do not to hold on to her and never let her go.

"Stay until I come back down?"

Something in Javi's voice made a warm spot open up in her chest and, although she knew she should leave, Ailani agreed.

Javi got Mabel washed up and ready for bed, trying not to rush yet wanting so badly to get back downstairs to Ailani.

Not that he was planning to do any of the myriad things

he wanted to do with her, but just because having her in the house had made the space feel, in a strange way, complete.

She'd fit so seamlessly, it was as though she'd always been there.

"Can Nurse Ailani read me a story, Papi? Please?"

How could he resist that pleading face? Those wistful eyes?

And when he called down, Ailani didn't hesitate.

Javi sat at the foot of Mabel's bed while Ailani read the story his daughter had chosen, and then Ailani sang Mabel a Hawaiian song, telling her that one day she'd show her how to dance to it.

By the time they closed her door, Javi was sure his daughter was already asleep, worn out by excitement.

"I've had a wonderful time," Ailani said as they went back downstairs. "Thank you so much for inviting me."

"Thank you for coming," he replied, hoping she realized how sincere he was being. "Mabel had a blast. As did I." He saw her glance toward the front door, and before she could say anything, he added, "You're off tomorrow, aren't you?"

"I am."

"So, stay and have a drink with me before you go."

Ailani turned those dark eyes his way, and for an instant Javi forgot to breathe. Then she smiled, and he clenched his fingers so as not to reach out and touch her face, knowing that if he did, he'd definitely kiss her.

Common sense be damned.

"Okay."

She had a glass of white wine, and after he'd poured it for her and gotten himself a beer, they meandered back into the living room and she curled up in front of the fire again.

"So, now you're all ready for Christmas," she said, sending him a sassy smile. "Finally."

"Still one or two gifts to buy," he told her with a shrug. "I haven't gotten anything for my niece and nephew, who're coming from California, and, of course, the cats."

"What did you decide about that? Are you getting them before or after Christmas?"

"I decided on after because we'll be rushing around and having people in and out of the house over the holidays. It'll be enough of a stress on Buster and Clara without putting them through that. I've already signed the paperwork and paid the adoption fees, and the shelter will take care of them for me until the twenty-seventh.

"They even said I should let them know if I want to bring Mabel to see them, and they'd help me arrange it."

"You're a good father." The smile she sent him was a balm to his soul. "You're so patient and loving with her. Not," she added quickly, "that there's any reason not to be. She's such a sweetie."

"Thank you for that." He looked down at the bottle in his hand rather than at the way the firelight caressed her velvety skin, giving it a rich golden hue. "Sometimes it feels as if I have no idea what I'm doing, and I can't help wondering if I'm doing right by her."

"Isn't that an intrinsic part of parenthood?" she asked, swirling her glass so the wine sent little dots of light flickering about the room. "No one really knows what they're doing half the time, even when they're doing it."

"True." For an instant his ex flitted through his thoughts and then was dismissed. "I was so worried when we applied to adopt that I wouldn't have the capacity to be a good father. That I might somehow not love Mabel the way she deserved. Now that's the only thing I'm one hundred percent sure of at any given point in time. I don't think I could love her any more than I do."

She nodded before tipping the last of her wine into her mouth.

"I really should be going." She sounded rueful and determined all at the same time. "It's been a long day."

"Of course. I'm sorry to have kept you this long." Getting up, he took the glass from her hand and walked over to place it on the table nearest to the kitchen. "Somehow, on the days I'm off, I seem to think the hospital just goes into stasis, waiting for me to get back."

That made her giggle as she got into the app on her phone so as to summon the rideshare. "I wish it had. We were incredibly busy."

When she was finished, she got up, slinging her bag over her shoulder, and they walked toward the door, even though she wouldn't be picked up for another five minutes.

"Thank you for wonderful evening," she said, sitting on the hall bench to pull on her boots.

"Thank you for coming over. You made Mabel's night."

She rose, her gaze searched his for a moment, and although it looked as if she might say something more, no words emerged.

Unable to resist, Javi stepped closer, watching her body language, waiting to see if she leaned or stepped away. Ailani held her ground, not moving, and when he cupped her cheeks, she was still looking straight into his eyes.

One kiss. Just one.

There.

Her full lips, soft and cool beneath his. Utterly still.

And then...

Suddenly, not even knowing how it happened, the kiss went from chaste to frantic between one hitched breath and the next.

Their mouths fit together perfectly. The fierce duel of their tongues aroused him, telling him Ailani wouldn't be a passive lover but would give and take in equal, thrilling measure.

He had her up against the wall beside his front door, and

her fingers clutched onto his back, pulling him closer, not pushing away.

And then, as quickly as it had started, they both froze as a little voice called from upstairs.

"Papi…"

"I…" He cleared his throat. "I'll be right there, Mabel."

Now her palms were flat against his chest, and for a moment he resisted, staying where he was, keeping her there in his arms. "Stay…"

"No. I can't. Please, don't ask again."

He knew she was right—smart. But everything inside him strained toward her, even as he let go and stepped away.

Her lips were fuller than usual, the deep pink of a woman who'd been kissed and kissed again, and his heart juddered, desire like magma in his veins.

The beep of her phone, and she reached for her coat.

"The rideshare is here." Her voice sounded as if it were coming from far away. "I have to go, and you need to check on Mabel."

"Yes."

Javi reached to help her with her coat, but she jerked out of his reach, dragging it on over her bag.

Before he could say anything else, with a swirl of cold night air, she'd opened the door and was gone.

CHAPTER SEVENTEEN

NEVER HAD AILANI been gladder to have a day off than she was the morning after she'd kissed Javi. Having hardly slept the night before, she'd have been useless at work. Every time she closed her eyes, all she could feel was Javi's lips, his body against hers, the heat of passionate desire rushing through her body.

She'd wanted him more at that instant than she'd ever wanted anything or anyone before.

But at the same time, she'd known she was gambling with more than she wanted to lose.

Already she was invested.

In him. In Mabel.

In a fantasy she hadn't even known she was harboring in her heart.

The dream of home, parenthood, love.

Things she'd thought to add to her list early on and hadn't bothered to because they'd seemed unrealistic.

As it was, maybe people would think a bucket list likes hers completely unrealistic. How would a nurse from the island of Molokai expect to see the pyramids of Egypt or visit Japan? Yet her mother had achieved those things through hard work and planning, and so, to Ailani, none of those things seemed unachievable.

But love? Marriage? Children?

She'd always hesitated to even think about them. Somewhere inside, there'd lain a barrier, holding her back from the emotional connection necessary to make those things worthwhile.

It hadn't bothered her before, but now, as she lay in bed, watching the weak winter sun make its way through the blinds, she knew she was in over her head. And in this case, she didn't know how to swim.

I'm only here for a short time.

I have too many things to do—to cross off my list.

I won't break Mabel's heart or my own.

Because the truth was she and Javi had no chance of a future together, and Mabel couldn't be allowed to become attached to a woman who'd be gone in a couple of months' time. Little hearts broke so much easier than big ones, and Javi should've known that, just like Ailani did.

Dragging herself out of bed, she wondered if she'd even hear from Javi again or if he'd simply decide it wasn't worth the hassle.

That she wasn't worth it.

So, it was slightly shocking when her phone chirped and she saw his name pop up.

I hope you're okay.

Heart pumping like crazy, she had to sink back down onto the edge of the bed so as to stop her legs giving out, and she replied:

I am.

I'm not apologizing. It was beautiful, but I know you were right to put a stop to it.

It took her a minute to gather her thoughts so she found the right words.

I don't need or want an apology. There's something between us, but it's best kept as friendship, for all our sakes. Especially Mabel's.

There was a pause, so long that she thought he wasn't going to respond at all.

I know.

And that was where they left it that morning, Ailani refusing to reach back out, trying to find some sense of equilibrium in a world that felt as though it had turned upside down.

The next day, for the first time in a long time, she dreaded going to work. Just the thought of facing Javi made her shiver, but there was no way to avoid her shift. Not that she really wanted to.

Work would keep her sane.

What they all did on the pediatric ward made a tangible difference in the lives of so many families. Those little bodies were precious, and helping to heal and care for them superseded any emotional turmoil she was going through.

To her total surprise, Javi acted as though that kiss had never happened. As though they were the same as they'd ever been.

"Lunch later?" he asked, as casual as could be. "I won't be able to leave until after one though."

"Sure," she replied, dredging up some acting skills from somewhere so no one would guess that inside she was a quivering mess. "Text me and let me know."

And they tried, very hard, to talk as though there'd been no change in the relationship. No moment of madness, threatening their peace of mind.

Or maybe, despite his texts, it was only her own that was threatened?

"I'm trying to figure out how to tell Mabel about her presents." Full of Beans was packed, but somehow Javi had been able to snag a table. "I don't want her to be disappointed on Christmas Day when there's no big present, and I think just telling her wouldn't be as effective. For all her intelligence, she'd still only six."

"Check online," Ailani suggested. "See if you can find two stuffed cats that have similar coloring to Buster and Clara. Then wrap those up, and when she opens it, tell her Buster and Clara are waiting for her to come get them. Tell her they're on vacation for a few days or something, so she doesn't insist you leave on Christmas morning to fetch them."

He'd laughed, just like he always did when she was silly, but even then she knew it took real effort on his part. If Javi could try so hard, then she could too.

Even though she was afraid everything really had changed and would never go back to the way it had been.

Javi didn't know what he felt, except that he knew he didn't want to relinquish Ailani's friendship, even though it would be best for all concerned.

Yes, he wanted her. And yes, he was ready to move on from his marriage and divorce. But was he ready for the type of temporary relationship Ailani could offer?

Well, maybe. But only if it didn't involve Mabel.

As a single dad, with a support system he felt he was already taking too much advantage of, there was no way to have that type of affair.

Besides, something inside kept whispering that Ailani

wasn't a short-term proposition anyway. That once they'd slept together, it could get serious quickly.

At least for him.

His feelings for her were already strong and seemed to grow each time they were together. Right now, his idea of moving on really didn't include another long-term relationship. He still had too many battle scars from dealing with the end of his marriage.

"Did you buy your Secret Santa gift yet?" Leigh asked him a couple days later when he was doing rounds.

"Of course. The party is tonight, isn't it?" He was wondering if somehow, in the midst of his mental turmoil, he'd gotten the days wrong.

"Yep, that's why I'm asking," the charge nurse replied. "*Some* people forget, and then it's a last-minute rush or we're a gift or two short. I'm reminding everyone on the list so no one gets left out."

"Mine's in my office so I don't forget it at home."

"Good man," Leigh said before hurrying off.

Javi wasn't particularly looking forward to the Christmas party. While he and Ailani had tried to pretend all was well, they both felt the tension, stretched like a vibrating wire, between them.

"At least the weatherman is calling for snow."

As though he'd conjured her with his thoughts, her voice came from just behind him, and his heart did that funny twist it always did when she was near.

Turning, he found her concentrating on the chart in her hand, and it took everything he had inside not to reach for her chin, tilt it up so she was forced to look directly at him.

"But do you believe him?" he asked, injecting amusement into his voice. "In my opinion, that's the only job in the world where you can get it wrong every day and people still listen to you."

That made her chuckle and finally meet his gaze. "That's true, but in this case, I think unless the storm that's been rolling across the country suddenly dies away by an act of God, they'll be right."

"So, you'll get your white Christmas after all."

"Looks that way," she said, but although she was smiling, it didn't go all the way to her eyes.

"I'll see you at the party later," he said, about to move on to the next patient on his round, for the first time glad he wasn't working with Ailani.

Afraid she'd be too much of a distraction.

"Yep," she replied, already walking away, unaware that he was watching her until he couldn't see her anymore.

CHAPTER EIGHTEEN

THE STAFF PARTY was in full swing, but Ailani turned her back on the revelries, unable to face it just then. Instead, she wandered to the window and stood looking out, deep in thought.

It was funny how often in life you thought you really, really wanted something, and then when you got it, there was no pleasure in it.

Outside, snow was falling. Thick fluffy flakes tumbling from the sky, clumped together, as though determined to completely coat everything in white.

She'd come to Boston to see snow and have a white Christmas. To build a snowman and make snow angels and maybe even try skiing. This was an opportunity to cross things off her list, and it should've been a happy moment, but truthfully, she felt nothing.

Around her people were laughing and chattering, drinks in hands and more than one Santa hat already at a rakish angle. The spirit of the season was evident, as was the family atmosphere she'd grown to expect in the pediatric department, but Ailani realized she wasn't the only one not feeling it.

Nick was staring out the window too, looking about as joyous as she felt. There'd been something brewing, she thought, between him and Bryn, but it seemed as though it'd gone wrong somehow.

Bryn hadn't confided in her, so Ailani didn't know the details, but when asked how they were, all they'd say was, "Fine."

Never one to pry, she left Nick to his thoughts and drifted off around the edge of the room, stopping to talk here and there, smiling so no one would guess what she was feeling.

A little lost.

Lonely.

Although he said he'd come, Javi hadn't turned up.

"I hate this soda," Izzy Jeong muttered, looking into her plastic cup. "You'd think medical folks would have some kind of fruit juice."

"Can I get you something else?" Ailani asked, looking across at the refreshment table where bottles of wine and other spirits sat, hoping for something to do to keep herself busy, even for a moment.

"No, thanks." Izzy gave her a little smile. "Don't mind me."

"Have you seen Dr. Pascal?" Leigh asked as she hurried up, looking frazzled. "I want to do the Secret Santa before people have to leave."

Having the party in the hospital meant that staff could come and go when they could get away, so even those on shift could get a taste of the festivities.

"No, I haven't," she said, just as there was a little eddy at the door and her heart turned over at the sight of him. "Oh. There he is."

"Thank goodness," Leigh said, obviously not hearing the hitch in Ailani's voice. "We can get started."

"Sorry I'm late," Javi said to the room at large as he bent to discreetly put a package under the tree. "I had a call I had to take."

Straightening, he looked around the room, his eyes lingering on Ailani's face for a long moment before moving on.

He started circling the room, greeting everyone, and although Ailani made sure not to stare, she circled too, keeping her distance, knowing where he was at every moment.

Leigh started handing out packages, calling out names so the recipients could come forward and claim their gift.

"I almost forgot mine," Dr. MacKenzie said to Ailani. He looked even more like a bird this evening, in a light gray suit with his red hair slicked back. "Good thing Leigh mentioned it to me today."

Before she could reply, Leigh called her name, and with a murmur she excused herself and went to get her gift, which turned out to be a bottle of coconut-scented bubble bath.

When Javi's name was called, she found a spot where she could discreetly watch him open it, almost holding her breath as he dug into the gift bag.

As he stood with the small, flat box in his hand, his gaze raced back and forth around the room, until he found her and stole her breath with his expression.

"Dr. Pascal. If I could ask you..."

As one of the other doctors distracted him, Ailani quietly slipped from the room, pausing outside to regain her equilibrium.

She'd bought him the traveling watercolor set he'd been looking at in the craft store and hadn't, at the time, considered it a very personal gift. But the way he'd looked at her when he'd realized what it was had suddenly made it seem positively intimate, and the entire encounter had shaken her to the bones.

I can't go back in there.

The thought came, borne on a rash of goose bumps.

Javi's expression had been so potent, so carnal, she was surprised she hadn't combusted on the spot.

It felt as though he'd somehow branded her from across the room, and if she went back into the party, everyone would be able to see it.

Making her way to the staff locker room, she changed her

shoes and put on her coat. Then, remembering Bryn had offered to drive her home, she pulled out her phone and texted her to say she was heading home on the train.

Making her way down to the staff entrance and out into the night, she paused outside the door, lifting her face to the sky. The heavy flakes dulled the urban sounds and created a strange, otherworldly glow around the lights. Ailani was transfixed. Transported to a new place. Her mind expanding to take in this exquisite, foreign scene.

She hardly registered the sound of the door behind her opening, and it wasn't until Javi spoke that the dreamlike state she'd fallen into was broken.

"How do you like your first snowfall?"

His voice was raw, the polish stripped away, and the sound of it made Ailani shiver. Not with cold or with fear but something deeper.

"It's glorious," she replied, her voice hardly above a whisper, tendrils of heat spiraling out from her core to suffuse every nerve and inch of her skin.

She didn't hear him move, his footsteps muffled by the snow, but she knew he had. It was as though she could feel him through her pores, she was so hyperaware of him.

"You bought me my gift, didn't you?"

It was more statement than question, but she answered anyway.

"I did."

"Why this?"

Strange how a simple question could sound like a hundred, given the number of answers one could provide. But, if nothing else, she'd try to be honest with him in this instance.

"You give your all, all the time. To the hospital, to Mabel, to your family. I... I thought you needed something that was just for you. I hoped you'd rediscover your love of art and in it, rediscover something about yourself, that maybe you hadn't realized was missing."

He was so quiet, she wondered if he'd reply. Around them the snow continued to fall, shrouding them in a cocoon of white so it felt as though they were the only people in the world.

"Come home with me." She shivered at the need in his voice, wanting to acquiesce, even as her better judgment warned her not to go.

"Mabel…?"

"Is with my mom tonight." He inhaled so deeply she heard it. Then he said, "I know I shouldn't ask, Ailani, that it's wrong for us both, but I'm doing it anyway. Come home with me."

She wanted to run. To hide from the tidal wave of emotion buffeting her. But instead, she turned to him and went into his arms without any hesitation.

Kissing Ailani in the snow was like heaven, but it couldn't last. Not with the cold wind that started blowing the flakes around so their skin was stung, nor with the chance that someone coming out through the door would see them.

"Is that a yes?" he asked into her ear, feeling her shiver as his breath touched her there.

"Yes," she replied, softly and yet clearly, without hesitation, and his heart sang.

Taking her back in through the staff door, he led her to the elevator. When it came, the car was empty, but he didn't try to kiss her again.

He was too much on the edge of losing control, his need for her overwhelming his senses.

In the parking garage, he guided her to his car and opened her door for her before rounding the trunk and getting into the driver's seat.

The drive to his home took longer than usual because of

the weather, but neither of them spoke. Javi was almost afraid to break whatever spell they'd fallen under, as though giving name to what they were doing would make it vanish, like the snow beneath a blaze of sunlight.

This desire for her was, he thought, a type of madness. Unleashed by her decadent mouth, her satin skin, rounded curves and sharp, sassy mind.

Maybe it was the long days of denial, the refrain of friendship and innocent enjoyment he'd repeated to himself that gave the anticipation additional strength. Whatever it was, he knew himself to be ravenous and hoped she was too.

That they could feast on each other and somehow, at the end of it, find surcease from the agonizing need.

When he finally parked in his garage, he turned to face her. Her eyes looked huge in the glow of the lights, dark and luminous, and her lips were still rose pink from his kisses.

Taking a deep breath, he said, "If you've changed your mind—"

"Shush," she said, like a teacher with an unruly pupil, reaching for the door handle to let herself out of the car.

As though in a daze, he let them into the house and paused only to lock the door behind them, then slip off his coat and shoes as she did the same. Up the stairs, her hand in his. Her skin felt almost hot to the touch, and he realized it was because his own fingers were cold.

Nerves? Or something else? Or a combination of physical and emotional?

The analytical part of his brain seemed set on tackling the question, until they entered his bedroom and Ailani tugged his hand, bringing him to a stop just inside the doorway.

"I should say the same, shouldn't I? Ask the same…" He couldn't fathom what she was asking, started shaking his head. "If you've changed your mind—"

He didn't let her finish.

If he didn't kiss her, feel her, *love* her immediately, he'd turn to dust or fade to a shadow. So he pulled her close, and when their lips met it was a sonic flare, a tornado, the elixir of life all in one.

He'd only known her for three weeks. How could it feel as though he'd waited a lifetime for this moment?

The sweet sounds echoing from her throat made torment out of desire, ratcheting his longing higher with each. And her hands were everywhere, undressing him, feathering over his skin, digging into his back as he found her throat with his mouth and scraped it with his teeth.

He pulled back, so as to tug off her top, and it was Ailani who reached back to unclasp her bra so she could shrug it off, leaving her torso bare to his ravenous gaze.

He wanted her in his bed, where he could look and touch and taste freely, so he picked her up and carried her the final few steps, putting her down on the duvet. In the light from the bedside lamp he'd earlier turned on remotely, her skin was the finest silk, gleaming smooth.

"Take off your clothes. I want to see you."

Her voice was breathy, but the demand in it was clear. He had no reason to deny her or to delay. He wasn't the type of man who was vain about his physique, so he felt no need to pose.

His entire being was focused on getting back to her and to feel her flesh against his, to give her pleasure.

As she watched him disrobe, she tugged off her pants and underwear, and as soon as he was naked, he joined her on the bed, reaching for her. They kissed and kissed, their hands roaming and learning and seeking until they were both breathless and Javi was aching for her.

But not yet.

"Tell me what you like, Ailani." He'd already learned how

sensitive her ears were, so he whispered into one, then traced the curl with his tongue. "Tell me what you like, and I'll do it."

So she guided him to all the most sensitive, erotic points of her body, told him how to position her, what to give her permission to do in return. He loved that she was so responsive, that her orgasms flowed, rippled, shuddered through her frame with consummate ease. His first came suddenly, unexpectedly, wrung from him by her surprisingly strong hands and tender, teasing mouth.

But that release was a gift to them both. Allowing them time for further exploration, for fresh desire to build, piling and piling until she cried out and Javi did too, as her pleasure propelled his into the stratosphere.

Exhausted, he pulled her close, threw a leg over hers, as though to trap her, he thought fancifully, and, with his face buried in the sweet scent of her hair, fell contentedly to sleep.

CHAPTER NINETEEN

AWAKENING CAME SLOWLY, as though she was floating up through a cloud of cottonwool. Or snow, she thought, the memory of it now indelibly stamped upon her brain. Not cold though, but warm—and surprisingly heavy.

Opening one eye, she realized first that she was in a room she only vaguely recalled. Secondly came the knowledge that she was the little spoon, and the big spoon was rather heavy.

Then it all came flooding back, and a firestorm of memories and sensations made her gasp.

Javi.

She was in his bed, having spent most of the night indulging in the most decadent sexual acts of her life.

Her face felt as though it was ablaze, but she didn't regret a single moment.

He'd been tender and passionate and demanding and giving. Everything she could have ever wanted, and then just that little *huna* more that could only have been found with him. That extra special bit that had taken it from sheer animal intercourse to something sublime.

From sex to lovemaking.

And somewhere in the midst of it, as she'd given voice to the pleasure firing like arrows through her body, she'd hazily thought, again, about the difference between dreams and reality.

The things we thought we wanted and the things we truly needed.

Now she knew if she could choose anything in the world, it would be this man, over anything else life had to offer.

The knowledge, however, gave her little delight.

To her mind, he'd made it plain he'd consider what they'd done a mistake, just like their kiss, interrupted by Mabel, had been.

And she couldn't blame him. Hadn't she told him, over and over, that all she wanted was adventure? To be free to explore the world the way her mother had?

To a man whose ex had left their comfortable life because it had been *too* comfortable—who clearly had been craving experiences unfound in their home—her ambitions must have sounded all too familiar.

All too hurtful.

There could be no future for her and Javi because even if she said she'd changed her mind about what she wanted to do with her life, he wouldn't believe her. There would always be that threat hanging over their relationship, the fear that one day, like Michael, she'd declare their life together boring and take off.

How could he be happy and secure in those circumstances?

And as time wore on and he kept a part of himself locked away out of that fear, how would she feel?

Would it be like battering her head against a brick wall, trying to convince him of her love?

It would kill her now that her barriers had fallen and she'd found her soulmate. While she would be all in, she'd expect no less from him.

There was an old song that said something about half a love being better than no love at all, but Ailani didn't subscribe to that theory.

She'd rather be alone than the only one a hundred percent committed.

Behind her, Javi stirred, sighed. His arm tightened around her, and she could feel his erection pressing against her buttocks.

One more time. For the memories.

And she rolled over and kissed him fully awake so they could make love one more time.

Afterward, as Javi fell back asleep, Ailani carefully slid out of the bed. Finding her clothes was difficult, but eventually she tiptoed out of the room and closed the door behind her.

It was still dark outside, and it was only when she got to the kitchen that she realized it was four thirty in the morning. Tempting as it was to call for a rideshare and go home, she wasn't sure that would be a wise thing to do by herself at that early hour.

She still had some time to get back to the apartment to get ready for work.

Finding her way around Javi's kitchen, she put on some coffee and then went to get her phone. That was when she remembered she hadn't told Bryn where she was, so she sent a quick text, telling her everything was okay and she wasn't to worry.

Ailani wandered into the living room, feeling almost disembodied.

Beside the Christmas tree was a wall of photographs, illuminated by the colorful lights that blinked and flashed. Without conscious thought, Ailani walked over there and stood looking at them.

Mabel was easy to spot, from a toddler sleeping in Javi's arms, her father beaming—so beautiful it made Ailani's heartache intensify—to her with lunchbox and backpack on what could only be her first day of school. There were two older couples and others she thought might be Javi's siblings. A group shot with one of the older couples in the middle, surrounded by two more generations.

Mr. and Mrs. Pascal, she thought, with their children and those children's spouses and children. And it was only in this picture she saw a man who she was sure was Javi's ex. A tall, handsome man with caramel-colored hair and a smile so wide and open, a person could be forgiven for thinking he would always be true and truthful.

But you weren't, were you, Michael? Instead, you made Javi believe in you, in what you had together, and when you left, you made sure he'd never truly believe in anyone ever again.

Unreasonable to blame the absent man, but as Ailani heard sounds she thought heralded Javi waking up, she brushed her silly tears away and prepared for whatever would come next.

Javi might never believe it, but she was determined to do the right thing for him and Mabel.

And herself, no matter how badly it might hurt.

When Javi woke up the second time, he realized he was in bed alone and, for a moment, wondered if he'd dreamt the entire night.

Then he knew he definitely hadn't, and the memories surrounded him, firing his blood again. But Ailani wasn't beside him, and after a moment of disappointment, Javi thought it might be a good thing.

He needed time to process what they'd done. Figure out how to handle it, whatever "it" turned out to be.

People said that sex changed everything, but it wasn't really true. Spending the night making love with Ailani hadn't changed the fundamental facts of their lives.

That his home was here and hers was in Hawaii.

That she craved adventure, while he needed stability, both for himself and for Mabel.

That whatever they ended up doing, Mabel had to be his first concern.

His daughter didn't need any more disruption in her life.

When looked at in that way, the answer seemed simple: He and Ailani couldn't have a relationship. Not a real, long term one. Firstly because she wouldn't be around long term, and secondly because she probably wouldn't want one, since being with him would take her from her family and tie her down in Boston.

For a woman whose professed ambition was to travel the world, that probably would sound like hell.

Besides, it was one thing to want to see snow and have a white Christmas; it was another to go through it year after year when you were used to balmy tropical climes.

But there was a part of him that wouldn't give up hope.

He'd never known anyone like Ailani. Something in her had reached out and captured its counterpart in him, and he knew he would never get it back. Maybe, just maybe, she might feel the same, and they could...

Here, his mind faltered.

Could do what?

When positions were so diametrically opposed, could there be compromise?

What right would he have to insist she give up her freedom and her dreams because of his responsibilities? The things he had to offer were things she either already had or had professed not to want.

He couldn't leave Boston, which was the only stable home Mabel had ever known. What right did he have, on the basis of a relationship a few weeks old, to ask Ailani to consider giving up her life, to live in his world?

The only thing he could do was follow Ailani's lead.

Sitting up, Javi listened for any sounds of habitation, but the bedroom door was closed and he couldn't hear anything. Getting up, he pulled on a pair of sweatpants and was hunting for a hoodie when the door opened and Ailani walked in.

"Morning." She was smiling, but Javi thought her eyes looked wary. "I brought you some coffee."

"Thanks." He took the cup from her outstretched hand. "You didn't have to."

"Of course not," she said briskly. "But I was making some for myself, so it's not a big deal."

"Been up long?" Putting the cup on the nightstand, he grabbed the first shirt he could find and pulled it on.

"Not really, but I have to go. I forgot to text Bryn last night, and she was about to call the police to report me missing. Besides, I need to get to work."

"Now that she knows you're safe, you could shower here and let me drive you to work."

The look she gave him was level, and if he didn't know her as well as he did, he'd think there was a hint of amusement.

"I'm not going to work in the same clothes I wore yesterday and turn up with the head of Pediatrics. Can you imagine the gossip?"

He could and, at that precise moment, didn't care. When he said as much Ailani shook her head.

"Javi, it wouldn't do your reputation any harm, but mine would definitely be in question. And while normally I wouldn't care either, I'm still very much an outsider at Boston Beacon and will have to live with the fallout, if there's any, until I leave in March."

Her words told him two things, neither of which made him

happy. She couldn't see them going public with their relationship, and neither had she any thought of staying longer than her allotted three months.

"I see," he said. "Okay. So where does that leave us?"

A flash of emotion crossed her face, but it was gone before he could decipher it.

"As friends who slept together," she said, her tone firm, no-nonsense. "But not friends with benefits. Frankly, you have your daughter to think about, and I've never been very good at sneaking around. I..." She cleared her throat and then continued in the same tone. "I'd love to see Mabel again at some point, but I don't want to take the chance of her getting attached."

He'd had an idea this might be the tack she'd take, but hearing it out loud made him feel as though the bottom had fallen out of his world.

Again.

But at least Ailani was being honest, unlike Michael, who'd waited seven years to come clean.

"Okay," he said again, nodding twice to emphasize his acquiescence. "We can do that. Still be friends, but no more..."

What should he call it? He knew he'd call it *making love*, but perhaps that would give his true feelings away, so he just waved his hand vaguely toward the bed and was ridiculously amused when her cheeks turned pink.

"No," she said. "No more..."

She made the same gesture, and Javi shook his head, feeling like someone had delivered a firm kick to his chest. Yet just below the surface, a manic type of laughter lurked. Needing a little space and time, he glanced at his watch.

"If you give me a few minutes, I'll shower and drive you home. We're due at the hospital the same time, but everyone's used to me coming in a bit early."

"I already have a rideshare coming." She glanced at her phone. "He'll be here in three minutes. See you at work."

Then, before he could do more than echo her farewell, she was gone.

CHAPTER TWENTY

BEYOND THE KITCHEN window the snow lay thick on the ground but had been blown off all the tree limbs, fences and other horizontal surfaces where it had accumulated. The sky, as blue as a robin's egg, heralded the effects of the cold front that had passed through. What had been fluffy snow now had a crisp, hard crust on top.

It had been two days since it snowed. Two days since the Christmas party. Two days since Ailani had walked out of the door, taking his heart with her. He'd tried not to think about it—tried to put it into perspective. They'd known each other for less than a month. Hadn't he learned not to succumb to his seeming innate need to pretty things up—to say *love* instead of *attraction*. *Need*, which indicated an inability to survive without rather than *desire*, which was a want.

Yet no amount of parsing, justification, shifting of angles had changed what he knew in his heart. Ailani had become important to him, and something inside him felt as if it were shriveling a little more every day.

It was Christmas Eve, and Mabel, trying so hard to be good but just picking at her breakfast, vibrated with excitement. Javi was working that day, to allow other staff members time to get their last-minute shopping and preparations done. His mother would be by to pick Mabel up in a little while, and Javi would head to Boston Beacon.

He'd already checked the schedule and couldn't make up his mind if he were glad or unhappy that Ailani wasn't working a shift.

Had it really only been twenty-three days since he'd sat here, wondering what the Hawaiian nurse would be like? Whether she'd fit in or be a good worker?

It felt more like a lifetime.

"Papi?"

Collecting himself, he shifted his attention to his daughter, unable to stop himself from smiling at her bright-eyed demeanor. No matter what darkness he was going through, Mabel drew him back to the light.

"Yes, *mija*?"

"Did you invite Nurse Ailani to Christmas dinner?"

He somehow kept the smile on his face although his heart wrenched, and he had to swallow the lump in his throat before he could answer. "No, *mija*."

Her brow wrinkled. "But Papi, she's our friend and so far away from home. I think she'd like to be with family for the holidays, don't you? Please ask her."

"*Mija*, I'm sure she already has plans. It's Christmas Eve."

Mabel rarely pouted or cried to get her way, but she had a way of looking at a person as though she held the scales of justice in her hand and you were being found severely lacking.

It was, in the final analysis, a very effect method of making her father feel like a worm, and it was working very well on this cold December morning.

"I like her," she said, still giving him that look. "And she likes me too. She told me so."

As though that was her final word on the subject, Mabel turned her attention back to her breakfast.

How he wished it were that easy.

I like her, and she likes me.

But he'd seen Ailani with Mabel, and he'd heard her argument, which aligned so well with his own—that no matter what, Mabel must be protected. As the adults in the situation, the little girl's needs had to come first.

That she shouldn't be hurt again.

A little voice in the back of his head whispered: *Who is it, really, that you're trying to protect?*

But Javi pushed it aside.

It was a relief to get to the hospital, to greet staff and patients, to feel as though no matter what was happening otherwise, this was where he was meant to be.

Everywhere he looked there were decorations as the staff attempted to give the children who were unable to go home for the holidays a sense of seasonal cheer. The children themselves had made paper stars, which were hung along the corridors, along with swags of greenery, balls and other ornaments. Most of the nurses were wearing deely boppers, reindeer antlers or Santa hats, and regular scrubs had, in some cases, been replaced with ones printed with winter or Christmas motifs.

Somehow, the hum of activity, the atmosphere of giving raised his spirits more than he'd expected.

The magic of Christmas had eluded him for the last few years. Longer, if he was scrupulously honest. Michael's discontent, which Javi had refused to see or acknowledge, had given the holidays a frantic, almost unnatural edge. As though his ex-husband had used the hubbub of baking and socializing and decorating as camouflage, while Javi had distanced himself from it all—and Michael too.

Then, when Michael had left, the holiday had seemed flat, as though all the fuss had been the most important part rather than the camaraderie of friends and family.

This year felt different. Better. More honest. Mabel was a big part of that, but so was Ailani. She'd come into his life at a time when he was opening himself back up to life and to change, giving him an honest friendship, without expectations.

He'd needed that, more than he'd have been able to admit even three weeks ago.

Still needed it, since he was self-evaluating.

Had he and Michael ever really even been friends? They'd gone straight from meeting to lovers to spouses. Yes, they'd shared their lives and some of their secrets, but had they shared friendship? The innate trust that came from genuine caring, and the knowledge that the other person would try to understand and do what was best, even at their own expense?

If they had, wouldn't it have been easier for Michael to open up long before their marriage had gone to hell? Couldn't he have been honest from the start, or as soon as he'd realized where things were heading?

"You're deep in thought." Iain had come right up beside Javi as he'd stood at the nurses' station without Javi even noticing. "Thorny case?"

"You could say that," he replied before nodding and going off to his next patient.

That thorny case was himself, he finally admitted. His preconceived notions and rigid adherence to the past—past experiences, past mistakes. The way things had been done before, and the consequences of those actions.

The past could inform the future, but Javi realized the real question was did it have to dictate it?

And was he brave enough to try to find out?

The sun set early in winter, and by five o'clock it was already dark outside the apartment windows, but the snow created a luminosity that came through the blinds into Ailani's darkened room.

Christmas Eve. Back home they'd be preparing for a feast, everyone pitching in when they could, pickups arriving at Tutu's house with tables and chairs, people bustling and teasing and laughter in the air. Just to annoy her grandmother, someone would play "Mele Kalikimaka" and everyone would sing as she gave them baleful looks.

She didn't know why that song annoyed Tutu so much. One day, when the time was right, maybe she'd ask.

Christmas held no excitement for her this year, for obvious reasons. In her fantasy world, she and Javi would wake up together and go downstairs to cook breakfast, while Mabel excitedly looked in her stocking to see what Santa had brought. And she'd be there when the little girl opened her gift and realized soon she'd have two kitties to play with.

Swiping away her tears with the heel of her palm, Ailani tried to turn her mind to other things. She was working tomorrow, having switched a shift with another nurse who had been invited to her boyfriend's parents for dinner unexpectedly.

"I didn't think it would get to this point so quickly," she'd said, beaming with happiness. "We've only been seeing each other for a couple of months."

Ailani had assured her it was no problem. After all, she'd turned down all the invitations she'd received, and Bryn was working tomorrow too. Maybe after their shift they'd do something together, but it probably wouldn't be terribly festive.

Bryn hadn't seemed to be too full of the holiday spirit herself the last couple of days.

When the buzzer downstairs rang, she almost ignored it. But having it go off again and thinking it may be a package for Bryn, she got up to answer it, bucking her toe on the sofa leg in the dark as she went.

"Ow, ow, ow, ow. Hello?"

"Are you okay?"

Javi's voice came through the speaker, making Ailani forget all about her aching toe. She must have pressed the button sooner than she thought.

"Hello?"

Almost reluctantly, her heart beating way too fast, her knees feeling a little shaky, she pressed the button again and said, "Hi. Yeah, I'm okay. Just hit my foot on the sofa."

"Can I come in?" How could he sound so cool when she felt like a mess and her voice sounded like a Smurf? "I'd like to talk to you."

She almost asked why but then asked herself if it really mattered. This man would always have a place in her heart, and if he asked something of her and she could oblige, she would.

So she pushed the button to let him in and hit the light switch so he wouldn't realize she'd been sulking in the dark.

When she opened the door and stepped back to let him enter, she couldn't help taking inventory. He looked as though he'd just come from the hospital, wearing his usual outfit of dress pants, a button-down shirt and smart wool jacket beneath his winter coat. But there were shadows under his eyes, and his mouth was set in a firm line.

"Sit down," she said politely, not wanting him to know that just his presence was making her body, heart and brain go haywire. "Would you like a drink? We have soda, hot chocolate—"

"No, thanks." He stood in the middle of the living room, taking up more than his fair share of space. Then she saw him take a deep breath, and he said, "Mabel wants me to invite you to Christmas dinner."

"What?" She sat down first, sinking onto the nearby sofa, before her knees gave out altogether.

Javi shook his head, and his hand slashed through the air as though cutting into his own argument. "We can get back to that because it isn't the main reason I'm here."

Gathering herself, she asked, "What is the main reason, then?"

He looked around, seeming almost lost for a moment. Then he caught her gaze with his and said, "I thrive on routine, on structure. It's how I've got to where I am at Boston Beacon."

Ailani nodded, knowing it was the truth. "It's served you well."

"Has it?" He shot the question at her so quickly, she was left floundering for a moment, and he went on speaking before she could respond. "It's fine in a work setting. But on a personal level?"

He shrugged, then lowered himself into an armchair, as though staying on his feet wasn't viable anymore.

"I kept thinking," he said slowly, as though trying to collate his thoughts. "Thinking about what you said your grandmother and uncle did after you came to live with them. How they were overprotective instead of letting you explore the world the way you wanted to."

"They did it out of love," she interjected, wanting that to be clear.

"And fear too, I think."

Hard to admit, but she knew now that was true, so she nodded. The air in the room felt heavy, and her heart, which had slowed once he'd started talking, began to race again. "What are you getting at, Javi?"

"I don't know," he admitted. "Except maybe it's the fact that they were wrong. They made calculations based on what had happened in the past and acted the way they thought would direct your life in the future. But those calculations were wrong. Although they'd deprived you of the freedom your mom enjoyed, you still ended up here, in Boston, on Christmas Eve."

He paused, his gaze dark and intent.

"On Christmas Eve," he repeated. "With me."

"Not—"

"Yes." He nodded, speaking over her. "Here with me, as I try to find a way to tell you that I want us to have a chance. That I don't want my past—my fear—to deprive us of the chance to explore this bond between us. A bond I can't and don't want to break."

Her heart was beating so hard and her mouth was so dry, she wasn't sure she'd be able to reply. Then the reality of it all came crashing down, and she shook her head. "I don't think you'd ever trust me not to run off, Javi. I can't live with you always worrying that just because I don't crave structure and routine the way you do, I'll one day up and leave."

He shook his head, the taut line of his mouth softening. "Michael was an all-or-nothing type of man. It never would have occurred to him to try to talk out what he was feeling—what he wanted. Instead, once he'd made the decision, that was it. And I..." He hesitated for a moment and then shook his head. "I was so afraid of losing the known, I never asked him what would have made a difference.

"I believe we could find a balance if we try hard enough. If we keep being honest and open with each other. I want the opportunity to find out if that's something we want, Ailani. I don't want to tie you down or pretend that us being together, trying to work this all out, will be easy. I know you have a life in Hawaii and that maybe you'll decide at the end of your three months here that you want to go back more than you want to stay here, but I'm willing to take that chance if you are."

Her heart was pounding in her ears, and she had to blink away the moisture that gathered in her eyes so as to see him properly. "What about Mabel? Would it be fair to her, if it doesn't work out?"

"Mabel already knows that not all relationships last forever. If we could do one thing for her, it would be to show her how important it is to be honest and to make the effort, if something—someone—is important enough, as you are to me.

"Will you take that chance on me? With me? We can start with Christmas dinner after your shift tomorrow and take it from there."

That deep voice, the emotion in his eyes was her undoing.

How could she resist when he was offering her exactly what she wanted?

"Yes." It came out a croak, her throat tight with anticipation, and she saw the corners of his eyes crinkle in amusement just as she started to giggle too.

Then they were both moving, meeting in the middle of the room, and suddenly she was right where she wanted to be, in the arms of the man who felt like home. Like family.

"Best. Christmas. Ever," she said as she lifted her mouth for his kiss.

"I agree," he replied, his lips already against hers, their hearts beating in tandem. "Completely."

EPILOGUE

One year later

FROM THEIR SPOT beneath a tree, looking across the sand, Javi and Ailani watched as Uncle Makoa gave Mabel instructions on how to stand on a surfboard, the two of them intent on the lesson.

Back at the plantation, everyone was preparing for Christmas Day, but Tutu had shooed Javi, Ailani and Mabel out of the house.

"You're on holiday," she'd said. "Away from that nasty snow. Go to the beach and get some sun. And take Makoa with you."

Uncle Makoa always found the bustle, even of family, overwhelming.

"Next year, you should come and spend Christmas with us, Tutu," she'd teased, not surprised when her grandmother had gone off on a rant, saying that as much as she loved them all, that wasn't going to happen.

It was no surprise to Ailani that her family had immediately accepted and absorbed Javi and Mabel. It was the Hawaiian way. *Ohana*, which meant *universal love*, took on a special aura when it came to accepting children into an existing family unit.

As though hearing her thoughts, Javi said, "If we don't get her back to Boston soon, Mabel will never want to leave." He sighed, leaning back and tilting his hat to shield his eyes better. "Honestly, at this point I really don't want to leave either."

"The lure of paradise," she said, rolling over so she was on her side on her towel, facing him. "Just imagine, back in Boston it's freezing, and here we are in swimsuits."

"Brr..." he said, sliding her a glance. "I have to say I prefer you in a swimsuit over a snowsuit."

"Same here," she said, giving him a grin. "I don't get to see your legs enough during winter."

That made him chuckle, but then he turned his attention back to the book he had in his hand, one finger holding his place.

"Your mom's diary is really moving. She was a wonderful writer, and she was particularly eloquent when it came to you."

"I love that part," Ailani said. "At first, I was more interested in her travels, but I think I needed to read about how I fitted into her life, if that makes sense."

"It does. You're lucky to have her feelings laid out so clearly for you."

"I am." Now she watched his face as she continued, "That journal I've been keeping for Mabel since I moved in with you both in May has been a great way to keep a record of our lives. Hopefully she'll be interested in it when she gets older. I'm trying to figure out whether to just keep that one journal or start a separate one."

"I don't know," he said, his concentration mostly on what he was reading. "Why would you need another one?"

She didn't answer, waiting until both the question and the potential answer penetrated through to that quick brain of his. Then his focus shifted, those hazel eyes suddenly intent, their gazes meeting and holding: his questioning, hers answering.

"Ailani. When?"

"August, I believe. I wanted to wait until we got home to

get a proper pregnancy test, but Tutu has already sussed it out, and—"

He'd rolled, the journal falling from his hand so he could pull her close, and she felt him trembling.

"Aloha wau iā 'oe," she whispered, holding him as tightly as she could.

"I love you too," he said in that raw, almost frantic tone that came out only when he was desperately moved. "I never knew I could be this happy."

And there was no need to answer because he knew, just as she did, they were meant to be together, and they'd make sure they stayed that way.

"Best. Christmas. Ever."

He whispered it into her ear, and she sighed, shivering with happiness.

"Until next year. Then that will be the best."

That made him chuckle, but he didn't let her go, just replied, "And every year after that will just get better."

And she couldn't help agreeing.

* * * * *

A PUPPY ON THE 34TH WARD

JULIETTE HYLAND

MILLS & BOON

For my team—you guys know the reasons!

CHAPTER ONE

"LIKE THE DECORATIONS?"

A staffer Dr. Nick Walker didn't know smiled brightly as they hung another pretend candy along the corridor of Ward 34.

He nodded, though the truth was that he didn't really care for holiday decor. "Quite festive."

"We're adding a few new things this year."

"I'm sure it will look great." The kids who had to visit the pediatric wing during Christmastime would love it. Anything to make little ones and their parents, who'd rather be anywhere else, happy was good with Nick.

However, he had no way of determining if this year was grander than the last. Since completing his residency, he'd spent no more than two years in any one place.

And today was his first full day at Boston Beacon Hospital. So the clock was already ticking. He might see Ward 34's decor next year, but after that...

His chest tightened at the thought of moving, even if it was his choice now. As a military kid, he'd moved almost every two years as his father had chased bigger and bigger assignments. Nick had lived in four countries and eight states at thirty-six.

Part of him always wondered if this was the last place.

Boston was nice. But so were most cities. That was one lesson he'd learned moving his things from one part of the world to another: Find out what made each place tick. Locate the best pizza joint, the ideal coffee hub and at least one fun hole-in-the-wall only the locals knew about, and anywhere could feel like home.

For a while at least.

"Dr. Walker." Dr. Javi Pascal raised his hand as he walked over with a young woman. A new hire… Nick knew the routine. He'd been introduced after his orientation last week.

"Dr. Nick Walker, this is Nurse Ailani Kekoa."

"Nice to meet you." Nick offered his hand. He'd been the new person in so many places—he understood the nerves. Not that the nurse with the bright smile looked nervous.

"Nick is our newest pediatrician," Javi continued. "Today is his first day on the floor, in fact."

"I guess that means you can't recommend any good restaurants or coffee shops?" Ailani gestured out the window to the Boston skyline.

"Fraid not," he offered without following her gaze. The Boston skyline was beautiful, but it was just another city, another layover point in life. "But if you hear of any, let me know."

"I'm sure my roommate will tire of me peppering her with questions, but if I find any, I'll pass them along. Newbies help each other out, right?"

"Right."

"Oh, I see another doctor…"

"That's my cue." Ailani waved goodbye as she followed Javi down the hallway.

Nick turned his attention back to the tablet chart. He had four patients he needed to see before lunch, and one was being discharged. Always a good day.

He clicked two more buttons, then felt pressure against his legs. Looking down, Nick blinked twice as the golden retriever wagged its tail. As a pediatrician, he was used to little ones grabbing his leg.

The occasional sibling getting loose from their understandably exhausted parents.

A dog, dressed as a Christmas tree and wearing a star headband, rubbed its nose against his leg again. This was a first.

"Honey!" The thick Boston accent was attached to one of the most beautiful women he'd ever seen.

"Sorry—Honey doesn't normally wander." The white woman made several hand gestures, and the dog sat, then lay at her feet.

Her green eyes met his, and Nick found himself at a loss for words. He'd connected with a few people in his nomadic life, but he'd never met someone and felt this gut punch.

The woman cleared her throat, and Nick shook his head. "Sorry—it's my first day on the floor."

"Bryn Bedford." She held out her hand, and Nick clasped it. The connection was brief but somehow intense.

Not that that made any sense.

"Nick Walker."

"Nice to meet you, Nick. This naughty one is Honey."

He pursed his lips as he looked at the dog. He hated being the bearer of bad news, but dogs—even ones dressed in such cute regalia—weren't technically allowed.

"It's nice to meet Honey, and she is adorable, particularly in her tree outfit." He cleared his throat. "But this is a hospital."

"Really?" Bryn's green eyes sparkled as he stated the obvious. Then she bent and lifted the tree, showing off the patch on the back that said Therapy Dog.

"Honey is one of the Paws for Hope therapy dogs."

"And dressed as a Christmas tree?"

Bryn laughed, a sound that seemed to go straight to his soul. "I'm afraid that's my fault. She loves dressing up, and I lose all willpower when I see a cute dog outfit. I think she has more outfits than I do. In fact, I know that's true as my closet is more than half hers, and I'm the one that buys the outfits.

"My…" She paused and looked at Honey. When she looked back at Nick, a bit of the sparkle had left her eyes. "Someone once told me I treat her as a dress-up doll."

She spoke to Honey, "But it's just because you are so cute."

The dog was adorable… Bryn even more so. "I've not had much interaction with therapy animals."

"Do you have a few minutes? I can show you what Honey can do. I'm scheduled to see Lucas before he's discharged."

"Lucas is on my rounds list, so why don't we go together?"

"Great." Bryn and Honey walked beside him.

"What support is Honey offering Lucas? I thought therapy dogs were usually here to see patients that were stuck here for a while. Discharge day is usually one of the best days."

"Usually." Bryn sighed as she rubbed a hand over Honey's head. "But one of Lucas's moms is in the army. They were being PC—something, it means *moved*…"

"PCS'd. Permanent Change of Station." It was a phrase Nick had heard so often around the dinner table. His father's life had revolved around receiving PCS orders. Once his siblings had gone into the military, they'd sent notes to the family group chat every time a new location had come in.

A group chat they'd kicked him out of when he'd left West Point Military Academy before his second year to pursue his own dreams.

Or quit…according to his father.

His life was the only one not controlled by orders. And yet he hadn't put down permanent roots.

"That's it! PCS'd. They were moving cross country when the appendicitis struck. It's why he's here and not at a base hospital somewhere. And his mom had to head onto her… I want to say office. That's not right, though. Starts with a *D*." Bryn tapped on her forehead, like she was trying to pull the phrase from her brain.

This was another phrase Nick could provide. "Duty station."

"You know all the lingo. That will help."

Bryn's words were bright, but Nick wasn't sure. Sure, he knew military lingo, but helping a kid sad about moving… there were no quick fixes for that.

"So Honey is along to cheer him up."

Bryn shook her head. "I prefer to think of it as Honey is here to offer what Lucas needs. She can give cuddles, pets, a soft place to cry. Or cheer, if that's what the patient needs."

Nick looked at the happy golden, its tail wagging as the star bounced on her headband. She looked cheerful, but he knew that not every patient was ready for cheer. Even one getting ready for discharge. "That is a nice thought."

"Honey has been a therapy dog for two years. She's quite skilled at recognizing what patients need."

"And how long have you been a therapy-dog handler?" The door to Lucas's room came into view. Nick had moments left with Bryn Bedford—and he wanted to savor all of them.

"Honey is my first therapy dog."

"What did you do beforehand?"

An emotion passed over Bryn's eyes that sent a knife to his heart.

How often had someone asked him something personal and he panicked? He was the black sheep of his family, the one who'd "refused" to serve his country, at least according to his father. The general had never seen a life outside of uniform as serving, never seen his children as more than an extension of his success.

All of that added up to a ton of questions Nick never answered. If one got trophies for creative ways to change topics, he'd have a wall full of gold.

"We've arrived." He made too big of a gesture as they got to Lucas's door. But he wanted her to feel comfortable, get them back on the easy footing they'd had before he'd dug too deep.

"So we have." Bryn's green eyes met his before she looked at Honey. "Shall we let this girl go first?"

"Sure." Nick was curious to see the dog in action. Most of his interactions with dogs were as service animals. Working dogs.

Honey was a working dog, but it was different. Her role was comfort.

"Hi, Lucas. Can Honey come in?"

Giving a choice. Nick smiled. That was something so many adults forgot to offer children.

"Yes!" The little boy's voice was bright as he patted the bed.

Honey looked at Bryn, who motioned with her hand, then jumped up and put two paws on the bed.

Lucas leaned over and kissed the top of Honey's head. "I'm leaving today. So I won't see you again." He said the words, then sucked back a sob.

How many times had Nick done that as a child? *Be strong, never quit* was the family motto.

"I don't see a lot of people again." Lucas's words were whispered, but his mother heard them.

Bryn stepped to his mother's side and offered her a hand. The woman squeezed it as she stood a little taller.

"I know it's rough, Lucas, but Fort Drum will be fun. It gets lots of snow." His mother's bright smile didn't quite reach her eyes, but it was clear she was trying to do her best.

The boy said nothing as he leaned his head against Honey's.

"I'm Dr. Walker."

"You're here so I can go to Fort Drum?"

"Yes." Nick stepped close and got down, so his face was eye level with Lucas. "My dad was in the army."

Lucas's head popped up. "You moved a lot?"

"Every two years." Nick hit the watch on his hand. "Like clockwork. I've lived all over the world."

"My mom has only been stateside, never OCONUS."

OCONUS—outside the Continental United States. A phrase only a military kid understood.

"My dad was everywhere."

But never at home.

Those were words that did not need to be spoken.

His father had focused on his career. And only his career.

And his mother, a career diplomat, had been gone nearly as much. The fact that they'd had four children when they'd spent years separated by continents was a miracle.

Besides, Nick's experience was not the path that most members of the armed forces chose. He'd watched many fathers and mothers in uniform pick up their kids from school. Attend school plays, do all the things civilian parents did.

"It's not fun to move, is it?"

"No." Lucas's lip trembled as his hand stroked Honey's soft coat.

The dog shifted a paw and looked at him. Nick could swear she understood all the words, though rationally he knew Honey was likely just responding to the tension in the young one.

"But this is the last one." Lucas looked to his mother, who nodded.

"The last one?"

"Mom is retiring after this station. She says we're staying in Watertown. That's next to Fort Drum. She grew up there." He sighed as he bopped Honey's nose.

"That's great. So one more new place, one more new school." Nick grinned. The last location was the best news a family constantly on military orders could get.

He'd met a few kids whose parents followed Lucas's mom's path—did their best to land their last duty location as close to home as possible.

"Where was the last place for you?"

There wasn't one. Not really. Though Nick knew what Lucas was asking.

"DC." The District of Columbia. His father had stationed at the Pentagon as the chairman of the joint chiefs of staff, literally incapable of achieving more in his career. His mother, not to be outdone, had spent the final years of her life rising in the ranks of the State Department, both more comfortable in White House briefings than their living room.

"Shall we look at your incision now?"

"Can Honey stay?"

Nick looked to Bryn, her smile eating away at the homesickness the conversation with Lucas had unintentionally brought on. "Can she?"

"Of course." Bryn stepped toward the bed. "But she needs to be at your feet while Dr. Walker looks at your belly."

Bryn snapped out a quick rhythm, and Honey pulled her paws off the bed, then jumped up and curled at Lucas's feet. A golden blanket over his legs.

Lifting his shirt, Lucas pointed to the three holes in his lower abdomen. "I've seen so many doctors. Even one I wasn't supposed to!"

Nick looked at Lucas's mother with a raised brow.

"A Dr. Murphy stopped in this morning. I think he meant to be in a different room. He was a tad flustered."

"Dr. Murphy is one of our surgeons. Always busy."

Bryn's voice was light, but Nick heard the unstated: *Great with kids, but a little gruff if you aren't his patient.*

"Why do so many doctors have to look at me?"

Nick let out a chuckle and motioned for Lucas to lower his shirt. "Well, your surgeon checks you out because he yanked out that yucky appendix using a special technique called laparoscopic surgery. I'm a pediatrician. That means I specialize in children's medicine. The hospital just wants to make sure you get to see everyone."

"So you don't get sued."

"Lucas!" His mother crossed her arms.

The little one hung his head, and Honey sat up so he could rub between her ears. "Sorry."

The mumbled word wasn't heartfelt, but Nick didn't mind.

"You're going to be sore for another week or so. If you notice anything coming out of the holes, if they itch or hurt really bad, you need to tell one of your moms, all right?"

Lucas nodded, not looking away from the therapy dog.

"The wounds are already scabbing on the edges. That's a

wonderful sign. Infection is rare, but if he spikes a fever over a hundred and one, take him to the ER. Otherwise, a nurse will be in shortly with discharge papers, and you'll be on your way."

His mom nodded and moved to Lucas's side. "Time to say goodbye to Honey now."

He leaned over the bed, gripped the dog's neck and let out a soft cry. "Bye, Honey. I'll try to remember you."

The phrase tore through Nick. He'd said exactly those words or heard them whispered through tears as a friend whose name and a face were gone from his memory had hugged him.

The life of a kid on the move.

"But this is the last stop." Nick offered the boy a smile but knew it didn't heal the hurt he felt right now.

Nick looked at Lucas's mom. "Good luck. I hope you enjoy the snow."

"We do." She ran her hand through Lucas's hair. "All right, sweetheart, you need to let Honey do her job and go see others."

Lucas squeezed her one more time, then pulled back. "Bye, Honey."

"It was nice to meet you." Bryn snapped her fingers again, and Honey padded to her side. Bryn picked up her leash, straightened Honey's star headband and headed for the door.

Nick followed. "Honey was great in there."

"She usually is." Bryn ran her hand along the dog's head. "However, you were the actual star. If her headband wasn't covered in dog fur, I'd offer it to you. You've really lived all over?"

"Four countries and eight states."

"Wow." She shook her head. "I've been in Boston my whole life."

"The accent kind of gives that away." Nick grinned, enjoying the tilt of her head and the fiery expression crossing her green eyes a little too much.

"*I* don't have an accent. You do."

"Of course." He laughed, enjoying the interaction. Bryn was gorgeous in her bright holiday sweater, with a sweet golden retriever at her heels. Picture perfect...and Nick was the furthest thing from it.

"I'm off to see Susie Cole. They admitted her last night. Do you want to see if she likes dogs, too?" The question was out before he thought it through. He was working. It was his first day, but he was hoping Bryn and Honey would tag along.

She looked at her phone, pulling up the note tracker. "Susie is on my list."

"List?"

"Yes. Honey is the goodest girl." Her tone shifted up, and Honey's ears tipped up, too.

Nick wasn't even sure Bryn was aware of the tonal shift.

She looked at him, and the hit of recognition rocked through him again. There was something about this woman that called to him.

Maybe he was just lonelier than he wanted to admit. He'd stayed in Phoenix for almost eighteen months. Gotten close to his colleagues, even briefly considered staying. But his mind refused to settle, so he'd set off again.

The military kid unable to stay still, even though he'd refused to wear the uniform.

That must've been it. The reason his mind was reaching for connection.

"Intake makes sure the patients and their grown-ups are comfortable with therapy-dog visits. You don't know about allergies or what home life is like. If a child fears dogs, it doesn't matter how sweet Honey is, that will just upset them." Bryn shrugged. "And if their grown-ups don't want them around dogs for whatever reason, you want to honor that."

"Their grown-ups?" She'd said that twice.

"Not everyone has parents." Lines pulled at the corners of her eyes, and her smile faltered a little.

Families came in all shapes and sizes. His family was technically what most people thought of. A mom and dad, with quite a few siblings, but it was far from picture perfect. "I always use the term *guardians*."

"That's good. But if a sister or brother raises you, or an aunt or grandparent... I don't know, a teacher friend of mine uses it in her classes, and I stole it."

They'd arrived at Susie's room. That wasn't a surprise. The pediatric wing took up the entire second floor, but it didn't take long to walk between areas. Still, he craved more time with the woman beside him.

Yep, loneliness was setting in. Luckily, Nick had a lifetime of learning how to deal with that. When he got home, he'd pop in one of his favorite movies, grab some popcorn and a soda, and chill.

"Ready?" Bryn's smile was perfection, and he had to take a deep breath.

Focus.

"Of course."

Bryn cut her eyes to Nick as they walked through Susie's door. The new doctor was the most attractive man she'd ever seen. His deep brown eyes seemed to peer right through her.

He looked like he belonged on the set of television drama. The kind where every doctor was hot as hell and the entire floor was dating each other. Drama and lifesaving antics happening constantly and all wrapped up nicely in an hour.

Or at least by the end of the two-part special.

Life wasn't that way. There was a reason so many books, blogs and Human Resources pamphlets recommended not dating in the workplace.

Not that Bryn needed reminding. One doctor ex-husband was more than enough.

Her thumb slipped to her empty ring finger. Almost a year since her marriage had ended. Two days into her honeymoon.

For reasons Ethan had never fully explained but that had

basically boiled down to her not being "the right fit." A harsh statement considering how much of herself she'd seemed to bottle up during their relationship.

"Puppy!" Susie's bright call broke through the unhappy memories.

The little one looked tired but not nearly as sick as her intake form indicated. Bryn didn't get many details, but as Ward 34's part-time therapy-dog handler, she had the basics.

And since she was a registered nurse, she could read between the lines better than most. She'd loved nursing. Another thing the implosion of her marriage had stolen.

Susie's blond curls were a mess, but her eyes were bright. No hint of the fainting that had brought her in.

"You look like you're feeling better this morning." Nick stepped next to Susie's bed.

"I want to go home." She stuck her bottom lip out and crossed her arms.

Her mother yawned, then frowned. "I know, Susie, but we have to find out why you fainted yesterday." The woman rubbed her hands together as she looked at Nick. "I'm Ellen. Susie's mom. I'm almost thinking I overreacted. It's been… been a year."

Honey nudged Bryn's leg, but she didn't release her. Dogs picked up on emotions, and it was clear that Ellen was deep in her feels. She had a daughter in the hospital, but that didn't explain the year comment.

If Ellen wanted to pet Honey, then she was more than welcome to, but Honey had to wait.

"Tell me a bit about what happened." Nick leaned against the wall, crossing his arms, his eyes fully directed at Ellen. Ready to take in the information.

Seriously, in blue scrubs with his stethoscope hanging from his pocket, the man was gorgeous.

"Mommy!" Susie looked over at Honey.

Nick looked at Bryn. "Can Honey sit with Susie while I talk to her mom?"

"Of course." Bryn dropped Honey's leash, then snapped out the release code she'd trained Honey with.

The golden wandered over to the bed, her tail wagging as she waited for Bryn to snap again, telling her it was okay to put two paws on the bed.

"My husband…" Ellen closed her eyes, taking a deep breath. "He's been gone."

"And he can't video chat," Susie interjected.

Ellen pursed her lips, then smiled at her daughter. "He's going to be so surprised at how much you've grown."

Her stance sent alarm bells through Bryn. How many times had her mother said something like that? *Daddy will be so surprised at how big you are. It's okay—his trip just took too long. He'll pick you up next weekend.*

It wasn't until she'd been almost a teen that she'd pushed back and called her father what he was. A deadbeat dad. A man who blew into her and her mother's life when he felt like it. And disappeared again when life got too hard or he met someone else who caught his fancy. Or when the system caught up with him for unpaid child support for her or the four half siblings she knew about.

"Anyway." Ellen looked at her daughter, then at Nick. "She was tired, but she's five. And while she doesn't nap anymore, sometimes…" She shrugged.

"Sometimes she needs one." Nick looked at Susie, making a silly face to head off the frustration Bryn could see in the girl's face. "I need one sometimes, too."

Susie's eyes narrowed, but then she refocused on Honey.

And this was why therapy animals were such a blessing. Calming influences that made life easier in one of the most difficult places in the world.

"I'm really starting to think I overreacted. That maybe she

didn't faint...but I know she did. She was standing in the kitchen arguing over a snack."

"I wanted raisins."

"I like raisins." Nick laughed. "Especially the yogurt ones."

"I've never had those—Mommy!"

"We'll see."

"That means no," Susie whispered to Honey.

Nick's eyes found Bryn's as she covered her mouth to hide the smile.

"I'm going to check you out, Susie." He pulled the stethoscope from his pocket and showed it to her. "Do you know what this is?"

"It listens to my heart."

"It does." Nick nodded, his focus on the child. "Your lungs, too. I can even use it to listen to your stomach growl. Want to see?"

Bryn's heart melted as she watched him put the earpieces in Susie's ears, then drop the diaphragm to her belly.

"Wow."

As a nurse, she'd worked with so many specialties. There were dedicated professionals in all of them, but pediatricians had some of the best bedside manner she'd ever witnessed. It was outside the hospital, though, that you needed to focus on. Her ex-husband could put on a good show when he wanted to, too.

Nick took over and started checking Susie, explaining what he was doing to both the child and her mother. Answering questions without getting upset or frustrated.

A perfect bedside manner.

Which was why Ethan dismissing his tiny patients should have been one of so many red flags. But she'd wanted to believe it had been just because he'd been focused on his career, on climbing the ranks so he could make changes to benefit all patients.

A catchphrase he used to make himself look better. Though

now she believed what he wanted was prestige. Not that it mattered. She wasn't his wife.

Not anymore.

"All right." Nick put his stethoscope back into his pocket and looked at Ellen. "The good news is she seems healthy. And the monitors last night caught nothing. Our night staff nurses said she did well."

"And the bad news?" Ellen's foot started tapping.

This was a woman well-versed in bad news. Her foot was tapping, but her shoulders were straight. Her face carefully devoid of expression.

"I don't know why she fainted. Sometimes episodes happen and we can't determine a reason. It never happens again, and it's a story that you tell her when she's a teen driving you up the wall."

"Other times?"

Nick looked at Susie, whose attention was focused on Honey. "Other times it takes another episode, or many episodes, for us to determine what's going on. I recommend following up with her pediatrician. If she faints again, has shortness of breath, chest pain, a fever over a hundred and one, bring her back." Nick shook his head, his shoulders dipping just a hair. "I'm sorry. I don't have a better answer. It could be stress. Children experience that just like adults."

"Yeah, well, there's enough of that to go around." Ellen caught a sob and shook her head. "Sorry."

"No need to apologize."

Bryn's eyes were getting misty as Nick comforted Ellen. She wasn't his patient, but the care in his voice, the extra time spent with her daughter, the acknowledgment that sometimes there wasn't an answer...

It was more than many doctors were willing to do.

The definition of a perfect doctor.

Bryn wanted to shake that thought from her mind. Nick

was a good doctor…to the two patients she'd seen. That meant nothing. It was his first day on the floor of Ward 34.

She knew that stress, hard cases, rough days—those were when you really saw someone's character.

"If you have questions, let the discharge nurse know, and I'll come back. It was very nice to meet you, Susie."

"I love Honey."

"Me, too." Bryn smiled and nodded to Nick as he walked out the door. "Does your mom want to pet her before I go?"

Ellen let out a laugh that sounded a little too close to a sob as she sat beside Susie on the bed. She ran her hands over Honey's head. Her shoulders relaxed, and the lines around her eyes disappeared as Honey worked her magic. "Thank you."

"This is Honey's dream job." The dog wagged her tail and dutifully stood as Bryn snapped three times and picked up her leash. Honey loved this, and Bryn loved helping people. Maybe she wasn't in nurse's scrubs now, but the thrill she got seeing Honey work made up for it.

Almost.

CHAPTER TWO

PULLING OFF HER COAT, Bryn tried to ignore the happy couples at each table as she slid to the bar seat. Myers + Chang was her favorite restaurant—it was also the perfect date night location. She came here by herself often. After years of almost never coming or having takeout, she refused to abandon her favorite place because she wasn't part of a couple.

She'd asked Ethan to come here with her so many times. Always getting her hopes up and then settling when he'd automatically refused. Three years and the man hadn't made such a simple thing a priority.

Never mind that she'd been willing to go where he'd wanted. Even for her birthday, he'd pouted, saying there was nothing he liked, and she'd canceled the reservations here and gone to the chain seafood place he preferred. Why was it, a year after they'd broken up, so easy to see what a terrible partner he'd been?

Because I wanted to believe that I'd found someone to stand by me.

After spending her teen years telling her mother she was better off alone than standing by her serial-cheater, disappearing husband, Bryn had believed she'd found happily ever after. A man with a stable job who wouldn't disappear on her. An illusion she'd clung to.

If her mother were alive, she'd apologize. It was easier to stay with less than you deserved than one realized.

Though Bryn had no intention of making the same mistake again.

Now she could eat here every night—though her pocketbook would balk at the idea.

Her phone buzzed, and she knew it was Indigo, a nursing friend from Brigham and Women's Hospital. The woman's annual holiday party was in a week. She and her husband threw a huge event. Decorations galore, people, spiked punch and a white-elephant gift exchange. Two years ago, they'd made the white-elephant exchange Bryn's bridal shower. And last year, everyone had been busy talking about the next steps for her and Ethan.

A year later, she was sitting alone at a bar. Divorced, living with a roommate, doing her best to avoid reminders that instead of celebrating her one-year anniversary, she was alone.

Still can't make it. Sorry.

She sent the text and set her phone down.

Ethan was Indigo's husband's best friend. Ethan would attend, despite hating parties, if for no other reason than to prove that the divorce didn't bother him...which it probably didn't. If she was honest, it wasn't dropping the two hundred pounds of dead weight that was her ex that bothered Bryn. It was everyone's questions. The not-so-quiet whispers, the pitying looks hidden not quick enough. It was just too much. So she was skipping Christmas this year.

The parties, the gifts, the gatherings...all of it. Maybe next year she'd pick back up the holiday traditions she'd enjoyed, but this year...nope.

"This is a busy place."

The words were smooth. Bryn couldn't stop the smile as she turned to find Nick.

"Nick. Or Dr. Walker."

"Nick, please." He grinned and shook a bit of rain from his hair. "I thought Boston got snow."

"We do." Bryn shrugged as she looked at the front doors. The rain wasn't hard, more of a mist than anything. "But most of it comes in January and February."

"So no white Christmas." Nick stepped closer as a couple moved behind him.

Her heart rate picked up, and her body coated with heat. He was fine. His full lips, dark skin, with just a hint of stubble on his chin. If she rubbed his jaw...

Bryn cut that thought off.

Nick was also a colleague. Which meant he was off-limits. *Fool me once, shame on you, fool me twice...*

Bryn had no intention of falling into the patterns that had burned her so badly.

"I can't tell you no white Christmas. It happens. But an icy Christmas or a cold, dry Christmas happen more often."

"Man, I thought I'd see my first white Christmas in years." Nick waved as the bartender stepped up.

"You getting a drink or eating at the bar?"

Nick's eyes slid to hers. "Do you mind if I join you?"

Yes. But only because he was so attractive. And she was already fantasizing about how he kissed. How his fingers might feel on her cheek.

Her skin prickled, but she could hardly tell him no because her body was awakening from the slumber she'd put it in after her divorce.

"Please." She gestured to the seat next to her. With any luck, he'd say or do something that pushed the sensitive, hot doc from her mind and let her focus on an undesirable trait.

Bryn wanted to slap the horrid thought from her mind. Nick had been perfectly nice. Her issues were not his.

"So, what's good here?"

Nick picked up the menu, and she tried not to focus on how

close he was. That if she shifted just right, her knee would brush his.

Seriously, maybe it was time to break out the dating apps. Though the very idea made her insides twist.

"Why did you choose this place?" Bryn looked at the menu in his hand. It was all good. The owners even had their own cookbooks. She'd tried a few of the recipes at home. They were good, but it wasn't the same.

"It's busy."

"'It's busy.' Nick. You walked in here because it was busy?" She laughed and leaned toward him before pulling herself back. "That's the whole reason? Do you like dim sum? Or fried rice, or ramen?" Myers + Chang was delicious, but if those weren't things his palate enjoyed...

"I'm not a picky eater. And yes, I chose it because it was busy. First rule of AreaFam—pay attention to what the locals like."

"AreaFam?"

"Area familiarization. It's a term my father used when we got to new places." A look passed over his eyes before Nick smiled at her. "If you move every few years, you figure out how to fit in. At least as much as possible."

"Makes sense. The nasi goreng is my favorite dish. It's a Southeast Asian fried rice and wicked good."

"Wicked." Nick tried to place the right inflection on the word, but it sounded off.

"Almost."

"That's a lie." Nick's smile lit up their little area of the bar, and Bryn giggled.

"It is. That was terrible." The term was one most Bostonians learned before they were two. It was also a word many associated with the city and tried to replicate. Usually without success.

"Give it time." Bryn winked, but the atmosphere around Nick shifted. Like time wasn't in his favor. The feeling made little sense—she was reading into things. Something she did far too often.

"Ready, Bryn?" The bartender, Bill, smiled as he stood in front of them.

A way to shift the topic—perfect. She pushed the menu that she hadn't needed to look at across the bar. "I'll have nasi goreng and a sangria, please."

"And you?" Bill looked at Nick, who peeked at the menu before handing it back to him.

"Nasi goreng for me too, and the pineapple-ginger soda with tequila please."

"So you enjoy moving?" Bryn loved the idea of travel, but she'd never ventured very far. She'd grown up in Boston, gotten her registered nursing degree at Boston College, then started working at Brigham and Women's Hospital. Her entire life had revolved around the city.

It was a good life. This was home. Even when the world collapsed on itself.

"Not really."

She must have made a face because Nick shrugged and leaned back, his features closing off a little.

"I just feel like I have to." He nodded to Bill as he dropped the drinks off.

"Have to?" There was a tone in his voice, an ache that pierced through the hum of the restaurant. She laid her hand on his, squeezing it, then pulling back. "What does that mean?"

His eyes shifted, looking at the minimal space between their hands. Was his hand burning like hers? Did he want to reach over and hold her, like she yearned to do with him?

"I don't know." Nick picked up his drink, took a sip, then shifted so his hand was on the back of his seat.

So she couldn't reach for him again?

"I just… I don't know what home feels like. Never found a place that fit."

"No family home?" Even with a family on the move, there

had to be somewhere they all congregated. Except there didn't. So many families never met up.

She and her mother had had dinner every Sunday before she'd passed, more out of obligation than love. And her father... Bryn wasn't even sure what state he was in. Hell, the man could've left the mortal plane and she wouldn't know.

"Nope. My father retired from the service but leads a big military consulting firm in DC. He technically has a condo in downtown DC, but in reality, he lives at the office."

"Wow." Bryn loved nursing. Being a therapy-dog handler was nice, too. Though it didn't quite fill the hole the same. But she wouldn't live at the hospital. Balance was too important.

"Yeah. The man is a certified workaholic. He got worse when Mom passed a few years ago." Nick reached for his drink, took a bigger sip, then set it aside. "And my siblings take after dad. All of them."

"All of them?" She'd begged her mother for a sibling when she'd been younger, not realizing that her father would need to be home...or her mother would need to choose another love to make that happen. Still, she'd always wanted a big family.

"Youngest of four!" Nick laughed as he pointed to himself. "And they live all over. My oldest brother is stationed at PACOM in Hawaii. My other brother is Special Forces, and who knows where he's at right now. And my sister was a fighter pilot, but she wants to keep climbing the ranks, so she's not in the cockpit anymore. She's at Wright-Patterson in Ohio, doing something she can't talk about. So family gatherings and home aren't really what the Walkers aim for.

"But you." Nick leaned over, but his hand didn't come closer to hers. "You're a homegrown Bostonian."

"Never left." The city was her place. She'd never doubted that. Even after Ethan had unceremoniously told her their marriage was over...on the second day of their honeymoon. That still infuriated her. He'd known before their wedding that he hadn't wanted to go through with it, but he'd still stood at the altar and made vows he'd had no intention of keeping. And Bryn had been so focused on trying to make him happy that she'd refused to see the signs.

At least getting dumped in such a way had cracked every rose-colored pair of glasses in her wardrobe.

When moving out of their home, he'd asked if she was moving away. She'd told him no. Though she hadn't elaborated, it wasn't his business. She'd left the hospital they'd worked at but not the city.

Luckily, Boston was large enough that she never ran into him.

The food arrived, and Bryn leaned over, inhaling the spice and savoring the moment. Then she took her first bite and sighed.

"I agree." Nick took another bite of the food. "You were right—this is delicious."

"Told you."

Bryn looked at her watch. Her plate was gone. She'd finished her drink, and it was nearly time to take Honey on her last walk of the night. Which meant she needed to say good-night to Nick Walker.

The problem was she didn't want to.

Conversation had been so easy. They'd talked of books and movies—Nick was a huge cinema buff. The night was simple, and for the first time in forever, she felt like someone heard her.

If this had been a date, it would have gone down as the best first date of her life. And it was so relaxed, probably precisely because it wasn't a date.

Maybe she had a small crush on the hot new doc, but that didn't mean the feeling was mutual. They were two colleagues who had run into each other and had an enjoyable time. No need to read anything more into the situation.

"You keep looking at your watch."

Her cheeks heated as she met his supple brown eyes again.

"I need to get Honey out for her nighttime walk. If Abbie was in town, I could text her, but she switched places with Ailani for three months. A nurse rotation with our sister hospital in Hawaii. Abbie won't have a white Christmas, but maybe she'll get sand in her toes." And now she was rambling.

Get it together, Bryn!

"I just don't think it would be fair to ask Ailani to do it. It was her first day today. She's been in town a week, still settling and all." She motioned for Bill.

"Ready for the check?"

"Yes, please."

Bill looked at Nick, then back at her. "Separate?"

"Yes." Her face was hot. This was not a date. That the bartender even suspected…

"We work together." Bryn's voice was rugged, and she tilted her head toward Nick. "Just colleagues." Why was she expanding on this? All she needed to say was yes. She pursed her lips, forcing herself to stop talking.

"Got it." Bill's eyebrows pushed together as he turned to her companion. "You ready for the check?"

"Seems that way." Nick leaned against the bar as he pulled his wallet from his back pocket.

"Sorry. I…"

"What are you apologizing for?" Nick raised an eyebrow, his whole body was relaxed, and if one snapped a picture, they'd capture the image of the most handsome man in the place.

"I'm not sure." She shook her head. "I need to take Honey out."

"You do. She's an integral part of Ward 34."

Such a simple statement. One that if she hadn't already had a sizable crush on the man would have created one. Ethan hadn't supported her choice to train Honey as a therapy dog. He'd said animals had no place in medicine—despite so many studies refuting such nonsense.

He'd gifted her the puppy. Looking back at it, though, Bryn wondered if that was because people liked golden retrievers. Honey looked great in pictures; he could talk about the sweet dog at home. But he'd never cared for her, never snuggled with her. To him, Honey was just an animal.

To Bryn, the dog was her universe.

"From telling me dogs aren't allowed in the ward to 'an integral part' of the team. Quite the turnaround." She playfully pushed against his shoulder, and fire lit through her body. For a woman who'd just loudly proclaimed this wasn't a date, she couldn't seem to convince her body.

"I didn't realize she was a therapy dog." Nick winked as he stood and grabbed his coat. "Sometime you'll have to tell me how you trained her. I've met a few therapy dogs but never asked many questions."

Bryn stood, accepting Nick's offer when he grabbed her coat and held it open for her.

Not a date...

"The training center is right around the corner. Honey and I are teaching tomorrow morning—nine to eleven—before doing an afternoon shift at the hospital. I always grab a coffee at the Full of Beans Coffee shop at eight thirty, then walk..." She cleared her throat—he didn't need a rundown of her morning plans. "If you'd like to join us, you're welcome to."

"I just might do that."

Bryn knew her smile was gigantic. She also knew that "might do that" was not *see you tomorrow*. Still, he seemed serious.

"Thank you, Bryn."

"For what?"

"Spending the night with me." He walked with her to the door. "It was nice not to eat alone."

It was. "Good night, Nick." Bryn looked at her feet, then made herself walk away. She reached the corner and couldn't stop herself from looking back.

She turned her head and saw Nick. Just watching after her. The light of the restaurant pooled on his face. He looked like a mythical being…an Adonis. And all his attention was focused on her.

He raised a hand; she did the same. Then he turned and walked the other way. Bryn shook her head and hurried home. It was already almost thirty minutes past Honey's walk time… At least her puppy was the forgiving type. Because Bryn wouldn't change a thing about tonight.

It was easy to spot Bryn in the coffee shop. All Nick had to do was look for the gathering of children and hear the exclamations of "puppy" and "Honey." Honey and Bryn must've been favorite regulars.

And why wouldn't they be?

Dogs were nearly universally loved, and Honey was a star. So was her handler.

And that was the reason he was coming into the coffee shop hours before his afternoon shift. Last night's dinner had been blissful. One of the best first nights out in his long history of new places.

He hadn't lied to Bryn, though he hadn't been exactly honest, either. Nick had walked up to the restaurant to look at the menu because it was busy. He might have eaten there. The menu looked good, and there was a crowd—always a good sign. But he'd seen Bryn taking off her coat and sitting at the bar.

Nick hadn't been able to open the door fast enough. He'd wanted to say hi. Wanted to eat with her. Wanted to spend time with her. It was a feeling so out of character. Nick moved on. It was his go-to.

The one constant in his ever-rotating location game.

His sister, Lisa, had once asked if he was chasing something. She'd been waiting to hear if she'd made Command. In that moment, she'd said she was looking forward to settling down. Finding some place warm year-round, her own home, maybe near a beach. Her eyes had held a sense of envy and judgment. Nick was the one not beholden to military orders. He was the one who could choose to stay.

And he never stayed.

Their father had walked in before Nick could answer. Holding the list of names for Command that Nick had known had contained his sister's. One perk of being the kid of the chairman of the joint chiefs—maybe the only one.

Lisa had bounded to their father, all hope for a different life fading as she'd heard that she'd made it. Commander of some center in Dayton, Ohio. Nowhere near a beach—and certainly not forever warm. In that moment, their father had looked so proud of her, and that was what mattered in the Walker house.

A look he never got.

Lisa had forgotten her question. But Nick hadn't. He wasn't looking for something—at least he didn't think so. Still, as Bryn looked up from her table, her eyes locking with his, he wondered if maybe staying in Boston longer was a good idea.

"Nick." Bryn's smile could light up a room. She wore a green sweater with a white snowman, matching Honey's snowman outfit. The two of them screamed Christmas.

"You look festive."

Bryn's smile faltered as she rubbed Honey's ears. "The kids love it."

"You don't?" She looked like she'd stepped out of a holiday catalogue. He wasn't an overly festive person. Decorations, holiday songs, bakery items sold in family-size packs with trees and wreath icing…they were fine.

There were people who lived for this time of year. Nick didn't mind it, but he didn't get excited about the shift from Halloween to Christmas. The trees and lights were pretty, but that was all.

However, if you had Christmas sweaters, surely that meant you loved the holiday.

Bryn ran her hand over the snowman, then looked at her phone. "We better get going. You ready?"

Nick held up his coffee. "Lead the way." She hadn't answered the Christmas question. Clearly a sore subject. That was a fact Nick understood.

People often asked why he volunteered for the holiday shifts. Why he never mentioned family. Why he moved all the time. There were no simple answers to those questions, and he was always grateful when people didn't push.

So he would let it go…but that didn't mean he didn't want to know.

They walked the couple of blocks to the therapy center in silence. It wasn't uncomfortable, though he wouldn't mind chatting with her more.

"Here we are." Bryn raised a hand, and Honey danced in front of a brightly colored door.

"So, is it okay if I sit in? I don't want to interrupt therapy. And I should have thought of that before just now." He'd been so focused on time with Bryn, on exploring something new with the beauty before him. As a doctor, he should have considered the implications of just dropping in on therapy.

Bryn shook her head. "This is the training center. People don't come here for therapy—we train the animals here. Then the handlers take the animals to the hospital, retirement center, schools, even workplaces."

"Animals?" He'd seen dogs in the hospital but nothing else. "More than dogs?"

"Yep." Bryn opened the door and motioned for Honey to stay while Nick walked in first. "Dogs are most common. But other animals go through training, too. We have a few cats, a rabbit, even a miniature horse."

"A horse!" The child in him wanted to scream with excitement. As a kid, he'd begged for riding lessons. The family had moved too much for that to become a reality. Still, there was something about the majestic beasts that called to him.

Bryn laughed. "Nick, does a mini horse excite you?"

"Who wouldn't be excited by that!"

"I hate to disappoint you, but Oreo, the mini horse, isn't scheduled for today."

"Ah." Nick shrugged as the excitement tapered off. "That's too bad. I'll have to tag along again when he's here." He shut his mouth. He'd just invited himself along... It was kind of Bryn to offer this visit once. For him to suggest—

"You're welcome anytime, Nick."

Pink coated her cheeks, and her soft smile sent heat straight to his heart. The world seemed to slow as her green eyes held his. His chest tightened as his breath caught.

"Bryn!" The call from the across the room broke the spell connecting them.

He could breathe easier...but he almost didn't want to. He wanted to know what the color meant in her cheeks. If she felt the connection between them, too.

"You brought a friend."

"Um." Bryn pushed a loose hair behind her ear as she looked over at Nick. "Yeah, a friend. And colleague. This is Dr. Nick Walker, the new pediatrician at Beacon Hospital. Honey's interaction with the kids fascinated him yesterday, and he wanted to see how we do things here. Though he's upset to miss Oreo."

"Oreo is only here on Mondays. He is a very busy horse." The middle-aged white woman held out her hand. "I'm Molly Anders, the director here."

"Nice to meet you." Nick gripped her hand. "I appreciate you letting me observe."

"Observe?" Molly shook her head, then looked at Bryn. "Wes, our volunteer, is sick, and you're here. So how about you help us train?"

Nick knew his eyes were wide. He'd planned to sit in the back, watch, learn what he could, but taking part? He didn't know the first thing about animals—let alone working animals.

"I've never had a pet." He'd asked. So many times, but the answer from the general had always been no. And an order from the general, whether directed at subordinates or family, was always followed.

"Not a requirement." Bryn winked as she waved to a woman passing them with an animal in a carrier. "In fact, it's good to have a range of animal expertise because the patients will, too."

Molly nodded as she pointed toward a bright blue door. "I swear it's really not that bad. You can be Bryn and Honey's partner."

Bryn opened the door, motioned for Honey to wait and then grinned at him. "I promise to go easy with you."

He wanted to laugh, make some cute comment. Instead, his tongue stayed rooted to the top of his mouth.

Stepping into the room, he looked at the six dogs, all sitting nicely on the floor. One was another golden retriever, but the other five looked to be mutts varying from lap dog to a hundred-pound fella who looked up at him, his tail whapping against the floor.

"So what exactly is the plan?" Nick didn't mind being helpful, but his therapy dog experience was primarily limited to Honey's unorthodox introduction.

"You're going to be the patient. We'll run Honey through the drills, and then the other dogs will follow. You just need to sit and walk as directed. Think of yourself as an actor… with furry friends."

"Sorry! Sorry!" A young man raced past Nick and slid into the chair next to the giant dog, a medium gray-and-white dog bouncing behind him. "The bus is running late, and I just…" He shook his head and let out a sigh.

"Good morning, Adam." Bryn put a smile on her face. "It's nice to see you and Pepper. Please instruct her to sit."

He motioned with his hand, and the dog did nothing. "We're

just a little hyped from the run in here." He motioned again and added, "Sit." Pepper ignored the instruction until he performed the same task a third time.

Adam scratched the top of the dog's head, then let out a clear sigh of relief.

Nick noticed a few of the other pet handlers didn't try to hide their frustration, but Bryn seemed unfazed by the issue. "Everyone, this is Nick Walker—our volunteer for the day."

The crowd clapped as Nick waved. Once more, Pepper popped up but sat again as soon as instructed. At least she was listening now.

"All right, Nick, you ready?" Bryn and Honey stood next to him, waited for him to nod, then started walking through the drills. Honey's tail wagged the entire time, and Bryn smiled at him several times.

There were far worse ways to spend the hours before a shift.

"Biscuit's turn." The gentle giant Nick had noticed when he'd first walked in stood with his handler and started going through the same drills he'd done with Honey, Scout and three other dogs. Laying his head in Nick's lap, accepting pets on the head, gentle tugs on the ear. Listening to the commands that his owner, Rachel, gave, before Nick followed, too. Finally, it was time for the last move: Biscuit walking beside Nick as they moved through a recreated playroom. Toys, bells and claps echoed all around.

"You're doing great. I owe you for this," Bryn whispered as he rounded the corner.

"Maybe you do." He winked. He wasn't sure how he'd ask for repayment, but if she wanted to buy him a coffee…or let him buy her one, he wouldn't turn the opportunity down.

"Nice work, Biscuit."

No sooner had the words left Nick's mouth than he felt something brush up behind him, and then the world seemed to shift as Biscuit's back legs pushed against his own. Shifting, trying to regain balance, he heard a yelp and pulled his foot up as Pepper darted between his legs.

The floor rose to meet him. Nick put out his hands to catch himself, a reaction he knew was wrong but couldn't stop in the moment. He blew out a breath as pain shot up from his left wrist upon landing.

"Nick, are you all right?" Bryn was at his level, her blue eyes searching his face before reaching for his wrist. "Can you move it?"

Pepper danced beside him, and Nick moved the fingers in his hand. It was sore but not broken.

"Good motion in the fingers." Bryn's hand was warm on his. If his hand wasn't aching, Nick would enjoy this.

"Now…" Bryn let go of his hand. "Can you rotate it? Don't force it."

"I am a doctor, Bryn."

"I know. And doctors make the worst patients."

The phrase echoed in his mind as he gingerly rotated his wrist. It was a line he'd heard from more than one nurse. Unfortunately, they weren't wrong. Doctors made terrible patients.

"That a quip you picked up being a therapy-dog handler?"

Her cheeks coated with color as she watched him move his hand. "Let's focus on your wrist."

Another question deflected…

"Sore but nothing too bad. Tomorrow it will probably ache, but it's not broken."

"But it could have been." Molly crossed her arms and looked at Pepper's owner. "Adam, can I speak with you, please?"

Molly, Adam and Pepper headed out of the room, Pepper clearly oblivious to the hanging head of her owner.

Bryn clapped her hands. "Thanks, everyone. See you next weekend."

"Bryn." Nick stood, dusting himself off. "I hope I didn't get Pepper in trouble."

She frowned, and his heart dropped. "It was an accident, Bryn."

"I know. But it wasn't your fault, it was Pepper's." Bryn dropped Honey's leash, and he dog stayed right by her side. After a quick motion with her hand, Honey sat. Another motion, and Honey lay down.

"That was impressive."

"Not really. *Stay*, *sit*, *lie down* are all basic commands for dogs. I trained Honey with words and motions in case I have situations where words aren't ideal. Those are the basics." Bryn looked toward the door. "Pepper is a wonderful dog..."

Nick heard the mental *but* she wasn't saying. "But she won't be a therapy dog?" He rubbed the back of his head. "I'm not a regular volunteer. She just got excited."

"Exactly." Bryn nodded. "You are not a regular. You're new and exciting."

"Right." Nick looked at the door again. The sweet dog and their owner had not returned.

"You're also tall, young, strong—"

"Are you trying to woo me?"

Woo? He'd landed on his hand, not his head. Still, the hint of pink brightening in Bryn's cheeks made him happier than he'd been in forever.

She cleared her throat. "The patients won't all be as fit or young as you are. They'll also be new and, if Pepper goes to a school, young and jumpy. So..." Bryn snapped her fingers in a quick pattern.

Honey grabbed her leash in her mouth and handed it to her.

"So Pepper isn't a good fit." He knew dogs failed at service training. Not every animal was meant to work, but...

"Sorry you were the last test. Not intentional, but I know it sucks."

"*Sucks*. That is a good word for it."

Bryn looked at her watch, then back at Nick. "Honey and I are in the ER this afternoon. Want to walk to the hospital together?"

"Absolutely."

CHAPTER THREE

"I DON'T KNOW what I expected of Boston in the winter, but walking through the park and seeing kids and families playing wasn't it."

Bryn laughed and pointed to the sky. "The sun is shining. It's not *too* chilly. You've lived so many places—you've really never experienced kids playing outside in December?"

"I have." Nick chuckled as a child raced across the path in front of them. "I guess I just figured there'd be more snow!"

"This is Boston. Not Maine."

Nick opened his mouth, but before he could deliver a witty statement, a scream echoed from the playground they'd just passed. He took off without thinking.

He turned and noticed Bryn and Honey keeping pace with him.

Reaching the playground, Nick could see a young boy between seven and nine on the ground. Blood coated the side of his head, and the boy didn't seem conscious.

A woman was kneeling beside him, tears streaming across her face. "Isaac. Isaac. Isaac."

"Stay."

He heard Bryn issue the command to Honey as he stepped toward the boy. "I'm a doctor."

"Call 911," Bryn stated behind her. "Tell them a doctor and nurse are on site but that we need emergency transport for a child."

"Nurse?" Nick raised a brow as she kneeled beside him. There wasn't time to discuss that, but when this was over…

Bryn put her fingers on the boy's wrist. "Pulse is rapid but strong."

That was a good sign.

"His breathing is consistent." Nick wanted the boy to open his eyes, but as far as he and Bryn could tell, the child was stable.

"His right arm is under him awkwardly, there's a cut above his eyebrow and, based on the surrounding blood, at least one on the back of his head, and…" Bryn looked at Nick, and he nodded.

The child had fallen. Potential neck injuries did not get moved without stabilization unless absolutely necessary. The cut was bleeding, adding to the blood on the child's face, but head wounds bled. It was possible it just needed a few stitches and looked nastier than it was.

"What happened?" Nick looked at the woman crying.

She hiccupped and said something, but it was unintelligible through the sobs.

Bryn motioned with her hand, and Honey moved beside the woman, pressing her body to her.

"Ma'am, I need you to take a deep breath." Her words were soft but direct. "Isaac is bleeding and unconscious. Can you tell Dr. Walker what happened?"

"He was doing tricks." The words came from behind him.

He turned to find a small girl—not the ideal firsthand witness, but he'd take anything.

"Tricks." Nick nodded. "Did he fall after the trick?"

She looked at Isaac, then back at Nick. "He was flipping. I told him I wanted a turn, and he looked at me weird. I told him to stop it. Then he dropped."

Looked at me weird…that could be anything from he'd made a face to rapid eye movement indicating something far more serious.

"Does your son have a history of seizures?" Bryn's words were firm. Clearly her mind had gone to where his had traveled, too. "We need to tell the paramedics."

"No." His mother fumbled for a tissue. "No, Isaac has always been healthy."

No history of seizures. That didn't mean much. Seizures weren't as common as television drama made them seem, and their causes were far vaster than the average person realized.

"His father was epileptic." The woman sucked in a deep breath. "It was well controlled, but then one night..." She blew out a breath and leaned against Honey.

He looked at Bryn and saw her bite her lip. Epilepsy was a difficult diagnosis. Even when the condition was well controlled, it was possible for the worst to happen. And Isaac's mom didn't have to finish the sentence for the medical professionals to know what she couldn't voice.

There was no way to diagnose it in the field, but the one bright point was that while epilepsy could begin at any age, its onset in childhood was unusual. It was family history the paramedics needed to know, but it didn't mean Isaac had had his first epileptic seizure.

"I hear the sirens." Bryn's shoulders relaxed.

She must've been feeling the same relief he was. There was little they could do for Isaac outside of assessing stability and getting frontline questions answered.

"Mom." The boy's eyes fluttered open, and he shifted.

"Stay still." Bryn laid a hand on Isaac's chest. Not pushing him down, but letting him know people were there. Head trauma often resulted in patients trying to get up and move. Some scientists believed it was an evolutionary leftover, the body going into flight mode. *Something injured me—must move.*

Nick wasn't sure, but he'd seen enough people and children follow the pattern to know Bryn's choice was a good one.

"Mom," Isaac repeated.

"I'm here." The boy's mother leaned over and kissed one of the few places free of blood. "I'm right here. But the nurse is right—you must stay still."

"What happened?" Isaac's voice was quiet with a thready, almost dreamlike quality to it.

"We're not sure," Nick stated. He and Bryn didn't have any answers.

"My head hurts."

"I bet it does." She smiled at the boy. "Can you hear the ambulance sirens?"

"Yeah."

"Well, they're going to take you to the hospital. You've got a cut on your forehead and at least one cut on the back of your head, too." Bryn looked up at his mom and then back at the boy. "You will probably have stitches."

Isaac moved his hand, but Nick caught it. "I know this is confusing, but I need you to stay as still as possible until the medics get here."

"Am I going to be all right?" The child's bottom lip trembled. "My dad."

"You aren't your dad." His mother broke in. "You're going to be fine. Perfectly fine."

Bryn snapped her fingers, and Honey moved from Isaac's mother's side and lay down next to him.

"She's pretty." He raised a hand and ran it along the dog's head.

"She is beautiful. And she knows it." Bryn used a mock high-pitched voice as she winked at Honey.

"I like her sweater." Isaac's voice was low. That was good. Adrenaline and stress were natural responses to trauma but not healing.

There was no way to know what exactly had occurred, but it was clear that Isaac and his mother were thinking of his dad. Worrying—which was understandable. And once more, Honey was here to offer a fuzzy ear.

"It's one of her favorites." Bryn flicked the headband the dog was wearing, causing the bells to ring.

"It matches your sweater."

"It does." Her voice wavered a little. Then she moved her hand to the sweater, pushed an unseen button and it lit up.

"Whoa!" Isaac's words were soft, filled with wonder. "It's so pretty."

Nick looked at their patient: Isaac's coloring was good. He was calm—mostly. There was more blood than Nick would like, but it wasn't gushing.

He looked over Bryn's shoulder. The sirens were getting closer, and he could see the ambulance coming through the park entrance.

Rationally, Nick knew it had only been a few minutes, fifteen minutes top, since the emergency call had gone out. But when a child was injured, time simultaneously sped up and slowed down.

"All right, the paramedics are here, Isaac." Nick shifted so Isaac could look at him and keep petting Honey without moving.

"When they get over here, they are going to put something around your neck. It will make sure that you can't move, and it can feel scary. It's necessary to keep you safe."

"They used it on my dad once when he had a seizure and fell." Isaac's bottom lip trembled, and he squeezed his eyes shut. "I can do this."

"You can." His mother kissed him again. "I will be right with you."

The first paramedic ran up, and Bryn stepped back and the lights on her sweater flipped off. She motioned for Honey to follow her and waved to Isaac.

The boy lifted a hand but stayed still.

Nick stood and quickly filled in the second paramedic on what they'd learned and observed. And in just a few minutes, Isaac was on the backboard and loaded into the ambulance.

He stood by Bryn as the ambulance pulled away. "So, you're a registered nurse?"

"Yes." Bryn started to cross her arms, then stopped herself. Beacon had hired her as a therapy-dog handler, but Javier knew she was an RN. He'd mentioned twice to her that Ward 34 needed nurses, that they could put her on the floor the second she was ready to slide back into her scrubs.

She'd considered it on more than one occasion when she'd been lying awake late at night. The urge to try it, to change the quiet pattern she'd slipped into pulling at her. But she hadn't taken that step.

"But now you aren't?" Nick's hands were in his pockets, his eyes trained on the departing vehicle.

She could tell from his stance that he wouldn't push her. And that upset her. Which made little sense. Part of the reason she was so happy that Abbie was in Hawaii was because that meant no one knew why Bryn had left nursing. Why she was spending Christmas alone with her dog. Why she was avoiding the magical things she normally so looked forward to.

"My ex-husband is a pediatric orthopedic surgeon at Brigham." The sentence flew from her mouth, and she had to fight the urge to hang her head. That Ethan had called an end to their union just after stepping off the plane on their honeymoon wasn't her fault. But how had she not seen that the man standing opposite from her at the altar had had no interest in getting, let alone staying, married?

How had she let herself change so much for him?

"I see."

"Really?" Even Bryn didn't fully understand her choice.

"No." Nick shrugged. "Lots of people get divorced and continue working in the field they were in before they got married."

"How many of them work with colleagues who danced at their wedding on Saturday and learned by Friday that the husband had already called it quits?"

Nick's eyes widened, but he had the good grace not to say anything.

"Everyone—and I mean everyone—at that wedding worked with us. My mom passed a few years ago. Ethan's parents aren't in the picture. He said it was because they didn't support him—not sure if anything he said was true. I just..."

Bryn swallowed the lump in her throat. She'd not voiced any of this in a year.

Because everyone I know knows this sob story.

"We got married the week before Christmas...and filed for divorce before New Year's. Before all the holiday decorations were even put away! You don't get a break on lawyers' fees based on the length of your union."

"That seems decidedly unfair."

"Thank you." Bryn pushed the button at the crosswalk and pulled her coat around her as the wind picked up.

Nick stepped forward. Not much, but enough to offer a windbreak. "I'm surprised you don't hate Christmas."

"I do." That wasn't exactly true, but the holiday had certainly lost more than a bit of its sparkle. Though Ethan had contributed to that, too. He hated fun decor. Hated homemade cookies. Pretty much all the things she loved.

"Bryn, that isn't true."

She put her hands on her hips and stared up at him, something that might've been intimidating if her heart didn't pick up as his cool brown eyes met hers. "You've known me for days, *Dr. Walker*. I think I know what I like about this season and what I don't."

Nick looked down at Honey...then flicked the antlers on the top of the golden retriever's head. "Your dog is in a holiday sweater, wearing antlers."

"She's a therapy dog."

"And you're in a matching sweater."

Heat flooded her cheeks, but she didn't look down at the snowman sweater. The bright, obnoxious snowman sweater that she'd flung on this morning without thinking. "It matches Honey."

"Yes. And it lights up, Bryn. No one who hates Christmas has a light-up snowman sweater."

The light changed before she could think of a retort. They hustled across the street as horns blared. They had the right of way, but that didn't mean the Boston drivers cared to give it.

"I took a break." The sentence was soft, but it echoed in her heart. A break. That was what this year was. A break from dating. A break from nursing. A break from holidays and celebrations.

"*Took* is past tense." Nick stopped as Beacon Hospital's entrance came into view.

"A figure of speech."

"Look me in the eye and tell me you don't miss nursing."

She couldn't do that. Bryn loved working with Honey. Loved seeing patients' faces light up when the dog walked into the room. But it wasn't the same as providing day-to-day care.

"You're signed up for the Santa Dash, the bake sale—"

"I know, but all that is for the kids. And to raise money for Camp Heartlight." The words sounded slightly hollow even to her. "The last year… I just… I just…"

"Put yourself in hibernation?" Nick's question hit her in the chest.

Hibernation. She rolled the word around her subconscious. The descriptor was accurate. She didn't miss Ethan. He was a jerk, something she should have realized before she'd been standing in white before all their friends.

Their friends.

His friends. Or rather, colleagues who thought his meteoric rise in pediatric surgery might help their careers—if he liked them. Not realizing that Ethan only liked one person.

Himself.

But she'd lost herself in that moment. Lost the free spirit that believed people were generally good. Yes, there were bad people. Her father was a disappointment, but after growing up without him, Bryn had thought she could spot the users.

Ethan walking away—on their honeymoon—had shaken her to her core.

"Hibernation is safe."

"And lonely." Nick rocked back on heels as he looked up at the building. "I've started over more than a dozen times in my life. Hibernation is a defense mechanism. Don't let it steal something you love."

"You sound like Javi." Bryn laughed. "He's eager for me to get back on the floor."

"A nurse quit a few days ago. It's got him worried. And he has a therapy-dog handler already through the hospital background checks, already employed by the hospital part time, who is a registered nurse. I'm stunned he's not following you around every time you walk onto the ward."

"That's not Javi's style." Bryn liked the head of Pediatrics. He was quiet, but he cared about his staff. Which was considerably more than she could say for her ex.

"What if we make a deal?"

"A deal?" Why did she say that? She should have said no. There was no reason to bring herself out of hibernation, as Nick had called it. She was safe.

Her world was small, but it was safe.

Still...

"I help you come out of hibernation, and you show me around Boston. The fun stuff. The touristy stuff and the hidey holes only the locals know about."

"And step one is talking to Javi about picking up nursing shifts?" Bryn's heart raced as she stepped through the entrance. She could start as soon as she wanted. If she wanted...

And Nick was right—she wanted to.

CHAPTER FOUR

NICK'S CELL BUZZED, and he reached over his couch to grab it. He couldn't stop the smile as he saw Bryn's name pop onto the screen.

Javi talked to HR. I start Friday.

It didn't surprise him Javi had talked to HR on Bryn's behalf. If the floor wasn't fully staffed, that meant that they couldn't admit as many patients. While the pediatric ward was never quiet, the winter months were very full. With people inside, children sharing germs at school and extracurriculars, influenza, RSV and other childhood illnesses cropped up more frequently.

For most children, this meant a few days off school, their parents making sure they drank enough fluids and took naps, but for some, it meant hospitalization.

That is fantastic. I can't wait to work with you!

As Nick typed back, his mind was already shifting to the other parts of this plan. Helping Bryn step back into nursing was the first step in pulling her out of her hibernation.

Why do I care so much?

That was a question that had rumbled around his brain for days. Nick was always polite to his colleagues. He considered a few of them friends, but he didn't get close. In any other situation, he might have suggested to a nurse or doctor that they return to the field, but he wouldn't have pushed.

Wouldn't have cut a deal with them.

I owe you some real Boston insights now. Want to grab dinner? Pizza?

Yes. He wanted to do that so bad. But he'd put off unpacking his apartment for weeks. Living in boxes was something he didn't mind. Hell, when he'd been in Atlanta, he'd not bothered to unpack half his stuff. It had just made it easier when he'd picked up and headed out again.

But the boxes had bothered him for days now. Since he'd met Bryn. Because inviting someone over while the only things unpacked were a week's worth of clothes and his movie collection was something he wouldn't do. And he wanted to invite Bryn over. Wanted to cook dinner and watch movies. As friends…

There was no point in lying. He was attracted to the woman. How could he not be? She was sunshine in a bottle, with light blond hair always pulled into some fancy braid, bright green eyes and a smile that seemed to push against his heart every time he saw it. However, you could be friends with someone you found attractive. And that was what he was going to be—friends with Bryn.

I want to say yes, but I finally started unpacking my apartment. If I stop now I might never start again.

At least he knew himself. If Nick didn't unpack the boxes, then he wouldn't invite Bryn over. So that meant this needed to be done.

Want help?

Two words on the screen. Two words that made his soul leap.

Yes.

He'd typed it and hit Send before he could think Bryn's offer through.

Then I need an address.

The smile emoji at the end of the sentence made him laugh. No one in his family used emojis in texts. His father had forbidden them years ago. Nick had never understood why the general hated them, but the family had followed the order.

He typed out his address, hit Send and sighed as she told him she'd see him in thirty minutes.

The knock at his door almost exactly thirty minutes later sent a lightning bolt through every nerve in Nick's body. Bryn was here. To help him unpack a life he never fully unboxed. His feet rushed across the apartment like they couldn't reach the door soon enough.

She was wearing dark yoga pants, a plain pink sweatshirt and she'd pulled her hair into a messy bun that sat on the top of her head. In short, she was breathtaking.

Man, he really had it bad.

"Bryn Bedford, reporting for duty." She made a fake salute, then giggled. "How was my salute?"

"As good as my *wicked*." He winked as she stepped into the apartment.

"Ouch!" She playfully made a motion with her hand over

her heart like she was pulling a knife from her chest. "Wow, you weren't kidding. This place isn't unpacked."

"Why would I lie?"

"I…" Her cheeks darkened as she looked toward the kitchen.

Had she been hoping he was looking for an excuse to invite her over? He was glad she was here, and if she wanted to just pop in a movie and chill, well, he wouldn't argue.

"Where do you want to start, Nick?"

"Kitchen? It's past time I stopped getting takeout to avoid doing dishes."

Laughing, Bryn moved toward the open kitchen. Then she stopped as she hit the living room, and he nearly ran into her.

"How many movies do you have?"

Her eyes were staring at the long wall in the living room, just opposite his kitchen. It was full of movies, from the baseboards to the ceiling. And those were only the ones he'd kept. Most of his library was on streaming services now. But these, well, these had come with him from place to place for too long to give away.

"I guess that number depends on if you're talking about just these or the online library, too. Though most of those I own on streaming, too. It's my hobby." Nick pulled at the back of his neck. Movies and film were his passion.

In a dark theater with the characters on-screen, a big fresh container of popcorn. It had been the perfect way for a lonely kid to lose a few hours.

"Do you like movies?" It was usually one of the first questions he asked on a date. Though this wasn't a date.

In fact, it felt much more intimate.

"Not as much as you." She smiled and walked to the wall. "You have everything here. Romance, horror, documentary, foreign…"

"Yeah. I don't really have a favorite genre. I just watch anything."

"What's your favorite?" Her eyes were bright as she turned to look at him.

"Favorite?" Nick let out a breath as he looked at the wall. "I don't think there's any way for me to choose. Almost every film has something I like about it. The story or the characters or the score. I mean..."

"I like holiday films. Or I did. I used to start watching them as soon as the turkey from Thanksgiving was put away. Ethan, my ex, wasn't a huge fan." Bryn let out a chuckle. "He wasn't a huge fan of anything. Funny how easy it is to see that now."

She clapped her hands, clearly trying to move past the words she'd said. "Unpack the kitchen. That's our goal tonight."

"It is." Nick grinned as he followed her into the kitchen. He didn't mind the statements about her ex. In fact, he enjoyed hearing them. Which was weird because that shouldn't have been the case. But he suspected Bryn hadn't talked about her ex in a while. Maybe since he'd decided their short-lived marriage wouldn't work.

Her talking about it with Nick meant she trusted him with the knowledge.

Or she's figured out I'm safe because I don't stay.

Nick wanted to pull that thought from his mind. No reason to seek the worst thoughts. Bryn was sharing with him. That was nice—no matter the circumstances. "Want me to put one on while we unpack? I've probably got any holiday movie you can think of."

Bryn put a hand on her chin, her eyes glowing. "That is such a challenge. What movie could I think of that you don't have?"

He crossed his arms, knowing his smile was gigantic. This was the perfect kind of challenge for him. With a woman who heated his blood and made him happy. A friend. Bryn was a friend.

Something he shouldn't have to keep reminding himself of.

"Come up with something?"

"No." She tapped her head again, then shrugged. "All I can

think of is *Miracle on 34th Street*. And that's the exact opposite of obscure."

"It is." He winked, picked up the remote he kept on the kitchen counter, turned on the television and quickly found the classic in his online stash.

"*Miracle on 34th Street* and unpacking. Not a bad way to spend the night."

Nick nodded. "Not a bad way at all, Bryn."

"Pizza should be here in about twenty minutes." Nick slid into the doorway by his study. His dark shirt had packing dust on it, but it couldn't diminish the beauty of the man.

Bryn!

She still couldn't believe she'd asked if he'd wanted help unpacking. Most women would have taken it as a blow off when they'd invited a man to dinner.

Not exactly *I'm washing my hair*, but close enough.

But she'd felt deep inside that he hadn't been lying to her. Hadn't been looking for an excuse. So she'd offered help, mostly expecting another rejection.

Part of her had kind of hoped for it. Nick was sweet, kind, intelligent and drop-dead gorgeous. And her colleague. Particularly since she was starting rounds on the pediatric floor this Friday.

He was off-limits.

If only her libido could get on the same page as her brain.

"Good—I'm famished." And she needed some kind of distraction. Though eating with Nick likely wouldn't diminish the blooming crush she had on the doctor.

She cut open the last box from the closet. It was full of coins, books and memorabilia from West Point.

His father had been in the army. So were his siblings. Was he storing stuff for them?

"Where do you want this stuff?" She held up an Army field manual.

"Oh…umm, nowhere. Just leave it in the box." Nick's cheek twitched as his jaw locked down, his easy-going stance shifting.

"Is this your father's stuff?" Bryn placed the field manual back in the box and closed it up.

"No." Nick pressed his hands together and cleared his throat. "I think that just about does it. Thanks for the help. Pizza. Pizza should be here soon."

"Nick?" Bryn stepped close to him. He was stiff, his eyes focused on the space over her shoulder. "Nick."

She reached for his hand, hoping to ground him in the present. "Look at me." When he didn't follow her command, she squeezed again and stated, "Nick, look at me."

"It's no big deal."

"I didn't ask." Bryn pressed her free palm to his chest. "Why don't you get us something to drink while we wait for the pizza?"

"I have a red wine. It's a dry wine." Nick cleared his throat as he shook his head, then pulled his hand from hers. "Since we unpacked the kitchen, I know exactly where the wine glasses and bottle opener are."

He grinned, but his features didn't quite light up.

"Red works well with pizza." Bryn wasn't much a wine person. She enjoyed the drink, but she didn't know if people recommended red for pizza. It didn't matter. Whatever memories this box had awakened were moving away now that he had a new focus. That was what mattered.

"I'll go pour, and just put…umm…" His eyes wandered to the box on the office chair.

"Back in the closet?"

In the trash? If it caused him so much pain, she wasn't sure why he carted the box from place to place, but it was his and she'd do with it as he asked.

"Closet sounds great."

"All right, then." Bryn deposited the box, then went to the kitchen. Nick was standing at the kitchen counter, gripping it with his eyes tightly shut.

She moved without thinking, placing her arms around his waist and just holding him. His fingers left the counter and lay over hers at his waist. He didn't move, didn't speak, but that was all right.

How often after her marriage had ended had she just wanted to be held? It was a simple thing. A connection—reminding you that even though you were at a low point, the world still thought of you. You still mattered.

They stood like that for several minutes before Nick turned. She dropped her hands. Her cheeks were burning. She'd just squeezed him, held him for minutes, and now she didn't know what to say.

"I owe you a glass of wine."

Bryn nodded, not quite trusting her voice.

He poured without saying anything, then passed her the glass.

"That was my West Point stuff." He took a deep sip.

"I thought you weren't in the military?" The wine was good, would go well with the pizza when it got here, but it could have been terrible, and it wouldn't matter. She was listening to Nick's story, one she was sure he rarely shared.

"I wasn't." Nick let out a long sigh. "I couldn't hack it. Not cut out for service."

Disappointment oozed off him, and she wanted to throttle whoever had told him that.

"So you started at West Point and left?"

"I finished my pleb year—the first year."

"Freshman year. That's the nonmilitary term for the first year."

Nick cracked a smile and his shoulders relaxed some. "Yeah.

The army called us yuks second year—sophomore year. Short for *yearling*, but not sure anyone ever used that.

"Pleb year you go through Beast—it's a six-week basics class. And if your dad is a high-ranking military member… that does not buy you leniency. I made it through, was top of my class my first year, but I dreaded going back for yuk year. Still, I showed up…started Buckner, the three-week cadet field training. After I finished it, just before starting the academic year, I broke."

"Broke?" Bryn raised a brow. "What does that mean?"

"Just what it sounds like. I realized I couldn't do it. I couldn't stay. Couldn't graduate. The only one of my siblings to walk away from the uniform. My father hasn't looked at me the same since."

"You're a literal doctor." Bryn knew nervous laughter wasn't great, but her brain couldn't stop it. "Seriously, Nick. You're a doctor. A man who saves children's lives. That's not even overstating it—that is legit your job."

"He didn't even show for my med school graduation. I stood there all alone while everyone took pictures with their family. My field isn't good enough for the general."

"Well, that is just too damn bad." She set the wineglass on the counter. How dare his family ignore such a momentous occasion. If they walked up to her right now, she'd given them several pieces of her mind.

Nick's brown eyes caught and held hers. He pursed his lips, then set his wineglass down and started laughing. The rich sound growing deeper as the laugh grew stronger. "It sounds ridiculous, doesn't it?"

It sounded cruel, but she kept that thought to herself. "I've seen you with patients, Nick. Watched kids, terrified children settle as you calm their—and their parents'—worries. You are exactly where you're meant to be."

"I could have gone to medical school after West Point. Served as an Army doctor."

"Would you have gotten to be a pediatrician?"

"I don't know. You serve at the needs of the armed forces when you go on their dime. If they needed pediatricians, then yes, if not…" He shrugged.

"If not, then you'd have gotten pushed into a specialty the army needed, right?"

"Yes."

"I think you were meant to be a pediatrician. So, it's a good thing you left when you did, but…" She paused, the question caught on the tip of her tongue.

"But?" Nick raised a brow. "Don't stop now. We've entered all new friendship territory here tonight."

Friendship. It was the right word. The word she wanted, too, but it struck her chest as she looked at him.

"But why keep a box that only brings you hurt?"

"I don't know." Nick finished his wine and poured a bit more into his glass. "My father wanted so badly for me to go, it felt wrong to throw it out."

"He didn't want you to be happy?" Why was that such a hard choice for some parents? Bryn saw loving parents all the time. But her mother had focused so much on her own happiness…tied to a man who wouldn't love her. And Nick's family wanted him to follow their path instead of their own.

Nick rolled his eyes. "Oh, he wanted us to be happy. Happy in the life he'd chosen."

"Was he happy?" The question popped out, and Bryn could tell by the snap of Nick's neck that he'd never considered the question.

"I…" He blinked over and over, like he was trying to funnel through a load of memories and coming up short. "I don't know."

A knock echoed through the apartment, and Bryn nearly jumped.

"That will be the pizza." Nick's body language shifted. The hurt son vanishing as he moved to answer the door. The confident doctor was back, the man secure in his place. But it was a shell, and deep inside was a hurt that she just wanted to wrap in a hug and force away.

Unfortunately, Bryn knew from experience that that was not how healing worked.

CHAPTER FIVE

BRYN YAWNED AS she walked up the steps to her apartment. Honey pressed her head against her legs, but she could tell the golden was tired, too. As the days got shorter, it was easy for her body to think that five was bedtime when the sun had set over an hour ago. Plus, she was putting in more hours with Paws for Hope since she was returning to nursing in three days. Three days to a new start.

Opening the apartment door, Bryn paused as Ailani waved...her hand full of the fake snow she was laying along the mantle of their faux fireplace. There was a small gas fire unit the landlord had sworn was a selling point.

A real fireplace, one with crackling wood...well, they existed, just not in apartment units in Bryn's price range.

Christmas decor. Usually by this time of year, her place looked like Santa had snapped his finger and turned it into a winter wonderland. She'd decorated her and Ethan's home every year...alone.

Bryn had sworn she wouldn't decorate this year. Sworn she was doing nothing. That her hibernation was keeping her safe.

The decorations were inexpensive, but they ignited a light in the dark room of her soul she was trying to ignore. Like Nick pointed out, she was wearing her sweaters. Dressing Honey is holiday cheer. Why keep herself from something she genuinely enjoyed?

"I hope you don't mind." Ailani's grin was wide as she held

up a plain red stocking. "It's December, and it just felt like the apartment need a little cheer."

Bryn looked at the decorations and pursed her lips. Ailani was only in Boston for three months. She didn't deserve a Grinch for a roommate. "Do you want to decorate? I mean really, really decorate?"

Ailani's dark hair fell to the side as she tilted her head. "What does 'really, really decorate' mean?"

Bryn giggled. "It means let me put Honey in her crate because she needs a nap, then why don't you come with me to my storage unit in the basement? We can make this place glitter!"

She clapped and nodded. "Glitter! Yes. This place needs some holiday glitter."

"You weren't kidding." Ailani wiped her hand over her forehead as Bryn put the star on the Christmas tree they'd decorated in the corner. "This place looks like a winter wonderland. And there are still boxes in the storage unit."

Bryn sighed as she stepped off the step ladder. "My old place was a house. My ex-husband barely noticed the decorations and didn't ask for any of them when we split our stuff."

Which was good because she'd had no plans to let Ethan have her precious holiday decor.

"Some of it is really unique."

"Like what?" Bryn looked at the lights, the stockings. Ethan had had very distinct tastes regarding decor. Most of her fun stuff had stayed in boxes when they'd lived together. Seeing it all out tonight stitched a little piece of her soul.

"You have bean holiday lights."

"Oh." Bryn shook her head as she looked at the strand.

"I thought Bostonians hated the nickname Beantown."

"We do." It was a terrible nickname, one more than a few opinion articles had recommended discarding, but nicknames were not things that one could just throw away.

"So the bean lights…"

"Were from a white-elephant party a few years ago. My friend Indigo found them, thought they were hilarious. The party all vied for them—you know how sometimes the silliest gift is the one people want the most."

"But you won them?"

"Traded a set of shot glasses for them." Shot glasses Ethan had, apparently, wanted. Not bad enough to bring his own white-elephant gift, but somehow that had been her fault, too.

"I triumphed." The aftermath of that triumph had been terrible, but in the moment, when the bean lights were hers, she'd felt such a rush.

"This is the first year I've hung them up."

"I like them." Ailani grinned, then turned and headed to their small kitchen. "Before we take the empty boxes back to the storage unit, I feel like hot chocolate. What about you?"

"Hot chocolate after holiday decorating? It almost feels like a requirement."

Ailani made the drinks, passing Bryn one of the Santa mugs they'd dug out and hand-washed just an hour ago.

"There is something about hot chocolate…" Bryn sighed as she moved toward the sofa.

"It tastes better when it's cold, too." Ailani slid onto the other side of the couch. "Funny how hot coffee is a thing everywhere, but somehow drinking hot chocolate when it's around eighty degrees just isn't the same."

"True. I love hot cocoa this time of year, but by mid-March, the drink loses all interest for me. It's just this time of year, it's cozy and grounding." Bryn was excited for the changes coming. Mostly.

"You ready for Friday?" Ailani's dark eyes held Bryn's over her identical Santa mug.

"Yes. And no." Bryn shook her head, wishing there was some way to make the conflicting feelings make sense. "I want to go back, I do. I just—"

"You're nervous?"

"Yes, like I was my first day at Brigham years ago. I mean, I was a nurse for almost a decade when I stepped away. I shouldn't be nervous."

"Sure you should." Ailani's face held no malice, no mean intent, but she said the words with force.

"It feels like I shouldn't. Like I should just be thrilled. And I am thrilled. Part of my soul feels like dancing at the idea of putting my stethoscope back in my pocket."

"Adventure is like that. It's thrilling and makes your chest pound, but it's terrifying, too. The what-ifs, the worries that you might choose the wrong path."

"Says the woman who left her warm, sandy island to come to frozen Boston, where she doesn't know anyone."

"Yeah, and part of that was terrifying." Ailani sipped her hot chocolate. "Still wouldn't change a thing, though."

There was the hint of something in Ailani's eyes. A far-off hope that Bryn didn't think was tied to hot chocolate, Christmas decorations or travel.

"I'm excited to be working as a nurse." Bryn swallowed, then added, "And the new pediatrician, Nick..."

She got those words out, then her mouth refused to let any other pass.

"He's cute." Ailani winked. "And he promised if he heard of any good restaurants, he'd let me know. Newbies sticking together and all."

"If you want recommendations, I'm happy to give them." Technically, she'd promised Nick she'd take him around Boston. Show him the hidden and not-so-hidden gems of the city. She could invite Ailani.

That would put her and Nick's outings in strictly friend territory. Force her to ignore the pull her body had when she was in his presence. It was the easy answer.

So why am I not offering?

"Javi has given me some recommendations, too." A little

color coated Ailani's tan cheeks, then she cleared her throat. "Ready to take the boxes down?"

Bryn set her Santa mug down and stood. She had questions about the color in the other woman's cheeks, but then Ailani probably had thoughts about her own statements about Nick.

And she didn't feel like sharing those, either.

Nick's lungs burned as he pulled in another breath of cold air. He privately swore at himself for signing up for the Santa Dash. He technically didn't need to train for the five-kilometer race fundraiser benefiting Camp Heartlight, and with each ragged breath he questioned just walking the race. But that meant even more time in the cold air.

It was an unfortunate reality that many children with chronic issues couldn't attend traditional summer camp. Camp Heartlight offered summer camp for children with chronic heart conditions. The staff for the two-week event were all nurses, doctors and paramedics. All trained to support the children if they had a medical emergency...but the camp was really about playing games, swimming, horseback riding and doing arts-and-crafts projects.

Nick had signed up as soon as he'd heard about the camp's mission. A five-kilometer race, starting in the park and ending with hot chocolate and doughnuts at the entrance of the hospital. No big deal...except it was December and his lungs had wanted to riot from moment his feet hit the pavement.

He knew the kids were planning to watch the race from the windows of the play area. And that was the only thing that kept his body moving as he pushed himself through the workout.

"Nick!" Bryn waved as she and Honey, dressed in outdoor running gear, passed him.

He'd known that she'd signed up for the Santa Dash, too. All right, maybe there were two reasons he was torturing himself in the frosty morning air.

He turned and headed toward Bryn and Honey.

She smiled as he came up beside them. Her nose was pink and her cheeks flushed, but the cold didn't seem to bother her as they kept pace together around the park.

When he thought his lungs might explode from the cold, he finally huffed, "How much longer you going?"

She sucked in a deep breath.

How did that not freeze her lungs?

"I have one more lap, then we go to Full of Beans for coffee, a blueberry muffin and a dog treat."

"Want some company?"

Her eyes glittered as they held his for just a moment before she focused on where she was putting her feet. A smart thought. "You are always welcome, Nick."

One more lap. He could do that. He could do anything if it meant more time with Bryn.

They ran the final steps in silence, and his body wanted to scream as Full of Beans came into view. Yes!

Bryn slowed, pulling up next to the shop. He started for the door, but she stayed in place, pulling one leg up behind her while she held Honey's leash in her other hand. "You need to stretch before you go inside."

Nick looked at the warm shop, the smell of coffee pulling at his nose. "I mean, it's warm in there... I could get us coffee, and that way you and Honey don't have to wait."

"What is it about doctors and not taking care of themselves?"

"Spoken like a true nurse." Nick shook his head, then mimicked her movement. She was right. He needed to stretch, and heading from the cold to a shop that was likely forty degrees warmer would play hell on his muscles.

"Well, I'm headed back onto the nursing floor."

Her smile warmed the frozen parts of him. She looked so happy. Nursing was her calling. Working as a therapy-dog handler helped, but it wouldn't give her everything she needed.

"Ward 34 will be even more lovely with you there." The pediatric floor was wonderful, and it seemed to radiate holiday cheer. There was always some fancy sweet treat in the staff break room. The giant fake tree had ornaments made by the kids, the staff was kind. It was the best place he'd ever worked.

"Ready for coffee?"

"I thought you'd never ask!" Nick pulled the door open and waited for Bryn and Honey to step through. "Grab us a seat. I'll get the coffee and treats."

"Nick—"

"No arguing. I wouldn't have finished my training session without you guys. Go." He waved them away.

Bryn hesitated for a moment, then tugged on Honey's leash, heading for the booth in the back as Nick turned to place their order.

"One coffee, blueberry muffin and yogurt dog treats." Nick set the goods on the table, then slid into the booth opposite Bryn. Her cheeks were still tinged pink, but the tip of her nose was its regular color now. "Warming up?"

"I think you were the one struggling, Dr. Walker." Bryn laughed, then handed a treat to Honey under the table.

"I've run for years but never in such cold conditions. Maybe my next stop should be somewhere warmer."

"Next stop?" Bryn's words were soft, and her green eyes focused on pulling apart the muffin in front of her.

"Yeah." The word was difficult to get out. That was new. He had a mental list of places he wanted to move. It was a running list he'd kept for as long as he could remember. Yet he couldn't pull any of the names to the forefront of his mind. Not while he was sitting here looking at Bryn.

"Ever consider staying?" She cleared her throat. "Never mind." She waved away the question and shoved a piece of muffin into her mouth.

He didn't want to wave away the question. Didn't want to see the acceptance crossing her face and realize that she expected he'd move.

I will move.

"So, why run outside if you don't like it? There are plenty of gyms around. You don't have to torture yourself in the Boston winter."

"The Santa Dash."

"Ah, Honey and I are running that."

"I assumed that was why you were out this morning." Who would choose to run in such conditions?

"You can go to a gym and run. Honey, however..." Bryn looked under the table, and he could tell she was smiling at the dog before she lifted her head. "The local gyms have some very specific requirements regarding animals on their equipment. Something about the fur."

The atmosphere around them shifted, the uneasy feeling his statement about leaving vanishing. Except there was still an uncomfortable pit in his stomach.

"Golden retrievers are natural runners, and it's a good way to help prevent hip dysplasia. Plus, that way we can crush the Santa Dash." Bryn chuckled as she passed the final dog biscuit to Honey under the table.

"But what will she be wearing for the 5K?" Nick leaned over, half joking, half serious. Honey was in a warm coat right now, designed for the cloudy cold day, but somehow, he doubted that would be the case for the Santa Dash in a little over a week.

"Her antlers are a big hit with the kids, so that and one of her sweaters." Bryn looked at the dog again, then up at him. "I enjoy dressing her. Maybe it's silly."

"I don't think so."

Bryn beamed at him, her hand starting toward his before pulling back.

Nick's fingers ached to reach over, run his hand over hers, connect whatever was between them. The easiness between them—it was something he'd never experienced.

"We should get going." Bryn tapped her finger, then pulled out her phone.

"Before you go—where's the best place to get a fresh tree?" He didn't decorate for the holidays, but Bryn was rubbing off on him. He'd looked at his place today and decided he needed at least a few things. "And decorations—because I don't technically have ornaments."

"A tree is easy. Mitchell's has fresh ones. Decorations... that's a different story. What kinds of things do you like?" Honey wacked her head against the table, and Bryn looked down.

"She's ready for breakfast and a nap. Why don't we go tomorrow after our shifts at the hospital? It can be a fun night out before I officially start on Friday."

That was the perfect plan. "It's a date."

Date...

The word slipped out, and he knew his eyes were wide.

"I'll see you tomorrow, Nick."

Bryn grabbed Honey's leash and waved a quick goodbye. She hadn't responded to his slip.

That was good. They weren't dating. And tomorrow wasn't a date...so why did it bother him so much that she wasn't even fazed by his response?

CHAPTER SIX

"YOU EXCITED ABOUT TOMORROW?" Izzy, one of the pediatricians on Ward 34, was smiling as she walked out of Beacon.

"Yeah." Bryn nodded. She was excited, and Ailani was right—the nerves were there, but she was ready for this next adventure. "Although it was weird to be here today without Honey."

"I'll admit that it's a little weird not to see you with a ball of golden fluff next to you." Izzy tightened her coat as the chilly air whipped around them. "I bet she'll be happy to see you when you get home."

"That feeling is very mutual." Honey had been her rock after Ethan had walked out. She'd curled herself into Bryn's side, letting Bryn cuddle her as she'd sobbed about the life she'd lost. Coming in for her meetings with HR and orientation without Honey felt a little weird.

"Big plans for tonight? Or are you just relaxing before the big day?"

Big plans... That wasn't a good descriptor for her night with Nick. How many times had she replayed his words? *It's a date.*

A figure of speech. An easy throwaway statement. They weren't dating. She was helping him put up his Christmas tree—that felt like something.

And maybe if he wasn't already plotting his next place, she might let her heart investigate it further. Some place warm. Nick had been in Boston a little less than a month. Not even long enough to unpack, and yet he was already thinking of the next thing.

Her father was that way. Always thinking of his next score, the next big thing. It never worked out, but that didn't make him change his ways. And Ethan...her ex-husband's focus was always the next step in his career. Neither was ever happy in the here and now. Never happy with her.

"I'm helping Nick—Dr. Walker—find a tree. He wants a real one." Bryn scrunched her nose. She liked the smell of fresh trees, but the fire hazard... Her brain just couldn't ignore it.

"Mitchell's is the place, then. Interesting date idea."

"Mitchell's is what I told him, but it isn't a date." Bryn kept her eyes focused on the parking lot, knowing Izzy's sweet, intuitive gaze was trained on her.

"Picking out a tree is a date—at least according to every holiday movie I have ever seen."

The wind was biting, but Bryn's face was warm. "Well, real life isn't exactly movie magic."

"Isn't that true."

The quiet words made Bryn's head pop up. The faraway look in the pediatrician's eyes sent a rush through Bryn's thoughts. She'd been so lost in her own wanderings about Nick.

"Izzy?"

"This is my car." Izzy's face was bright, though her smile wasn't quite full. "Enjoy your not-date tonight, Bryn. See you tomorrow—on the floor."

Bryn raised a hand and hurried to her own vehicle as the wind cut through the parking structure again. She and Nick would have fun tonight. That didn't make it a date.

Not a date. Not a date. This is not a date.

The fact that Bryn had had to remind herself of that fact as she strolled to Nick's door was not a good sign.

He's leaving. He just got here, and he's already thinking of leaving. Focus on that.

Boston was her place. She'd love to travel, vacation abroad or visit all fifty states, but this city—it was where she felt at peace.

And part of her wished Nick felt that, too.

She raised her hand to knock, not nearly as secure as she wanted to be in her determination that this friendship with Nick was just that. A way to pull her from her hibernation and help him get familiar with Boston before he vanished and started the process all over again.

"Bryn." His smile was infectious, and the invisible chain that seemed to tug on her heart whenever he was around tightened a little further.

"I really can't thank you enough for choosing a tree with me." He closed the door and stepped into the hallway. "No Honey tonight?"

"Oh." Bryn blinked and looked to her side, well aware that she'd left Honey at home but not quite knowing how to respond. "I left her at the apartment. Afraid all you have tonight is just me." Guess that should've cleared up any questions she had about this being a date. No one expected someone to bring their dog, even one they'd trained as a therapy animal, on a date.

"Well, 'just Bryn' is wonderful, too." Nick leaned closer, his spicy scent wrapping through her before he yanked his head back.

For a moment, she'd thought he might kiss her. She'd nearly closed the distance between them. That would've been an embarrassing gaffe.

It didn't happen.

But that she thought it could…

"So, Mitchell's sells the best trees?"

"Yes. And it's close. By the time you find parking, it will probably be easiest to get one we can carry back here on our own."

"That's fine. If you don't mind." Nick buried his hands into his pockets. No chance of holding hands...which made sense.

So why did it bother her? "Of course not."

"Did you get your tree there?"

"Oh, no. I have a fake fir." The idea of a real tree made her shudder. She'd never have one, not in any place she slept. Not again.

His eyebrows pulled together. "Really? I would've pegged you as a real-tree gal."

"Nope. My mom liked real trees, but the danger with them..." She shrugged as the horrid night their apartment had nearly caught fire ran through her memory.

A week after Christmas, her father had called her mother after Bryn had gone to sleep. Popping in like he did. And like always, her mother had gotten excited that maybe this time was different. Maybe this time he'd stay. He hadn't even wanted to come to the apartment...a red flag her mom should've seen.

But then, who was Bryn to judge missing red flags?

"They aren't dangerous if you keep them watered, make sure the lights aren't on when you aren't around and get rid of them right after Christmas."

"Said like someone who never put a fire out." Bryn laughed, but there was nothing funny about the situation. It was only because she'd gotten up after a bad dream that she'd been awake for the first spark.

"You put a fire out?"

"A small one." She bit her lip. "I was looking for my mom." She hadn't found her, but that wasn't information she needed to share. "There was a little smoke on the tree. I think I thought I was still dreaming. I pulled the lights...which was good because after the spark caught, I threw water on it. The smoke alarm went off, but there wasn't any damage beyond the tree."

"That would make me purchase a fake tree, too." Nick's hand swung by hers.

What would he do if she reached for it?

Bryn mentally shook that thought away. *Not a date... remember.*

She hadn't held hands with anyone in so long. Hadn't really touched someone. It was a funny feeling. She gave hugs and small touches to her patients when they asked. And she'd hugged Nick the other night, held him tightly while he'd dealt with his own internal turmoil. But how long had it been since someone had reached out to her?

Offered her comfort?

The answer was, sadly, far too long.

"Where was your mother?"

His question shook her morose thoughts loose. Unfortunately, there was no happy answer there, either.

"Out with my father. He wasn't..." What were the best words here? Her father lacked so many things. "Wasn't around much." That was one way to put neglectful, mean, vindictive, absent.

"And not like mine?" Nick's arm slid around her shoulders. "Mine slept at the office far too often, but his home, the one he'd claim—even if he rarely rested there, was ours."

He squeezed her, and she leaned her head against his shoulder. The support he was offering was sweet. "No. Not like yours. Richard Bedford wandered throughout his thirty-six-year marriage. Mom always thought he'd come around. She really loved him. He...he loves himself."

Nick squeezed her one more time, then dropped his arm. Bryn lifted her head, grateful for the comfort, even if she wished he'd hold her a few minutes longer.

"So, you made a good point regarding safety issues. I think maybe we should grab a fake tree. We can pick up some ornaments, too."

"Nick..." Bryn hit her hip against his as she pointed to

Mitchell's up the corner. "My issues with real trees don't have to impact what you put in your apartment."

"They don't have to, but..."

The silence that hung on that *but* was nearly deafening.

She wanted to push. Wanted to pull whatever words he wasn't saying into the open.

"But..." He looked at her, his brown eyes staring directly into her soul. "But..."

"Three *buts*. Off to a good start there, Nick."

"Real trees make you nervous, right?"

"Right." Bryn shook her head, not quite understanding where he was going.

"Well, if I plan to have you in my place, you know, for area familiarization and everything, I don't want you to be uncomfortable." Nick's dark cheeks were just a shade darker, and Bryn suspected they were full of heat.

Her cheeks certainly were.

"That's very kind of you."

Nick offered his arm, and she took it as they walked back to his car and headed to grab a tree. A fake tree.

Her throat tightened. It was the kindest thing anyone had done for Bryn in forever.

"It's bright."

Bryn's words were kind, but Nick knew she was searching for more and not finding them. There wasn't a lot you could say. His tree was fine. That was the best descriptor he could use for the blue-and-red monstrosity.

"Why did I only buy red ornaments?"

Her giggle made up for the very un-holiday-looking tree in the corner. "Well, if you had bought a regular green fir-looking one, it would look festive in the traditional way."

"They had blue Christmas trees, Bryn!" He pointed to the tree. How could he possibly choose a plain tree when there were other options? "And purple and orange. I mean, if you're going to have a fake tree, why not go snazzy?"

It would've been a good argument if he'd picked different ornaments.

"Snazzy is great...but the bright red on the electric blue is...a look."

A look was as good descriptor for what was happening in the corner of his apartment. "It *is* a lot."

"Sure." Bryn stepped next to him, tilting her head as she looked at the tree. "I bet it's brighter than any tree you've had before."

"We didn't have trees."

Her head shifted, and her body moved just a bit closer to his. Not quite touching, but close enough to add comfort quickly after his words.

His family celebrated Christmas, just not with much fuss... and that included trees. It was hard to complain when they'd had stockings and piles of presents in the corner.

But presents didn't compensate for growing up alone. Nick wondered if his parents had used so many gifts to make up for not being around, for pushing them to become the picture of service...their vision of service.

"I see."

"Mom was often stationed in different places than us. Dad..." Nick crossed then uncrossed his arms as he looked at the tree. "Well, Dad's attention wasn't ever very focused on decorations."

Unless we were performing something he could brag about or salute.

Her hand slipped into his, and she squeezed it.

It was nice. No, that wasn't the right descriptor. It was so much more than that. Something had shifted the day he'd met Bryn. It was like his heart had met a kindred soul.

A person it wanted in his life. A person supposed to be in

his life. But was that fair when he knew he wasn't planning to stay where Bryn would always feel at home?

And was it selfish that so much of him didn't care? He wanted Bryn in his life. Needed her in a way he couldn't put into words. At least for as long as he stayed in Boston.

"Well, then maybe this is a new tradition for you. Each year, you do your best to add one new Christmas decoration."

"What goes with this tree?" Nick laughed. It really was the opposite of what he'd been going for. But he'd spent the night hanging out with Bryn, so he couldn't get too upset that this tree wasn't like the ones he'd seen in friend's houses and magazines growing up.

The general might not've been big on decorations, but he would hate this one!

Part of Nick wanted to celebrate that. The rebel in himself. The one who'd bucked the family tradition.

Another part wanted to put the tree back in the box, return it and get something more "traditional." Which wouldn't matter because it wasn't like his father would ever see it.

"There are people that do themes for their decorations. You could make yours the decor version of the ugly Christmas sweater." She giggled, then covered her mouth.

"What's your theme?" Her green eyes caught his, and Nick couldn't look away if he'd wanted to.

The world seemed to hang on this moment. This pinpoint in time that was just for them. The universe holding its breath as they looked at each other.

It was a moment of nothing and everything all at once. Such a fancy phrase. One he'd heard romantics utter some variation of but he'd never experienced it, never believed in its existence.

Until he'd met the woman beside him. How was it possible to share not one but multiple versions of this with a person?

"I don't have one. Not really. Ailani says my decorations make the apartment feel cozy."

Cozy.

What a descriptor. He bet her place felt like a home. Warm and cozy.

"I buy the decorations that make me happy. My tree is full of these angels. They release a new version each year. My grandmother used to give me one every year as part of my Christmas presents. My ex always got upset because he said the tree was half angels."

Nick put his arm around her waist, and she leaned her head against his shoulder. This should've felt awkward. In theory, they were closer to strangers than anything else. He'd worked with colleagues in med school for four years knowing nothing more than their names and the specialty they'd wanted to practice.

With Bryn, everything felt like a puzzle piece clicking into the perfect place.

"When she passed, my mom continued the tradition, and a few years ago when she died, I bought them for myself."

Because her ex wouldn't.

She didn't say the words, but he could hear them on the edge of the soft tone.

"I haven't bought this year's." She let out a sigh. "With everything from last year and my not-stuck-to plan to ignore the holiday, I never got it. Missing that one won't make much of a difference. Like I said, my tree is nearly full of them."

She needed that ornament. Pure and simple. He wasn't exactly sure where to find it, but he would.

She looked at her watch, and he knew this signal. Bryn was getting ready to leave. It was late, and they'd been together for hours. Yet it wasn't enough time.

He was starting to suspect there might never be *enough* time with Bryn.

"Honey needs to be walked?" His voice was soft, the question hanging between them.

"No. Ailani said she'd handle it." Bryn pursed her lips as her green eyes connected with his.

What would she do if he leaned his head? If he dropped his lips to hers? She was so close. A head tilt, a lowering of the gaze, movement universally acknowledged by lovers as they led up to a first kiss.

"Bryn." Her name on the tip of his tongue made him ache to follow through with the motion.

This was the moment. The one he'd remember forever. Long after he'd left Boston.

The thought was enough to make him start.

And she pulled back. A look passing across her features that he couldn't quite register. Hurt? Or relief?

Nick didn't know. But the moment was lost, and his heart ached that he might never find it again.

"I look forward to seeing you in nursing scrubs, Bryn." He slapped his head with his hand. "I swear that was not the worst pickup line. It was real—"

"A real pickup line?" Her blond brow rose.

"No." Well, he'd found awkward. Found it and dived right past it into the pool of shame.

"I just meant it will be nice to see you on the floor. Nursing. Though I know everyone will miss Honey, too." He blew out a breath, knowing that hadn't salvaged the interaction.

From nearly kissing to sticking both of his feet in his mouth.

"I'll see you tomorrow." She raised her hand, and for the longest second, he thought she might cup his cheek.

If she did, he'd drop his lips to hers and explore whatever was between them.

Instead, she pushed her hand against his shoulder. "It's a nice tree. Bright, but nice. And yours. Good night, Nick."

"Good night, Bryn."

CHAPTER SEVEN

"You ready?" Liz's bright smile did little to ease Bryn's mind as she stepped into the locker room. That wasn't the radiologist tech's fault, though.

She was starting nursing today. Stepping back into the role that felt so foreign after Ethan had walked out on their relationship. And once again she was crushing on a coworker.

She'd been so sure Nick was going to kiss her last night. So sure his lips would brush hers. Her body had ached for the moment. Then he'd pulled back.

Hurt and relief had rushed through her all at once. Then she'd had to stop herself from cupping his cheek. Who did that!

Someone who wanted to be kissed.

"Ready as I can be." At least that was true. "My roommate told me adventure can be thrilling and terrifying."

"That's a good line." Liz pulled off her coat.

"I can't believe I'm here without Honey." The hospital was keeping her as a nurse seventy percent and a therapy handler at thirty percent. So she'd still be here one day a week with Honey, but it felt wrong to be here without her furry friend by her side.

"It is a little weird. I know you spend most your time on the pediatric floor, but everyone in the hospital loves her and her cute little outfits."

"How could they not!" Bryn laughed as she searched for

her allocated locker. Thinking about Honey almost drove her thoughts away from Nick. Almost.

"Oliver." Liz raised a hand as the other radiology tech pushed through the door. "He's quite the cutie, huh." The last comment was muttered in an undertone.

Liz had waved with such fanfare Bryn couldn't stop the giggle rising in her throat. The radiologist tech was pure fun. It was a shame she didn't get to work with her more. Liz, like Nick, had lived all over. Bryn loved hearing her stories about starting over, finding new things. Ailani had done the same—chosen her own adventure.

Maybe it was something Bryn should investigate more closely. Even if it meant leaving Boston?

Her heart clenched at the idea, and she pushed it aside.

Oliver smiled at Liz, his eyes rooted on her.

It looked like Liz's crush was reciprocated. If only it were as easy for Bryn to read Nick.

Her belly did a little flip as she saw the doctor himself step into the room.

"First day should be pretty easy for you." Liz grinned. "No awkward meeting-your-new-colleagues moments."

"Because everyone already loves Bryn," Nick stated as he eased into the conversation.

"*Love* is a strong word." Bryn knew her cheeks were flaming, and she hoped Nick would chalk it up to nerves from the first day, rather than the mountain of emotions pressing against every nerve in her body as the gorgeous pediatrician stepped to her side.

"But an accurate one," Nick said.

Bryn dipped her head and waited as a Liz and Oliver rushed out with a wave. The air in the small room seemed to evaporate as Nick stood next to her and a small silence descended.

Bryn consciously breathed in and out, hyperaware of the man beside her. Had he thought about last night? Did he even realize she'd thought he was going to kiss her? That she'd wanted it?

Probably not.

Nick had promised to help her step out of her hibernation. He was doing brilliantly, but for reasons she hadn't expected. She was supposed to be stepping back into nursing. Experiencing the holidays...

And instead, it was her heart wakening. That was not supposed to be in the cards.

The windows were open, but the heat between the occupants didn't seem to cool at all.

"I wonder what new treats are in the break room this morning." Nick's eyes were bright as he glanced at her. "It always smells like sugar. Whoever made the molasses cookies was an artist." He put his fingers to his lips, kissing them, then letting his hand open. The gesture was so relaxed. So loose and perfect.

And all Bryn could focus on was his lips. Nick's full, luscious lips that had been so close to hers less than twelve hours ago but not connected.

She needed to focus on something other than the hot doc. Which should've been easy since she was working the floor today. If she was at a new hospital, it might've been, but she knew everyone. This was a new position, not a new job, and those first-day butterflies were not an available distraction from Nick.

"I keep meaning to make iced sugar cookies." The words came out as Bryn slid her bag into her locker. She'd worn her holiday scrubs today. Technically the hospital provided scrubs, but floor nurses could wear their own, if they paid for them.

Like clothes for Honey, Bryn had an entire closet of candy-cane, Santa and cookie scrubs for this time of year. It was festive, and the patients loved it.

"Iced cookies?" Nick leaned his shoulder against the other side of the locker. "Like splattered with icing and sprinkles or fancy decorated?" He raised his brows, his smile ripping through her.

"Fancy." Bryn shrugged. "I told you I used to holiday out! I took a class a few years ago on cookie and cake decorating. They are very pretty. Want to help me make some?"

The question flew out, and she couldn't help the hope that he'd say yes. Maybe that wasn't the smartest move after thinking he'd kiss her, but technically she was showing him around Boston and he was helping her find herself.

"You bet. Though not sure I'll be any help on the frosting side."

"It's how they taste that matters. And people buy the cookies no matter what. After all, Camp Heartlight is a good cause." Bryn shut her locker; it was time to get on with the day.

"It is." He righted himself and smiled. "Have a great first day, Bryn."

"Thanks, Nick."

Bryn was smiling as she stepped into a patient's room. Nick had caught a few glimpses of her today while he'd done rounds. Each time, she'd had a grin on her face.

Nursing was a noble profession. However, Nick thought it was important for people to understand that it was a job. One that should be respected, like all professions. If it was just a job for some individuals, something that they did because it was interesting or made a good wage, that was all right.

For some, though, it was a true calling—the place where their spirit felt most at home.

And Bryn was one of those people. It was why she'd not been able to fully leave the profession after everything that had happened with her ex.

"Dr. Walker?"

Nick turned to greet Dr. Izzy Jeong. "Yes, Dr. Jeong?"

"You treated a patient named Susan Cole—she goes by Susie, right?"

The name sent his spirits tumbling. "Yes. She presented with fainting..." He closed his eyes and tried to think through his days before it clicked. "Exactly a week ago. She was here my first day."

"A week ago. Exactly." Izzy looked at the tablet chart and let out a sigh. "You couldn't identify the cause?"

"No." Nick looked down the hall, not knowing which room was Susie's, but knowing she was here. And that meant she'd fainted again. Another fainting spell meant something was going on. But what?

"Her labs were perfect. Her EKG showed nothing. I told her mother that sometimes fainting spells happen. There is stress in the family."

"What family doesn't have stress?" Izzy tapped a few things out on the tablet.

"True." Everyone had things going on, but there'd been a look on Susie's mother's face. A sadness that had permeated the room. "The father isn't in the picture, but I don't think it's a divorce or dead-beat situation. Susie said she can't video call with him."

"Prison?"

Izzy's suggestion was possible. More than a million children in the US had an incarcerated parent, something that would add stress to any family.

"I don't know. But stress on any body, particularly a little one, could cause a fainting spell. However, more than one a week apart?"

"Not unheard of." Izzy frowned and looked down the hall to the patients' rooms.

"But unlikely." Nick blew out a breath. "I take it she's your patient for this admit?"

Izzy nodded. "I've called for an internal-medicine consult. The blood work the ER did isn't hitting any red flags, and once again, the EKG is perfect."

"I hate this kind of case." Nick crossed his arms, then uncrossed them. People expected doctors to have all the answers. It was why they went to school for so many years. They knew a lot, and usually the answer was discernible.

When it wasn't... A chill sunk through his nerves. They hadn't exhausted the options. He'd not travel the route of worst-case scenarios. Not yet.

Maybe Internal Medicine would crack the case.

"They're sending Kalista Mitchell—second-year resident in Internal Medicine. She should be here within the hour, or so they say."

Nick agreed with the frustration. It wasn't the specialty department's fault. They were in high demand, but when given a time estimate, he often mentally doubled it.

"I hate not being able to give her mom an answer." Izzy's hand ran along her belly, then darted back to the tablet chart.

"Susie's back." Bryn's distressed voice was soft as she stepped next to him.

He must've been worried to miss her walking up. "Dr. Jeong just told me. And once again, she's presenting as fine."

Bryn let out a noncommittal noise. Was she traveling the worst-case-scenario lines, too?

"I've requested a consult from internal-medicine." Izzy looked at Bryn. "She saw Honey—that was in her chart. Did you notice anything when she visited with the dog? I'm grasping at straws, and I understand that."

Bryn closed her eyes and crossed her arms. "She loved Honey. She complained about not being able to video chat with her dad. Her mom seemed stressed. If there was anything else, I don't recall it."

"You and Dr. Walker are on the same wavelength. That's almost word for word what he said." Izzy chuckled.

"Not helpful, but at least our memories are probably accurate." Bryn's eyes caught his, then looked away.

Izzy was right. They seemed to be on the same wavelength, the same chord, the same everything.

"Someone call for an IM consult?" The resident with red hair power walked toward them.

"Yes." Izzy looked a little surprised.

Honestly, Nick was, too. "That was quick. The order went in less than twenty minutes ago."

"I'd just finished with a patient, so could come straight here," Kalista explained. She nodded to Bryn, "It's nice to see you in nurse's scrubs, Bryn, but a little weird not to see a ball of golden fluff at your side."

Bryn gave her a broad smile. "That's what everyone says, Kali. I do sometimes find myself looking at the ground or snapping to bring her to my side. Habit."

"Bryn, can you come with us for the consult?" Izzy looked to Kali. "I really would like to get Susie's mom an answer, if we can."

"Absolutely."

"You'll fill me in?" Nick caught Bryn's gaze before she started off.

"Of course."

"Still no puppy."

Susie crossed her arms and glared at Bryn as she followed Izzy and Kalista through her door. It was the first thing Susie had said when Bryn had come to do vitals check.

"Susan."

The little girl's shoulders slumped as her head hit her chest. Clearly, her full name was only used when Susie was misbehaving.

"Sorry, Susie. Honey stayed home today."

"I want to go home, too."

"Of course you do." Kali slid next to the bed and offered Susie a smile. "My name is Dr. Mitchell. I'm going to ask you and your mom some questions and see if we can figure out why you keep visiting the hospital."

Visiting the hospital.

Bryn loved that terminology. Hospitals were scary places for kids and adults. Visiting seemed to lesson that some. She'd have to steal that line.

"I want to go home, and I want Daddy."

Susie's mother closed her eyes and bit her lip so hard, Bryn feared she was tasting blood. Then she seemed to shake herself and offered her daughter a watery smile. "I know, baby. Me, too."

Bryn looked to Izzy and saw the pediatrician shift her focus to Ellen, too.

"Have you eaten anything this month that's new? Anything you've never eaten before?" Kali asked Susie.

"Sugar cookies. I had sugar cookies. They had sprinkles. One was shaped like a tree, and the other was a round one with red icing. It turned my teeth red."

"You've had sugar cookies before, Susie," her mom interjected. "They just looked like regular cookies instead of Christmas cookies."

"The trees taste better. They do."

"They do." Kali nodded to Susie, then looked to Ellen. "Can you think of any new food introductions?"

"No. I haven't had a lot of time to experiment. It's been mostly boxed mac and cheese and hot dogs."

"Mac and cheese is one of my favorites, too." Kali's words were bright and directed to Ellen.

Bryn knew parents feared judgment when their kids were in the hospital. That parent blogs and social media had made some feel inadequate if they couldn't make a homemade three-course feast three times a day with organic fruits and veggies.

Kids needed love and attention. Mac and cheese was fine.

"All right, so no new food introductions. Tell me what was happening right before each fainting incident."

"I wanted raisins and to talk to Daddy."

Kali tilted her head as she looked at Susie. Kali had posed

the question to Ellen, but Susie answering was fine, too. It also meant that she remembered the incidents.

"How did you feel then?" Izzy directed her question at Susie but looked toward Ellen briefly.

"Mad. I know that's bad, but I feel mad sometimes."

"Being mad isn't bad," Ellen's voice was tired, and Bryn stepped beside her. Susie's mother looked like she needed to sleep for three days and then spend a week at a day spa.

Unfortunately, there was no way for Bryn to offer such relief. If Honey were here, she could park her right next to Ellen and let her pet the dog. It wouldn't clear all the stress, but it would help.

"That's right." Kali added, "It's an emotion we all get. But when you were mad, did your body feel anything?"

Susie's eyebrows narrowed. "It felt like my body." The tone was one only a small child could offer. Like she thought the adults were asking the dumbest things.

"I know it sounds like a silly question." Kali winked, then looked at Izzy. "The EKG was fine?"

"Yes. And we ran another this morning."

Kali nodded, then pulled a sticker out of her pocket. "Thank you for answering my questions, Susie."

"No other doctor gave me a sticker." She ripped the back off and stuck it to her gown, her grin brilliant.

If she hadn't fainted twice, Bryn would say Susie was in perfect health.

Kali looked to Izzy, then to Ellen. "I'm going to run my thoughts by my attending. They will be in sometime later to talk to you."

"Thank you." Ellen nodded, but Bryn could see the frustration pooling in her. She wanted answers, and the two doctors didn't have one.

"Will they have stickers?"

"I don't know, Susie, but I'll let them know you like stickers." Kali offered the little one a smile.

"And dogs. I like dogs."

Bryn had to cover her lips to keep from laughing. There was no way to promise Susie that she'd bring Honey to see her. With luck, Susie wouldn't be here the next time she had the therapy dog.

"I'll tell Honey you said hi when I get home." Bryn could tell Susie didn't like that answer, but she didn't argue as the medical professionals left for the hallway.

"So, what are you planning to tell your attending?" Izzy's voice was tight. "Because I want to give Ellen some idea of what is happening if we can."

"Honestly, I wonder if it's heart related. She looks very healthy. Many things can cause fainting. Lung and brain cancer, kidney disease to list just a few of the most dangerous, but it can also be brought on by stress and is fairly easy to correct."

"The mad comment?" Bryn raised a brow. It didn't surprise her that Susie didn't have words to describe how her body felt. At five, it would have to be a big pain moment. That it wasn't… well, that was actually a good thing. Though it added to the mystery of the diagnosis.

"An EKG only catches the heart in real time. Not a previous episode. I'm Internal Medicine. I'm not saying it isn't an infection or a chronic condition, but I think ruling out heart conditions is step one."

"Any idea how long the wait is to get a pediatric cardiologist? With multiple clear EKGs, she doesn't qualify to see one here. And pushing it as a priority will be a difficult sell with the insurance company." Izzy looked like she wanted to stamp her feet.

Bryn knew she was frowning. The fact that insurance and a patient's ability to pay were such drivers was difficult for most medical professionals, but it was an unfortunate part of the medical systems.

"Maybe my attending will have a better answer. I'll talk

to them, hopefully get some answers soon." Kali walked off, and Izzy leaned against the wall.

"You all right?"

Izzy was usually bright and sunshiny, but she looked a little worn today. Maybe it was just Susie, but Bryn wondered if there was something else.

"Just a little tired."

"'Tis the season." Holiday cheer wasn't the only thing passed around this time of year, after all.

"True." Izzy smiled, but Bryn could see that it was an effort.

"You'll let me know if you need anything?"

"Of course. Thanks for checking, Bryn." She pushed off the wall and headed to her next patient.

Bryn looked at the closed door, wishing there was something she could do for Ellen and Susie, but coming up with a big fat nothing.

CHAPTER EIGHT

"FIRST DAY OVER!" Nick beamed as Bryn stepped beside him to wait for the elevator.

"It is." Bryn closed her eyes for a moment. "It was a good day, other than not finding an answer on Susie's fainting spells."

"Izzy told me they're recommending Susie see a cardiologist."

Bryn blew out a breath as she looked back over her shoulder.

The first day was always exhausting. He was glad that Izzy had filled in the information for him. But he also understood how unsettling a shift without answers for a patient was.

Kali's attending agreed that a heart condition needed to be ruled out before they went further down the medical-oddity list of conditions. They also thought it was safe to discharge her with orders to follow up with a pediatric cardiologist.

Nick didn't know if Ellen had been told that yet, but assuming her vitals remained stable, Susie was going home soon—again.

Hopefully, she wouldn't be back at Beacon. It was one of the weird things about this job. You got close to patients, helped them on the road to health and then, if you were lucky, you didn't see them again.

The elevator doors opened, and Nick frowned. He hadn't gotten to see Bryn much on the floor—the nature of the job keeping them busy. And he wasn't quite ready to say good-night.

They started toward the parking garage, and he wondered if it was too much to ask if she wanted to grab a drink or some dessert after a long day.

"Just answer your damn phone!"

Bryn was moving before he could quite register who'd called out.

"Ellen." Bryn's tone was commanding but gentle. "Ellen."

Susie's mother turned, and Nick's heart broke at her red eyes and tear-stained cheeks.

Bryn didn't say anything else. She just opened her arms. Ellen waited only a microsecond before stepping into them and bursting out sobbing. Bryn held her.

And Nick waited. He wasn't sure his presence would be helpful, but until he knew why she was so upset, he wasn't leaving.

"So-sorry." A sob broke the word as Ellen stepped back and wiped at her eyes. The action wouldn't do much, but it was a comforting motion.

"It's fine." Bryn's voice was soft now, the understanding nurse rather than the commanding one. "Nick—Dr. Walker— and I didn't have any plans. Right?"

"Nope. No plans." He'd been trying to think of one, but that wasn't the point right now.

"Were you trying to get a hold of your husband?"

"Oh." Ellen crossed her arms around her waist. She looked tiny and so worn out. "No. Jack can't..." Her words trailed off. "He's not available right now."

Not available right now.

Such a cool statement. One that could have dozens of meanings.

"I was actually trying to reach one of our senators." Ellen let out a bitter laugh. "Not that they ever answer. That voicemail won't see one of their staffers reaching out. Though all of my polite requests haven't gotten me return phone calls, either."

"Is there anything we can do?" Bryn looked at Nick, and he shrugged.

If Ellen was calling senators, he didn't know what the two of them might be able to do. His father was connected to more politicians than anyone else Nick knew. But that level of contact was reserved for so few. It was the reason his father's military consulting business made so much money following his retirement.

"Either of you know the president?" Ellen pulled on her neck, then looked at her watch.

"No," Bryn and Nick said at the same time.

"Why do you need the president?" Nick wasn't sure why Susie's mother would need to contact senators, let alone ask if they knew the president in a way that he was fairly sure was a joke but also a hopeful statement that maybe, just maybe, she might get lucky.

"It doesn't matter." Ellen shook her head. "I need to get back before Susie wakes up. If I'm not there, she'll worry."

She looked at Bryn. "Thank you for the hug—I didn't realize how much I needed it." Then she headed back inside before either he or Bryn could say anything else.

"What just happened?"

"Honestly... I have no idea." Nick looked at the closed hospital doors, not sure what to make of this encounter. "But your reaction was perfect. She needed that hug."

"Just doing my job."

But she wasn't on the clock. It was like Bryn instinctively knew what people needed and acted to ensure they got it. It was admirable, but he suspected it was also exhausting.

"Any chance you want to grab a drink?"

Her question sent most of the worries about Ellen from his mind. "I'd love one."

"Great." She made a face, and he held his breath. "Oh no. I need to go home—Honey."

"I understand." And he did. Honey had been home by herself today. He was sure Bryn had worked out a way for the dog to get fed and walked, but that wasn't the same as having her person home.

"Do you want to get a drink at my place? I have wine."

Nick couldn't think of anywhere else he'd rather be. "Point me in the direction and I'm there."

Bryn pulled out her phone, and a few seconds later his phone dinged. "That's the address. Give me an hour, then…" She shrugged, and there was a hint of color in her cheeks.

"I'll see you soon." Nick thought he might be dancing on air as he headed for his car.

Bryn's hair was still wet as she looked in the mirror and assessed the fourth outfit she'd thrown on after taking Honey out for a walk and grabbing the quickest shower known to humankind. Maybe she should have told Nick to give her two hours.

That would only have given her more time to overthink the outfit she was wearing.

Ailani was out tonight, but still. Her place! What had she been thinking?

It had just seemed like such a natural response. One her heart had offered before her brain could work through any of the potential complications.

So now she was standing in front of her mirror in a plain white T-shirt and comfy athleisure pants, wondering if she was too dressed down for this. Maybe a pair of jeans…but she was off work and just wanted to relax, and that meant no buttons.

Still… Bryn started toward the closet when her phone buzzed.

Here.

Such a simple text, but her heart skipped a beat. She looked at the pants and huffed. Honey tilted her head at the noise, and Bryn petted the dog's head before heading to the door. "I guess this will have to work."

She opened the door and nearly let out a sigh as Nick stood before her in a light blue T-shirt and jeans that hugged his waist so perfectly.

"Hi, Honey." Nick bent down and rubbed the dog's ears.

Bryn's face heated—she'd been worried about what she was wearing, and the first thing Nick had noticed was the dog.

It's a good thing, Bryn.

This was a simple crush. One she needed to push past. Nick was a coworker and one that rambled to new places when the urge to run struck. A man she could fall for. So easily. And that just meant getting her heart broken.

One heartbreak per life was more than enough.

"Why don't you come in? If you sit on the couch, you can give Honey all the love while I get the wine."

Nick stepped into the apartment and immediately moved toward the tree. "So, these are the angels?"

"Oh." Bryn moved to stand beside him as he gazed at her tree. It was a hodgepodge of ornaments. No theme—angels from her grandmother and mother, a few penguins she'd found funny and ornaments some children at Brigham had made her.

"It's homey and much cuter than mine."

"Well—" Bryn chuckled "—it's certainly not as loud."

Nick's hip bumped hers, and desire pushed through her. How did he kiss? With softness…or a possessive drive that made you forget all your thoughts and sink into a need that was simply Nick?

Her body burned, with no outlet for release. "Do you prefer red or white?"

"Whichever you like."

Bryn shook her head. "You really should choose. I prefer sweet reds. The brand I like is pretty cheap. And it's not for everyone. I remember the first time I poured it for…" Her words cut off.

Ethan wasn't here, and it didn't matter that he'd flipped out that she'd buy such cheap wine, never mind that she enjoyed it.

"I always keep a few bottles for guests that are nicer quality."

Nick was frowning, the deep lines in his forehead making her nervous. She'd gotten good at reading Ethan's and her mother's moods. Bryn knew exactly what each frown meant, what the smile that was just a tad off indicated.

"Are you all right? If I did..."

"Bryn, I'm not your ex. Who, honestly, if I met the man, I'd say some pretty sharp things to."

"Oh. I know you aren't." That wasn't something Bryn worried over. Nick was about as far away from Ethan as possible. She just wanted him to feel welcome in her home. Wanted...

The urge to clear her throat pulled at her, but Bryn just smiled.

"You watch my moods, don't you?" Another expression she couldn't read passed across his gorgeous features.

"I watch everyone's moods. Nurse superpower." This wasn't a big deal.

Nick raised a brow but didn't comment. "The sweet red is fine. I'm here for the company."

Honey pressed her head against his thigh and let out a soft bark.

"Honey." Bryn pursed her lips as the dog laid a good portion of her weight against Nick. "That isn't polite. Though he came for your company."

"I came for yours. Honey is just an added fluffy perk."

She moved into the kitchen, grabbed the glasses and poured. When she came back into the living room, Nick was looking at one of the angel ornaments.

"You're really fascinated with the angels." She handed him the glass, very conscious of his fingers touching hers.

The heat of the connection, the look in his dark eyes. If

energy fields were real, she was certain that hers and Nick's would burn brightly every time they were near each other.

"They're important to you."

She bit her bottom lip as she felt it tremble. Four words. Four words no one ever said to her. Her mother had loved her. Bryn had never doubted her, but she'd been an extension of her father in some ways—something that had kept her mom tethered, for better or worse, to a man she'd loved but who couldn't love her back.

"You can see that whoever is designing them has changed their art over time. The more recent ones," Nick held up the box with last year's date, "have much more descriptive faces versus this one." He pointed to the oldest in her collection.

"Yeah." Bryn took a sip of her wine, the sweet taste hitting her tongue. "I don't have the oldest one. It came out the year I was born, and my grandmother didn't start my collection until my first birthday. I looked for it once. You can find them, but the few that are out there are true collector's items."

Nick made a face, then, in a joking voice, said, "Unopened, new in box."

Bryn giggled. "Yes. Exactly."

"I had a friend in college that loved this comic character—not sure which one. But he'd go to conventions and always get frustrated. The prices put a lot of the collectors' items out of reach for those that truly loved the comic."

"It can seem like a status symbol. Though who would think Christmas ornaments would be so desirable?"

"True." Nick winked. "So now we have something very serious to discuss."

Her breath caught in the back of her throat. "We do?" Was he going to broach the heat between them?

"What day are we frosting cookies, and do you want to do it at my place or yours?"

Bryn knew her mouth was hanging open. Every thought

had left her brain. Her mind knew she needed to say something. Anything.

Cookies. She was thinking of kisses. Of running her hands over his glorious body. Trailing her mouth across his jaw. And he was thinking of cookies for the bake sale.

What was she supposed to say? Something. She needed to say something. Like now. Words. She needed words.

Speak!

Wow, the silence was really deafening.

"We *are* baking cookies, right?"

"Yeah. Of course. Umm… Frosted cookies need to be baked the day before. I can bake them tomorrow. Then we can decorate them the day after. You have the bigger kitchen, so I can just bring them there. And Honey won't get in our way."

There—she'd said the words. Forced them out. Now it was time to change the subject.

"So, why don't we watch a movie? I've been dying to watch a sappy made-for-television movie."

"Operation Get Bryn to Celebrate Christmas is working." Nick beamed as he moved with her. "I love watching movies after a long day. It's my top way of relaxing."

She nodded, not quite trusting herself to speak the truth. Holiday movies were the last thing on her mind—it was just the first thing she'd thought of. But putting on a movie would keep the conversation down, lessen the chance she might say something embarrassing or, worst of all, confess her crush.

She grabbed the remote and saw a look pass over his face as she slid into the oversized chair next to the couch. Was he disappointed she was in the chair? Or was Bryn was reading into something, hoping…?

CHAPTER NINE

COOKIES. NICK HAD asked Bryn about when they would be decorating cookies. Two days later and he still wanted to slap himself. That was the exact opposite of the question he'd wanted to ask.

He'd wanted to ask if he could kiss her. If she felt the heat between them. If she thought of him as often as he thought of her. If her life felt right when he was with her.

If the answer was no, he'd move past it. She was a person he wanted in his life.

The other night had been the perfect opportunity, and he'd misstepped from moment one. Bending down to look at Honey, to keep from telling her how beautiful she'd looked. How tempting the relaxed outfit had been.

Then he'd asked about cookies, and she'd sat in the chair instead of beside him during the movie. The one good thing was he now knew exactly which kind of angel ornament he was looking for.

At least she was coming to his place after this shift. Cookie decorating and maybe another chance...

"Dr. Walker?"

Nick turned to greet Dr. Iain MacKenzie, the man's thick Scottish accent always reminding him of the year his father had been stationed in England. He still wasn't sure what his father's job in North Yorkshire had been, but Nick had gotten to cross the border into Scotland nearly every weekend. The country was beautiful, and the people were exceptionally welcoming. It was one of his favorite places.

"You're taking over for me on this shift."

"Yep. You ready to head home?"

"So ready." Iain's voice was strained, so that meant there'd been a difficulty. Twelve-hour shifts were long no matter how they went, but some were longer than others.

"The patient in room three—Logan Anderson, sixteen. There's a surgeon coming from Brigham. His mother requested a second opinion regarding the surgery Dr. Lowes recommended for his broken tibia."

"A second opinion on a broken bone?" Second opinions weren't unheard of, and Nick encouraged them for difficult diagnoses. However, a broken bone rarely required one.

Iain nodded. "Dr. Lowes isn't thrilled. I guess it's a pretty cut-and-dry break. They need to put pins in to stabilize."

"And the sooner, the better." Bones tried to stitch themselves back together when they broke, and the process moved even faster in small limbs since kids hadn't stopped growing. If the bones started healing, the surgeon would have to re-break the bone to get it set—extending the healing time.

"That's what Dr. Lowes said. However, the mother is insisting and called the surgeon. A Dr. Pierson—know him?"

"No." Boston had twenty-five hospitals and twenty medical centers. There were doctors, surgeons, nurses and just about every other medical profession all over the city. Even if he'd been in the city for years, it was unlikely he'd know a quarter of the medical professionals outside of his own colleagues.

"Dr. Pierson is the best—at least according to Logan's mother. She wants him to look at the break and see if he'll accept the transfer to Brigham."

"Can't she just request a transfer? Patient's rights?" Nick looked at the notes on the tablet chart. Logan had broken his left leg in a skateboarding incident. He and another skateboarder had collided at an indoor track, and the other kid had landed on his leg at just the right angle.

"The parents are going through a divorce. His dad brought him here because it's the closest."

"Ah." Nick finished reading over the notes. Divorce was hard, even when people felt they were better off separated. When it wasn't amicable and children were involved, he'd seen some terrible things done for "the child's best."

"Does his mom feel Brigham is the better hospital, or is she mad at Dad?"

"Not sure, but she has primary custody. There's another twist—Dr. Pierson doesn't take every case. He's very much sought-after."

"I see." Nick barely controlled his desire to roll his eyes. Most physicians went into medicine to help patients. To solve complicated cases and bring people hope.

A not-insignificant number went in for prestige. Those were sometimes selective in the patients they took on—a way to add to that "prestige." It was something Nick had witnessed a handful of times but never understood.

"Not sure when he'll be here. I've instructed the nurses to keep Logan as comfortable as possible." Iain looked toward the room and frowned.

"We got it from here. Hopefully by the next time you're on shift, all this will be worked out without Logan going through the pain of transferring and he'll have had surgery and be getting ready for physical therapy." It would be nice to think that Logan might be discharged by then, but unfortunately an orthopedic break requiring pins likely meant the teen would be at the hospital for a while.

Iain nodded, looked at the room's closed door once more, then back at Nick. "Good luck."

"Thanks."

Bryn slipped out of room three, and Nick's feet moved before he could think through what he was going to say.

"How is Logan?"

Her green eyes seemed to look through him as she shrugged her shoulders.

"Bryn?"

"He's sleeping. Not overly restful, given his raised leg and the pain that even powerful narcotics won't fully dim."

"That's the best we can hope for, at least according to what Iain told me. So what's wrong?" Because something had upset her.

"His mother is difficult."

"Iain mentioned that as well." Bryn started down the hall, but Nick reached out and grabbed her arm. His touch was light and brief, but he wanted to pull her into his arms. Whatever the mother had said, it must have been short. "Bryn. Talk to me."

She looked at the place where his hand had just been, then ran a hand over where he'd touched. "Mom wants her son at Brigham. She thinks we're all mediocre, for reasons that don't bear repeating, and she's upset that her son is so heavily medicated."

"He has a compound fracture." Nick blinked, knowing his face must've been a mixture of horror and shock. What parent wouldn't want their child as comfortable as possible in this situation?

"He does. But she's focusing on making a point to her soon-to-be ex-husband."

"A point. What point could that possibly be?" Fury rattled through him as he took a deep breath. His parents' union had been unique. Most marriages would not have survived the distance and sometimes years apart. It certainly wasn't the type of union Nick would want, but it seemed to work for them. And his parents would never have proved a point to each other by weaponizing their children.

"That he needs her. That without her people get hurt, that he isn't capable." Bryn looked over his shoulder back at the room. "It's clear she's using Logan as a pawn. It's the image of the family, though, I think. Not love that she's upset about. But then, I don't know, she just screamed at me, not at her husband—who wasn't in the room, and asked why her son was so sleepy."

That was a piece of intel that was good to know. "At least most parents aren't concerned with the family image."

She let out a sound that caused Nick's head to swivel. "Far too many see their children as pawns for the union they want. Not for the individuals they are."

"Bryn..." His heart broke at her tone. It felt like this wasn't about a difficult mother. At least not Logan's difficult mother. "Bryn," he repeated when she didn't look up, "you're enough." He wasn't sure what else to say.

Her eyes lifted, and she offered him a smile, though it was far from the brilliant one he saw so often in his dreams these days. "Thanks." She let out a sigh and looked back at the door. "I'm going to grab a quick cup of coffee in the cafeteria and push off this mood. I'll be back in ten minutes, all right?"

"We still on for cookies?" He understood that she needed a breather. Hell, there were days when all you could muster was a few minutes in the corner of the break room, but you took it—gathered the feelings patients brought up and moved forward.

"We'd better be. I have two dozen stars and two dozen trees we're supposed to make pretty." She nodded, then started down the hall. She looked back over her shoulder once, and he offered her a wave.

"You the one in charge of Logan Anderson?"

The gruff tone had to have come from Dr. Pierson. If the doctor took Logan and his mother signed the paperwork to move him, it would make the lives of everyone who was dealing with Logan's case easier. But based on Bryn's statement, Nick wasn't sure that was the best choice for the teen.

"Dr. Walker." He held out his hand as he turned. The tall white doctor didn't bother to offer his.

"Dr. Pierson, surgeon at Brigham Women's Hospital." His eyes held no friendly camaraderie, no warmth. "The patient?"

Perhaps he was an accomplished surgeon, but his mannerisms didn't make the best first impression. "He's in room three. Dr. MacKenzie got the full report from our ortho—"

"His mother called me. He has a fractured tibia. Not my usual case."

Usual case.

Nick hoped his face didn't display the disgust that statement brought. Private practice afforded doctors more choice in the types of patients they saw, but most used it to control how much time they had and to lower their caseload. Not to see a certain "type" of case.

"Do you specialize in ankles?" That might explain the frustration he saw from Dr. Pierson. If he specialized in ankles, he could do the tibia reconstruction, but it wouldn't be his typical case. Nick was trying to find something to let him give the surgeon at least some grace.

Anything.

"I specialize in complicated cases." Dr. Pierson cleared his throat. "Where is the patient?"

"Room three. His mother and father are with him."

Dr. Pierson walked off, and Nick moved with him. According to Iain, he had privileges at Beacon, but there was something about the doctor that made Nick uncomfortable. An air that screamed, *Not a good bedside manner.* Logan and his father had been through enough with the bad break—another ear to hear what the surgeon had to say wouldn't be a terrible thing.

"Nina." Dr. Pierson nodded to Logan's mother as he came into the room. The surgeon stepped to the side of the bed but didn't acknowledge Logan.

"Ethan, I'm so happy you made it."

Ethan? The name buzzed in the back of Nick's brain, but he couldn't quite understand why. He looked at the clock. A full minute in the room and Dr. Pierson had still not introduced himself to Logan.

"Yes, well…" Dr. Pierson let out a sigh. "Craig made sure I knew you wanted me to take a look. You could have asked for him, after all he is also an orthopedic surgeon—though not as good as me. Anyway, since he is looking for a new partner for his practice, I decided to indulge him."

"Yes. He and I have grown close." Nina's eyes shifted to her soon-to-be ex-husband.

Nick knew his eyes were wide, and Logan's father made eye contact with him. The man looked as horrified as Nick felt.

Logan needed surgery to set his leg, to make sure it healed properly. That was what mattered here, not some quid pro quo.

"Our divorce will be finalized in a few weeks." Logan's father sighed. "What matters is Logan's leg and getting him cared for."

"Which is what we're doing, Jeff." Nina offered a smile she didn't even attempt to make real. "You have your girl, and I am—"

"Linda is a colleague, not my girl—" Jeff held up his hands. "Nope. We aren't having this conversation. Dr. Pierson, thank you for coming. Are you going to take Logan's case?"

"No."

"Ethan!"

"Nina, this is a simple reconstruction—there is no need for my services. Transporting him will be painful and potentially do more damage."

Finally, something that was about the patient. Nick made a note in the tablet chart. Hopefully Logan could have surgery tomorrow at the latest.

"Simple!" Her face turned bright red, and she shook her fist in the air. "I will tell Craig."

"I'm sure you will, and I will ensure he understands that he's being used to make your husband jealous. Everyone will understand what is happening." Dr. Pierson's words were cool, but the daggers were clear in the tone.

"Have a good afternoon." He dipped his head, then turned and left without another word.

"When will my son get the surgery?" Jeff looked drained as he typed something out on his phone.

"Are you letting your lawyer know, still hoping for more custody?" Nina typed something out on her cell phone, not even looking at her son.

"I'm letting the office know that I won't be in for a few more days. And yes, I will use this with the lawyers. I'm thankful Logan slept through this, but he should be our priority."

"I'll make sure someone updates you when possible." Nick wanted out of the room, it was uncomfortable. He felt for Logan, but at least his father seemed focused on the boy.

He closed the door and saw Dr. Pierson at the end of the hall, leaning against the wall, his back to Nick. The posture made it clear he was talking to someone.

The surgeon had privileges at the hospital, but there was something about his posture, as if his purpose was intimidation.

Suddenly Bryn tried to step around him, but Ethan moved, blocking her.

Ethan.

The name clicked as Bryn's eyes met Nick's from across the distance. Ethan Pierson. Her ex-husband. The man who'd dumped her on their honeymoon.

Nick's feet were moving before he could think through his plan. Get to Bryn. Nothing else mattered.

"I see you've gone back to wearing ridiculous scrubs."

It was only as Bryn heard the words coming out of her ex-husband's mouth that her brain finally registered that he was here. At her hospital, looking at her with the same disappointed eyes.

A look that once would have sent her mind into overdrive trying to figure out what slight she must have done. She'd bent herself backward trying to be the perfect version of the wife Ethan had wanted. Broken herself to be what he'd desired. Bryn hadn't liked herself then, though she hadn't wanted to admit it. And it hadn't made Ethan love her, either.

So it didn't matter that he didn't like her fun scrubs. Not anymore.

Still, she felt her shoulders turn in, and the urge to make herself smaller hovered in her chest. The desire to apologize pulled at the back of her throat. Bryn wouldn't give into that, though. Not this time.

She liked the scrubs and so did the children. That was enough. But she also wasn't going to debate it with her ex-husband.

"If you'll excuse me, Ethan." She started to go around him, but he shifted, catching her just off guard.

Why was there no one in the halls? She swore this place was always busy, but it felt deserted now, when she needed someone…anyone!

"It's good to see you, Bryn." The tone was disingenuous, but if anyone passing heard it, they likely wouldn't think anything of it.

"Do you need something?" She was proud that she hadn't said *It's good to see you, too.* If the raise of his brow was an indicator, he'd expected that. Good. He deserved to be the one feeling out of control for once.

"I was seeing a patient. Broken leg that needs surgery. Basic stuff, really. At least for me."

Making a boy's trauma about himself. How typical. He hadn't even said the patient's name. Honestly, he might not've known it.

Logan. The teen who'd barely woken when she'd entered his room, despite his mother's constant complaints. And he'd tried to make his mother feel better, even exhausted and in pain.

How many times had she done that with her mother—tried to ease a pain that she couldn't ease? A pain her mother had held on to because letting it go would be even more painful.

"Logan." Bryn cleared her throat. "His name is Logan."

"I didn't check." That confirmation did not make her feel better. The same old Ethan.

"It's the bones that matter."

Bryn didn't bother to respond to that.

"Excuse me." She moved to the side, and her eyes caught Nick just before her ex's body cut him off from view.

Had Ethan always been this controlling? Maybe. Or maybe she'd just done whatever he'd asked.

That still makes him controlling, Bryn.

Ethan was too tall for her to see over his shoulder, but she hoped Nick was on his way. Things had been awkward since she'd thought he might kiss her, but she wanted him right now.

And only him.

"It's interesting seeing you in scrubs again. I thought you hung up your stethoscope after our divorce."

The harsh look in his eyes sent a chill down her spine. Their union had set a land-speed record from the altar to divorce court, but she still wished him well. Hoped that whatever it was he was looking for, he found.

She'd assumed he'd think the same for her. Apparently the age-old statement regarding assuming was far too accurate.

"It's new. I'm getting myself back—stethoscope included." It felt good to say.

So good.

"Bryn!" Nick's voice was bright as he pulled her to him, his lips pressing against hers possessively for just a moment before pulling back. "You were right—the blood work came back on Paisley. Thank you!"

She didn't know what to say. There was no patient named Paisley. No blood work. Nick was stepping in with flair.

"Sorry." Nick winked at Bryn before looking at Ethan.

Her ex-husband's cheeks were bright red. The relaxed posture he'd used to trap her had vanished into a rigid man oozing jealousy. He didn't want her...but he didn't want her to want someone else.

Well, too damn bad!

"We've been working on that case for a week, and Bryn... she's amazing."

Ethan opened his mouth, but Nick didn't wait for him to say anything.

"We still on for tonight, angel?"

"You know we are." Bryn smiled back, grateful for the gift he'd given her. Witnessing a speechless Ethan was priceless.

"When you get a moment, can you meet me in room seven? I need to discuss the results with Paisley's father."

And now he'd made a point of getting her away from Ethan. Nick was exactly what she needed...in more ways than one.

"Of course." Bryn nodded, knowing the room was empty.

Nick strolled off, and she didn't bother to hide her grin. Let Ethan think what he wanted.

"You're seeing someone?"

Bryn looked at him, finally seeing the monster she'd cried so many tears over. He wasn't owed any of her life. He'd given that up when he tossed his ring onto the bedside table on their honeymoon.

"That's not any of your business, Ethan." It was shocking how easy the words were, even though her brain was screaming, *Screw you.* "I've moved on. I suggest you do the same."

His mouth opened, but like Nick, she didn't stay to hear what he had to say. All her ex-husband's words had been exhausted—at least as far as she was concerned.

Her fingers ran along her lips. A kiss at the hospital wasn't exactly professional. And if anyone had seen it, she might've been a little perturbed. Though, honestly, probably not.

She'd thought of kissing Nick for the last week—really, since the moment she'd laid eyes on him.

Her only gripe about the encounter was how short the connection had been. But it had been powerful.

Possessive—but in the best way, like he'd claimed her, showed Ethan he had no power.

And he didn't. Not anymore. Nick had tossed the last of her reserve away when she'd met him. It was like he'd pulled the final cord on the box and let the real Bryn out.

That transformation was the reason there was a stethoscope in her pocket. The reason she'd pulled out her fun scrubs and decorated her tree the way she wanted to for the first time in years.

She was stepping into herself for the first time since she'd moved out of her mother's place, and she liked herself.

"Is he gone?" Nick's question was out before Bryn fully opened the door to room seven.

"He is. Listen, Nick—"

"I'm so sorry, Bryn. I shouldn't have kissed you. That was inappropriate. If you want to report me to Human Resources, I understand."

Nick's words sucked the heat from her body.

"It's fine." She heard the words leave her mouth, but her body locked down. Bryn was tumbling. The place she'd thought they'd been, the reason…

An apology. The first thing he'd given was an apology. And an offer to report himself to Human Resources.

Not a comment on how it had been too short. Or how it was a shame they'd had to have her ex-husband force the issue, even though it felt like they'd been moving to this point from moment one.

He leaves.

She was just supposed to help him adjust to Boston. It wasn't Nick's fault she was crushing on him. He'd broken up the encounter with Ethan in such a way that she'd never have to worry about him again. That should've been enough.

"Bryn."

She plastered on a smile. "It's fine, Nick. Better than fine. Ethan looked gobsmacked. I've never seen him speechless. Best early Christmas gift ever."

"And the kiss?"

What was she supposed to say? He'd apologized for it. So quickly.

"Was a kiss." That was an answer...not a great one, but better than blurting out that she'd wished it had been longer. That it had happened outside the hospital. In a place where they could explore.

"I'll see you tonight, all right?" She smiled but didn't wait for his response as she pulled on the door to leave.

Today had already been too much, and somehow she had to put her mask back on before they decorated cookies tonight. Maybe the kiss had been inappropriate. A thing to apologize for.

But Bryn had enjoyed it. And she craved more. So much more.

CHAPTER TEN

"THAT IS A lot of cookies." Ailani laughed as she helped Bryn pack up the last of the supplies for tonight's decorating extravaganza.

"It is." Bryn looked at the cookies, the icing, the little baggies she was planning to drop two cookies into apiece. "But it's for a good cause."

"Did you get any of Kali's solstice cookies?" Ailani closed her eyes and sighed. "They were so good. I could have eaten a dozen of them, but they were gone when I went back."

"I missed them. I had some of Leigh's lemon cookies, though. Very good."

"Well, I'm sure these will be delicious." Ailani followed Bryn down to the garage. "Think Nick has a knack for cookie decorating?"

"I don't know, but he seems to really want to try."

"Or…he wants to spend time with you."

The cool garage couldn't stop the heat flooding her cheeks. "He *does* want to spend time with me. As a friend."

"Uh-huh." Ailani chuckled. "The way he looks at you, like he's contemplating kisses… I'm sure friendship is exactly what's on his mind."

"Javi looks at you, too. I've seen it…when you walk by and aren't looking. More than friendly, some might say."

Now it was color flooding Ailani's cheeks. "I hope you have fun decorating, Bryn."

So they were officially disregarding this conversation. That was all right with her. After all, Nick had kissed her this afternoon, then promptly apologized.

"I don't know when I'll be back. Cookie decorating…"

"I've got Honey. Enjoy yourself. No one has a curfew tonight." Ailani waved before darting back to the stairwell.

Maybe she didn't want to hear Bryn's retort, or perhaps she was worried Bryn might bring up Javi again.

The man looked at Ailani. It was sweet, like he was thrilled she'd landed at his hospital. Which, if one thought of it, the odds of finding someone you connected with were so small. It was why her mother had tried so hard, too hard, to keep her father.

And it was the reason Bryn had tried to mold herself to fit Ethan's perfectionist ideal. Billions of people in the world and only one or two were really meant for you.

A fraction so small it was amazing anyone ever found lasting love. Nick's teddy-bear-brown eyes popped into her brain.

She cleared her throat and started the ignition. Her car rumbled to life, and she turned on the radio station that played holiday music twenty-four hours a day for the entire month of December.

Bryn belted out the tunes she loved, hoping they might ease the tension in her belly and knowing there was nothing that was going to stop her brain from thinking about Nick.

"I admit I didn't think there'd be so many cookie supplies." Nick's chuckle rumbled through her as he grabbed the bags of decorating supplies Bryn had hauled up to his front door. "If I'd known, I'd have just met you at your place."

But Ailani was at her place. Maybe that was the safest answer, but Bryn wanted to be here with him. Exquisite torture she might regret tomorrow, but that was future Bryn's problem.

"Is this your way of saying you've never held a piping bag?"

The flirty tone came so naturally around him. Was it even flirting if she was just being natural?

Another problem for future Bryn to ponder. Tonight she was just having fun.

"I don't even know what that is, Bryn." Nick set the bags on the floor, opened his apartment door and ushered her in.

Christmas music floated out of speakers. The tree they'd decorated was lit up in the corner. It still looked terrible, but he'd kept it.

"This is festive." And he'd done it for her. Nick wasn't into Christmas, at least not like Bryn. This was meant for her.

"Figured you'd like decorating to music. Though, if I'm wrong and this requires silence, then we can do that, too."

"This is perfect." She took the supplies to his kitchen, waited for him to set his stuff down, then opened the bag and pulled out a piping bag stuffed with green icing. "This is a piping bag, and it's going to be your best friend tonight."

"I kinda figured you'd be playing that role."

"I—" Words refused to trip from her tongue as she looked at him.

"But I can make friends with this, too." He winked and took the icing bag from her hand, setting it to the side. "I'm just glad you came."

"Why wouldn't I?" Bryn grabbed the box of sugar-cookie trees and put it on the table. "We'll start with these."

"Because of this afternoon."

"Please don't apologize again. Okay? I don't want an apology." The words were tighter than she'd meant them to be, but if he apologized again, she might spill all her emotions.

"But I am sorry. Sorry that our first kiss was rushed. That it was at the hospital. For an audience. I saw him, and it clicked who he was. And I couldn't stop my feet from moving to you."

"First kiss?" Bryn turned, her back against the table. She latched onto it with her hands. It was an awkward pose, but it steadied her.

"I've wanted to kiss you for days, Bryn. Since nearly the moment I laid eyes on you." Nick took a step toward her, then paused. "Maybe that isn't fair. I know this is supposed to be friendly—you helping me acclimate to Boston, and me supporting you as you step back into nursing."

Her eyes burned. It was all the right words. The ones she'd wanted to hear for so long. "Nick..."

"If you want to be friends, I can be that for you. I can. But I needed to say this. Needed you to hear, at least once, that my apology was for kissing you *at the hospital*. Not for kissing you. I'll never regret that."

"What if we call a mulligan?"

He stepped beside her, but she still didn't release the grip on the table.

"A do-over would be wicked good."

His *wicked* was still terrible, but she didn't care. Bryn released her hands and closed the distance between them. "Kiss me."

His hand rose, cupping her cheek. His eyes seemed to drink her in as his head slowly made its way toward her. The soft brush of his lips was the exact opposite of the possessiveness this afternoon. "Bryn."

Her name had never sounded like a worship before.

Pressing her lips to his, she pulled him as close as physically possible. She needed to know how he kissed, how he truly kissed.

"Nick, kiss me. Really kiss me."

The words broke whatever dam he'd been holding himself behind. His mouth claimed hers, and she melted into the moment, certain that there was no better place in the universe than being held in Nick's arms while his lips ravished hers.

His fingers skimmed her braid as her hands slipped down his hard stomach.

Finally, he broke the connection. Leaning his forehead

against hers, they stood there just enjoying the heat and time together. It was magical.

"That was the best do-over ever." Bryn laughed at the silly words. "That sounded so dumb."

His thumb ran along her bottom lip, lightning sparking through the touch. "That was perfection. Plain and simple."

"We have dozens of cookies to decorate." Bryn pursed her lips as she looked at all the supplies she'd lugged up here. She'd promised to bring them in tomorrow.

Camp Heartlight was the perfect place for kids with heart conditions. It let them be themselves and let their parents give them an experience so many kids got without fear of the worst happening. Plus, Ailani knew she was here, so if they didn't bring in any cookies…

"Show me how to hold the piping bag."

"Was that a double entendre?" She giggled and playfully pushed at his shoulder.

His cheeks darkened. Though if she wasn't paying such close attention, she wasn't sure she'd notice. She put her hands on his cheeks, feeling the heat. "Was it, Nick?"

"No. Though that hasn't stopped my body from flooding with heat."

She knew better than to question that statement.

"All right—we ready?" She waited for a minute, then added, "For cookie decorating."

"I'm ready for whatever you want, Bryn."

She put the icing bag in his hand and pointed to the box of trees. "Those are yours."

"Yes, ma'am." Nick saluted and opened the box. "How do I do this?"

"It's really not that hard." Bryn grabbed the other green icing bag she'd made, outlined the cookie with royal icing, then filled it in, moving onto the next one while the first dried.

After doing six, she picked up the yellow icing, added a star at the top and lights. Finally, she grabbed the brown, outlined the trunk and held it up for Nick's examination. "See—easy."

"Sure." He laughed and pressed a kiss to her lips. "If you say so."

"Those look good."

"That's a lie, Bryn!" Nick dropped a kiss on her cheek. This evening was the definition of perfection. He'd kissed her, really kissed her, and the universe seemed to beat in rhythm with his heart.

The last few hours he'd kissed her freely. The only issue was that they were nearly done, which meant Bryn would leave soon. He wasn't ready for that.

"It's only because you're so stiff." Reaching her arms around his waist, she placed her hands over his and guided the bag of icing across the cookie.

"Relax."

How exactly was that supposed to be possible with her breasts pressed against his back? His body was hyperaware of every curve pressed against him. Cookies were the furthest thing from his mind.

"Nick."

"You can say *Relax* all you want, sweetheart. It's not happening when your body is pressed like that against mine. All I can think of is putting this icing bag down, turning and letting myself drown in your beauty."

"That is quite the line." She pulled back, and he set the bag down, reaching for her.

"Not a line." His fingers ached to undo her braid, to run through her long locks. To see them draped over his pillows. His mouth crushed hers.

Need, desire, it all blended into one with this woman. He'd always held himself back with women, not fully giving in to his wants. Bryn met each swipe of his tongue, each press of his hips against hers. She anchored him.

Kissing Bryn was nice, better than nice, but he craved so much more.

She pulled back, and he feared he'd gone too far. Let his ache escape.

"I need to text Ailani." She looked at the cookies, then at him.

"Of course."

Bryn held up her phone. "Should I ask if she can take care of Honey for another few hours, or..." She bit her bottom lip.

"Or?" He wanted her to stay. Wanted it desperately.

"Or should I ask her to take her out tomorrow morning, too?"

"I am always going to choose option B." Though if she was going to stay more often, he'd need to find out exactly what Honey needed. There was a pet store on the corner. Surely he could find everything there.

Or they could stay at her place, provided Ailani was all right with it.

Bryn's cheeks turned the most delectable shade of pink. She typed out a few things, then put her phone down.

"While we wait for an answer...we should finish assembling the cookie pouches."

Cookie pouches. He could focus on those...maybe. She'd made a promise, and he'd sworn to help her. "I still feel bad, putting one of your cookies in the pouch with mine. Yours are a work of art. Mine are..."

"Edible." Bryn's lips glided across his. "That's what matters, Nick. They're edible." Bryn turned, focusing on the cookie pouches.

"If you say so." He stepped behind her, wrapped an arm around her waist.

"You're right." Her words were thready.

He pressed his lips to her head. "Right?"

"It is hard to concentrate with you behind me." Her head leaned back, and he took the invitation of her mouth.

She tasted like sugar and holidays and everything he'd ever needed.

Her phone dinged, and he wanted to weep with relief as she moved to grab it.

Bryn laughed and shook her head.

"Can she walk Honey tomorrow?"

"Yes, she says, *Told you so*."

"Told you so?" He reached for her hand, pulling her close as soon as her hand was in his.

"She told me she sees the way you look at me. That it was more than friendship in your eyes."

"Ailani is very observant." Nick ran his hand along her back. At the hospital, he had to actively force himself not to look for her.

Bryn's eyes shifted to the cookie pouches behind him. "We still need to pack up the last dozen pouches."

He spun her so she was in front of the table, him directly behind her. "Nothing's stopping you," Nick pressed his body to her back, letting out a sigh as her butt rubbed against him with extreme deliberation.

His hands ran along her belly before dipping under the holiday sweater she wore. Her soft skin under his fingers was a waking dream.

"You are so beautiful." His lips feathered kisses along her neck.

Bryn let out a soft cry and moved her ass against him again. "Two can play this game."

"Good." He cupped her butt with one hand and let his other hand trail along the edge of her breasts. He was already hard. Already dangerously close to completion, and they'd not even discarded a single stitch of clothing. "I want nothing more than to spend the rest of this night turning each other on."

"All you have to do is look at me to turn me on."

Bryn's admission nearly turned his legs to jelly. This everyday woman whose mythical hold on him was so precious wanted him as much as he craved her.

"You're my own personal siren." He slid his hand over her breast, rubbing the nipple through her bra.

"And you are doing an excellent job distracting me." Bryn leaned her head back, giving him perfect access to her incredible neck. "The quicker I finish these..." Her words caught as he slipped a finger into her bra.

"Or you could just say you have enough already. Three dozen, in fact. No one's going to fault you."

Her body tensed, but not in the way he wanted.

"Finish them, baby. It's fine. It gives me more time to find exactly what turns you on."

"Thank you for understanding." She kissed his cheek, then bent back over his table. The woman had been a people pleaser her entire life. With him, he wanted her to be herself. There was no way she could relax if she was worried about the cookies.

And Nick wanted Bryn relaxed as he explored every bit of her amazing body.

"Last one." She jiggled her butt again as she tied the ribbon.

He'd never considered himself such an ass man, but damn, the motion drove him mad.

"Finished!"

She turned in his arms, and Nick did not waste a single second. He lifted her, moving with as much speed as he could manage into his bedroom with her lips devouring his.

Laying her on the bed, he grunted, "Don't move." He didn't wait for an answer as he moved to the bedside table and turned on the lamp. "I don't want to miss a thing."

Bryn slid to her knees and lifted her sweater over her head. Then she unhooked her bra. As he stood in front of her, she grabbed the edge of his shirt and ripped it over his head.

"My siren is demanding."

"You've spent the last twenty minutes touching me through

my clothes and under them. Grabbing my butt and stroking my nipples. My body burns."

The words turned him on nearly as much as the sight of her perfect breasts.

Her hands skimmed over his stomach. "You are the hottest man I've ever seen."

"No one has ever said that to me." Nick lazily stroked her breasts, running a thumb over her nipples, enjoying the tightening bud.

"They were thinking it. They had to be." Bryn's mouth captured his, pulling him onto the bed.

"Bryn." His hand gripped her waist as her legs wrapped around him. They were still clothed from the waist down, and the urge to rip her pants down, claim her warred with the instinct to savor every moment, every touch.

Her hand reached between them, fingers flicking along his hardness. "Nick…" She nipped at his neck. "I need you inside me."

All thoughts exited his brain. She truly was a siren. He pulled her pants and panties down together, dropping them on the floor without thinking.

"Your wish…" He trailed kisses along her breasts as he slid a finger inside her. "Is my command."

"Nick." Bryn's eyes widened as he stroked her inner core. This wasn't what she'd meant, but her body moved against his hand, lost in the motion as she sought release.

He pressed his thumb to the top of her mound and couldn't stop the smile as he felt her tighten and let out a moan.

"You are perfection." Nick undid the buttons of his pants, slid them down and reached for the top drawer of his nightstand.

Bryn followed the motion and pulled the drawer open. She lifted the small gold package and carefully ripped it open, pulling the rubber out. Her green eyes held his as she cupped him and slid it down his length.

Her fingers skillfully caressed him before she guided him to her entrance. "Nick, I need you. All of you."

She wrapped her legs around him, and he lost himself in the haze with the beauty beneath him.

CHAPTER ELEVEN

"SWEET GIRL, you are so bouncy." Bryn laughed as Honey practically danced into the elevator. She felt the same excitement, but for different reasons. Nick was on shift this afternoon.

Not that she hadn't seen him every day since they'd decorated cookies. Two nights since he'd made her body sing. He saw her—the real Bryn—and liked her. It was intoxicating. She ached to wake next to him as she had after that night.

But that wasn't fair to Ailani. Honey was Bryn's responsibility. A responsibility she loved—Honey was family.

Ailani had casually mentioned before heading to the hospital this morning that she didn't mind Nick staying over. Bryn planned to take her up on the kind offer but ensure they didn't abuse Ailani's hospitality.

She didn't want to get her hopes up too much, but it was impossible not to when they felt like they belonged together. Like they were meant for each other.

It was a wild feeling to have, period, but after only knowing each other two weeks...

The elevator doors opened, and Kali was standing right outside. "Hi, Honey." She bent to pet the dog, then looked up at Bryn. "You look happy today."

"Do I?" Bryn felt like she'd had a perpetual smile on her lips since Nick had first kissed her.

"Yes." Kali winked. "Almost glowing."

A doctor walked up, looked at Honey and shook his head. "A golden retriever in a Santa sweater."

"This is Honey. Honey, Dylan." Kali beamed as she looked at the doctor.

When she turned to pet the dog again, Bryn noticed a similar look in Dylan's gaze. Romance seemed to be blooming on Ward 34…or her own happiness was putting romance goggles over her eyes.

"And I'm Bryn. It's nice to meet you, Dr. Geller." She knew of the visiting pediatrician but hadn't worked any shifts with him.

"You, too."

"I need to get to my next rounds. Life of a resident!" Kali smiled, but there was a hint of tiredness in her soul. Residents were too often overworked and exhausted.

"Take care of yourself, Kali." Dylan got the words out before Bryn, but she was glad someone had said them.

Kali didn't say anything, but she raised her hand as she headed for the stairwell.

"I need to see a patient. Have a good day, Bryn, and very nice to meet you, Honey."

Honey wagged her tail as Dr. Geller walked away.

"All right, girl, you ready to see some patients and work your magic?"

Honey's deep brown eyes looked at her, and her tail wagged harder. Rationally, Bryn knew Honey couldn't understand the words, but it often felt like she did.

Stepping into the pediatric ward, Bryn was happy to see the all the holiday decorations. This unit was always brightly colored, but it still gave off *hospital* vibes—just *vibrantly painted hospital* vibes.

The tree, the pretend wrapped candy, the snowflakes the kids had made on the windows…it coated the feeling some. Though she knew the parents and patients would rather be anywhere else.

She and Honey walked to the nurses' station to check in. Instead of a nurse sitting in the main chair, there was a small child.

One not wearing hospital garb and coloring what looked like a worksheet from school.

"This is Mabel." Ailani strolled to the desk, and the little girl looked up and smiled.

"Nice to meet you, Mabel." Bryn smiled and offered the girl her hand for a high five.

Mabel hit it and let out a subdued laugh.

"Javi's babysitter fell through, so she's hanging at the nurses' station until her grandmother arrives." Ailani looked at the worksheet. "Looks like you've almost finished your homework."

"You don't look old enough for homework." Bryn laughed and looked at Ailani.

She shrugged in a way that made Bryn think she thought the same.

"Do you want to meet Honey?"

"Honey?" Mabel peeked over the desk and let out a squeal. "You have a dog!"

"She's a therapy dog. She visits with the patients to give them a smile."

"I'm not a patient." Mabel frowned.

"I know. But I need to look over the paperwork to see who wants to see Honey this afternoon. So you can keep her company while I look, all right?"

"I can do that." Her head bounced with the sincerity that Bryn found so heartwarming in children.

Somewhere between childhood and adult life, most humans lost the ability to just be themselves. Not to care about what others thought. She knew older individuals often rediscovered that trait, but that meant a lot of years not living authentically.

Something she'd done for far too long. A trap she still sometime felt like she wanted to slide back into.

"Do you have many patients today?" Ailani smiled over the counter, looking at Mabel.

"Not a lot, but I want to check on Logan first."

Her roommate looked up and pursed her lips, "His surgery went well, but his heart seems to hurt. Maybe Honey can help."

"I hope so." Bryn leaned over the desk. "Thank you so much for keeping Honey company, Mabel." The girl was rubbing Honey's ears and smiling.

Javi walked by the desk and looked over the counter.

"Careful, Javi. Someone will be asking you for a golden retriever soon."

His dark eyes cut to her, and he shook a head before looking at Ailani—a look that seemed to speak for itself.

"Come, Honey." Bryn snapped, and the dog dutifully stood and moved to stand by her. "All right, Miss Floofy, it's off to work for us."

"Bye, Honey!"

Bryn waved, laughing. This wasn't the first time—and it wouldn't be the last—that someone said hello or goodbye to the dog and not her. She saw Nick step out of the staff break room and raised her hand.

"Nick!"

He turned. There was a look in his eyes—a sadness not hidden quickly enough.

"What's wrong?"

"Nothing."

Bryn tightened her hold on Honey's leash as she tried to adjust to the rough sound in his voice. "Nick, I can tell—"

"It *is* nothing. My father emailed. One meant for my siblings. I read it before he could recall it."

"Recall—"

"Yeah, recall. I got the notification while I was reading the invitation that he was recalling it. Trying to pull back what he'd sent. So…" He shrugged and blew out a breath. "Like I said. It's nothing."

That was a lie, but this wasn't the place for it. "Why don't you come to my place tonight? We can do dinner, then walk Honey and put on a movie. Just a nice, simple night."

"Sure." Nick nodded. "Though I hope I don't have to receive a bad email to get an invitation."

"Of course not. You're welcome anytime." Bryn reached out and squeezed his hand. "I'm off to see Logan."

"Good luck." Nick squeezed her hand back before dropping it. "His mom—" He paused, seeming to weigh his words. "She's not there, but it also feels like she is."

"The vibes are off. Got it." Bryn gave the leash the slightest tug as she and Honey headed to the room.

She knocked and waited for the permission to enter before heading in. Logan was in the bed, his leg up in traction with an external fixator keeping the pins in place. It was going to be a long road to recovery.

"You aren't wearing scrubs." Logan's eyes were sleepy, but he gave her a lopsided smile.

"I'm here today as a therapy-dog handler. You marked on your day sheet that you'd like an animal visit, if possible."

Logan laughed as he tried to lean over the bed.

"Nope. You stay there. She comes to you." Bryn held up a hand. There was a reason Logan was in traction. His leg needed to stay as still as possible.

"I hate being in this bed." Logan crossed his arms, but his smile grew larger as Honey stepped to the bed and put her paws on her the edge.

"I know. Staying still for so long must be hard, but Honey's here to release some of the boredom."

"I love dogs. I didn't do the paperwork—that was probably dad."

"Oh." Bryn kept the tone even. Kids talked more than adults, but teens were often hardened shells. Asking the wrong question could shut all communication down, so she'd gotten good at noncommittal phrases.

"He got a dog as soon as he moved out. A lab mix called Midnight. She is the cutest thing." Logan rubbed Honey's ears. "She'd be too excitable for the hospital, though."

"Honey has had a lot of training."

"Mom hates dogs. All animals, actually. I won't tell her you and I are best buds." He leaned his head against Honey's.

Bryn had no words for that. People might not like animals or could be allergic, but to hate them... Teens could be dramatic, but she suspected Logan watched his mother closely, trying to please a person who was unpleasable was a constant torture.

"What do you like doing? Skateboarding?"

"I did like it." He looked at his leg, his bottom lip wobbling before he focused all his attention on Honey. "Mom wants me to stop. She says this should be enough for me to focus on what's best for me."

What's best for us is Daddy staying home. You need to look pretty, be quiet, be sweet. Help me make him want to stay.

Her mother's voice echoed in her mind, but Bryn didn't know what to say. She'd spent her childhood trying to be what her mother had wanted. Trying to be perfect so her father would stay—something she knew now had had nothing to do with her. Her mother should have wanted what was best for Bryn, what made her happy.

It was such a low bar to get over, and it never stopped shocking her how many parents saw their kids as extensions of their wants and dreams.

"What do you want?" He'd had a serious injury. If giving up the sport was something he was thinking of, that was understandable.

"To get back out on the ramps." He glared at his foot. "I know it's dangerous, but so are other sports. I enjoy skateboarding."

"You're right. Other sports have injuries, too." She'd treated kids with injuries from soccer, football, gymnastics... There was a risk with everything. That was life.

"Sure. But other sports have college scholarships. They have respect. They make her..." Logan stopped and wiped a tear from his cheek.

In other words, his mother saw other sports as prestigious and skateboarding as a hobby that got her nothing. At least Nick had his father in his corner, but one loving parent didn't always make up for one unloving one.

"I just want to make her happy, and I never seem to do that. And now I'm in traction, and I have months of physical therapy, and she and dad are fighting, and—"

"And none of that is your fault." Words that were so easy to say, but Bryn knew sometimes took a lifetime to fully accept.

"She's always unhappy with me, and I just think sometimes if I made her happy, maybe they'd figure it out." He sniffed and looked at the ceiling.

"I thought the same with my parents."

If I say the right things or love them better. If I make the house just like Ethan likes... People-pleasing was something she understood all too well.

"It really isn't your responsibility." Bryn snapped her fingers, and Honey hopped from the bed. "You are enough. Just the way you are."

"Doesn't always feel like it."

"I know." She shook her head. Broken bones healed—broken souls took much more work. "But when you doubt it, try to remind yourself. It's the best gift you can give yourself."

"Thanks." Logan's tone was one of a teenager, so sure they knew the world, sure they could find another way. She'd been that kid once, too. It was a lesson she hoped he learned sooner than she had.

"Will you bring Honey back?"

"I will. She'll be here in three days, and I will be back in scrubs tomorrow."

He closed his eyes, and she let the rest of the conversation she wanted to have float away. The teen had confided in her. That was a precious gift, and there was no telling if he'd do it again.

Stomping up the stairs to Bryn's apartment, Nick tried to push away the gloom cloud that had hovered over his head all day. But it persisted, reminding him over and over of the email.

His father was coming to Boston—for business, of course. After the new year, and he'd wanted to know what Nick's siblings thought of him stopping in to say hi to Nick. He'd said he figured he'd have a free night for dinner but didn't know if he should see Nick.

Then he'd made a joke about them all being busy serving on duty twenty-four hours. Before ceding that surely Nick kept himself busy, too.

Perhaps it was a joke, a bad one, meant for his siblings in uniform. He might've even pushed off the hurt if not for the *surely*. Like somehow them being forced to be on the clock twenty-four hours a day was a major flex.

Like most doctors, he worked twelve-hour shifts. It was exhausting and rewarding. And he loved it, so much more than he'd loved standing in uniform.

Something his father would never understand. Nick accepted that—even so, for his father to be so close and think of stopping in, ask his brothers and sister their thoughts and then recall it after he'd sent it...

Nick looked at his phone once more, wondering if his father might send a text or another email. Some acknowledgment that Nick had seen the email. Because he'd have gotten a notification that he couldn't recall the email. So he knew Nick had seen his words.

The silence ached.

The door to Bryn's apartment opened as he hit the top of the steps. "Honey could tell you were on your way." Bryn smiled, but he could see the worry in her eyes.

"Are you trying to tell me my footfalls are too heavy?" Nick chuckled, determined not to let his father's dig impact his night with her.

"It's an old building." She reached for his hands, pulling him into the apartment. The lights on the tree were lit, and the place smelled delicious.

She handed him a wine glass and opened the red. "You tell me when."

A heavy pour was what he wanted, but he didn't want to waste any time with Bryn while sloshed. "That's good."

"You sure?" She held the bottle up and raised a brow.

"Yes." He waited while she poured her glass, then clinked her glass with his. "My dad's email is bothering me."

She stood still, and he let out a breath and told her its contents.

When he was done, Nick waited for her to say something. Anything. Instead, she snapped her fingers, and Honey pressed herself against his legs as Bryn went to pull the salmon from the oven.

"Nothing to say?" He wasn't sure why that bothered him so much.

Bryn pursed her lips as she set the salmon on top of the oven. "When did you last talk to him?"

"It's been at least three years. A few months after mom passed."

She nodded. "Your choice, right?"

"I just got tired of him being disappointed in me."

"That's fair." She moved, wrapping her arms around him. "You're amazing. A fantastic doctor, kind, hardworking…"

"A great kisser." Nick dropped his lips to hers.

"Fishing for compliments." She pulled his head to hers, deepening the kiss, her body molding to his. A little slice of perfection in the difficult day.

"All right, Bryn. What's the 'but'?"

She pulled back, and he could see her weigh her thoughts.

Moving back to the salmon, she grabbed two plates, quickly putting the fish and vegetables on one before passing it to him and walking to the small table.

She sat and took a deep breath. "I'm sorry he hurt you. That was unfair. But have you considered that he might want to see you?"

"See me?" Nick laughed. "My family was built on service,"

"You are serving, *Dr.* Walker. Just differently."

"Not according to my dad. You should have heard him when I left West Point. He couldn't even look at me. He graduated from West Point, my brothers and sister followed in his footsteps at West Point or other academies. I chose a different path, and that…"

"Nick—"

Now that the words were spewing forth, he couldn't seem to slow the flood. "He joked that I wasn't busy. Like somehow what I am doing is less important."

"Do you think what you're doing is less important?"

Nick's head popped back. "I…" Arguments formed in his mind. A loud *no* that he couldn't quite get out.

She reached her hand across the table. "Why are you hesitating?"

"I don't know." This should've been such a straightforward answer. A quick response.

"That's okay. But you didn't answer my question. Do you think he might want to see you?"

"He joked about me not being busy." Why couldn't Bryn see that?

"I know. The joke was in poor taste. But what if it alleviated the nervousness he felt? I'm not excusing that, but if he wants to see you, do you want to see him?"

Yes. His heart cried out at the idea. He wanted to see his dad. Wanted to know he was proud of him, though that wasn't something Nick thought was possible.

"You don't have to answer the question, Nick. Not to me,

but you need to know the answer. You're an adult, you get to choose who you associate with, but maybe if you settled that part of your past, you might feel more comfortable staying in one place."

"Staying in one place?" He shook his head. "Bryn…"

"Just saying." She cleared her throat. "There's an ice cream shop around the corner. If you want an after-dinner treat, we can go there." She smiled, and he felt the air shift.

She'd pushed him, then backed off. The tough conversation wasn't done. His heart urged him to hash it out. Tell her that Boston was great, that he felt more at home here than he had anywhere else. But permanence wasn't really something he felt he did.

Heck, that was the argument his father had made when he'd left the academy. That he couldn't commit. That he was a quitter. Maybe his father had been right. He'd certainly left more positions than anyone he knew.

Bryn made him feel different, but that didn't mean the urge to move on, to go somewhere else wouldn't return.

"Ice cream sounds great."

"Perfect." Bryn grabbed her empty plate, but he waved her hand away when she reached for his.

"You cooked. It's only fair that I do dishes." He took her plate, letting his fingers trace her wrist before walking to the sink.

"I could get used to this." She grinned as she stood next to him.

Get used to this…

The words sent his heart racing. He wanted her to get used to this. She deserved it…but what if he let her down, like he'd let his family down?

"I'm going to hook Honey up." Bryn stood on her toes and kissed his cheek. "Ice cream in December. I'm so glad that you want a cold treat on winter day."

"Ice cream is good no matter the temperature."

"Agreed." She laughed and went to grab Honey's leash.

The easy conversation should've been nice. But it felt off, like she'd cut off a potential disagreement in midstream. He watched her hook up Honey and mentally pushed at the gloom cloud again. It wasn't as dark around Bryn, but it hadn't burst, either.

In fact, it felt more stuck in place than ever.

"Enjoying the milkshake?" Nick eyed her drink for the third time.

"Yes. Wishing you'd gotten a milkshake?"

"I think I chose okay." The man had stood over the counter for nearly five minutes before selecting regular chocolate ice cream. The Scooper hadn't hidden her smirk when he'd asked for a chocolate cone with chocolate ice cream.

"All those holiday flavors, and you choose chocolate." Bryn shook her head as he held the door to her apartment complex open. She was currently sipping a Christmas Cookie milkshake, enjoying the tiny pieces of cookie the blender hadn't quite crushed up.

It was an inane conversation. The same kind they'd had on the walk to the shop and back. The kind that kept them from diving back into her questions about his father's emails and the emotions it brought out in the man beside her.

The man she'd pushed further tonight than she'd pushed anyone in a long time. Her heart fluttered each time she remembered the hollow look on Nick's face as she'd asked him if he wanted to see his father.

She believed what she'd said. Blood connection didn't equate to family. But she also believed people could change. The email, and particularly recalling it, had been wrong. But his father had been asking about contacting him—it was a big deal.

And Nick wanted the connection. She could see it in his

eyes. That didn't mean it was good for him, but he wanted it. Only he knew what that meant.

"I like chocolate. It's my favorite, and I got a fancy cone." Nick wrapped his arm around her as they walked to the stairwell.

"A waffle cone dipped in chocolate with chocolate ice cream. It's a lot of chocolate. Want to try the sugar-cookie milkshake?"

"How about I try it like this?" Nick used his free hand to put the keys into the door before dropping his head to hers.

His mouth ravished hers. The taste of chocolate on his tongue set her body ablaze. Like it had each time he'd kissed her, her body seemed to slide into his, her flesh aching to discard the barriers between them, just giving in to the desire.

"Bryn…" He said her name between kisses as he pushed her apartment door open.

She unhooked Honey's leash with one hand and snapped the command that send her to her crate. It was only after Nick lifted her into his arms that she looked over her shoulder to see if Ailani was there. No sight of her, so need to explain—though this needed very little explanation.

CHAPTER TWELVE

"THIS PLACE SCREAMS *BRYN*." Nick felt his eyes widen as she led him into the Christmas market. When she'd suggested this outing, he'd agreed because it made her happy. And making her happy was all Nick wanted, particularly because it felt like he'd misstepped the other night when she'd asked about his dad.

"I love it here. It's like holiday speed dating. There are so many independent stalls. The mixture of food and handmade gifts... There's something magical about the Christmas markets."

"So this is a yearly pilgrimage for you?"

"It was until Ethan and I got engaged. He was so weird about the holidays. Parties were fine, provided they were work colleagues, a way to schmooze his way to the top. Decor had to be picture ready."

"So you gave up something you loved because your fiancé... Sorry. Too personal."

"Is it?" Bryn frowned, then shook her head. She coughed and looked at her feet before saying, "Arguing about it was uncomfortable. So I just didn't."

Her quick shift last night about his dad popped into his brain. She'd shifted as soon as he'd gotten upset. Like she hadn't wanted to push him too far.

"Not overly proud of that choice, but it is what it is."

Nice going, Romeo. You've embarrassed the woman you care about.

Nick kissed the top of her head, trying to soothe the feeling that she was bending herself for him. That wasn't what he wanted, what he needed.

And dropping a question because your partner was uncomfortable was the opposite of cruel.

"So, what are we seeing first?" They followed the steps into the market, the holiday music blasting.

"The old ornaments. I always look for the original angel. I know the odds of finding it are super low." She laughed, but there was a hint of sadness in her tone. "But I always hope that someone will have it—and be willing to part with it for a price I'm willing to pay. You'd be shocked what the value of some ornaments are."

Except he wouldn't. Not anymore.

"Maybe we'll get lucky this year." He'd found this year's ornament and already wrapped it for her. She wasn't participating in the Secret Santa, but he planned to put it under the tree then anyway. And he'd set up an alert on several online sale sites for the original angel ornament—all with no luck so far.

However, the price tag on several ornaments had raised his eyebrow. Still, he'd paid a small fortune for the movies in his collection. What people prized was their choice, and he wasn't judging.

"Izzy!" Bryn raised a hand waving, then he saw her head back up. "And Dr. Murphy. I mean Ben. It's so nice to see you two."

"Bryn and Nick. Checking out the markets?" Izzy's smile was brilliant as she looked from her friend to Nick. The pediatrician was one of the sunniest people he knew, and that was saying something since he was standing next to a woman who practically radiated friendliness.

"It's Nick's first time." Bryn hit his hip with hers, then laid her head against his shoulder. "I worry it might overwhelm him."

It was such a couple action. Nick thought his heart might melt.

Izzy let out a chuckle, and Ben smiled.

At least Nick thought it was a smile. It was over so quickly.

"This place can be a bit much." Ben gestured to the gathered crowd as he seemed to pull into himself a bit.

"Don't worry, I'll keep you safe." Izzy kissed his cheek.

Ben cleared his throat and pulled a little away from her.

"I'll keep *you* safe, too." Bryn kissed Nick's cheek, her eyes moving from her friend to the uncomfortable-looking surgeon beside her.

"Well, it was good to see you guys." She squeezed Nick's hand.

"Have fun." Izzy waved before she and Ben wandered down the aisle toward a stall with holiday-themed children's items.

"Ornaments!" Bryn cheered, pulling him along.

"Ornaments." Nick dutifully followed, enjoying the sight of her giddiness. The music was loud, the place was crowded, food and holiday candle smells mixing in interesting ways. It was the definition of *overwhelming*, and watching Bryn love every minute was the best gift.

The booth they stopped at was overflowing. Even if her angel was here, he wasn't sure how'd they locate it. "All right." She held up her phone, the image of a tiny angel in a yellow dress sitting on a cloud in the forefront. "This is our mission."

Nick covered his mouth to keep the laughter from bubbling up. This meant a lot to Bryn, and he knew exactly what that angel looked like. Though he wasn't going to mention that. When he found it, he wanted it to be a surprise.

When.

The word clung to his heart as he started looking through his section of the booth. He'd always considered this an *if* project. If he found her angel. If he was still here. If...

Nick lived his life in *ifs*, not *whens*. Not absolutes.

Never absolutes.

A small heart ornament caught his eye. It was a red heart with the words Our First Christmas engraved over the center.

The bottom of the heart had a little box where it said to write the year or names. A way to personalize it.

It was simple. Each year there were probably a few dozen ornaments produced like this for lovers. There was nothing special about it—until you added the names.

Nick needed it, wanted his and Bryn's names written on the bottom. The urge was so deep in his soul, it felt like if he didn't purchase it, he'd always regret it.

When. He wasn't sure when it had happened or how, but Bryn was his *when.*

Looking over his shoulder, he saw Bryn talking to the owner of the booth and showing her the image on the phone. He could tell by the movement of her shoulders that it wasn't good news.

He waited for her to finish her conversation with the woman, then opened his arms. "No luck?"

"She doesn't have it, but she knows someone that does. Seven hundred dollars." Bryn squeezed him, then stepped back. "No ornament is worth that."

He didn't agree. "I mean, that is a steep price, but you've been looking for so long. You could think of it as an investment."

"Nick." Bryn reached up on her tiptoes. "I want the ornament on my tree. Not in a box to stay precious with the hopes someone might pay me more for it. After all, it's only worth what someone will pay for it."

"We could ask for the contact. Maybe we could negotiate?"

"You're sweet." Her hand cupped his cheek as she shook her head. "But no. I'll keep looking. What's in your hand? Did you find an ornament? It's red. That matches your tree!"

Nick felt his mouth fall open. He hadn't even thought of that. The ornament matched the color scheme he'd inadvertently started.

She reached for it, her eyes widening as she looked at the box, then at him.

"It matches my tree, though that isn't why I want it." His cheeks blazed, and there was no way to blame the crowded Christmas market. Nick monitored Bryn's face, saw the tips of her lips move up and the corners crease on her eyes.

"Nick…"

"We should get it." He wanted it, and he wanted her to want it, too. Yes, their relationship was new. So new. But that didn't matter.

"These are meant for people that plan…" Her voice fell away as her thumb ran across the image on the box.

"Meant for people with more than one Christmas, right?" His voice was surprisingly steady as he asked the question. This moment was nothing and everything all at once. Nick knew what he was saying…what he was asking.

Her face stayed focused away from the ornament. He wasn't even sure she could describe it fully if asked. "Nick—"

"Bryn." He dropped a kiss on her forehead as she worked out what she wanted to say.

His heart hammered as he waited.

"Honestly…" She blew out a breath, her green eyes capturing his. "They're meant for people planning more than two holidays together."

A lifetime. All the holidays. The future. Home.

That was what these were supposed to mean.

He should put it back. They'd been dating less than a month. Yes, he was considering staying in Boston for more than a year…but that didn't mean forever. It just meant—

Nick didn't know what it meant. He'd never felt this before. Still, his brain screamed for him to find a funny joke, use laughter to escape the tension he'd created, but his heart seemed incapable of setting it down.

"I think we should get it." *We*—a word he'd never used in a relationship before—felt so perfect with her. When she said nothing, Nick continued, "As you pointed out, it goes with my tree."

"It does." Bryn's fingers brushed his as she looked at the ornament. It was a cheesy, but he wanted her to want it to. "Will it make you happy?"

It was a weird question, and he didn't quite know how to respond. *Yes* was the answer, but what if it didn't make her happy?

Bryn pleased people. She was stepping into her own power again. But he wanted this to please her, not an agreement to please him.

"I want it, Bryn, but not if it makes you uncomfortable. I know this is new and this ornament is a lot. It means—"

Her finger pushed against his lips, shushing his words. "I want the ornament, Nick." Then she kissed him.

In the bright light of the stall, with Bryn's arms around his neck, time seemed to stand still. Like the universe recognized what this moment was. What they were.

"Get a room!" The child's voice carried over the music, as did his mother's quick shushing noise.

Bryn burst into laughter as she pulled away, covering her mouth. "Maybe we should get the ornament and take the kid's advice."

Nick pulled her to him, dropping a soft kiss against her lips. "That sounds like the perfect plan."

"Stop pulling at the collar. You look fine!" Bryn smiled as she and Nick stepped up to the starting line for the Santa Dash. The Camp Heartlight fundraiser was well attended, which was good, but Nick might not have counted on so many people seeing him. Snow was likely on the way.

"Brr… Even in this outfit, I'm freezing." Bryn looked at the sky. Not a cloud in sight. But maybe, if it kept getting colder, they'd have a white Christmas after all.

"Nick!" Kali's bright call lit up behind them as the resident and Dylan pushed through the crowd to step next to them on the starting line. "I thought wearing Santa hats made us festive." She elbowed Dylan, then gestured to Nick.

"A full Santa suit." Dylan rubbed his gloved hands together, the tip of his nose already red in the wind.

Bryn squeezed Nick's hand as he fidgeted. The Santa suit had been her idea. Sort of.

She was wearing white pants, a frilly tutu and a snowman sweatshirt. Honey was in one of her sweaters and reindeer antlers. She'd mentioned wearing something festive to Nick, meaning a fun sweater or elf ears. Still, her heart had nearly exploded when she'd opened her door this morning.

It was clear he'd done it for her, to make her smile. It had worked! She was falling for him. Who the hell was she kidding? She was tumbling headfirst in love with Nick Walker.

"You don't think it's too much?"

The Santa suit was perfect, but she knew he was hyperaware that no one else was in a Santa suit. He stood out!

In the best way possible.

"You should stop and see kids when we're done. I bet they'd love that." Ben rolled his shoulders as he joined the group at the starting line, his eyes focused straight ahead.

"Did I miss the memo on Santa hats?" Nick chuckled.

"Santa hats?" Ben touched his head and blinked as though he'd just remembered the hat. "Right. Uh. It was Izzy's idea."

"Where is Izzy?" Bryn looked at the crowd. So many faces in the mixture, though she suspected that if Izzy was running, she'd be by Ben.

"Not feeling up to a race this morning." Ben cleared his throat, his gaze still focused on the man holding the starting gun. "She's meeting me—us—at the finish line."

"Smart move." Nick jumped and blew into his hands. "If it's going to be this cold, it should at least be snowing! When are they blowing the starting gun?"

Honey barked, and he pointed to her. "She's ready to be warm, too!"

"She's ready to move." Bryn laughed and reached up to drop a kiss on the tip of his nose. "There are a lot of people here, and she's very excited."

"Santa!"

A little boy pointed to Nick, and he bent and spoke to the child for a moment. The scene was enough to melt her heart.

"All right, I think Ben is right. We should stop by and say hi to the kiddos." Bryn thought Nick would enjoy the moment, too.

"I am usually right." Ben pulled one arm across his chest, then the other.

"Runners ready?" the race master called.

"Yes!" The chorus of cheers echoed across the gathered crowd.

"Is this a joke?" Nick jumped again, still trying to keep himself warm. "Of course we're ready!"

The starting gun sounded, and the crowd took off.

Dylan and Kali shot out of the gate. If they kept that speed they might not win, but they'd have nearly first choice of the doughnuts.

Ben hung with Nick, Bryn and Honey for about half a mile before he pulled away, too.

They were making a solid effort, but Bryn didn't want to push Honey too much.

"You don't have to stay with us." Honey could run the full 5K, but Nick was faster...and highly motivated to reach the warming tents set up in the hospital parking lot with hot cocoa and doughnuts.

"I know." Nick looked at Honey before focusing on the pavement. "But I've no plan to leave my best girls."

He was talking about the race. Bryn knew that. Nevertheless, her heart leapt at the words. For once, someone was staying in her life. He'd insisted on hanging the ornament on his tree. Front and center.

She glanced over at him, her whole body heating as she

took in the Santa suit. She wasn't falling for him…she'd fallen. Head over heels in love with the man beside her.

"You make a pretty good Santa." Logan rubbed his hand over Honey's head. "Particularly with your reindeer." The teen's voice was high pitched, and Honey's tail wagged and wagged.

She would collapse once they made it back to the apartment, but for now, she was in doggy heaven.

"Pretty good?" Nick shook his head. "And to think I came with candy canes."

Bryn still wasn't sure where he'd found the bag, but it added to the fun as they visited the kid's rooms.

"Candy canes?" The teen rolled his eyes. It was playful enough, and Bryn was glad to see the interaction. Logan was moving from the hospital to a rehabilitation center in a few days. He'd not taken the news well.

Which Bryn understood. He wanted to go home, but that wasn't safe yet, something that was difficult for the teen to understand.

"All right, we have to head to the next patient's room." Nick passed Logan another candy cane. "Maybe they'll like my Santa outfit more." He winked and offered a wave.

"I appreciate it. I just like Honey more."

"Story of my life." Bryn laughed as the dog pulled her paws off Logan's bed.

They wandered out of the room, and Javi waved them over. "Can you stop in and see Jiyan? He's a four-year-old waiting for heart surgery and he's quite excited to see Santa."

Ailani walked up, and Bryn could see the worry on her face before she said anything. "Susie is being readmitted. The staff is transporting her from ER now. Maybe a visit from Santa will lighten the mood, if you don't mind another visit."

"Of course I'll see Susie." Nick's shoulders slumped, and Bryn wondered if her body language showed the same concern. Susie was meant to follow up with a cardiologist, though it could take weeks to get an appointment.

"We'll stop in after Jiyan." She blew out a breath and laid a hand on Honey's head, who sensed the tension and leaned her body against hers. "Good girl."

"All right, let's see Jiyan!"

Bryn followed Nick, hoping her smile looked good.

"Santa!" The little boy with dark hair clapped as he sat up in bed, a coloring book slipping from his lap.

His mother, Amita, leaned forward in her chair, smiling as she clapped in the same rhythm as her son. "It's Santa!"

"Hi, Jiyan."

The little boy looked at Nick, waved, then turned his attention to Honey. "Puppy!"

"And once more I'm outshone," Nick whispered as Honey walked over and did her magic.

"I'd say you get used to it, but…" Bryn made sure Jiyan didn't hear what she said—though, as usual, Honey was the star of this show.

Nick held up a candy cane and moved over to the bed to talk to Jiyan.

Bryn moved next to Amita, but the two of them said little while Nick and Honey worked.

After about ten minutes, Jiyan yawned, and Nick moved quickly. "Time for us to let you rest."

"But—"

"Rest is good, Jiyan." Amita's words were soft as she stood and pressed her lips to her son's forehead. "Tell Santa bye."

Jiyan smiled at Honey and waved at Nick before lying back in the bed. "Bye, Santa and Honey."

"See, that time you got mentioned before Honey." Bryn chuckled, but she knew the sound was off. They were headed to see Susie. Anytime a patient was readmitted, it was difficult. But this was Susie's third admit in three weeks. And there was still no diagnosis.

"Time to see Susie." Nick pulled out two candy canes. "In case her mom wants one, too."

It was a good thought. The parents of chronically ill children were often exhausted. A candy cane wasn't much, but including Susie's mom meant a lot.

Nick knocked on the door and entered after Ellen called to come in.

Susie shifted in the bed, glaring at the cords monitoring her heart. Crossing her arms, she bit her lip, then turned her glare on Nick.

"I don't want to see Santa. Santa isn't real." Tears coated her eyes, and Ellen moved to her side.

"Susan—"

"It's fine." Nick looked to Bryn, passing her the candy canes. "I promise." Then he stepped out.

"That was rude, Susie." Ellen's scold was half-hearted, and she immediately dropped a kiss onto Susie's head. "I know you're upset about Daddy."

"If Santa was real, he'd bring Daddy home." Susie let out a sob, and the heart monitors started going off. Her heartbeat was skyrocketing.

Javi, Ailani and Nick all stepped into the room.

The private rooms weren't that small, with equipment, patient, parent, and four medical professionals and a dog. It was nearly claustrophobic.

"Take a deep breath for me." Ailani's voice was calm as she moved past Bryn and Honey.

Javi looked at the dog and raised a brow.

Bryn gave Honey the order by snapping her fingers, and the dog immediately moved and jumped onto the end of the bed. She curled up tightly between Susie's legs.

"Focus on Honey." Javi's eyes were trained on the monitors, and Ailani coached Susie to breathe. Slowly, the child's heart rate started coming down.

"Good job, Honey." Javi checked the monitors one more time, then at Nick. "Can I talk to you for a moment, Santa?"

"That's not Santa."

"You're a very smart little girl." Nick took off his Santa hat and smiled at Susie. "After you, Dr. Pascal."

"Thank you, Dr. Walker."

The men filed out as Ailani checked the monitors on Susie's chest.

"I hate these." The words were soft and laced with tears.

"I know, honey." Ellen sat on the other side of the bed and gently stroked her daughter's hair. "But we have to make sure you're okay."

"I want Daddy."

Pain hovered in Ellen's eyes, but her voice was strong as she said, "Me, too."

Ailani offered them a sympathetic look and held up the Call button. "If you need anything, just push this."

"Thank you." Ellen lay with Susie and Honey. She and Bryn sat in silence, and eventually the little one drifted off.

"Please tell Dr. Walker I'm sorry about Susie. She asked Santa to bring Daddy home last year and…" Ellen closed her eyes, a tear slipping down her cheek.

"But Santa couldn't deliver." Bryn finished the words.

"No one can. No one will even take my calls anymore."

Bryn and Nick had heard one side of this conversation the last time Susie had been admitted. Bryn hadn't wanted to push then, but it was clear that Susie's heart condition, whatever it was, was impacted by stress.

If there was any way to facilitate a call with her dad or something… Bryn would do her best to make that wish come true.

"Where is her dad?" Bryn slid into a chair while Honey snoozed with Susie. "You don't have to answer, but if we can help…" Her words died away, she wasn't even sure what she meant.

"I don't know."

Bryn pursed her lips. She'd seen that look on her mother's face so many times, not knowing where the man she loved was hurt her deeply. At least for Susie, it looked like Ellen was putting her daughter first.

Ellen sucked in a deep breath as she ran her hand over Susie's cheek. "She looks so much like Jack. Susie has his eyes and his nose. She looks so different now. He went on assignment thirteen months ago. Jack's an independent journalist. There was a hot story about a narco-terrorist on the island of Saloda. I didn't want him to go, but the pay…" Ellen wiped a tear from her cheek. "It was a lot."

Saloda had been in the news last year. Bryn hadn't paid much attention as she'd prepped for the wedding, but she'd seen a few reports. And suddenly the name Jack Cole clicked.

"Because it was so dangerous." She looked at Susie and recalled the news story of Ellen standing with a senator, begging for her husband's release from the narco unit—and the radio silence that had happened after.

"Always be wary of a deal that seems too good to be true." Ellen's laugh had no humor in it. "We got a proof of a life six months ago, but the news cycle has moved on. So my senators, both federal and state, have stopped taking my calls. The State Department says they're monitoring the situation, whatever the hell that means, and I have no contacts in the Department of Defense."

But Nick does.

"I just want someone to answer. I know the odds—I know the situation is dire and he might be gone forever. But I feel in my soul that he's still here. My heart swears it."

Maybe it did. There was so much about the human body that was still unknown, let alone the metaphysical world.

"And now Susie's heart condition… If Jack was here, he'd know what to do. We weren't able to get in to a see a pediatric cardiologist until the new year. Jack knows everyone—

he probably even has some fancy contact from a story he ran years ago that could have squeezed her in. It's not fair, and our medical system needs a full overhaul, but I'd take it if I could get to know what is going on."

"I understand." Bryn knew better than most that the US healthcare system needed changes. Knowing that and also accepting that if you had a contact you'd use it for your child didn't make Ellen a bad person.

Bryn wasn't sure there was anything she could do, but maybe Nick knew someone. His family was rooted into the Defense Department. And his mother had worked for the State Department.

Susie was sick, but perhaps fate had dropped her at a hospital that could care for her physical self and her mental need for her father. Christmas was a magical time of year…maybe, just maybe, Bryn could grant this wish.

At the very least, she could ensure the hospital counselor talked to Susie and Ellen.

Standing, she rubbed Honey's head to get her attention. The dog stood slowly and gently stepped to the edge of the bed, where Bryn could lift her off without waking Susie.

"If I can help, I will."

Ellen offered Bryn a smile she knew meant *Thanks, but I doubt it.*

There was nothing left to say, so Bryn slipped from the room and ran directly into Ailani.

"Dr. Walker and Javi think they know what's wrong. Still need to talk to a cardiologist, but if she's in the early stages of aortic stenosis, the dizziness and fainting when stressed makes sense." Her smile was brilliant.

Bryn understood. Figuring out an unknown was a big deal.

Javi joined the small group, looking settled and at ease, certain that they were on the right track. It was reassuring, though she didn't see Nick.

Where is he?

"I've contacted Cardiology and Ben. Hopefully by Monday, we'll have an answer and a treatment path forward. Until then, we need to keep her as unstressed as possible."

Bryn looked at Ailani, then at Javi. What Ellen had told her wasn't in confidence, and Jack's detainment by the narco-terrorist group had made international news once upon a time. "I know why Ellen and Susie are so stressed...on top of the medical condition." She reached for Honey, running her hands along the dog's ears as she recounted what she'd learned.

"Wow." Ailani's face was devoid of color. "That's a lot."

"It is." But with Nick's connections, Ellen might get an answer, a contact who would at least return her phone calls. Bryn looked down the hall and still saw no sight of him.

"Last I saw him, he was in the break room." Ailani nodded in that direction. "Maybe grabbing some bake sale items after the run!"

"Probably." She needed to get to Nick. She wasn't sure why, but something felt off. He should've been out here. He and Javi had found a path forward for Susie, so why was he hiding in the break room?

Bryn headed over there, opening the door she called, "Nick?"

She moved the moment she saw the slump of his shoulders, pulling him into her arms. No questions, no recitation of what she'd learned.

"My dad's plans accelerated. He'll be in town starting Wednesday. He emailed—again." He let out a bitter noise. "At least this one he didn't recall. Told me to reach out to his secretary to schedule a time."

Oof. Bryn didn't know the man, but telling your estranged son to contact you through your secretary wasn't the best look. "Do you want to reach out?"

Deep down she thought he did. He wanted what his father had given his siblings—acceptance. Bryn didn't know if that was possible, but if he never reached out, Nick would never know.

"No." He shook his head. "The man is here for work. I'm a side project, just like always. So no, I do *not* want to see him."

"All right." She loved him. If he didn't want to see his father, then he didn't have to. Though it made helping Susie and Ellen more difficult. She'd find a way—one that didn't upset the man she loved.

CHAPTER THIRTEEN

NICK FELL AND let out a grunt as his butt hit the ice…again.

"If you want to go, we can." Bryn skated around him as he brushed his hands against his knees. She'd tried helping him up the first few times he fell, but he'd unintentionally pulled her down with him and then spent the limited time he remained on his feet apologizing.

He'd wanted to see the Kelly Outdoor Rink. It was decorated for the holidays, and people were rushing around the rink. Or slipping and falling like Nick.

He slid to his knees, then managed to get back up onto his feet. "I don't think this is much of a date. Maybe it's time to move on."

"A new activity it is." Bryn looked at the rink exit. She could be there in three seconds, but Nick… "Do you think holding on to my arm will help you get to the wall and then the exit?"

"Absolutely not!" Nick shook his head, then held his arms out as his feet started flailing. Somehow, he kept his balance.

He was probably right. She'd be just another impediment to his already slow movement. Still, not being able to help him was frustrating.

Bryn held her breath as they started the journey. Little kids whizzed past but avoided taking Nick out. By millimeters, they made it to the wall.

"I feel like I've won some award!"

She couldn't stop her chuckle. "The wall—great reward."

"Says the woman whose ass isn't freezing and aching."

Bryn kissed his cheek. "Poor baby. Why don't we go back to my place, and I'll take care of you." She winked as she skated backward. "Unless you're too sore?"

"Such a tease." He pulled himself along the wall. "If I was faster, I'd skate up, pull you into my arms and kiss away that playful smirk."

"That is very *Christmas movie* of you." She stepped out of the rink, then waited for him.

When he finally made it, she reached for his hands. "And you can always kiss me on unfrozen ground."

"Your wish." His lips were chilly as they met hers, but her body heated anyway.

"Bryn!"

Nick's hand wrapped around her waist as he looked past her. She didn't need to follow his actions to know her ex-husband was behind her. Why he was calling her name when he could just pretend not to see her like he'd done so often in their marriage?

Still, she turned, appreciating Nick's arm sliding around her waist. Twice in one month after not seeing Ethan since the divorce was really too much.

His arm was wrapped around the waist of a blonde with green eyes. The man certainly had a type.

Ethan's date looked at him before looking at Bryn. "Umm… I'm Daisy."

"Bryn." She pointed. "This is Nick."

"Right." Daisy's gaze was hyper-focused on Bryn, never leaving her face.

"Well, we're just leaving. Have a good night." Bryn and Nick wobbled off to grab their shoes from their locker.

She waited for a moment before letting out the nervous chuckle she felt in her throat. "That was awkward for him, right?"

"I think he called your name by accident, then didn't know

what to say." Nick shrugged as he pulled the skates off his feet and flexed his toes.

"Maybe." Bryn wasn't overly concerned with it.

"You ever think of moving? Then you'd never have to worry about awkward interactions again."

The question hit her heart, and she kept her head down as she pretended to focus on tying her shoes.

"Bryn?"

There was an edge to Nick's voice. A point of pressure, like he was hoping she'd say yes.

Or I'm reading into things because I worry he'll move.

She'd given up her job at Brigham. It was hard to regret that because it had led her to the man beside her. But she wasn't leaving the place she'd always called home because her ex-husband resided in the same city.

"No." She pulled him to his feet. "Lots of people stay where their exes are. I'm not seeking him out but not running, either."

"It's not running. It's moving on."

Moving on. Was that how he thought of moving? And was it because he was restless or did something else happen?

"Why did you leave the last place you lived?" They'd talked of so many things but never what had led him to Boston.

"It just didn't fit anymore." Nick leaned his head onto hers. It was comfortable and easy, but it felt like he was trying to ground himself.

"But why?" If she knew, maybe she could sense the changes in him. Give herself a heads-up. The next time he moved on... if he asked her...maybe she'd go with him.

Boston was home, but maybe it could be somewhere else, too.

"I don't know. It just felt like time to move on."

"Just felt like it?"

"Yeah." He shrugged, like none of this was a big deal.

Maybe it isn't?

What happened when he felt the urge again? What might that mean for them?

Her phone buzzed, and she was grateful for the interruption. "Oh, it's an email from one of the state senators." She'd sent off a flurry of emails about Jack after her shift yesterday, hoping that another contact might yield results.

"It's a no, isn't it?"

"I haven't even read the…" Her voice died as she looked at the form letter telling her they appreciated her contacting them about this important issue and to be sure to remember to donate for reelection.

"Bryn."

"It's just the first contact. It's fine." She meant the words, but the sting of rejection still burned. Her gaze shifted to Nick, but his face was turned away. Once more, she swallowed the urge to ask him to reach out to his father. Nick had to cross that bridge.

Bryn's head was bent over her laptop as Honey laid her head in her lap. He watched her absently rub the dog's head as she scrolled through the internet, searching for contacts who might help Susie's dad.

Like Ellen hadn't exhausted every road.

Nick felt for the family. However, he also was realistic about the odds of getting Jack home soon. The quickest prisoner transfers took months. Many were yearslong endeavors with backdoor negotiations that only high-ranking diplomats ever knew about.

And that was when you were dealing with another government. Which the individuals holding Jack were not.

The US government had a standing rule that it did not deal with terrorists. At least not directly.

Bryn hadn't asked for his help. That stung. But he couldn't figure out why.

And even if Nick emailed, it didn't mean his father would

help. The general made time for those who mattered—a tiny list that included his siblings, a handful of colleagues but not Nick. A lesson he didn't need to be reminded of.

His father's last email was a single line. No *Would love to see you*. No *Miss you*. No *Love you*. No *I'm proud*. He'd had emails from colleagues with more warmth.

Hell, even his father's assistant could have crafted a better message. If he'd let his assistant do it, then there might be more affection in the note.

Nick knew if it had contained microscopic evidence that his dad wanted to see him, he'd set up the time. Even if it meant asking his dad's assistant to "schedule" him in.

Was it too much to want his father to want him to stop by? To say that?

Bryn yawned, and he moved quickly.

"Take a break, sweetheart." She'd been at this for days.

"I will. In a few minutes." She reached for the coffee cup at her fingers, but he pulled it away.

"You need to rest. Adding caffeine at this hour—"

"Please!" Bryn giggled as she gently pulled the cup from his hand. "Are you really telling me that caffeine still affects you? How much did you drink as a resident? They live on the stuff, and so do nurses."

"Medical training abuses residents too often. That doesn't mean they should have to rely on caffeine to meet their ever-increasing workload. And nurses shouldn't need to, either."

"It's just coffee, Nick. I need to find—"

She was going to burn herself out. This wasn't sustainable. If by some miracle she found a way, this was a marathon, not a sprint.

"I'll pass it back if you can look me in the eye and swear that if it didn't offer you some sort of stimulant, you'd still drink it."

Her cheeks colored, and she opened her mouth, then closed it. "I'm trying to help Ellen and Susie."

"Why?" The question popped out before he could catch it.

He cared about his patients and their families, but this project was literally international.

"Other staff members grant wishes to the patients at Christmas. It isn't required, but I mean, think of this as me granting a wish for Susie and Ellen."

Nick knew his mouth was hanging open. What was he supposed to say to that? A wish! "Bryn—"

"I know it's a long shot."

"A long shot!" Nick shook his head. "Bryn, other staff members find a way for a person dressed as the kid's favorite superhero to surprise them. They get visits from the museum staff with items they can touch. Zoo animal visits. They do not facilitate international agreements! That would take a literal Christmas miracle."

"I know I won't get him home—I just want someone to tell Ellen and Susie they haven't been forgotten. Someone to notice that they're still waiting for the person they love. To pay attention to them. Is that so damn hard?"

"Yes."

She stood as his harsh word hit the room.

"Bryn, you have to be realistic. You can't please everyone and—"

"You think I'm being a people pleaser here? You think that's what this is?"

"Is it?"

She looked at her feet, then shifted on her heels. "No. It's trying to provide some relief to a parent who's been through more than she should have this year. It's about trying to bring a smile to a child who yelled at Santa to get out of her room." She let out a breath. "Nick, I might fail. I get that."

"Do you? Do you understand that you might not be able to bring anything to the table here? Sometimes you have to just move on."

"I don't *move on*." Her whole body seemed to shake as she

stared at him. "When I care about something, about someone, I don't move on."

They were dangerously close to talking about something other than Ellen and Susie.

Pulling at the back of his head, Nick tried again. "You don't know anyone who can help."

"Not true." She closed her eyes, her bottom lip shaking, before she straightened her shoulders and looked at him. Her green eyes said the words before her mouth could.

"Bryn."

"I know you. And *you* know someone. Your family has connections."

Connections. There it was. The fact that his family had access to a part of the world almost no one else did. His family, but not Nick.

He got recalled emails and one-line statements telling him where his father would be. Nothing that let Nick call in this kind of favor. Was that why Bryn hadn't asked him to help?

Was that why she'd waited until they were arguing to even bring it up? "And yet you didn't ask me, did you?"

Bryn shook her head, and for the first time in their short relationship, she didn't quite meet his gaze. It was the same action his father had taken when Nick had explained he wasn't returning to West Point. Looked past him.

"Would you have reached out? Will you?" Bryn sounded too hopeful.

"No." Nick hated how fast the word slipped from his mouth.

Seeing his father, asking him for a favor…one he probably wouldn't be able to grant. Assuming he was even interested in trying.

"All right."

Her soft answer sent shock waves through him. Where was her anger?

"All right? Just 'all right'?"

The lines around her eyes deepened, and he hated the frown on her face.

"Yes. Just 'all right.' You get to decide what you need from your family. I can't make that choice for you."

Nick's chest ached as she turned back to the computer. The slump in her shoulders gave away her disappointment, but she didn't argue. She was giving in—just like she'd done with her ex-husband. Reading him and giving him what she thought would make the situation go away.

"My father might have access to someone. At the very least, he could probably pull a string to get a senator's aid to return a call." He didn't know why he was doubling down here. She'd let him off the hook—he needed to drop this.

"Given what I've learned regarding the joint chief of staff, the Department of Defense and the group holding Jack, probably." Bryn grabbed the coffee mug, tipped it up, finishing it before she started typing again.

A freight train seemed to blow through his mind. What was happening? "So you aren't mad at me for not reaching out?"

Bryn shook her head but didn't look at him.

"I think you're lying. I think you're angry and you're trying to please me like you did Ethan." He was not her ex-husband. He cared about her. Full stop.

He wanted Bryn—all of her. The fun, joyful woman who brought him so much life, but also the tough woman. The anger, the sadness. Those emotions were part of life, and he didn't want her hiding them.

"Do you want me to be angry?" Bryn rubbed a hand over her forehead before she looked at him. "Do you want me to make you see your father? I'm your girlfriend, not your mother or your counselor."

"I want to know your actual thoughts. I want the words you're holding back. What do we have if you aren't honest with me?"

"I can't help you with this. Until you realize that your achievements are worthy no matter what your father thinks."

"I am not looking for my father's approval."

"Yes, you are. Whether you're lying to me or yourself right now, I don't know. But you want it."

"I don't need him. He turned his back on me. I graduated from med school, and he didn't even come. If a success doesn't happen in uniform, it doesn't matter." Nick's hands were shaking as he looked for his keys. He needed to leave before he said something worse.

"You asked me for honesty. You wanted the words. You can't get upset with me for giving them." Tears hovered in her eyes, but they didn't spill over. This was the woman who'd found herself again after her husband had turned from her on her honeymoon.

The strong woman he'd fallen in love with her.

"What are you looking for?"

"My keys."

They hit his chest a moment later.

"Bryn…" Her name on his lips nearly broke him as he grabbed the keys from the floor.

"I wasn't trying to please you. I was trying to protect you." A tear slipped down her cheek. "And now you're running."

"I'm not running."

"Then why the keys, Nick? This is our first fight. They happen between people who…" Her fist pulled to her chest as she sucked in a deep breath. "Who care for each other. If you run now, will you ever stop?"

The room's walls were closing in, the air thickening. His mind refused to listen to his heart's command to stay. To tell her it wasn't her he was running from. To explain that he didn't even know what it was pushing him toward the door. But he needed to leave.

"I need time."

"Time? Nick…"

"I'm sorry." His emotions were all out of whack. It felt like the shell around his soul was cracking. And he didn't know if anyone would like what was underneath.

He was in his car, sitting behind the wheel with no memory of exiting the apartment or running down the stairwell, when his final words echoed in his brain.

Had he told her goodbye? Kissed her cheek? Given any indication that he'd meant he needed time tonight?

Did I just break up with her?

Leaning his head against the steering wheel, he let out a soft sob. His soul urged him to go back upstairs, apologize, make her understand that he didn't need his father's acceptance.

Except what if she was right?

She wasn't. The fear, the sadness—none of it was tied to that. He was going home. Getting a bit of sleep, putting himself back together.

He'd call her first thing. Ask her for coffee. Put everything to rights. It would be fine. It would.

CHAPTER FOURTEEN

"WHERE'S HONEY?"

Susie's frown didn't bother Bryn as she stepped into the room. She wasn't the first patient—and she wouldn't be the last—to look a little sad when Bryn didn't walk into a room with the ball of fluff beside her. "She's at home."

Holding up the stethoscope, she smiled, though her heart wasn't really in the motion. "I'm your nurse today."

"And you want to check my heart?" Susie rolled her eyes, then looked to her mother.

Ellen was giving her the look all moms seemed to develop. It said *Behave*.

"Everyone is listening, checking your heart, aren't they?" Children picked up on so much more than adults gave them credit for. And children who spent time in the hospital seemed to grow up even faster.

"Everyone." Susie lay back and adjusted the lines of the monitors on her chest like a pro. "I hate these."

"That's normal." Bryn moved to the side of the bed. Her job this morning was to make sure the electrodes monitoring for any decline or acceleration of Susie's heartbeat were properly attached.

The door opened, and Nick stepped in with Dr. Jarod Keegan, an interventional cardiologist.

Bryn saw Ellen sit up straight, her hands grasping the

edge of the chair that she'd rarely left over the last few days. Two doctors.

She knew Javi had explained the aortic stenosis, commonly called AS, the diagnosis they were scoping out. And Ben had consulted, too. That it was Dr. Keegan here and not Ben was an actually a good sign.

Dr. Keegan had completed his schooling at Howard University. The black man's hair was graying at the temples, but he was one of the top cardiologists in the country. And if he was here, it meant open-heart surgery wasn't necessary.

Nick's eyes stayed focused on Ellen, away from the bed where Susie was. Away from Bryn. Silence from the man she loved could be the loudest sound in the world.

"Ellen, I want to introduce Dr. Keegan. He's an interventional cardiologist."

"I know the polite thing is to say *Nice to meet you, Dr. Keegan*, but…" Ellen looked at Susie and then the two men before her.

"But it's not." Dr. Keegan nodded. "I know. Trust me, you aren't hurting my feelings by acknowledging that you'd rather be anywhere else."

"Another doctor?" Susie bit her lip and pulled a small stuffed animal to her chest.

"Yes." Dr. Keegan moved toward her. "I'm here to talk to you and your mom about what we have to do to help your heart."

"An interventional cardiologist—what does that mean?" Ellen's foot was tapping, her eyes laser focused on the cardiologist.

"The echocardiogram confirmed Dr. Walker and Dr. Pascal's suspicion of aortic stenosis." Dr. Keegan looked at Susie and explained, "Remember when the nice lady with the big machine came in here and used a wand on your chest to see your heart?"

She nodded.

"Well, that showed that one of your heart valves isn't as big as it needs to be. So we're going to put a balloon in your heart to widen it."

"Will it hurt?"

"No. You'll be asleep, and when you wake up, your mommy will be there."

While Dr. Keegan was comforting Susie, answering all her questions, Bryn looked at Nick. The man had been silent this whole time. Which made sense, if she was honest. He was here as Susie's pediatrician of record during this shift. This was Dr. Keegan's show. But she wanted to hear his voice.

She'd started so many texts, pulled up his number at least a dozen times since he'd walked out of her and Ailani's place two days ago. And she'd not followed through with any of them.

I need time.

She didn't know what that meant. But she wasn't going to push him. She'd adjusted herself for Ethan. Molded herself into a model for him. She wasn't doing that again.

She was looking for ways to help Ellen. Maybe she wouldn't be able to, but she wanted to help. And it wasn't people-pleasing because Ellen hadn't asked and didn't even know.

Bryn knew what it was like to feel forgotten. If she could help Susie and Ellen avoid that, particularly around the holidays, there was no stopping her.

"If you have questions, let me know. I've got the OR scheduled for the twenty-third. We'll let Santa know you'll be home a few days after Christmas."

"He's not real." Susie's tone was just as strong as it had been when she'd made the comment to Nick after the Santa Dash.

So young and disheartened.

Dr. Keegan didn't argue, he just patted Susie's leg. "You'll be home in time to enjoy watching the New Year's Eve fireworks."

Susie nodded but didn't say anything else.

Dr. Keegan headed out, and Ellen looked at Nick. "Is there anything I should have asked?"

"No. You did great." They were the right words, said in the right tone, but his bedside manner was lacking.

Was that because she was standing here?

A year ago, maybe even a few months ago, she'd have ensured that it wasn't her. Hell, she'd left Brigham to please her ex-husband! She wouldn't be doing the same here. Ward 34 was her place.

But she was also worried about Nick.

"If you need anything, please let me know, sweetie, all right?" Bryn squeezed Susie's hand and then walked out.

She hovered outside of the door. Nick stepped out and nodded, his brown eyes not quite meeting hers.

"Nick…"

All her words seemed locked deep inside. "Are you going to the staff holiday party this evening?"

"I'd planned to."

Bryn waited, but he didn't say anything else. "Nick—"

"Dr. Walker!" Leigh Wachowski, the head nurse, waved a hand, "Teen in room six can't stop throwing up. I think we need to start IVs to prevent dehydration. Can you take a look and write up the order if you agree?"

"Of course. Have a good day, Bryn."

Have a good day. On the outside, they were nice words. Friendly words between colleagues.

If she'd had any doubt that he'd meant *time* as a reference for a breakup, this shattered the illusion.

People walked past her in the hall. She registered their presence but little else. Her heart still beat, even though her soul swore it shattered. Life moved on. She wasn't sure how she was going to do that, but that was a question to answer in a few hours. Or a few days.

Today she'd do her best not to be alone with Nick. And she'd skip the holiday party. Ailani could bring along the cookies she'd made for the party.

But that was the simple answer. The safe answer. It was also the route she'd taken at Brigham. Stepping aside so Ethan had his place.

She and Nick could coexist here. Or he could move on. Her broken heart nearly collapsed at the thought of him leaving. Eventually he'd leave. Find another place. A new adventure. Away from her.

This was her place. Which meant sticking around. Going to the party. Putting on a happy face. She could do this. Somehow.

"Bryn." Izzy smiled as she passed over a tablet chart. "Can you start meds on my patient in room two?"

"Yes." She took the tablet chart, but before she could turn, Izzy's hand was on her shoulder.

"Are you all right?"

"Fine." The word women had used for generations to mean *no* but say *yes*.

Izzy squeezed her hand. "If you need to talk, I'm here."

"Thanks." Bryn tapped the chart in her hands. "Let me take care of your patient."

"Just remember to take care of yourself, too."

Holiday music blasted from the staff speakers. Paper snowflakes were hung on the windows, and the Christmas spirit seemed to fill everyone except for Nick. He placed the small present for Bryn and the envelope with his Secret Santa gift under the tree with the other gifts. The tree had giant red balls and blinking lights, and the array of boxes underneath it was impressive. Which made his small envelope for Secret Santa look a little sad.

He'd drawn Liz, a radiology tech, who, according to the intel he'd received, loved coffee. So he'd gotten a gift card to

Full of Beans. It was a fine gift. One that would make the radiology tech smile. It wasn't deep, though. Not personal.

Not like the small box he'd just laid under the tree wrapped in paper covered with brightly colored Christmas trees. An inside joke about his tree. The gift he'd hoped to share with Bryn following her shift on Christmas morning. A dream that wouldn't come true now that they weren't speaking.

Nope, the gift he'd found, the one he was so proud of, was going with the other Secret Santa gifts. At least she'd have it, though. That was what mattered.

He'd thoroughly messed all this up.

His plan to call her the next morning had fizzled in a ball of nerves. He'd always joked that movies made too much out of the hero and heroine not talking, called it unrealistic.

He'd wanted to believe he was immune to such things. As days of silence had grown between him and Bryn, he'd realized how human it was.

The real pain was knowing there was an easy way to fix it. Call his dad. Get the contact.

Easy…

"Bryn."

He heard Izzy's bright voice saying her name, and his head turned. Bryn wore a green sweater, brown pants and a star headband. She looked professional and like a Christmas tree. A look only the woman he loved could have pulled off.

Loved.

He loved her. And now he was standing on the opposite side of a holiday party with no idea how to bridge the cavern he'd dug between them.

"Look at these cookies!" Izzy held up what looked like the cookie Bryn had talked about making for tonight. Not as fancy as the ones she'd made for the bake sale, but much better than the ones he'd tried to decorate back when he still could.

"I think we might have too many sweets." Bryn's laugher made his heart sing, while it sent shards through his soul.

He shouldn't be here. Except the only place he saw Bryn now was on Ward 34. It was bliss and torment wrapped into one.

"It finally snowed." Ailani's voice was soft as she stepped next to him.

"It did." Nick had waited the entire month to see snow. Bryn had told him Boston rarely had a white Christmas. Today he should've been throwing snowballs at her, watching Honey roll in the wet stuff while Bryn playfully scolded her.

"You doing all right?"

There was no succinct answer to Ailani's question. *No* might be a complete sentence, but it was so much deeper than that.

"Fine." He crossed his arms, then uncrossed them, then crossed them again.

"You certainly seem fine," Ailani murmured, her eyes focused on the thick snowflakes falling outside.

He wanted to ask how Bryn was. Except he wasn't sure there wasn't a non-creepy way to do it.

If she was all right, if the laughter he'd heard a minute ago was real, that was a good thing. But it also meant she was fine and he...well, he very much wasn't.

"Bryn says she's fine, too. It's like you guys are running off the same script."

Ailani waited a minute, then wandered off.

Nick counted snowflakes, giving himself to the count of fifty before he had to turn around and put on a cheerful face. Or a happy enough face.

His phone buzzed, giving him one more reason to ignore the general holiday feeling around.

Pulling the phone from his back pocket, Nick felt his heart drop at the email.

Something came up—in town until the day after Christmas.

Another one liner with no personal message. At least the general was consistent.

"Time for Secret Santa!"

The peppy call came up, and Nick instantly regretted putting the present under the tree. He needed to step out. Just for a moment.

He swore when he came back, he'd be as jolly as St. Nick. Somehow.

"Happy holidays." Kali held up one of the holiday paper cups from the punch table.

"Happy holidays." Bryn raised her own cup, ensuring her eyes never strayed to the window where Nick seemed to be camped out.

"And it's snowing!" Kali pointed to the window.

"It is." She tried to sound happy. A white Christmas was truly magical. And Nick had wanted it. Was he excited?

"Delivery for you, Bryn." Leigh gave her a small box.

"I didn't do Secret Santa." She passed it back. It was a fun tradition, one she would absolutely take part in next year.

But she hadn't been a full employee and hadn't been in the holiday spirit when she'd seen the signup.

Leigh shrugged and handed it back. "It has your name."

Pink, blue and green trees covered the paper. Her eyes filled with tears as she rubbed her fingers over the images. It wasn't pretty paper. It was pretty horrid. And she loved the hidden meaning behind it.

A hidden meaning that meant she knew just who had left her the present. A present from Nick, under the staff tree. Not under his tree. Not under hers.

"Are you going to open it?" Kali was all grins.

"No."

Kali blinked and gripped her wrist. "Bryn…"

"Just going to wait until I get home. I…umm… I didn't get a gift for anyone else, so…"

"I didn't, either." Kali nodded, but Bryn could tell the resident knew she wasn't being quite honest. "I think I'm going to check on Dylan again. Jiyan's still in surgery."

"Right." She blew out a breath and slid the small box into her purse. Tonight she'd open Nick's present. And grieve the second message that seemed to call from the gift.

Goodbye.

CHAPTER FIFTEEN

"Bryn, do you have any acetaminophen? My feet are aching, and I still have another six hours on this shift."

Bryn peeked over the fridge door as Izzy leaned against the locker bank. "If you open locker fourteen, my bag is in there. I have acetaminophen, or if your feet are aching, you can grab the ibuprofen." Ibuprofen was better for aches and pains, but as a physician, Izzy knew that.

"Acetaminophen will work."

"Izzy?" Bryn's mental radar raced. She'd been feeling under the weather, not drinking…and now avoiding ibuprofen.

Could Izzy be expecting? Before Bryn could travel too far down that mental road, Izzy held up the small angel ornament. "This is so cute."

The little angel was wearing a yellow dress, sitting on a cloud with her eyes closed. The first in the series. Nick's gift for her. It was the sweetest gift she'd ever received. Something she'd tell him, if she ever saw him.

It was strange. After seeing each other every day for several weeks, it was like he'd poofed out of existence. She saw his names on charts, but since the staff party, she hadn't actually worked a shift with him or laid eyes on him.

"It's the first in a series for the ornaments I collect."

Izzy's eyes widened as she looked at the ornament. "Really? Why is it in your purse?"

That was an excellent question. One she didn't really have

an answer for. Nick's gift should've been on her tree. Or packed away where she didn't have to see it every day. Instead, she was carting it around like a comfort item.

A comfort item from the man she loved but hadn't seen or talked to in days.

"Nick gave it to me." Bryn bit her lip and squeezed her eyes closed, refusing to allow the tears to fall.

"I see." Izzy's voice was quiet, but Bryn felt her arms slide around her shoulders, squeezing them tightly.

Her lovesick pain was probably very obvious to everyone.

"I'm all right." She had told Ailani the same thing when she'd asked. And Izzy's look was so similar to her roommate's that she knew her words weren't convincing.

"What happened?" Izzy grabbed a bottle of water and downed the two pills before sitting back on the bench.

"I don't know." How dumb did that sound? Things had been fine, and then they'd been arguing and he'd walked out. "Nick's father is in town. He's reached out a few times, but Nick isn't interested in connecting. I did my best to give him space on that, but then it was almost like he got mad at me for doing that. It was so hard to read."

"Hard to read?" Izzy's brows rose. "Do you read people often?"

"Of course." Bryn shrugged as she peeled the banana she'd grabbed from her lunch bag. Medical staff rarely had time for a full break, but she kept easy to grab snacks in the fridge.

"Of course..." Izzy flexed her feet, then added, "You realize not everyone does that, right?"

"Does what?"

"Reads people's emotions."

"Yes, they do." How could one interact with others if they weren't gauging their reactions? Understanding how things might affect them...pleasing them.

Bryn rubbed her hand over her brow. She'd grown up with an inconsistent mother. Always trying to game how she might handle a situation. And she'd done her best to be what Ethan had wanted…doing the same thing.

Izzy pulled the pager from her hip and looked at the numbers. "I'm sure reading people has its uses."

But it also kept her from fulling connecting, let Bryn hold back rather than fully embrace others. Rather than tell Nick she'd like his help or explain that it would be nice if he reached out to his father or gave her the contact, she'd held back.

Intent on making sure he wasn't uncomfortable.

Guessing that asking him would upset him. But upsets happened. That was life.

"I need to see a patient." Izzy rotated her feet one more time before standing. "If you need something, you'll let me know?"

"I feel like it's me that should say that." Bryn winked as Izzy's cheeks colored before she headed out the door.

Bryn lifted the angel and gently placed it back in the locker. When her shift was done, she was texting Nick. It was time they had a conversation. If it didn't go the way she wanted, well, she'd deal with that when she had to.

"It's Christmas Eve. Please. I just want to know my husband hasn't been forgotten." Ellen's voice shook as she leaned against the wall of the garage. The same place he and Bryn had seen her weeks ago. Fighting the same battle.

"Ellen?"

"Oh, Dr. Walker." She let out a soft sigh. "I stepped out for a few minutes while Susie was resting. She came out of surgery yesterday. It was successful, but she's still tired."

"She will be tired for a few days. It wasn't open-heart surgery, but it still takes a lot out of a little body." Nick moved to stand beside her on the wall. "But you don't not have to feel bad about stepping out here to check on your husband."

"'Checking.' More like 'screaming into a void.'" Ellen kicked at a rock. "Nothing feels right with him gone. The world is a little darker, the music a little dimmer. Jack—Jack is my home, and for the last year no one, except Bryn, has even given me the time to listen to our story."

Bryn.

"I mean, she can't even do anything, but she listened and even called a few senators."

She'd done more than that. He'd watched her search everything she could. He could only imagine what she'd done in the days since he'd left.

"She's a special person." The description didn't come close to describing the woman he loved. The woman he'd accused of people-pleasing, when she was the one who'd seen what Ellen and Susie really needed—someone to notice them. And he'd let his own issues with his father get in the way.

"I need to get back to Susie. Thanks for chatting for a minute."

Nick raised his hand as she stepped back into the hospital. He looked toward the rows of parked cars, then pulled the phone from his pocket.

He blew out a breath, then pulled up the text he'd gotten from Bryn.

Can we talk?

Three little words that sent a rainbow of emotion through his body. His fingers hovered over the digital letters before he backed out of the texts. There was something he needed to do first.

So he pulled up the number he hadn't reached out to for years.

If you're available, I'd like to talk.

Nick put the phone back into his pocket, and then it vibrated. It couldn't be his father. He never got back to people this fast—or rather, he didn't get back to Nick this fast.

Still at the office. Will be here a while.

Working. In the local field office. On Christmas Eve. Technically, Nick was working, too, but at the hospital. It was different.

Before he could type out a fine or think of a way to ask for a favor via text, his father texted again.

This time it was an address.

It was probably as close as he was going to get to an invitation. So he should take it.

On my way.

The office building was like so many around Boston, though it lacked any company names on the walls and there were more than a dozen cars in the parking lot long after hours on Christmas Eve. The formidable-looking security guard sitting behind the desk didn't look pleased to see him. He'd been in enough places like this as a kid to recognize the signs.

Secure building. One he didn't have clearance to enter.

Here.

His father had likely been notified the moment he'd stepped through the door, but the text at least gave him something to do while the guard sized him up.

"Let him in."

Nick's heart nearly split in half as it tried to decide if it was excited or terrified to hear his father's voice over the guard's radio. There was still time to turn around.

But Bryn needed him to follow through for Ellen and Susie. So his feet moved forward.

"He hasn't even shown any ID. And he isn't on security's list for tonight." The guard didn't take his eyes off Nick. His left hand held the walkie-talkie, the right hovered close enough to his waistband to draw the weapon in the holster.

An entry list for Christmas Eve. How very Dad.

"I'm aware, Tristan. I said let him up."

"Fifth floor?"

"Third."

So whatever "party" was going on was happening on the fifth floor. Some late-night secret operation? Probably. Did his siblings know?

Maybe. Though if they did, they wouldn't be able to tell him, either.

Nick swallowed, trying to force the weight of unworthiness down. He was here for Bryn. For Ellen and Susie.

He wasn't a quitter.

Tristan didn't bother to say anything as he walked to the elevator, punched a set of numbers into the keypad and stepped back.

Nick slid into the elevator, the *3* already lit up. Pushing the other buttons would have no effect, but Tristan pointed to them anyway.

"You go to three and then right back here."

Nick barely resisted the urge to offer him a salute as the doors closed.

Not like it's my fault my father is in charge of whatever is happening here tonight.

When the doors opened on the third floor, Nick pushed himself off the back wall of the elevator, then gave a little wave to the camera in the corner.

The long hallway had four doors, and only one was open. Apparently meeting the son he hadn't seen in over ten years in a place other than an office building wasn't an option his father was choosing. Fine.

Walking through the open door, Nick paused, taking in the general behind the desk. The man wore civilian clothes now. The touch of gray at his temples had taken over his father's entire head. He looked somehow smaller than the man in Nick's memories.

"Seems like you have a lot going on tonight." Maybe that wasn't the best way to address his father for the first time, but nothing more traditional seemed to want to make its way out.

"Christmas Party."

Nick raised a brow but didn't call out the lie. Even the Department of Defense didn't usually work on Christmas Eve.

"So, what do you need?"

Right to the point. He wanted to call his father's bluff, wanted to point out that his father had sent the first email. And let him know he was staying in town longer. Nick hadn't initiated this.

Unfortunately, he was right. Nick was here for a favor.

"I need you to ask a senator or someone with connections about a man named Jack Cole." He knew those words were off, but he didn't know who exactly his father needed to ask. "And have someone call his wife, Ellen."

"Jack Cole? The journalist taken captive by the narcos?"

"You know the case?" His father was well connected, but even he couldn't know everything. Nick had expected his father to ask a few questions at least.

"Yeah. I've been briefed on it. Recently, even." His father looked at his watch and cleared his throat. "But I'm not allowed to discuss it. Hopefully someone will call Ellen soon."

"Soon!" Nick shook his head. "No, that's not the answer you're giving me. Ellen and Susie have heard nothing. Nothing. Not even a proof-of-life or an email to let them know they aren't forgotten."

"No need to get upset." Why was that always the statement? Don't get upset. Focus on the next thing—move on.

"Damn it. No one is returning Ellen's calls. It's Christmas Eve. Their daughter just had heart surgery, and no one will call her back about her husband." This shouldn't have been that difficult to understand.

"Contacting families…not really my line of work." His father's hip beeped, but he pressed a button, silencing whatever message was coming through.

"When has that ever stopped you?" Nick moved toward the desk and put his palms on it, emotion clouding his brain as he laid it all out.

"You were the chairman of the joint chiefs of staff. The literal highest military rank. You're going to sit there and tell me you can't call in some minor favor with a representative or colonel so someone tells her Jack hasn't been forgotten?"

"There's no need to raise your voice."

"Why not!" Nick shook his head. "We're family. If you can't be vulnerable with family, then who can you be vulnerable with? Family is supposed to catch you when you fall. Supposed to stand with you when you make big life choices. Not run when you need them. Or throw them out when you choose…"

Nick cleared his throat. He was here for Ellen and Susie. And Bryn.

Bryn… Family.

He stepped back and took a deep breath. Bryn had been vulnerable with him. Let him into her heart after her ex-husband. And the first time she'd asked him to dig deep, to dig really deep about wanting his father's approval, he'd turned and run.

He'd moved on, instead of focusing on what really mattered.

"The US government doesn't deal with terrorists." His father's voice was even. No hint that Nick's outburst ruffled him at all.

Focus on this moment, then next stop, Bryn's.

"There are back doors in every policy. And last I checked,

you work for a contract company now. Plausible deniability is your game. Besides, it's not like I'm asking for a rescue. Just a freaking phone call to his wife and daughter. Hell, it doesn't even have to be for Christmas. Before New Year's. Just make it happen."

"Mitch."

It was weird to hear someone call his father by his first name. For Nick's entire childhood, he'd been *General*. Nick turned to see a man standing in the doorway. He was wearing civilian clothes, but his carriage was either military or *very* recently ex-military.

"I need five minutes, Peyton."

"Don't have it. It's lockdown time."

Lockdown. No. Nick knew what that meant. No communications. Everything stayed still until whatever op was over. It was Christmas Eve. This couldn't be happening. "Dad."

His father's eyes softened for just a moment. Or maybe they didn't. "An op sped up, and I need your phone. Now."

"No." He'd done what he'd meant to. This was not where Nick was spending Christmas Eve. He needed to get to Bryn. Needed to return her text.

"I'm leaving. At least I can tell Bryn I tried. And that I know the answer to her question."

"Who is Bryn and what question did she ask?"

"Mitch!"

"I'll be in the command room in three minutes. Everyone has their orders. Follow them."

Peyton didn't salute and he seemed less than thrilled, but he turned on his heel.

"What question?"

"She's my...was my girlfriend." The word was stung as it passed his lips. "She asked if I needed your approval. I told her of course not." There wasn't time for this discussion, and honestly, it was Bryn he wanted to have it with. "But I was wrong. I wanted you to see me. To be proud of the choices I made. But it's not what I need. Not anymore."

Bryn's smiling face floated in his memory. "I have someone that wants me for me. That sees my value." And he was going to do whatever it took to win her back.

"Mitch!" The call came from down the hall, and he saw his dad's eyes switch to the doorway.

"Stay here until this is over. Phone." He held out his hand, and Nick put the phone into it. He'd seen the look often enough to know that arguing was pointless.

His father paused at the door. "I'm glad you came. I know it doesn't seem that way."

It didn't, but he wasn't going to press his dad about it.

"It shouldn't be more than six hours. No one in or out. Can't run the risk of any leaks."

Nick had no intention of leaking anything…not that he'd get the chance. "Fine. And I don't get to know what it is?" Nick slid into the chair across from the desk. This was the worst way to spend Christmas Eve.

"Sorry. Maybe there will be a Christmas miracle." His father's words were soft, but he didn't look back this time.

Christmas miracle. Cryptic words from a cryptic man.

Nick blew out a breath. No answers on Jack, but Bryn would understand. And they'd find someone else to help them. Nick wasn't sure how, or who, but he had six hours to think it through.

Nothing to do but close his eyes and wait.

"Your father sends his regards. You're free to go." The man placed Nick's phone back into his hand, then turned and walked out of the room.

He didn't want any more family talk anyway. But to send a lackey… At least Nick could close this chapter and move on to the new one.

The most important chapter—Bryn.

"Merry Christmas." Nick muttered through a yawn. He looked at his watch and his spirit sank. It was far too late to call Bryn or show up at her door. Which was exactly what he wanted to do. So he'd get a few hours of rest, then tell the woman he loved Merry Christmas…and that he needed her.

CHAPTER SIXTEEN

"Bryn!" The sight of her blond braid sent happiness through his exhausted brain. Honey was walking beside her on Ward 34. Reindeer antlers and a Santa sweater made them look like they'd stepped out of a holiday card.

She turned, surprise written across every part of her face. "Nick? Oh, my."

He knew he looked like hell. He'd fallen asleep as he'd waited for the clock to reach an appropriate hour. When he'd jolted awake an hour ago, all his soul had wanted was to be with her.

"Merry Christmas, Bryn."

"Merry Christmas." She rocked back on her heel. "I sent you a text yesterday."

"I know. My father confiscated my phone." That sounded wild, an actual truth-is-stranger-than-fiction situation.

"What?"

"I actually don't have a great deal to add to that. Saw my dad, pleaded for him to have someone call Ellen. Pretty sure that failed. Then some op or something started. He took my phone, and I was locked down for six hours."

Bryn's eyes were saucers, and her mouth was hanging open. "What?"

Yeah. Repeating that question made sense.

"Wildest Christmas Eve ever...and the most boring. But

that's not why I'm standing here." Nick stepped closer, yearning to reach out to her.

Honey pushed her head between his legs. "It's good to see you too, Honey."

"Why are you here?"

"For you. I'm done running. You were right—I wanted my father's approval. I think I've kept moving because I didn't feel comfortable with myself. Like I wasn't enough. No matter what place I work or the achievements I get, it isn't in uniform, and he'll probably always consider me a quitter."

"You are not a quitter." Her right hand formed a fist. This woman. This brilliant, loving, beautiful person was ready to go into battle for him, even after he'd walked out.

"I know." The words were cleansing.

Her eyes roamed his face, looking for a break or a worry that he didn't mean it. The woman was a mood reader, a trauma response she couldn't help. One that she'd tried using to help him and he'd thrown in her face.

"I'm glad you know that. I really am. It's a wonderful Christmas present." Nick stepped closer, moving Honey with him. "I love you, Bryn."

Her mouth fell open, and he hated the surprise on her features. He was going to spend the rest of his life making sure that she was never again surprised by how much he cared for her.

"You're my person. I shouldn't have fled the other night. I should have called the next morning. I should—"

Her finger lay against his lips. "I love you, too." She stepped into his arms—as close as Honey would allow.

"I should have asked you for help right away, too. I was worried how you'd react."

He kissed her head, loving the feel of her in his arms. "With good reason."

"Still, you aren't my parents or Ethan. I trust you with all my feelings."

"All our feelings." Nick brushed his lips against hers. He'd needed to see her. Waiting until her shift was over had not been an option, but he wished he could seal this moment with more passion.

"Honey!" Susie's call made Bryn chuckle as she stepped back.

"It's always about Honey." Nick kissed her again, then pulled back.

"You get used to it." She wrapped an arm around his waist as Ellen wheeled Susie up.

"Merry Christmas, Susie." Bryn moved to get down on her level.

"Merry Christmas." The little one sighed as she ran a hand over Honey's coat. "I secretly asked Santa to bring Daddy home—at the window when Mommy was out. She thought I was sleeping."

"Oh, baby." Ellen rubbed her daughter's head.

"I know he isn't real, but…" She shrugged, then leaned toward Honey.

Such sad words. Maybe her dad wouldn't be home for Christmas, but Nick would find some other way. One of his siblings might know someone.

"Ho! Ho! Ho!"

Nick froze as the sound echoed behind him. He'd never heard his father make Santa noises. And he wasn't hearing it now. It couldn't be…

"Ellen. Susie!" A man with long, light brown hair pushed past Nick and Bryn.

Cries of "Jack!" and sobs filled the air as the small family reunited.

"Nick." His father's voice was right behind him.

He turned, his hand squeezing Bryn tightly. His father was here. In a Santa hat. A group of men were behind him—a few he recognized from last night.

There was an expectation that he'd speak. But Nick's synapses refused to offer him words.

"You must be Nick's dad. I'm Bryn. Welcome to Ward 34."

"How?" The simple word was difficult to force out.

The op last night. Clearly, they'd been ferreting Jack back to the States, but Nick still couldn't quite believe it.

"Some Christmas miracles are classified." His father offered a wink that actually looked jovial.

"Santa must be real!" Susie clapped as a nurse led the small family to an empty room to give them some privacy.

Bryn covered her mouth, and he saw a tear slip down her cheek.

"You got your wish." Nick kissed her temples.

"I had nothing to do with it." She let out a laugh as she squeezed his hand. "But this is the best Christmas morning ever."

"Technically, I think you were part of it, Bryn. I doubt my son would have given his speech to remind me of the importance of family without you." His father shrugged. "Jack still has to go through debriefing, and the med check is being done at this hospital. The reunion wasn't scheduled for today, but Nick reminded me that family is most important. And I think *you* had a lot to do with that."

"She had everything to do with it." Nick's heart leapt as Bryn looked at him.

"I have a small roast in my crock pot. Why don't you come to dinner with us, General?"

Nick held his breath. If his father said he was busy or unable to make it, that was fine.

His father's dark eyes, ones he knew were identical to his own, met his. "I'd love that. But, please, call me Mitch."

Another Christmas miracle.

EPILOGUE

"I've got something for you." Bryn's giant smile was contagious.

Any worries the urge to pack his things would reappear had fled as his and Bryn's relationship progressed. The day she'd moved into his Boston apartment was still the happiest of his life, followed closely by the day they'd gotten engaged.

"A present?" It wasn't his birthday or Christmas, but Bryn loved gifting things, and he loved watching her excitement when she did.

"Sort of. It's outside." She looked at her phone, then back at him.

"Outside?" Nick looked to the window. Two years in Boston and he still didn't know which he disliked more, the steaming heat of summer or the biting chill of winter. Spring was gorgeous, though…something easy to forget as the heat seemed to radiate off the sidewalks today.

They'd treated more heat stroke this week than in his entire career. What could she have outside?

"Come on!" Bryn pulled him to the door.

"It's melting outside, sweetheart."

"I know, so we should move fast." She wagged a hand, and Honey lay back on her bed.

Too hot for Honey, but not him. All right, then.

They raced down the apartment steps. Sweat was already

beading on his temple. And the woman he loved was nearly bouncing with excitement.

Stepping outside, he saw a miniature horse standing in the shade.

"Oreo and his owner, Cedric, came to say hello." Bryn waved to Cedric before petting Oreo on the head.

Nick clapped with a childlike excitement. "Oreo. The therapy horse."

"Yeah, sorry—your building has a *no mini horses* policy, so we had to do this out here. Which also means the little guy and I can't stay too long." Cedric patted the chocolate mane.

Nick understood, but just meeting the therapy horse was a dream come true.

"Bryn pointed out that with her nursing schedule, we kept missing you at Paws for Hope." Cedric smiled as Oreo let Nick rub his neck.

That was true. He'd gone several times, and it was always fun, but each time he'd hoped to meet Oreo. Running his hand over the horse's mane, Nick let out a sigh. As a child, he'd dreamed of riding, but then he'd not known little horses existed. If he had, he would have begged for one from sunup to sundown—to hell with the consequences.

"Thank you." Nick stood and shook Cedric's hand. It was too hot to make the little horse stay out, even in the shade.

"And thank you." He pulled Bryn to him, dropping a kiss onto her lips, enjoying the taste of her, the feel of her. That this was his life was a gift he'd never expected.

"There's more."

"Bryn…"

"Shush!" She pulled an envelope from her back pocket and handed it to him.

He opened it and stared at the gift certificate for riding lessons. "Bryn."

She pulled another envelope from her other pocket.

"This is too much."

She shook her head. "Nope. This one is mine. I get the bigger horse!"

"All right. But we're waiting until the heat breaks." Nick sighed. "Let's go back upstairs."

"I love you." Bryn put her hand through his.

"I love you, too."

* * * * *

COMING SOON!

We really hope you enjoyed reading this book. If you're looking for more romance be sure to head to the shops when new books are available on

Thursday 23rd November

To see which titles are coming soon, please visit
millsandboon.co.uk/nextmonth

MILLS & BOON

MILLS & BOON®

Coming next month

HEALED BY A MISTLETOE KISS
Alison Roberts

Pedro smiled but he was turning away already to pick up his kit. Nikita followed him to the door of her cottage.

'Thank you,' she said.

'No need to thank me,' he said. 'It was my fault you hurt yourself in the first place.'

'That wasn't what I was thanking you for. You've given me quite a lot to think about.'

He was giving her that look again. The one that seemed to be melting its way through all the protective, healing barriers Nikita had so carefully constructed over the last year.

Did he really believe that she was, deep down, the person she'd always been? Was that why he could say things that gave her more hope than hundreds of hours of counselling had achieved? Why he could touch her without her feeling the need to flee?

The skin-to-skin contact they'd had as he'd examined her foot and ankle would have been her worst nightmare not long ago. She'd never thought she would ever, ever, be able to allow a man to touch her again.

Or had that been because it was purely professional, in order to make a medical diagnosis?

A personal touch…like a hug, or getting anywhere near an intimate touch, like a kiss would undoubtedly be an entirely different matter.

That thought was in Nikita's mind at the precise moment that Pedro turned to say goodbye as he reached the door. And maybe her balance wasn't perfect because she was trying to keep the weight off her injured ankle because she didn't stop right away and Pedro put his arm out to steady her.

Another touch that didn't scare her was enough for something to shift inside Nikita's head. Or her heart? Whatever…she needed to know…

So she used her good foot to stand on tiptoe.

And she kissed Pedro Garcia.

On his lips.

Continue reading
HEALED BY A MISTLETOE KISS
Alison Roberts

Available next month
www.millsandboon.co.uk

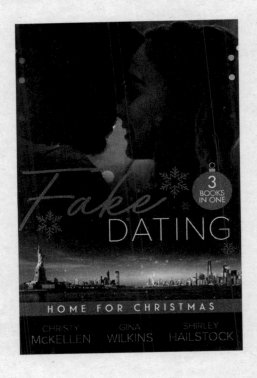

LET'S TALK
Romance

For exclusive extracts, competitions and special offers, find us online:

f MillsandBoon

🐦 @MillsandBoon

📷 @MillsandBoonUK

♪ @MillsandBoonUK

Get in touch on 01413 063 232

GET YOUR ROMANCE FIX

Get the latest romance news, exclusive author interviews, story extracts and much more!